BEAUTIFUL VILLAIN

PIPER STONE

Copyright © 2022 by Stormy Night Publications and Piper Stone

All rights reserved. No part of this book may be reproduced or transmitted in any form or by any means, electronic or mechanical, including photocopying, recording, or by any information storage and retrieval system, without permission in writing from the publisher.

Published by Stormy Night Publications and Design, LLC.
www.StormyNightPublications.com

Stone, Piper
Beautiful Villain

Cover Design by Korey Mae Johnson
Image by 123RF/tverdohlib

This book is intended for *adults only*. Spanking and other sexual activities represented in this book are fantasies only, intended for adults.

CHAPTER 1

Kirill

Blood.

Strings of crimson washed over my eyes, the rage becoming uncontrollable.

Wham. Wham.

Wham. Wham. Wham. Wham.

I jerked back, taking deep breaths as I studied the punching bag swinging in a wide arc. I rubbed the sweat from my forehead with my arm, flexing my fingers before fisting them again. Then I issued several brutal punches against the dense piece of stuffed leather, dancing around to the other side then slamming my fists against it several more times.

My hands already ached, but the burning pain also allowed me to feel alive, freed from the ugliness of the dreams that had strangled me with sharp claws for years. I pummeled the bag again, losing count of how many times I'd thrown a brutal punch. Still, it didn't ease the ache inside or the rage that kept me on edge.

An attack on my men.

Six of them murdered.

The perpetrator still at large.

Wham. Wham. Wham.

Fuck. I walked into the attack like a fucking idiot.

And I'd been one of two left alive.

The hunger for revenge tore through me, the ugliness of it evil and I was out for blood. I could almost taste the coppery sweetness in my mouth.

However, that wasn't the only reason for my aggression.

I took a step back, stalking toward the bottle of water, almost crushing the thin plastic before I was able to open the cap, guzzling more than half. After splashing some of the frigid liquid in my face, I returned to my task. I was determined to rid myself of the memories, if only for tonight.

Even as I smashed one fist after another, putting all my weight into driving away the demons, the visions kept coming, one bloodstained frame after another. The past was more than just a terrible nightmare.

It had turned me into a monster.

Years had passed, my entire adult life a statement, or perhaps a retelling of what I'd endured as a child, the carnage left behind after a savage attack on innocent families, ripping away all the people I'd loved. The mother who'd nurtured me and a father who'd protected me against the tyranny gone in an instant.

Then there'd been my baby sister, innocence personified.

I could still hear their screams, the wretched sound echoing as much as the barrage of gunfire. Nothing had been able to stop the nightmares. Not liquor. Not women. Not violence. There hadn't been a single moment of existing that had extinguished the stench of blood or managed to alleviate the damning horror of seeing their vacant eyes. At least I'd been able to use my rage to my advantage, settling scores as necessary.

What I'd yet to be able to accomplish was hunting down the men responsible. That would come. One day I would take everything from the bastards who'd destroyed all that I cared about.

Wham. Wham! Wham!

Only on that day would the nightmares end, at least for the last surviving member of the Sabatin family.

* * *

Candy

. . .

Stop. Stop. *Stop!*

The noise was like bottle rockets going off in my brain. All I'd had to do was get out of the elevator and I'd heard the same thunking noise I'd put up with for several nights in a row. I was working long hours, my legs hurt enough I wasn't using the stairs, and the jerk making the noise only adding to the misery. I glared from one door to another, also furious no one had bothered to try to get the asshole to stop. Were they all in comas?

When there was a moment of silence, I lifted my middle finger toward the ceiling. Maybe the jerk had heard me. I yanked my keys from my pocket, taking two steps toward the door and…

Whap whap.

The. Same. Shit.

I jammed the key into the lock, cursing a blue streak. My mother would say I needed to have my mouth washed out with soap. Well, if she was standing here, she'd be doing the same thing.

Whap whap.

I closed my eyes, albeit briefly. At this point, I was pretty certain that by the end of the night, I'd be in jail, especially since the only thing on my mind was murdering the asshole above me who'd just moved into apartment Four-F. I knew exactly where the scumbag lived since I was in Three-F. Directly below him. A new neighbor. A loud neighbor. One who didn't give a crap what time of night it was. *Welcome to the neighborhood, you son of a bitch.*

I'd never even met the dude and I was ready to send him to his maker. That didn't make me a very nice girl, but at this moment, I didn't care. All I knew about him was from a booming male voice echoing in the hallways and a new name slapped onto the mail bin by the superintendent of the building.

I remained just inside the door to my apartment for a full minute and all I could hear was…

Whap whap.

Whap whap.

Whap whap.

If the sound wasn't so regular, I'd think he was beating someone to death, which is what I would do to him. He obviously didn't understand the power and wrath of a redhead after a long night serving jerks sucking down beer like it was the last night on Earth.

Well, the new neighbor was about ready to get a lesson in an Irish temper.

I tossed the food I'd brought home from the restaurant with me on my kitchen counter, taking long strides to the small closet and grabbing the broom. Then I glared up at the ceiling, jabbing the wooden handle toward it. Oh, yeah, like that was going to work. The entire building had high ceilings. And I wasn't that damn tall. I grabbed a chair, dragging it across the floor and directly underneath the horrific noise.

Even after rising onto my tiptoes, well, at least as much as my Converse sneakers would allow, I was at least six inches shy of fulfilling my task. I'd need to use the up close and personal approach.

After tossing the broom and jumping off, I headed straight for the door, stopping short when I heard my mother's voice inside my head.

"Never forget you can catch more flies with honey than you can with vinegar."

While I'd never really understood what she'd meant up to this point, as I glanced over my shoulder, a smile brightened my pissed-off mood. Bribery. There wasn't a man alive who wasn't hungry for a juicy roast beef sandwich oozing with delicious au jus and topped with just the perfect swirl of horseradish sauce. Eh, maybe the fruit salad would be tossed, but a girl could try.

I snagged the bag, planted a smile on my face, and took the stairs. When I was standing in front of his door, I shored my shoulders, fisted my right hand, and pounded on the door like the entire building was going up in flames any second.

The heavy footsteps weren't as loud as the odd guttural sounds, but as he came closer to the door, I could swear I heard him speaking a foreign language.

"Kto, chert voz'mi, bespokoit menya?"

I refused to back down in any way. Nope. Not this girl.

Until he threw open the door.

While I tried to keep an angry sneer on my face, I was robbed of that beautiful moment by the sight of the giant standing in front of me. I wasn't short by any means, but standing inches away from Mr. Barbarian, I felt tiny.

His chest, his bare and very muscular, perfectly carved chest, heaved as he glared at me with murder in his eyes—his gorgeous emerald-green eyes, his pupils almost iridescent. We had a stare down for a few seconds, but it seemed interminably longer.

Even worse, as he allowed his gaze to drop to my scuffed red tennis shoes, moving so slowly I thought we were in a time warp, I couldn't stop quivering. If he didn't have such a savage scowl on his face, I'd said he was probably the best-looking man I'd ever seen, but it was tough to tell given his flared nostrils.

Yet as he huffed and puffed, his muscles gleaming in the track lighting hung way above, I could envision him on the cover of *Sexy Convicts of New York*.

While he was checking me out, I was doing the same, blinking rapidly at the way his hard body glistened from sweat, beads trickling down his muscular arms and broad chest. Dear God, the man looked like Adonis on steroids, especially given the colorful ink sweeping down from his neck onto both forearms. While every part of his body was carved to perfection, I was certain his jawline could cut glass.

His eyes were full of something that I couldn't place. Mystery? A firestorm? No, they were cold just like ice, penetrating in a frightening way yet I was barely able to blink let alone breathe. For a few seconds, a strange but solid buzzing sounded off in my ears, the noise deafening.

If I didn't know better, I'd say the handsome barbarian wanted to swallow me whole.

I took a deep breath, holding it as I dared to scan the rest of his sculpted body. I knew proper ladies didn't stare at men's crotches, but I couldn't help myself, especially since he was wearing tight-fitting shorts and nothing else.

Oh, my God. I couldn't believe I found this monstrous man attractive. I tried to keep from breathing at all, which would allow him to know he'd managed to intimidate me, but it was almost impossible.

He reminded me of one of those famous actors in the summer blockbusters, only he wasn't one of the good guys. He was the villain, one beautiful villain.

Huffing, he cocked his head, lifting a single eyebrow as he concentrated on the bag in my hand then shifted his heated gaze to my chest.

I was used to men gawking at my chest given the ridiculously tight bright green tee shirt that every employee wore. It just happened that the name of the bar and grill, Killian's, was plastered straight across my breasts. I watched as a single bead of sweat trickled down to his lips and the way he dragged his tongue across the seam of his mouth was the most provocative thing I'd seen in a long time.

If not ever.

"Does this mean you're my treat for the evening? I admit, I *am* famished."

Not only were his words dripping with a heavy overtone of sexuality, but the deep bass of his voice and the thick Russian accent were a dangerous combination. I wasn't the kind of girl who got flustered over a boy, but this was no boy.

This was a man, a real man, the kind who didn't take no for an answer.

I tried to form words in my brain so I didn't sound like an idiot when I responded, but everything I thought of sounded like gibberish inside my mind. I'd never been this flustered around any man, no matter how good-looking they'd been.

My lungs could no longer accept any additional air, my throat starting to shut down when he grabbed me by the arm, yanking me inside his apartment.

Inside his lair.

Holy crap.

"It's a…" *Oh, Jesus. Get a damn grip.* "It's a peace offering." My words sounded like they'd come from the twelve-year-old me, timid and asking for forgiveness. And what was with offering the brutal man anything?

"For what?" he growled.

Why the hell was he still staring at my breasts?

"For you shutting the hell up. I need some sleep. I work long hours."

Every ounce of oxygen seemed to drain from the room as he took several deep breaths.

When he slammed the door closed, tugging the bag out of my hand, I stumbled backwards, which was the wrong way. I should have fled toward the door, only I doubted Mr. Barbarian was ready to let me leave.

"Killian's," he grunted then opened the bag, pulling out the sandwich, tossing the satchel onto one of the chairs then peeling the layer of foil from around the roast beast. *Beef.* I tried to look away, but with his intense stare, his eyes piercing mine, I couldn't force myself to take my eyes off him. I was frozen like a stupid kid just before her first kiss.

When he bit into the sandwich, tearing half of it away and chomping down, I realized my mouth was watering. As he chewed, I was lost in the moment, my breath skipping as subtle growls rolled up from the base of the beast. His nostrils remained flared as he swallowed, the animalistic sounds getting louder. When he popped the remainder in his mouth, I was forced to chew my bottom lip to keep from making a strangled sound.

Like a moan.

I'd never known any man to consume food with such passion.

I folded my arms across my chest, trying three times before I was able to swallow. I noticed a dribble of the sauce on the corner of his mouth and damn if the wicked side of me didn't want to offer to lick it off.

That was crazy. This man could be a serial killer for all I knew. I threw a quick glance around his apartment, realizing where the sound was coming from. He had a huge hanging punching bag positioned in the middle of his sparsely decorated living room. The long, thick chain dangled from a massive steel girder suspended from the tall ceiling. All I could think about was the alternative uses for the chain.

That certainly didn't make me feel any better.

I studied him, watching as he chewed like some barbarian then glanced toward the swinging punching bag a second time. The thumping noise. "You're a boxer."

He grunted his reply.

His hands weren't wrapped and there was no sign of any gloves. He was using his naked fists. While I knew sound echoed, the power he'd used on punching what looked like a professional grade bag should have given him scrapes or bruises. His hands, while just as masculine as the rest of him, showed no signs of wear and tear.

That wasn't the case for his entire body. He had a nasty-looking scar on his chest. If I had to guess, I'd say there were others crisscrossing his body, but they were weaved into the various designs. What in the hell did this man do for a living?

You know what he does. He kills people.

The little voice inside my head wasn't helping in the least. I was genuinely curious about him, maybe too much so, but I was here. He was standing right in front of me.

He was gorgeous.

And I was completely irrational.

"Right handed? You're putting too much weight on one side. That makes you unbalanced. You need to practice more with your left arm. That will make you a more even fighter." I was surprised how authoritative my voice sounded.

The sudden silence sent chills trickling all the way down to my toes. I shot him a look, involuntarily licking my lips. Damn it. I could tell by the twinkle in his eyes he'd caught the obvious gesture of attraction.

"Um, if you're wondering how I know this…" Now I was blabbering on like some scaredy cat. Great. "My cousin's a boxer, amateur but he's pretty good. He's a southpaw and can't use his right arm for shit." Heat swept along my neck, oozing on both sides of my jaw until they flamed scarlet. Oh, my God. I wondered in the warm glow of light if he was able to notice.

Tick. Tock.

How much time had just been sucked into the wind?

"Now, do you want to tell me why you really interrupted me, *moy malen'kiy ognennyy shar?*"

Everything coming out of his mouth was dripping with sexual innuendoes and this time as his hooded gaze shifted to the floor, I knew he was undressing me with his eyes. That brought out the fury I'd felt earlier.

"I don't know what the hell you just said, but it sounded like an insult and that's not acceptable. I already told you the *real* reason. Noise. That noise." I pointed toward the still swinging punching bag, giving him a nasty look.

"I would never insult a creature so beautiful."

"Do you always flirt with women you don't know?"

"Isn't that what flirting is all about?"

How the hell would I know? I usually shied away from wasting my time, but with him, everything seemed different. Dirty. Sinful.

And far too delicious.

"You don't know me," I countered, catching his look of amusement.

"But it would seem you'd like to get to know me."

"Don't flatter yourself, buddy."

I was rewarded with a flash of his gorgeous eyes, although they seemed darker, more ominous than they had before.

"I assure you that I have no need to provide myself with compliments," he growled. Again. Could the man sound more like an animal in heat?

Why was it that almost everything that came out of his mouth was frustrating? "Of course you don't. You're far too handsome and debonair." I couldn't believe I'd just told the dangerous-looking man he was handsome. While it was the truth, I needed to learn to control my mouth.

"I'm surprised you're giving me a compliment."

"Don't give me that."

"What am I giving you?" he sneered.

Why did I have the feeling he had several disgusting ideas in mind?

"Bullshit. You're well aware of how handsome you are. I'm certain women tell you that all the time."

He cocked his head. "Women aren't usually as forthcoming as you are."

"Well, I'm glad I can be of service."

"Service. I like the sound of that."

This was getting out of hand. There was a spark of electricity soaring between us that made me as uncomfortable as I'd ever been, and I knew rivers of red streaks were sailing up both cheeks. I was usually very good at bantering, but with him, everything seemed ten times more difficult.

"Just because I brought you food doesn't give you the right to think I'm going to service you with anything else."

When he did nothing but lift his head, I continued to launch into him. To hell with the fact that he was one big, scary-looking dude who could break me into pieces with one hand tied behind his back. "I think I've had enough bullshit for one night. Furthermore, it's after two-thirty in the goddamn morning. Most people, you know, *normal* people, are trying to get some hard-earned sleep. I happen to be one of those people, although I just got home. The noise you make every night for hours on end is unacceptable, your behavior atrocious. You are going to stop boxing or beating someone to death or whatever it is you do at this ungodly time of night. Do you hear me? If you keep it up, there will be consequences."

I couldn't believe I'd just thrown out a threat, albeit a small one, to a man I'd cross the street to avoid at night.

I planted my hands on my hips, refusing to back down.

He said nothing, did nothing for a full twenty seconds, which had to be the longest twenty seconds of my life. Then a slight smile curled on his upper lip. Still, he remained completely silent.

But my sixth sense told me to run. Fast.

"Well, then. I'm glad we got that straight. Welcome to the building. I'll just see myself out." I took a wide berth around him, almost making it to the door. 'Almost' being the operative word.

When he snagged my arm, spinning me around and crushing his chest against mine, every wisp of air was dragged from my body. His masculine scent was ripe with a heavy dose of testosterone and musk, which instantly made me lightheaded. I slammed my palms against him, but it was all in vain. He was an unmovable force.

I'd caught sight of ink covering his back, the figure reminding me of a horrible prehistoric creature with fangs and claws, the beady red eye the signature of a living breathing monster.

"What I called you was my little fireball and I'm afraid you aren't going anywhere. While the meal was somewhat enjoyable, I prefer something much sweeter."

"Sweeter?" I managed, my heartbeat pulsing in my mouth.

"Yes, *malen'kiy buntar'*. Now, it's time for dessert."

CHAPTER 2

Candy

I'd been out of my mind for coming here. There was no other reason for being so stupid, especially in the middle of the night.

This was bad, extremely bad. It was the kind of *really* bad that might end up with my body disappearing in the back of his trunk, tossed in some dark location where no one would find me. His little firecracker? Was he kidding me? He had no idea what kind of spirited girl I was.

"I suggest you get away from me," I said as boldly as possible. I didn't even know his name. What was I supposed to call him or tell the police? This big scary dude called me dessert?

"And why should I do that?"

"Be-cause. Be... I have roommates. We watch out for each other."

"You live alone."

How the hell did he know anything about me? Was he watching me, stalking me? This was much worse than I thought.

"I do not."

"I don't like lies, especially when they come from the mouth of a beautiful woman."

"I'm not lying to you. And stop calling me beautiful." I struggled, but the immoveable force was determined to keep me exactly where he wanted. He was also goading me. Why?

"Why don't you believe how luscious you are?"

Luscious. There hadn't been a single man who'd ever called me anything so... decadent. Why did my mouth have to remain so dry?

"I'm just average, nothing more. That's beside the point."

What the hell is wrong with you?

"No, that is the point, the entire point." He swept the rough tip of his index finger across my upper lip then floated it down the side of my neck, circling my pulse. Was this his way of explaining how he was going to kill me? He studied me intently, the intensity of his gaze burning a hole straight through me.

While I didn't pull away, I gave him the harshest glare I could, even though I was quivering to the core. Even our prickly conversation wasn't enough to stop the electric vibes swimming back and forth between us.

"Thank you for the compliment but it's time for me to go."

"Interesting. Tell me something, *moya krasota*. Why do you have a quiver in the corner of your mouth and why is the gorgeous pulse on the side of your neck throbbing? Is that from the desire burning deep inside of you?"

His chuckle pulled me out of some vacuum. What the hell did he just say to me? Desire? For him? A monster? Fat chance in hell. And what the hell did he call me?

"You're crazy. There's no way I could desire someone like you," I barked, allowing my usual personality to kick in. He was serial killer crazy.

"Absolutely. I am stark raving mad, *printsessa*, which is exactly why you should have known better than to come to a mysterious man's apartment in the middle of the night. Dangerous things could happen to a pretty young thing such as yourself. Don't you know there are some very bad men on the streets of New York?" He kept the sexy smirk on his face as he trailed his finger further down my neck to the edge of my tee shirt, sliding it back and forth twice before dipping it just underneath the material. "Unless you have a hidden reason for your visit. If that's the case, then it's very likely we won't get along."

What hidden reason? His personality seemed to change every few seconds. One minute he was amused I'd bothered him, the next he was pissed. However, I didn't need a lesson in Russian to know what he'd just called me. "I'm nobody's princess, especially yours. And it's obvious you're one of those bad men I've read about in the news, but I was here first, renting the apartment months ago, and you aren't driving me away. But you are driving me nuts. Just promise me you'll cut the noise at midnight, maybe one in the morning. Is that a deal?"

His chest heaving, I could swear he was contemplating what I'd told him, gauging whether I was lying. I was the one who couldn't trust him.

He cupped my neck and a good portion of my face, his big hand grasping and holding me in place. Everything about the man was terrifying, but especially his eyes. He had a desperate, unforgiving look in his iridescent eyes, but his gaze seemed soulless. Maybe he'd already sold his soul to the devil. "What's your name, little fireball?"

"Candy," I spouted off without thinking. My God. I must have lost my mind.

"Candy. The name isn't regal enough for a woman of your stature, but it's delicious enough."

Every word out of his mouth oozed with seduction.

"What's yours?"

"Kirill."

He said his name with such savage force, the tone deep and guttural, that it took my breath away. Only monsters had such a dangerous name, while I was named after something far too sweet. I could tell by the sly smile he issued that my name pleased him.

"Yet your name is appropriate given the circumstances, little beauty," he whispered as he swept his thumb back and forth across my lips. "My favorite dessert is candy, rich chocolate to be exact, a treat meant to be savored by taking several licks before biting into the rich center. Tell me, Candy. What flavor will I taste when I feast on your pretty pink pussy?"

He was mad. Absolutely insane. And I was nuts for thinking I could deter a man like him from doing everything he wanted. As he pulled me onto my tiptoes, I was helpless against the brute, even though I beat my fists against his rock-hard chest several times. "You're going to let me go or I'll scream for the police."

His grin was even more disturbing, the sparkle in his eyes allowing me to know in no uncertain terms that he controlled the area. He wasn't just a criminal. He was much worse, the kind of darkness only nightmares were made of. I was no fool, especially given what one of my cousins did for a living. Finnegan faced bastards like him almost every day as a New York City police detective. He'd committed his career to hunting down monsters just like this.

And Kirill was definitely one bad-ass criminal, maybe an assassin. My mind was fuzzy, but odd questions surfaced in my brain.

Why would an assassin live in a crappy apartment building in Brooklyn?

Why would he be boxing in the middle of the night?

Duh. He was honing his skills as a killer.

Kirill took a deep breath, holding it as he studied me, reveling in keeping me in his full control. When he breathed across my face and neck, my knees buckled, my heart thumping so loudly the sound echoed in my ears. As he lowered his head, his scent filtered all the way through my system, tossing a cup full of gasoline on flames that shouldn't exist.

"I have no issues making deals, especially in the middle of the night. While I enjoyed the sandwich, I have another idea in mind."

"I'm sorry. I'm not in the habit of talking to dangerous men in the middle of the night. There are no more deals to be made." My insistence was met with another sly smile.

"It would seem you don't understand. You aren't allowed to change your mind. You've already made a deal with the devil."

"What are you talking about?" I no longer recognized my voice. When he dragged his tongue across my lips, my legs began to shake even harder. The devil. At least he was giving me a warning. He was stupidly gorgeous, and I sensed he knew it. Suddenly, I felt like a piece of juicy tenderloin in a large platter ready to be served.

"What am I talking about?" he repeated, allowing his gaze to shred every ounce of clothing as if he had a knife in his hand. "You're a beautiful woman, Candy, and I'm going to enjoy teaching you about the power of passion."

Passion? Wait a minute. He thought I'd really made some crazy kind of deal with him? Oh, hell, no. I'd walked from the frying pan into the fire.

I soon found out his bold intentions when he brushed his lips across mine. As insane as it was, firecrackers went off in my system, vivid colors of the rainbow shooting across the periphery of my vision. I was completely unprepared for this man, any man for that matter, to treat me like a possession, like he'd claimed me because I'd dared to knock on his door.

When he pressed his lips against mine, I found myself leaning into the far too intimate moment, my breath skipping in time to my rapid pulse. He slipped his other hand around the back of my neck, holding me in place as he towered over me, taking his damn sweet time before pushing his tongue past my pursed lips.

I didn't want to like what he was doing to me, but within seconds, I'd yielded my mouth to him, allowing him to taste me. I was paralyzed by his actions, swooning from the way he held me. I wasn't the kind of girl to have fantasies like my friends back home had cooed over. I'd been taught to be practical, finding a boy after I'd succeeded in life who was financially stable and would keep his good looks as we grew older. This was a bad boy fantasy on steroids.

It was also unacceptable.

As he crushed his mouth over mine, pulling me even tighter against his body, I'd never felt so small or inconsequential in my life. My nipples ignored what rationality I had left in my mind, so aroused and aching that with every slight movement he made, a jolt of raw anguish sliced through me. Ridiculous visions rushed into my mind of the man tearing off my tee shirt, licking and sucking first one hardened bud then the other.

Good God. What the hell was wrong with me?

He made the kiss an artform, sweeping his tongue back and forth across mine, his actions dominating, but strangely romantic.

In some psychotic crazed killer kind of way.

I continued to lean into him, my fingers slipping across his slickened skin, making my actions seem like I was caressing him.

Encouraging him.

No. *No!*

This was the nuttiest thing I'd ever gotten myself into. I bucked hard against him, wiggling back and forth as I struggled, trying to find a way to get enough room to knee him in the balls. Somehow, I doubted that was going to do much damage. He was obviously made of steel or some other indestructible component. Yet the harder I fought, the tighter his hold became. Now the bastard was mimicking my moves, grinding his hips against me. The intense sensations tingling every inch of me were from the feel of the hard ridge of his cock slicing into my stomach.

No man could be that large.

No way.

He was like a giant in every aspect, perfectly fitting the Adonis appearance. As he made several guttural noises, I realized he was growling.

Like a beast in the wild!

Holy shit, the man was serious.

The second he slid his hand down my back, the tingles shifted into overdrive, shooting straight into my pussy. Within seconds, I was mortified as I caught a whiff of that very desire he was talking about. I could already feel a rush dampening my panties. This had shifted from bad to disastrous. Nothing good could come out of this, but his touch was warm and inviting, filling my mind with filthy, delicious thoughts.

This wasn't me. I'd never had a one-night stand in my life. What was I talking about? I'd never even had a thirty-minute stand.

Kirill sucked on my tongue for several seconds before breaking the kiss, nipping my lower lip.

I jerked back, gasping for air. "I'm sorry. There's been some misunderstanding."

"So you were lying to me."

"No. I mean… I was trying to be nice bringing you food, not suggesting anything else."

I could tell by the blank look on his face that he either didn't understand me or didn't care.

His next words were finally the last straw.

"You need to learn a lesson in caution and in telling the truth. And I'm just the man to teach it to you. Then, *moy malen'kiy ognennyy shar*, I'm going to enjoy my dessert."

The audacity of the man.

Finally, something kicked into my hapless brain, and I managed to rear back, issuing one hard punch to his jaw. Of course. His face was made of steel as well. Almost nothing changed, but the look in his eyes, a combination of fury and amusement. "Don't call me your little fireball."

He released his hold, rubbing his jaw, a huge grin crossing his face. Strangely, even when he smiled, he looked like a dangerous criminal.

I backed away, then sprinted around him toward the door. This time, he was on me in a flash, pushing me against the thick wood, planting both hands on either side as he crushed his full body weight against me, cutting off my air supply.

"Tsk. Tsk. That wasn't very nice of you. I accepted your peace offering, but in my world, the server comes with the food. You see, my beautiful girl, I take what I want, and I definitely want you. All of you."

His words weren't threatening as much as they were a promise.

I managed to swallow, doing everything I could to keep from making a single sound.

He took several deep breaths then pulled me away from the door, tossing me over his shoulder.

"Let me go!" I knew my cry was in vain.

My outburst was met with a brutal smack on my backside. I kicked out, pummeling my fists against his back, but the formidable structure wasn't budging. He cracked his hand against my backside several more times. I wanted to hate what he was doing, but the slight pain only added to my arousal. How could I feel this way?

"You're going to obey."

"No. I will never obey."

His chuckle was dark, adding to the wild desire swelling from deep within. When he delivered four more in rapid succession, the sting was enough to bring tears to my eyes.

"Now, be a good girl."

His heavy footsteps as he took long strides deeper into the lair would forever remain in my memory. Suddenly, everything was surreal. He was the caveman, and I was his mate being taken to his cave. While the thought was horrifying, it was also exciting. The man reeked of passion, and I'd fallen into a haze of lust, incapable of fighting in earnest what he was doing to me.

Did that make me a willing victim?

God above, this was insane.

"Why are you doing this?" I muttered as his strides developed a rhythm. I tried to grab onto the chain holding the boxing bag in place, but that forced him to smack me again, this time the hard swat shifting from stinging sensations to outright pain.

"Why? Because I can. Because you offered."

"No. No! That's not what I meant." I lifted my head, trying to find anything I could use as a weapon. Oh, yeah. What did I think I would manage to do, beat the brute over the head? What good would that do?

My words faded away as he moved down a hallway, passing by two open doors to the last one. When he walked inside, I was thrown by the luxuriousness of the room. Gorgeous ornate and huge furniture was positioned against almost every wall, the deep shade of purple on the walls as shocking as what I was dealing with.

The room didn't seem to suit him at all. He stopped just inside, turning just enough I was able to see the massive bed. Holy shit, it was huge, the vivid purple comforter thick, the material like velvet. I pushed against his back, tossing my head over my shoulder when I felt him yanking one tennis shoe off my foot.

"What are you doing?"

"If we're going to become acquainted then we'll need to be more comfortable." His words were a statement, the thickness of his accent sliding over me like he'd yanked the comforter from the bed, sliding it against my naked skin. *Girl, what did you get yourself in the middle of?* There was no dignified answer.

I was dizzy, my stomach full of butterflies.

After yanking off my other shoe and both socks, tossing them aside as if his effort was bothersome, he dumped me directly into the middle of the bed. I sank into the softness, stunned from the revelation of what was about to happen.

Move. Get a grip.

My little voice was jarring.

I wasted no time, scrambling to try to get to the other side. What was I thinking? He simply wrapped his fingers around my ankle, tugging me all the way back to the edge.

"I can see I'm going to need to punish you even more before we can enjoy each other's company."

"This is crazy. You don't have control over me."

Kirill crawled onto the bed, hovering over me possessively. He snagged my hair, holding me in place as he rolled the tips of his other fingers down my spine, moving them along my buttocks then sliding them underneath.

"Oh," I whimpered, taking shallow breaths as he eased his hand between my legs. I was overcome with a deliriously exciting rush of vibrations, clawing the covering as he rubbed up and down the length of my pussy. Everything he was doing added to the extreme embarrassment. The bastard now knew that his roughness had enticed me, luring me into his darkness. I closed my eyes, trembling as he slid a single finger under the thin elastic. His touch was surprisingly gentle, the tip tickling my clit as he swirled it around the tender bud several times.

As he held me, he took his time continuing the spanking, moving his hand from one side to the other. I couldn't breathe, had no sense of what I'd been thinking, but as the scent of my desire floated between us, I was mortified.

"Yes, my good girl." With every hard crack of his hand, I fell more and more into a blissful state, my mind a complete blur. The pain had already morphed into something sinfully delicious, which was crazy.

He gave me six more, each smack of his hand harder than the one before. By that point, I could no longer breathe easily.

Everything about the man aroused me, which was horrible to admit to myself. He took his time, enjoying the moment, the rumble coming from his chest indicating his hunger was increasing. When he pulled his hand away, a ragged breath escaped my mouth.

"That's where you're wrong, my sweet, delicious Candy. As of now, I've become your protector."

"What the hell is that supposed to mean?"

"That means I never intend on letting you go."

CHAPTER 3

Kirill

She blushed for at least the sixth time, the simple, innocent action adorable. She was a little hellion, sassing people her method of protection. Even though I'd made a bold claim, she couldn't understand there was no protection from a man like me. I was used to rebellious women, most of them acting as if they had every right in the world to be haughty in their mannerisms, demanding in their actions. But they'd taken it to an artform, which usually bored me after ten minutes.

This girl was different, her defiance a natural protective element, although she hadn't expected that I would open the door. It had been obvious by the flash of terror in her eyes. Yet she'd recovered quickly, another adorable trait like the way she was chewing on her lower lip, trying her best to figure me out.

BEAUTIFUL VILLAIN

To date, no one had been able to do that.

Women like this had never attracted me before, but everything about this girl was enticing. The moment she'd opened her eyes wide, I'd been lost in them. We'd instantly connected, the harsh thrash of electricity a bolt of lightning crashing down from the sky. Her eyes were luminescent, so large my cock ached even more. While mine were green, often described by other women as the perfect jewel, hers were soft in nature. More inviting. The hue reminded me of murky ocean water, only a hint of green capable of being seen from the naked eye, but the draw so powerful that I couldn't resist swimming toward it.

Even thought she'd denied the attraction we shared, pretending she was offended by my words, I'd seen the look of desire in her eyes if only for a few seconds.

But there was no doubt in my mind that she wanted the experience of spending the night with a dangerous man.

"I know you want this," I said with the arrogance she expected me to have.

I was grateful at that moment I'd changed into gym shorts, or my cock would be pinched in my zipper. In a few short minutes, she'd managed to awaken the savage beast inside of me.

Her mouth twisted, her eyes wild with a combination of indignation and excitement, but she couldn't seem to find the right retort, which up to now, she'd had no problem with.

"I think you're mistaken," she snarked. I could tell by the flash in her eyes that she was proud of herself for finding her voice.

"How's that?"

"I didn't come here to…"

"To?" I encouraged.

"To be hassled by a Neanderthal."

"Tsk. Tsk. Now you're insulting me, and I thought we were getting along so well."

"Then you thought wrong."

"I'm never wrong."

"But you're always an asshole," she huffed, shaking her head.

"I believe we've already established that, and I have no intentions of hassling you. What I have in mind is more carnal in nature."

"You're impossible. Insane. I don't know you. This isn't going to happen."

"You seem to know me pretty well, or at least you don't mind making rude statements."

She was even more flustered, wiggling in my hold, which only aroused me even more.

"That's because you make it easy to do."

Everything about this was a bad idea.

I'd had a lot of them over the years, but this one was likely to bite me in the ass. It didn't matter. The moment I'd opened the door and witnessed the creature standing in front of me, I'd nearly lost my mind. She was perfect, a creation sent from God himself. Very few women had caught my eye over the years, but this one had yanked at the brutal man inside of me, dragging the sadistic beast to the surface.

I'd caught a glimpse of her once before, her long sun-kissed hair swinging back and forth in a ponytail as she walked. My cock had ached then just as it did now, but I'd made it a point to stay away from temptation. If she hadn't knocked on my door in the stark middle of the night, none of this would be happening.

Now it was too late, my hunger off the charts.

Everything about her called to me, stirring the darkness I'd attempted to shut down. Her light green eyes reminded me of early morning grass as first light shifted over the horizon but tinted with a delicious blend of fire and ice, a dangerous combination for a man like me. They stared at me with fear laced in them, but there was also a continued look of defiance. That made my balls tighten even more.

What continued to nag at me was the obvious. If she worked for Killian's bar, the fuckers who owned the joint might have sent an innocent creature to check out what the hell Dimitre and I were doing residing just outside enemy territory. The Russians and the Irish had always had a beef, especially when the *Pakhan*, Vladimir Kozlov, had barreled into the country, taking over a good portion of land surrounding them. The Irish lived in several boroughs inside the city, but this one was by far the most populous, which allowed a decent observational post.

It was no mistake that Dimitre and I had been stationed at this apartment for a tentative duration of time. We were seeking information as well as retribution for the execution of my men, all trained assassins. The majority I'd trained myself to be the fixers of the Bratva, carrying out necessary exterminations in the dead of night, which prevented unnecessary bloodshed in the streets.

The attack had been unexpected. I continued to blame myself for the oversight. I'd spent years training to face any scenario when it came to eliminating our enemies. Gone were the days of simply going in with guns blazing. While war in the streets was always an option, the silent kills without witnesses had proven to be most successful.

All hand selected for their loyalty and brutality, my team's skill had been unequaled by the Italians, the Armenians, or the Polish mob. Everything about the attack reeked of betrayal. Only the Italians had the ability to decimate the secure building housing our massive collection of weapons and other instruments. Yet there remained a tentative truce between us, peace that the city needed. My team and our company had been shrouded in secrecy, the location only known by the highest officials in the Bratva.

The attack had been well executed, leaving only two survivors and the building in flames. Members of law enforcement had arrived within minutes, a further indication whoever had planned the massacre had hedged their bets with calling them ahead of the assault.

That night had been nothing abnormal, the mission we were on simple in terms of the Bratva: the removal of three snitches in three different locations. We'd never had the opportunity. I'd finished the deed myself after the horrific event, taking out my anger on the bastards, but it hadn't robbed me of the guilt.

The bastards responsible had hoped any survivors would be arrested for illegal arms charges or worse. Our only saving grace, if such a thing existed for the Bratva, was that we owned the law enforcement officers who'd been sent.

When four different informants had indicated the Irish were involved, that had made things dicey. There was no indication the attack had to do with the Irish mob, the group significantly smaller and less organized than the Kozlov Empire. That left us with the powerbrokers of the unions, people we called the Saints. They were powerful in a different way, controlling the unions and a good portion of politics.

While they weren't immune to getting their hands dirty, an operation of that size indicated a much larger and more deadly plan was in the works.

It was my task to find out what the fuck that was.

Mistakes weren't an option.

While getting this close to their territory wasn't part of our typical duties, it could prove helpful. In addition to hunting down the motherfuckers who'd killed my men, we also needed to ascertain what plans certain members of the Irish clan had with regard to several construction projects that were ongoing. While we had had significant control over dozens of members of law enforcement, we hadn't made a dent in the unions.

The fuckers controlled almost every aspect of the business, requiring every worker in the city to become a member or face consequences.

That was about to change.

The union leaders had no idea what kind of consequences they would face if they continued to cause problems.

I thought about how Candy had entered my life and exhaled. Women were used as pawns all the time. The act was popular in my home country. I was no fool and had never fallen for anything so egregious, which is why the timing bothered me.

While I doubted that she was being used given her real surprise when I'd answered the door, I'd keep it in the back of my mind. Or maybe that's what I wanted to believe.

Not that it would matter. She was mine. That decision had already been made.

I'd wrapped my hand around her ponytail, dragging her head back after making the proclamation. Her reaction was exactly as I'd expected. She'd hissed at me, as if she had any choice in the matter. As soon as I ripped the red elastic band from her hair, she tossed her head, allowing the limited light in the room to add a luminescent hue to her long locks. Damn, the woman was beautiful, more so than she'd appeared in the scruffy blue coat and ridiculous Converse sneakers.

She had the kind of body men fantasized about, her hourglass figure built exactly as any red-blooded man would envision in his mind. I wanted to explore every inch, taking hours to learn all her nuances in order to make her moan from my touch alone. She held a vibrancy inside that ignited my passion. There was nothing worse than a meek woman pretending to be an innocent flower, waiting for a man to save her from the ravages of others.

This girl could fight. That much I'd already seen.

"Damn you," she snarled.

"I'm already damned, *printsessa*."

"Stop calling me that. I'll never be your princess."

"You'll learn soon enough that there is nothing you can do to prevent it."

What she knew about boxing had surprised me. Somehow, I knew I was in store for additional shocks along the way as I indulged in our combined pleasure. But first, the little fireball would need to accept that I controlled her. I inhaled her sweet aroma, my mouth watering at the sinful thought of driving my tongue past her swollen folds. The fact she was already wet pushed away any sanity. It was no use around her. She'd awakened a need that could never be shut down again.

As soon as I eased back, Candy attempted to crawl away from me again. "You're a very naughty girl."

"You have no idea, buster," she snarled in return.

I allowed her to scramble away by several feet, grinning as I watched her, my balls tightening even more. She was a handful and then some. The rowdy bar wasn't a fan of Russians, so visiting her at her place of work could prove to be toxic. Not that I gave a shit. She was now my woman, and I would frequent whatever establishment suited me.

"You really do need to start obeying me if we have any hope of getting along," I said in an even gruffer voice than normal. I did enjoy toying with her, but my patience would wear out soon enough.

I dragged her toward me, spanking her bottom over the far too short khaki skirt she wore.

"Ouch! That hurts."

"As it should, *printsessa*."

"I just told you. Stop calling me that. I'm no princess. I pay my own way, do my own thing."

I wasn't certain who she was trying to convince, but her spiteful words only enflamed my raging desire that much more. I was finished with wasting time, my needs increasing with every passing second. After climbing off the bed, I pulled her to the edge, reaching underneath to unfasten her skirt.

"You're crazy," she whispered, but there was no animosity in her tone, just a breathless wonderment of what was about to occur between us.

"We've also already established that." I jerked on the zipper, finally able to drag the dense material past her rounded hips.

She picked that moment to start another little quarrel between us, doing everything she could to get out of my clutches. I wasted no time spanking her bottom several times, the sting in my hand giving me a wide smile.

Candy stopped moving altogether, but as she twisted her head over her shoulder, the venomous look she gave me allowed a jolt of electricity to soar into my system. I'd had burly men who didn't issue anywhere close to the ferocity she was showing. Everything the woman did enticed me even more.

After removing her skirt, I took my time rubbing my hand across her buttocks. I wasn't romantic by nature, certainly not considered gentle with anything I did in my life, but with this girl, I wanted to take my time without interruption, indulging until I was fully sated.

If that was possible around her.

"Tell me, Candy. Have you ever had a man show you what true ecstasy feels like?" I breathed in her scent once again, dragging my tongue across my lips as I thought about the sweet kiss. She'd yielded to me, but she hadn't fully let go. That would come with time, when she was insatiable with need.

"I..." The warm flush cresting along her chin was just as delightful as the adorable pink panties, blushing pink to be exact.

"It's alright to be honest with me, *moya krasota*."

"You have no right to ask me that," Candy insisted, although she made no attempt to move away. "I don't know you."

"Ah, but you soon will." Using the flat of my hand, I continued roaming from one side of her bottom to the other before easing the material of her panties away. "Answer me."

I could see just enough of her pinched expression to tell she wanted to be open with me. I gave her a single smack as a reminder of who she belonged to.

Her ragged whimper was sweet music. "Yes. Okay? Yes."

"But you've never found anyone who took the time to learn every beautiful inch of you in order to find out what makes you tick."

There was something adorable about the way her lower lip trembled when she tried to hold back the truth. I pulled her panties down her long legs, barely able to control the barbarian inside of me. I'd never been this aroused, beads of sweat rolling down the back of my neck.

When she remained silent, I cracked my hand against her porcelain skin twice. It was enough she jerked forward, tossing her head back and forth.

"No. No!"

"That's about to change." It had been a long time since I'd been able to show a woman how a real man should behave, especially in the bedroom. When I allowed her to leave my apartment, she would be completely satisfied, sore, and already hungry for more.

"I don't... want you."

"And I don't believe you. I can still see the tiny tic in the corner of your mouth. There's no sense in denying your attraction. We're both adults." I smacked her four additional times, but I'd grown bored with disciplining her. I had plenty of time to do that if necessary. Now was all about satisfying our shared needs.

"But you're a horrible man."

The tone of her voice had changed, as if she was trying to convince herself she could never want such a repulsive man like me in her life. I used a single finger, sliding it up and down her glistening pussy, allowing my simple touch to release the truth.

"Oh…" she whimpered, clamping her eyes shut.

I eased my finger past her folds, my cock pinched against my tight gym shorts. I would need relief soon, but I'd force myself to wait until she was completely satisfied. The first time had to be special, something for her to remember for months, years to come. As I pumped deep inside, I could see her resolve crumbling before my eyes, her breathing rapid and the pulse on the side of her neck thumping rapidly. It was all I could do not to drive my cock deep inside without hesitation.

When I added a second finger, she lifted her head, her face glistening with a light sheen of perspiration, her luscious lips pursed as she continued to fight the sensations rushing through her. She was tight, impossibly so. I'd need to make certain she was extremely wet before thrusting my cock inside.

I couldn't take my eyes off her as I thrust inside, my chest tightening from the anticipation of burying myself into her wetness. The way she arched her back, shifting backward and forward was almost too much for the savage inside of me to take. My breathing had become labored, so much so my muscles tensed. I was given a delightful gift only minutes later when her fingers tightened around the comforter, a blissful smile crossing her sweet face.

I was already bringing her to an orgasm. She was like a perfect flower, finally opening to the sun. I snarled

BEAUTIFUL VILLAIN

inwardly from the poetic thought, shoving it aside for now. As I slipped my other hand under her shirt, she issued a tiny mew. With a few more strokes of my hand against her pussy, I could tell she was close. Curling my fingers, I shifted the angle of my hand and almost immediately her body reacted, tensing at first, her breathing ragged.

"Oh. Oh. Oh." She sucked on her bottom lip, the slight action more provocative than anything else she'd done. But it was also adorable because she had no idea what kind of power she had in the flash of her eyes and the cutting words dripping from her mouth. No woman had defied me so blatantly.

And that made my hunger that much more intense.

I was mesmerized by her beauty and the way she was reacting. I wouldn't be able to get enough of this woman. When she threw her head back, I pressed my thumb against her small asshole, pushing it just inside.

The lovely Candy didn't need any further encouragement. As hard as she tried to keep from exclaiming, she failed, her glorious whimper floating toward the high ceiling. I was even more delighted when the single climax erupted into another, her entire body trembling.

She had no idea what kind of powerful hold she had over me. I could do this for days without a break. When she stopped trembling, I returned to the bed, easing my arm around her head, brushing my slickened fingers back and forth across her tight lips. While she didn't fight me when

I pushed them inside her mouth, I could tell by her clawed hands that she was angry with herself for letting go even for that long.

I pushed the strings of hair away from her face, lowering my head until I was able to press a series of kisses against her skin. As I dragged my tongue toward her ear, she laughed softly as if I'd tickled her.

"Now, I think you understand that we are good together, *moy malen'kiy ognennyy shar*. I'm going to enjoy fucking you."

"This can't... I mean you are... I don't know you."

"Mmm... That's about to change and all for the better. What I just gave you was a mere taste. Soon, you'll be spiraling out of control."

"I'm a good girl."

"I'm certain you are, but there's nothing wrong with embracing your bad side, now is there? Life is all about taking chances. I sense that's how you've wanted to be but felt strangled by a fake requirement to follow the rules. Yes?" Before she had a chance to respond, I turned her over onto her back, remaining aloft as I peered down.

Seeing her long hair splayed out across the dark purple comforter, my balls ached to the point of sheer agony.

"Maybe," she whispered, trying to look away.

I gently pulled her chin back to center. "My little rebel, you never have to look away. Answer me."

"It's what I was taught."

"Understood; however, tonight is about taking what you want. Do you think you can do that?"

She seemed tentative at first, but finally pressed the heels of her hands against my chest, using her fingers to caress my skin. As her eyes darted back and forth, I realized I was smiling all over again. She had that kind of effect on me, providing a sense of joy where I'd had none for as long as I could remember.

No one would dare try to take her away from me. They wouldn't be that stupid.

Her breathing still skipping, she traced the ink from my neck down my right arm, her small tongue darting out several times. Whether it was another nervous gesture or not, it was driving me closer to the edge of rationality.

I lifted one of her arms over her head then the other, easily able to wrap my fingers around her small wrists. She arched her back immediately, which put strain on the tight tee shirt. I raked my gaze down from her face, savoring every minute of the way her body responded.

She chewed on her inner lip as I crowded between her legs, fanning my fingers then pulling them down her face, the tips barely touching. She never blinked as I continued crawling my hand down further, swirling the tip of my index finger around one taut nipple. When I shifted to the other, taking my time flicking it back and forth before pinching it between my thumb and forefinger, she twisted her head away, panting.

I eased my finger under her chin, slowly turning it until she was forced once again to look into my eyes. "Don't look away from me, beauty," I commanded, issuing a hearty growl after saying the words. Her expression of defiance continued to excite me. I never wanted to drive the spunk and fire from her.

I lowered my head, blowing across her jaw before capturing her mouth. Her lips were tight as they'd been before, refusing to allow my tongue entrance. But as I gently teased open her mouth, keeping the moment of intimacy soft and sensitive, I felt her entire body relax, allowing her lips to part.

The taste of her from before hadn't been nearly as sweet. As I swept my tongue inside, I was reminded of juicy cherries as they popped inside my mouth. She was so damn delicate, the aura of innocence about her entirely different than I was used to. I could kiss her for hours, which certainly wasn't like me.

I allowed the kiss to continue, even though I was losing control. When I finally let go of her wrists, I was certain she'd claw my skin. Instead, she slipped her hand over my shoulder, dangling her fingers.

As I pulled away, I gave her a stern glare before rising off the bed. "Stay right there."

"What if I don't?"

I shot her a look, taking exaggerated deep breaths. "Then you won't like the consequences."

* * *

Candy

The treachery of my body remained in the forefront of my mind. One minute I'd tried to break free of the criminal's hold. The next I was succumbing to him like some wanton sinner. What had happened to the good girl inside, the one who refused to take crap from anyone?

He'd happened, the brutal Russian with a voice like an opera singer. I was appalled by the scent of sex permeating the room, until I was forced to accept it was my sex, not his.

Yet.

He'd peeled away far too many layers, able to see the truth behind the shield I'd forged a long time ago. He'd seen my blatant desire, encouraging me to open up to him. And I'd allowed that to happen.

As Kirill walked away from the bed, heading for his dresser, it was the first time I realized he was wearing a watch. I found it intriguing that he took his time removing the oversized piece, placing it gingerly inside a box on the dresser. I was right about his scars. There was another long one going down the back of his leg. I could only imagine how that had been caused. Whatever did likely kept him out of action for a long time, the wound cutting nerves and tendons.

When I shifted on the bed, moving closer to the edge, he lifted his head, staring at me with darker eyes than before. He was daring me to try to make a run for the door. One minute he was tender, sweet like a lover. Then his true personality rushed to the surface. He was a true savage.

Russian.

What was he doing in an Irish neighborhood? Well, technically the apartment building was outside the invisible circles, but it still didn't make any sense. The Irish community was tightly knit. There wasn't a thing that went on without everyone else knowing about it. That had been the very first thing I'd heard from more than one member of my extended family almost immediately after I'd moved to New York. It was their way of warning me where I was safest. Maybe that's why I'd purposely chosen an apartment just outside the limits.

When Kirill turned around, his gaze seemed heavier than before, his stare reminding me of a wild beast in the jungle. He wasted no time removing his boots, tossing them aside. I jumped both times he dropped one to the floor, but I still couldn't take my eyes off him. I doubted he would enjoy being called beautiful, but this was the epitome of the term, even with his scars and constant scowl.

My throat tightened as he slipped his fingers under the elastic of his shorts. Dozens of filthy thoughts raced through my mind. They were so depraved that I knew I needed to go to confession this Sunday in order to feel cleansed. There wasn't water hot enough to rinse away the pure sin.

I could still try to convince myself that he didn't excite me or that I hadn't enjoyed the orgasm, but it would be the biggest lie of the night. As he lowered his shorts, I slapped one hand over my mouth to keep from exclaiming. He'd been created as the perfect image of man, his muscles so chiseled that from a distance he appeared to be carved out of stone. I swallowed several times when his shorts went down past his hips.

Oh. My. God. There was no chance in hell his big cock was going to fit inside me. No, it wasn't just big, it was huge, long and thick just like the rest of him. I tried to look away, I really did, but how can one be exposed to something so incredible then not want another glimpse? Heat seemed to rise from the depth of my being, shooting into every cell and muscle. Or maybe it was the other way around, the rush of adrenaline and tiny explosions going off in my body stealing a good portion of my breath.

As he stood completely naked, I started shaking all over, my teeth chattering as he approached. When he returned to the bed, he eased me further up on the bed until my head rested on a pillow. I thought brutal men didn't care about a woman's comfort? Now I was thinking completely irrational thoughts, maybe in an attempt to keep my mind from dropping into the pits of hell.

Kirill hunkered over me, remaining on his elbows as he peered down just like he'd done before, but there was something entirely different. More concentrated. He remained silent as he drew his finger down my neck, rolling the tip along my side all the way to my waist. As he slowly started to roll the shirt up and over my breasts, I wrapped my hand around his wrist.

"I'm going to make you feel so good, *moya krasota*," he whispered.

"What is that?"

"My beauty."

He continued to call me his. What if he never allowed me out of this room, let alone his apartment? I wanted to laugh at the ridiculousness of my thought, but was it? Everything about him was possessive. I closed my eyes, not bothering to fight him as he pulled the material over my head. I halfway expected that he'd part my legs, driving his cock inside me in one brutal move, but he continued his exploration.

The lightness of his touch continued the way it had been before, gently rolling over my curves as he traveled between my breasts. I could still taste his kiss coupled with my pussy juice. I'd thought the combination would be revolting, but it'd been sweet and tangy at the same time.

"Very beautiful," he muttered before finally dropping his head, swirling his tongue around my nipple. When he eased my arms over my head again, he didn't hold them in place, but I knew better than to dare try to move them.

I stared up at the ceiling, prickles of sensations riding up and down from my toes to the tips of my fingers and back down again. His scent was stronger than before, the musk and testosterone becoming a drug I wasn't certain I could live without.

He was as tender as he was before, laving my hardened bud for a full minute before pulling the tender tissue inside his mouth. When he sucked, the sound he made was erotic, evocative. I was pulled into a sweet buzz, all reality shutting down around me. I wanted to touch him, to feel his rippling muscles beneath my fingertips. I longed to drag my nails down his back, making my own marks. The thought was as outlandish as the moment we were sharing.

No, this wasn't exactly sharing. We weren't entering into a relationship of any kind. This was just sex. Or was it?

I bit back a series of moans when he pinched my nipple, twisting it until I was forced to cry out in discomfort.

"Shush, little one. Allow the pain to take you to the cusp of ecstasy."

Was he kidding? Is that how he thought it worked? I shifted my legs, surprised when he rolled his arm under my thigh, lifting and pulling my leg out to the side. I'd never felt so exposed, another flush creeping along my cheeks. I turned my head, gasping for air as he brushed his lips to my already bruised nipple, sucking until he eased the pain. He was watching me so intently, only moving when I did, reacting to every tiny shift or my ragged breathing.

There was no way to stop moans from escaping no matter how hard I tried. He nipped my bud, sucking even harder before lifting his body a few inches, growling as he dragged his tongue down my stomach. I was thrown by how sensual he'd made the experience, tossed into an even thicker fog as he swirled the tip around my belly button.

I realized I'd arched my back, as if I was begging him to lick me. Mortified, I wanted nothing more than to hide under the covers, but my beautiful villain would never allow it. He took his time pressing his hot, wet lips from one side of my hips to the other. By that point, I was panting, lightheaded from the intense pleasure rolling through me.

Time seemed to stand still as he gathered my legs into his hands, pushing my knees against the covering. I dared take a quick look down and when he licked the inside of my thigh, I threw my arm over my face, openly disobeying his silent wishes. I couldn't stand to watch, even though I was tingling all over as wave after wave of pleasure trickled through me.

I had no idea how much time he took before darting his tongue against my clit, but the moment he did, I jerked up, a scream ready to erupt from my throat.

He growled as a response, digging his fingers into my skin. I'd never been stretched so wide open, exposed for a mysterious man I didn't even know. I resisted laughing, biting my lip as a string of stars floated in front of my eyes. How could anything so bad feel so good?

As he flicked his tongue back and forth across my tender nub, I bucked against the bed, lifting my hips. I couldn't help myself. He sucked on my clit, every sound he made a string of guttural noises. The man was a true animal, barbaric in every way, but as he continued licking, drawing his tongue up and down the length of my pussy, I realized he was an expert in providing ecstasy.

He knew exactly what made the sensations rush to the surface, changing the speed and roughness every time I responded. No man had ever bothered to care this much, dragging me close to ecstasy then backing off, elongating the incredible experience.

I was breathless, my head pounding given the savage reps of my heartbeat. Everything was a huge blur as he drove at least two fingers inside of me, pushing me closer and closer to nirvana. I wasn't the kind of girl who had regular orgasms. As another one powered toward the surface, I realized just how much I'd been missing out on. I slammed my hand on the comforter, struggling to breathe as a climax finally rushed into me like a bolt of lightning.

"Oh. Oh. My. God!"

He held me down, his fingers kneading my skin as he feasted like a rogue, licking up every drop of cream as the single orgasm pushed into a wave. All rational thoughts were tossed aside, the pleasure more extreme than anything I'd ever felt before.

I was exhausted, elated and furious with myself all over again. I kept my head to the side, fisting my mouth as the weight on the bed changed. I could feel his heat from a hundred yards away. He was made of fire and brimstone, exuding the kind of power reserved for those in charge of everything and anyone in his vicinity.

Now that included me.

I knew after this he would never let me go. I'd been captured by the devil himself.

I continued to tremble as he pressed his weight against me, although I sensed he was doing his best to keep from crushing me. His eyes were no longer focused, his full lips holding the sheen of my sex. When I tried to look away, he cradled my jaw in his hand, brushing his thumb back and forth across my lips.

"You're afraid of me," he half whispered.

What did he think I was going to say, that I wasn't afraid of anything? Maybe I hadn't been up until the point I'd knocked on his door. I'd lived a relatively sheltered life until coming to New York. Even though my parents were far away in a tiny town in Pennsylvania, several of my relatives were always close by, one owning the bar where I worked. That had been the only reason my parents had allowed me to come to New York in the first place.

So maybe I was a little scared of him.

Okay, so a lot.

He could still kill me if he wanted.

"Yes. Does that make you happy?"

He sighed then leaned down, replacing his thumb with his tongue, swiping it back and forth across my lips before capturing my mouth. As it had done before, my body reacted instantly, arching toward him. This time, disobedient or not, I raked my hand over his shoulder, scratching his back hard enough I hoped he'd feel it for days. Maybe I'd been lucky enough to draw blood.

Kirill didn't seem deterred at all, his kiss even more passionate, his growls permeating the air around us. The man could kiss, I'd give him that. As if in response to what I'd done, he eased his hand down, pulling one leg to the side. Then I felt the bulbous head of his cock breaching my swollen folds.

I stiffened, still uncertain I could handle his size. As he slipped the tip in by several inches, I was shocked how my pussy muscles reacted, stretching immediately to accommodate his large girth. I moaned into the kiss, shifting my hips back and forth, my actions only driving him in even deeper. The electricity shooting through me was magical. There were so many dancing vibrations skittering through me that I had difficulty breathing.

He took his time as he'd done with everything else, allowing me to get used to his massive size. When I felt his balls hitting my bottom, I gripped his arms, hanging on for dear life. That's the moment everything around us vanished. I wasn't entirely certain I could even remember my own name.

He brushed his lips to my ear, licking the shell then whispering words in Russian that I couldn't understand but everything coming out of his mouth sounded sexy, filthy in every way.

When he pulled almost all the way out, I gasped, bucking my hips against him.

"My little insatiable rebel," he said, laughing in a deep, sensual tone. "You'll get all you can handle, my fireball, but you're not in control. Get that through your pretty little head. You'll accept what I demand and come when I tell you to. Do you understand?"

The sound of his voice remained hypnotic. When I didn't answer him, he squeezed my throat, but gently, a reminder of just how dangerous he truly was.

"Yes."

"You feel so damn good and you're all mine."

Every time he acted possessive, I cringed deep inside, but the words also excited me even more. He teased me, remaining barely inside as he peered down. Then he thrust brutally, the force driving me into the bed by several inches. When he repeated the move, I wrapped one leg around his thigh to feel grounded.

Over the course of the next few minutes, he developed a rhythm that was both savage and soothing, driving deep inside like the brutal man he was. We were locked together in the ultimate sin, our bodies made for each other.

The thought was just as crazy as everything else had been, but I'd never been driven into a state of euphoria before. He refused to stop, plunging harder and faster, pushing me to the point of no return. Never in my wildest imagination would I consider doing something like this on my own. I fought every emotion, every ugly thought as my pussy muscles clamped and released several times, keeping his delicious cock buried deep inside.

I was lost in the moment, ecstasy rolling through me for the third time.

"Yes. Yes. Don't stop. Yes."

"I won't stop, baby, until you take all you want. Now come for me, *printsessa*."

I felt the brush with ecstasy coming closer, vibrations dancing through me. And closer still. His fucking was even harder than before, our hips smashing together, our combined sounds unrecognizable.

His command resonated throughout my body, driving me into a beautiful windswept climax immediately.

I could tell I was digging my nails into his arms as the orgasm powered through me. He pounded into me long and hard, refusing to let me go. I was driven to some kind of madness as the hard fucking continued, his growls mixing with the slam of the headboard against the wall.

When his body tensed, I held my breath, easing my other leg around him. As he began to shake, rising onto his elbows, he pressed his face against my neck.

"My beautiful *myatezhnik*."

As he erupted deep inside, I blinked several times, a single tear sliding past my lashes. What had I just done?

CHAPTER 4

Kirill

Structure.

Organization.

Discipline.

I practiced all three in my profession. I had to in order to keep my edge as well as remain alive. While living and working in the US was somewhat safer than in Mother Russia, there were still dozens of men who'd enjoy the sight of blood oozing from the wounds they'd inflicted. While I usually refrained from alcohol, as I stood in front of the floor-to-ceiling window in the living room, I was already on my second drink of the night. I'd turned off the lights, preferring the darkness when I worked through a problem in my mind.

And Candy was a definite problem. While I'd enjoyed feasting on her body, I couldn't get the strange nagging out of my head. Maybe I'd lost my touch in being able to see treacherous actions within a few seconds of meeting someone.

As I rolled the glass across my forehead, I allowed my thoughts to drift to the possibility she'd come to seduce me. While there was nothing of real importance for her to find inside this shithole of an apartment, simply knowing the layout might prove to be beneficial to some fool who was determined to bring down a portion of the Kozlov family.

I tossed back the shot, heading for the bottle for another round. On this night, I knew I wouldn't feel the effects of the liquor to any degree. As I took a deep breath, I was able to gather her scent all over again. It was intoxicating, even if it had a slight hint of stale beer and roast beef. I snickered and poured the third shot. A peace offering. The girl had balls. Yes, she did.

With what the Kozlov family was going through with the unions, I would need to tread water carefully with her. How the hell had I managed to get myself into this situation? Sighing, I took a smaller sip, allowing the alcohol to remain in my mouth for a short time before swallowing. The slight burn felt damn good, but not nearly as amazing as being inside of her. It had been a hell of a long time since I'd enjoyed being with a woman. Tasting and fucking Candy had been a real treasure.

When I heard a sound, I powered back the drink, slowly turning my head toward the door leading to the bedrooms. Candy walked closer, her timid gait indicating she was still embarrassed by what we'd shared. I'd removed her clothes from the room and the sight of her naked body aroused me just as much as before. Although she couldn't get out of the apartment without getting past me, she was a clever girl so I wouldn't put anything past her.

And I wasn't finished with her yet.

"You took my clothes. Does that mean you plan on keeping me here?" She had one arm crossed over her voluptuous breasts, the other hanging in front of her sweet little pussy. Like that was going to keep me from taking what I wanted. Her attempt to maintain some of her dignity was adorable, my cock already throbbing from the thought of taking her again.

"Come here," I instructed.

She hesitated, as I knew she'd do but even in the darkness with only the light of the moon coming in through the windows, I could tell she'd dropped her gaze to my fully erect shaft.

"I said. Come. Here. Do not make me ask you again."

Her continued act of defiance was going to irritate me at some point. She would soon learn that she was fully under my control whether she was appreciative or not.

When she started moving in my direction, I put the glass on the bar, remaining at the window. She needed to follow my directions. I wouldn't meet her halfway. That wasn't my style.

"Are you going to allow me to leave?" she asked when she was only a few feet away, still far enough I wasn't able to reach out and grab her without lunging forward.

"When I'm ready."

"That's not fair."

"Who said anything in this life is fair, Candy?"

"Who are you?" She dared come to within arm's reach. When she did, I dragged her close, pushing her up against the window.

"The question is who are you? Did you come here for a reason?"

She seemed to sense my question wasn't about the noise level, but when her mouth twisted, I wrapped my hand around her throat.

"Do not lie to me again, Candy."

"What do I have to lie about? I told you why I came. Now, I'm sorry that I did."

"And Killian's bar. What the hell are you doing in that place?"

A hint of confusion crossed her face. "I work there. That's where the sandwich came from that you inhaled. Where the hell do you work, a prison? Oh, no. You should be the one behind the steel bars."

I half laughed, squeezing for a few seconds then releasing my hold. "You don't want to know details regarding my profession. I suggest you refrain from asking questions that could cause you distress."

"Does that mean you're an escaped criminal?"

"That means I'm capable of really bad things. I didn't lie to you before and I don't have any intention of doing so now. However, there are things you will never learn about my life."

"You make it sound like we're going to be a couple."

I fingered her mouth, rubbing with enough pressure that her eyes opened wide. "I hope you're telling me the truth. If I find out otherwise, you won't like the consequences." A couple. She had no way of knowing what it would mean if I kept her as anything other than a possession. She'd become a weakness, an instant target that even a bastard like me wouldn't want to force onto her life.

However, I could keep her a secret for a length of time.

If she wasn't lying to me.

I'd find that out soon enough.

To her credit, she didn't seem afraid. She didn't shake or whimper, just stared me in the eyes rebelliously.

That only made me want her even more. Unable to resist, I crushed my body against hers, sliding my hands down then lifting her up by several feet. I was easily able to slip the tip of my cock just inside, pushing her all the way against the window. She mewed her response, clinging to my shoulders, her eyes darting back and forth across mine.

"To answer your question, I am a man you don't want to cross. I suggest you keep that in mind." When I thrust the entire length inside, I was amazed how her tight pussy muscles clamped around my shaft, drawing me in even deeper. I could fuck her for hours and still never have enough. I kept her pinned to the window, sliding in and out. I planted my hands on either side of her, rolling onto the balls of my feet as I drove as deep inside as her body would allow.

"Bastard," she whispered.

My chest heaving, I kept my hard glare on her beautiful face. "I'm glad you're beginning to understand your place. I'm going to fuck you and often."

She was such a slight little creature but rounded in all the right places. I had a feeling she had no idea just how gorgeous she was. I could imagine how the men at the bar reacted to her, how they manhandled her. I couldn't allow that to happen any longer. She was mine.

As I started fucking her in earnest, she said nothing, but she didn't have to. Her body responded as it had before, her breath skipping and the pulse in her neck throbbing. Just the heat from her skin alone was enough to keep the fire burning deep within me. She was wet, her pussy muscles yielding to me. I was still insatiable with need, unable to control myself around her. I wanted every part of her, to drive her to the furthest realms of ecstasy over and over again. As I continued fucking her, I realized that even if I was required to toss her aside, that would be a command I wouldn't be able to follow.

I would simply need to find a way to protect and shield her from my world. If that was possible. I slammed my hands against the window, using the friction and the power of my muscles to keep her in position. Nothing had felt so good as being inside of her. Candy continued to study me, trying to dig her way into my soul. Even if she managed to do so, what she would find would certainly terrify her even more than she was at this point.

There was a softness to her that had nothing to do with her glorious body. Even the lushness of her lips was appealing, a reminder that I was usually nothing more than a bastard when it came to women. This beautiful girl deserved the finer things in life, rather than living in a shitty apartment or working in a seedy bar.

I could make that happen for her. Hell, I could rock her entire world, allowing her to live in the lap of luxury. Maybe that's what I needed to do. I couldn't concentrate, the sensations rolling through me explosive in nature. I wanted to chain her to my bed, keeping her prepared for my return, but I'd need to learn everything about the beautiful vixen before I felt comfortable that she wasn't a plant.

That was the way of my jaded life, never being able to enjoy the freedom the money and power should allow. When she pressed her knees against my legs, squeezing her pussy muscles, it was her way of attempting to take control. I lowered my head, allowing her to hear several guttural growls before I captured her mouth. She wrapped her hand around my neck, her fingers caressing my skin as I continued fucking her.

She had no way of knowing that she was melting away a layer surrounding me, solidifying her place in my life.

There wasn't a chance in hell I'd be able to let her go.

As another orgasm swept up from my balls, this time I threw my head back with a primal roar.

Candy had been brought into my life for a reason. Now it was time to find out why. If she wasn't the charming flower that she portrayed herself to be, the consequences she'd face would be harsh as well as irreversible.

She would then realize she'd crossed the wrong man.

* * *

As I moved into the living room, I was surprised to find Dimitre drinking coffee. Since we'd moved in, he'd spent a single night in the apartment we shared, his duties as security officer of the patriarch of the Kozlov Bratva often keeping him working late into the night and crashing in his room at the main estate.

I didn't acknowledge his presence as I moved toward the coffeemaker. It was another libation I rarely indulged in, but after the night of passion I'd shared with the rebellious woman and the day ahead, caffeine was the least of my worries.

"Any news on the bastards who tried to destroy us?" Dimitre asked. He had a penchant for being overly dramatic, which usually didn't bother me but today, I remained on edge, the bitterness and rage nearly consuming me. Anytime I was forced to come in close contact with the Irish, it dragged out my demon.

With a single exception.

Damn it. I had to get Candy out of my mind, but her tough, contrary demeanor coupled with her utter innocence continued to call to me.

"We've been here six fucking days, Dimitre. I'm not a goddamn miracle worker."

"Whoa. You're in a surly mood," Dimitre muttered, laughing afterwards. He knew my moods better than most. We'd become friends, although there'd been little time to do anything but work. The Kozlov family were harsh taskmasters, although I enjoyed the various tasks more than most.

"Actually," I said, taking a cup of coffee and hissing from the taste. "I had a good night for a change." Three weeks had gone by since the attack. Three fucking weeks. While my men's extermination was the underlying cause of my sleepless nights, the barrage of gunfire in the confined space had brought out memories that I was best served not to think about.

"Meaning what?" He darted his gaze toward the bag I'd insisted be hung in the living room. While we didn't rent the fleabag apartment to provide a statement to anyone, he considered my hobby overkill since I used my fists almost every day keeping the peace.

"Meaning, I had a late-night visitor." I allowed myself to grin, my cock twitching as I thought about her again. Even after a scalding hot shower, her scent remained covering portions of my skin. I'd fucked her a third time before allowing her to leave, satisfied when she'd screamed out my name in passion. I would do it again, only I craved taking her virgin ass. The thought allowed another smile, vile and filthy thoughts better than bitter coffee as a wakeup mechanism. Maybe she'd be able to soothe the savage beast.

Or keep him on the edge.

"Really? The loneliest man on the face of his planet had a date?"

"Not a date. A happening."

"You mean you had sex. You are glowing," Dimitre chuckled.

"What the hell are you doing here?" His jokes usually fell flat on me but given my usual mood swings, I was already ready to clamp my hand around his throat. And we were buddies.

"A change of clothes. We have that important meeting today." He snorted after reminding me. Neither one of us believed that it would do a damn bit of good.

"You meant you were sent here to make certain I didn't forget about the meeting."

He laughed, shaking his head.

Important. Storming into any union office was a bad idea in my opinion, but Alexei was determined to try to reason with the president of the sordid trade council. Out of any of the dozens of unions, they were almost as corrupt as the Bratva, but they were regaled by construction workers throughout New York. In my opinion, we needed to use force in order to help them understand we refused to accept their politics or their threats. They were fooling themselves if they didn't think we'd retaliate at some point. They would not stop our construction projects.

It was also another method of garnering information about the attack.

"It's bullshit and you know it." I dumped the coffee, the bitter taste forming bile in my mouth.

"Yeah, well, Alexei is insistent. He's trying to legalize our activities."

I threw him a glare. "Do you really believe that?" Alexei was a cunning man, tossing out enough information to try to pacify members of law enforcement. I doubted he would ever completely legalize the family operation even after his father passed his ruling torch.

That is if Alexei's older brother didn't return from Russia to claim his rightful place.

Dimitre walked closer, a smirk on his face. "It doesn't matter what I believe. We follow orders."

He was well aware how much I hated following anyone's rules, but I owed the Kozlov family my loyalty and that never wavered. Besides, men whose did disappeared. However, there was another more personal reason I'd stand beside the patriarch until the day I died. In addition, Alexei Kozlov always had a second plan, including how to handle Michael Walsh and the building and construction trade council if pushed. We would annihilate the executive board if necessary, although he remained just as hesitant as his father to demand blood flow in the streets.

Even if there wasn't a single person inside the Bratva who didn't hunger for retaliation.

"Yeah, we do. We need to find the snitch in our organization." I studied him for a few seconds. Even though we were friends, as the head of security, he certainly knew of the plans and the location of the former warehouse. Shit. Maybe my guilt was getting in the way. Dimitre was another loyalist if for no other reason than the love of Vladimir's daughter.

"Sevastian is in charge of fleshing out the asshole."

Sevastian. The youngest brother was almost as brutal as I was. I sneered at the thought. He had a way about him that terrified even the most seasoned soldiers.

"So tell me about this girl," he chortled.

I glared at him again. "Maybe a plant."

"You've got to be kidding me? So, you added seduction to your repertoire? Not bad."

"As I said, meeting her just happened. At this point, it's a wait and see." I rubbed my clenched jaw, still uncertain what the hell I wanted to do with the woman.

"And she's still alive?"

As I leaned against the counter, I mulled over the question. "What do you know about the Walsh family?"

He snorted. "As much as you do. They are bad news for Alexei and his endeavors. I have no doubt they know enough people to create a group of assassins. Even though they act like they don't, they have a shitload of money. Their old man is formidable, his firm hold on the construction market a stumbling block. As I said, you already know all this."

Stumbling block. If Michael Walsh was assassinated, it would alleviate several of the issues we faced. I'd suspected him the minute the warehouse had been attacked but proving it was something else entirely. "And the family? Do you know all of them?"

"One son is a highly respected and totally clean detective. The other children are considered disappointments to the high and mighty Michael Walsh. Why?" When I didn't say anything, he burst into laughter. "Please don't tell me you hooked yourself up with Walsh's daughter. She's beautiful but a real piece of work. Although not a bad idea, if you ask me. Am I right?"

"No, it's not the daughter, but I do think she's close to the family. Just a gut feeling. She works at Killian's and lives downstairs under us."

He stared at me for several seconds then looked away. Dimitre knew the family politics better than most. After he whistled, he shook his head. "I'm going to give you a piece of advice. Talk to Alexei. Don't keep your relationship from him. He'll be pissed if you do, and you know what happens when he gets angry."

It was funny that he wanted me to talk to the brutal brother over the patriarch. He knew just how close my relationship had always been with the man, something else to piss Alexei off. When dealing with Alexei, even I tempered my dislike of him.

Crossing him wasn't an option. People didn't just disappear; their entire families did as well. Well, I had no family, at least that I knew of. They'd been taken from me years before during a massacre. I would never forget the blood staining my hands or the horrible sound of gunfire popping all around me. The screams of my family continued to echo in my ears, especially my little sister's as she begged for me, her tiny cries of anguish changing me forever. "I don't have a relationship with the woman. I'm just fucking her, and I intend on doing so as often as I fucking want." I was starting to lose control around the edges and that couldn't happen.

"Then it might be your funeral."

"While I appreciate your concern, I'll give you the same advice. Stay away from Tatiana. She would only cause you pain." As the only daughter of the Kozlov Empire, she was off limits to everyone, including the hired help. While Dimitre hadn't confided in me regarding his love for the girl he was tasked to protect, my keen observation skills had provided me the information he'd prefer to keep hidden.

He glared at me, prepared to offer a challenge. I simply kept the same expression on my face. We both knew the score, although it was often difficult to tolerate, let alone accept.

His laugh was just a way of hiding the truth. "Fine, Kirill. Have it your way, but don't say I didn't warn you."

I moved from the small kitchen, heading for the bedroom to dress, my thoughts drifting to Candy and the night before. Tonight, I would gain answers. No matter the outcome, my questions would be handled.

Period.

* * *

The project was only a third of the way to completion, the new casino meant to rival those owned and operated by the Italians. The best architect had been hired, the sleek design and planned amenities likely to exceed every other facility located in

New York or Atlantic City. With billions on the line, it was imperative the construction schedule was maintained.

The singular problem with achieving the goal was the fact the Kozlov family refused to hire union workers. They'd balked at the idea at least a half dozen times, preferring to use those whose loyalty could be easily measured and controlled by the family. The pay was good, the benefits even better, but the other side had added additional pressure.

"Just imagine. This time next year, we'll be operational," Alexei said as he stared out the window of the construction office.

"As long as there are no additional hiccups." I could tell my statement annoyed the man, but he simply shook his head.

"You worry too much, Kirill. Nothing is going to stand in our way."

His defiance was admirable but even he did wishful thinking. The threats were getting out of hand.

"This is just a meeting with Michael Walsh?" Dimitre asked.

Alexei gave him a look, grinning as he usually did when he had something up his sleeve. "Absolutely. For now. So far their threats have been everything I'd expected."

"That too can change," I muttered as I glared out the same window, noticing two of the superintendents heading quickly in the direction of the office. All three of us bristled as they walked in.

"Boss. I think we have a new issue." Jeff Parker was a solid worker, never causing problems, but I still had my doubts about his full loyalty. He glanced from Dimitre straight to me, swallowing hard as he stared into my eyes. Why did I have a feeling the man was hiding something?

"What now, Jeff?" Alexei asked.

Jeff raked his hand through his hair. "It was after quitting time last night. I stayed late to handle some paperwork. Suddenly, two men walked into my office."

"What two men?" I growled, inching closer.

"I don't know. They wore masks and carried weapons." Jeff was antsy as fuck, shifting from one foot to the other. The other man, some asshole I didn't know, couldn't find the balls to look us in the eyes.

A red flag was raised in my mind.

Alexei shot me a look, a curl forming on the corner of his mouth. "What did they say, Jeff?"

"They demanded the workers join the union by the end of the week or there would be consequences."

Consequences. The word held special meaning today, especially since Candy had dropped into my life unexpectedly. That also meant the idea another plan was in motion wasn't farfetched. I bristled, glaring at Jeff. The fucker better have more details than that.

I sensed Alexei's rage increasing. "Did they happen to mention what that would entail?"

Jeff swallowed hard for a second time. I was about ready to shove a weapon against his forehead. It was obvious he wasn't telling the entire truth. "No, sir. They just told me to make certain I let you know."

Alexei walked closer, taking the time to adjust the man's partially lifted collar. When he spoke, his voice held none of the anger I knew he was carrying. "And you just found it necessary to provide that information to me, Jeff?"

"I'm sorry, boss, but we had a late shipment today, several workers who didn't show. I was ass deep in alligators."

I sneered at his analogy.

Alexei sighed, choosing not to discipline the man for ignorance. "From now on, I don't care what time of day or night it is, you will either provide that kind of information to myself or to Kirill. Do you understand me?"

The mention of my name made Jeff shudder visibly. It would seem my reputation had preceded me.

"Of course, sir. I'm sorry. I'm used to threats, but this one was… different."

"I understand, Jeff. We'll take care of it." Alexei said nothing else until the two men walked out the door. Then he turned toward Dimitre. "Make certain additional security is provided and I don't care how many people you need to hire."

"You got it," Dimitre said.

When Alexei shifted in my direction, he shook his head. "Something is different. I don't like this and certainly can't trust Michael and his goons."

"I don't like Jeff's lackluster attitude. Do you trust him?"

"As much as I can trust anybody. I'll have his bank accounts checked. If he received a payoff, he wouldn't be smart enough to try and hide it. I'm telling you. It's like they feel they suddenly have the upper hand."

I thought about how to broach Candy's appearance. "Would he use a pawn to try and discover information?"

"I would put nothing past him. Why?"

"Because a chick who works at Killian's Bar and Grill showed up at my apartment last night out of the blue. She claims it was about noise."

"Noise?" he asked, laughing.

"His desire to be a heavyweight boxer," Dimitre teased, his laughter cut short when he noticed my harsh glare.

Alexei took a deep breath. "Did you extract information?"

"From what I can tell, she has no real connection to the Walsh family."

"I assume you handled her."

I exhaled, staring him in the eyes. "In my way."

He took a few seconds before laughing. "Let me guess. You plan on keeping her on a leash."

"So to speak. However, I do think she could be used to flesh out who's responsible." It was the only way to handle her that made any sense, but doing so would place her life in danger. The thought wasn't acceptable.

"I like your style. However, don't get close to this girl."

"I don't get close to anyone, Alexei. You know that." He should know better than to give me directions.

After a few seconds, he nodded. "Let me know what you find out."

Exhaling, a bitter taste formed in my throat as I thought about her. My blood boiled for a second time. Questioning idiots who betrayed us was my specialty. What I had planned for Candy was entirely different.

But it would prove to be equally effective.

My cock throbbed at the thought.

* * *

I stared up at the mirrored building, my anger just as close to the surface as it had been the entire time I'd spent in the vehicle with Dimitre. There'd been no need for discussion. We knew what we were facing.

Alexei grinned as he lifted his sunglasses, staring at the entrance to the building. "This shouldn't take long."

We entered the building as any other group of professionals, moving silently toward the elevators. The union office was on the top floor, which didn't surprise me. Those elected to hold the upper-level positions fashioned themselves to be above the law, enjoying the perks of their powerful status. They had the ability to halt every construction project in the city, thereby bringing the Big Apple to its knees in a matter of hours.

The shutdown of our operations wasn't acceptable.

Fortunately for the two women sitting at the front desk, they didn't bother to try to stop our advance into the posh suite. They'd been made aware of the established meeting. It would seem everyone in the set of office suites knew who we were, all scuttling behind closed doors as we walked by.

While Michael spent limited time in his office, the man usually found on a golf course, the fact he kept regular hours made it easier to handle corporate conversations. Besides, he'd called for the meeting days before.

As civilized people should conduct business, Alexei had mentioned more than once. In the old days when I was growing up, business was often handled in back rooms and cellars. Times had changed.

We burst in through the closed door, standing just inside. Michael remained behind his desk, two men I'd never seen before standing behind him. The scene was laughable, the scruffy dudes incapable of passing for enforcers.

I glanced around the office, making certain we weren't in for any additional surprises.

"Alexei," Michael said after a full minute had passed.

"Michael. How good to see you." He walked closer to the man's desk, leaning over. "I'll make this meeting short since I have several other more important meetings this afternoon. If you ever threaten any of my workers again under any circumstances, the wrath you will face will not only rock your family but the entire city as well. Do you understand me?" I knew why Alexei hadn't mentioned the attack. We'd done everything we could to clean up the mess without other organizations learning of our mishap. That would also damage our reputation, something we couldn't afford.

I noticed a slight twinge of fear, the same nervous tic Candy had displayed. However, Walsh regrouped quickly, moving to a standing position. "Oh, I understand, Kozlov, but what I don't think you understand is how much power I control in this city. I suggest you consider another line of work."

The man was either stupid or goading us. Either way, he would also learn a valuable lesson.

And I would be the one to teach it.

CHAPTER 5

Candy

I stared at my reflection for the umpteenth time that day alone. My grip on the ugly Formica counter was so tight my knuckles were white. I wasn't certain I recognized the face staring back at me. She was entirely different than the day before. Why?

Because she'd not only accosted a huge gorilla of a man who had to be a serial killer, she'd liked it. Why were the stupid lyrics, *'I kissed a girl and I liked it'* floating around in my mind? This was entirely different.

And the brute was all male. Every. Single. Inch. As I wiggled, the cotton panties I'd chosen for the night couldn't prevent the dense khaki fabric of my skirt from scratching my bottom. Even after over twelve hours, I could still feel the burning sting from the spanking he'd given me.

He. Him. It. Monster.

Kirill.

There. I'd finally thought his name, but I couldn't say it out loud. Not inside the bar anyway. There were some things a girl just couldn't do. Sure, she could fuck a savage but not speak his name because of his heritage. I rolled my eyes before tugging my ponytail holder from my pocket, yanking my hair behind my head. I could still feel his rough fingers touching me, stroking me.

Although it was impossible given the two showers I'd taken, I was able to gather a whiff of his masculinity.

And I wanted more. God help me, I did.

After finishing my hair, I took a deep breath, allowing faded visions to swim through my mind.

He'd been so... authoritative, controlling yet easily the most passionate man I'd ever met. I closed my eyes, tilting my head until the air conditioning vent tickled one side of my neck. Other than the temperature difference, the sensations reminded me of when he'd blown across my face seconds before devouring my mouth.

Just thinking about his gorgeous body, including the best-looking ass in the world made me tingle all over. I shifted my fingers down the side of my neck with a deep sigh. How the hell was I going to get him out of my life now that he'd claimed me as his own?

"Girl. Are you alright?"

I jumped, almost hitting my head against the glass. A rush of embarrassment flooded me, scooting up both sides of my face. Damn it. This was getting ridiculous. What had happened was an atrocity, disgusting. That's the way I had to look at it. Then I'd be forced to try to ignore his advances.

Advances?

Who the hell was I trying to kid? He wasn't going to take no for an answer. Short of moving out of the city, or better yet, out of state, I doubted Kirill would leave me alone. I made a face at the girl entering the bathroom. Tanya was another server, one of the few who bothered to talk to me.

"I'm fine. Just… I'm just thinking."

The look on her face mischievous, she glanced around the bathroom then lowered her voice. "If you ask me, it looks like you got lucky last night."

Another rush of embarrassment almost knocked me over. "Nothing like that." Almost everything he'd said to me continued to play in my mind as it had since I'd closed my eyes in my own bed. That hadn't been until well after dawn.

"Uh-huh. Did anyone ever tell you that you're a terrible liar?"

"All the time as of late." I took several deep breaths, trying to get the man out of my head. What also bothered me was the fact he thought I'd been sent by somebody. To do what? What in the hell could a girl half his size do?

"Come on. We have a few minutes. Confess."

"There's nothing to confess. I had a drink with somebody, and we hit it off."

"Get out of town and I don't buy it for one second," she snorted and pushed her arm against mine. "You have that glow, a bright shining aura surrounding you. You know that only happens for two reasons. Right?"

I narrowed my eyes, glaring at her.

"After wicked wanton sex and when you're pregnant."

The last word almost made me want to vomit. "I assure you that I'm not pregnant. It takes good sex to do that." As soon as the words had flown out of my mouth, I sucked in my breath. Was I still thinking I'd dreamt the entire thing? I rubbed my forehead, longing to scratch out her eyes as she chuckled, the sound more like a cackle.

"Whoever he is, the dude must be pretty damn hot. Maybe he has a twin brother," Tanya cooed.

Dear God. I hoped to hell he didn't. The world couldn't handle one of him as it was. "Ha. Ha. Let's get to work."

"Careful. It's already rowdy out there."

"It's Wednesday. What the hell are they celebrating?" While the bar always seemed packed, as soon as I opened the door, I knew it was going to be one of those evenings

—late and exhausting. Maybe Kirill wouldn't notice when I got home.

Then again, he had evil eyes. For all I knew, he had another set in the back of his head.

As I grabbed my apron from behind the bar, I took a few seconds to scan the room, breathing a sigh of relief.

At least the shift would give me time to think about how to get the man off my back.

And into my bed.

Nope. That would never happen again.

* * *

I was wrong. Completely wrong. Lately, all I'd been was wrong. My brain was already mush and there was more to endure.

Barely two hours into my shift, I was thankful we were allowed to wear tennis shoes. Between the huge and very rowdy crowd, enough beer had been tossed on the floor to make the place a skating rink.

I was shocked my cousin allowed certain behaviors, but this was New York, or so Rian had told me on several occasions. It had been his subtle way of warning me that I wasn't in Pennsylvania any longer.

And thank God for that.

While I usually enjoyed the raunchiness of the crowd, tonight the dozens of men and few women seemed downright crazy. The customers guzzled drinks, forcing one of the bartenders to cut an entire table off, which had then led to a near brawl. That had been followed by the manager bringing his steel bat from behind the bar, forcing everyone to cool down.

With Sean Doyle's six-foot three-inch frame and bright red hair, with the right expression, he was able to create a deranged look with no problem.

There were so many customers, they seemed to illegally filter out the front door since the patio had yet to open for the season. What the hell was going on tonight?

Then there was the yelling, the demands.

"Hey, toots. Another beer over here."

"Hey, sugar, can you deliver your own personal Killian to me?"

"Such a beauty. How about we get to know each other after you get off. Then I can get off."

I'd heard just about everything, almost none of which bothered me. My skin was thick enough I usually managed to brush the trash talk aside. Tonight, I was ready for a fight myself. Maybe the fact asshole number fifty-seven had just 'accidentally' bumped into me, sending an entire small pitcher of beer splashing down the front of my shirt was the last straw.

Or possibly his shit-eating grin.

"You did that on purpose," I hissed, forced to lift my head several inches to try to look him in the eye. I'd be damned. By the jeers from the assholes at his table, I could tell the man had been egged on, perhaps dared to do something so... so... stupid!

"Of course I didn't, sugar."

That was the last time I would tolerate being called sugar. After giving the sloth a huge smile, I reared back, fisting my hand.

"Whoa. Whoa," Sean said as he grabbed my offending arm, tugging me away from Neanderthal boy. "I think that's enough. Buddy. You and your friends are out of here."

"That's not fair," he wailed.

Why was it that drunken men always resorted to acting like children who'd been scolded?

"I said. Outta here." Sean pointed to the door, still trying to keep me from attacking the pompous asshole.

I shifted around the man, planting my hands on my hips. "I'll be happy to show you to the door."

"Woo hoo!" one of them whistled.

"Not so fast," Sean snapped, glaring me in the eyes. "Why don't you get another tee shirt from the back room and take a minute and change?"

At least Neanderthal boy was swaying back and forth. I only hoped one of his friends would help carry him back to whatever sleazy location he lived in.

"Fine." I walked away, my ponytail swinging back and forth.

Tanya lifted her eyebrows as I passed, trying to keep from laughing. Maybe I'd made her night. Who knew? Exhaling, I realized by the time I made it into the storeroom that I was shaking, only able to almost engage in a fight because of adrenaline. I grabbed my size, cursing under my breath as I headed to the bathroom.

Even the new shirt wasn't going to keep me from stinking like beer for the rest of the night. I jerked off the dirty one, fighting to get the other one over my head. Then I remained exactly where I was hours before, staring into the mirror as if the strange feeling pooling in my stomach and tickling sensations would pass. The bastard had managed to break through my hard shell, finding the ooey-gooey center inside. That seemed like weakness to me and not something I wanted to partake in.

I tucked the shirt into my skirt, lifting my middle finger at the mirror. At least that gave me a slight laugh. Fortunately, there were just a few short hours left before I could slink into my apartment and lock the door.

Then I'd crawl under the covers, ignoring the rest of the world, especially Mr. Four-F.

When I walked down the hall, a strange sense of foreboding washed over me. Someone was watching me. I sucked in my breath, moving into the main room, taking a few seconds to scan the area.

"They're gone," Tanya said as she flew by.

I wasn't worried about them. The vibe skittering through me was entirely different. I half expected Kirill to be sitting at the bar, or at least one of the closest tables, but he wasn't. Maybe I was imagining things.

Or maybe it was wishful thinking.

"Uh-oh." Tanya's voice got my attention a few seconds later.

"What is it?"

"Trouble with a capital T." She nodded toward one of the back tables. I had no idea what she was talking about. "They are with one of the unions, like the big boys. They make or break careers, companies, and kneecaps if you ask me, but don't tell anyone I said that."

"O-kay. So?" Kneecaps? I knew some unions were rough in years past, but was that practice still going on today?

"So when they're around, it seems trouble follows. Just be careful. That's your station."

Careful. I shifted my gaze. Sean wasn't paying any attention, which usually meant they weren't an issue. While I knew part of the Walsh family was involved in at least one union, I hadn't talked to Rian or anyone else about their involvement. What bothered me was that a dude had been waiting in the corner closest to the hallway. Just standing there. When he passed, he gave me a look that sent a series of shivers down my legs. When he sat down at the very table I was supposed to service, I froze for a few seconds before my resolve kicked in. I hoped he enjoyed the view because that was as close as the prick would ever get.

I moved through the crowd to their table, planting my usual Barbie doll smile on my face.

"You should have seen the Russian pricks today. They thought they were going to lay down a threat and have Michael cower. They learned," one of the guys as the small table said, or maybe I should say pontificated. The others laughed.

"Yeah, that might be true, but you've heard stories about the Bratva," another one said. "They are nothing but animals."

Bratva.

The smile was put away, a smirk replacing it. Still, I swallowed hard, a tiny bead of perspiration trickling down the back of my neck.

"What can I get you, boys?" I asked after I was ignored for a full ten seconds.

The first guy lifted his head, grinning at me like half the other patrons had all night long. "What are you offering?" He was the gawker and the look in his eyes remained malevolent even though his words were said in jest.

"Don't give her any crap, Rory." The third guy offered a genuine smile. "Don't mind him. He's trying out his usual Wednesday night asshole status."

"Shut up, asshole," Rory snarled. "Why don't you give us a round of Killian's? Sugar pie." He stared me in the eyes as if he was memorizing my face or as if he'd recognized me from somewhere.

"Sure thing, dick weed." While I'd muttered the last two words, I couldn't give a shit about a tip. As I was turning to leave, the front door opened. While Kirill wasn't trying to make a statement with his entrance, he did. Within seconds, you could have heard a pin drop inside the bar.

"Fuck me," good ole Rory hissed.

As soon as Kirill walked inside, he turned his head in my direction, darting his eyes toward the table of men who'd just ordered. I'd already witnessed his cold, hard stare several times. Tonight, his aggressive look was entirely different, the darkness of his eyes startling.

Everything was at a standstill, including my heart. He locked his eyes with mine, his jaw clenching.

"Speak of the fucking devil," Rory huffed from behind me.

I dropped my head slightly, comprehending what the asshole was insinuating. A lump formed in my throat as Kirill lifted his head, his expression even more possessive. For about a million reasons, I expected him to grab me by the arm, tossing me over his shoulder like a caveman. He didn't, although as he walked toward the crowded bar, I could sense he was doing it on purpose, protecting what he believed belonged to him.

He couldn't have picked a worse night to stalk me.

I bit my lip, jumping slightly with every heavy bootstep he took.

Finally, the crowd started talking again, but I heard their grumbles. The insults were disgusting, but in every one of them, I heard real fear. I waited, watching as the two bartenders snubbed the brute, acting as if they hadn't seen him.

That was bullshit.

Since I still didn't see Sean, I made my way through the crowd, easing behind the bar and heading toward Kirill. At least the closest people around him had made a wide berth, giving him two full arm lengths of space. I threw a look at the two bartenders, giving them an evil eye. What the hell was the Russian going to do inside the bar?

Kill every person here.

I rolled my eyes at my stupid thoughts. Now I was incensed. Unless Kirill had come into the bar before killing people, he was still a paying customer. I used it as an excuse to crowd over the surface, glaring at him.

"What are you doing here?" I asked, trying to keep my voice as low as possible.

"The last time I checked, this was still a free country," he answered, the sound as deep and ominous as it had the night before.

He continued to stare at me with his hooded eyes, making the entire situation uncomfortable as hell.

"Are you drinking?" I asked, finding it difficult to catch my breath.

"Bourbon. Neat."

While he'd happily issued full sentences the night before, his few word answers gave me an intense wave of shivers. He was angry, even more so than the night before. I backed away, prepared to grab a bottle of bourbon, watching as he turned his head toward the three men I was going to serve. Maybe what good ole Rory had said was true. Shuddering, I moved toward the computer, typing in both orders. As they flashed across a screen, one of the bartenders moved to fill the beer order.

And left Kirill's order alone.

I grabbed a bottle, pouring him a hefty amount. He deserved a little hospitality after the way he'd been treated. A laugh tried to push to the surface. My mother had called me far too naïve to live in New York. Maybe she'd been right. Organized crime was everywhere. I'd seen *The Sopranos* and documentaries. I'd read stories. That didn't mean I understood their organizations.

But I did sense the danger.

After sliding the drink across the bar, I whispered the amount of the bill, uncertain what to expect. He lifted his gaze from the glass to my eyes as he wrapped his hand around the base, twirling it from side to side. Even though it was impossible, I could swear I heard the scraping as the tumbler shifted across the wooden surface.

As he lifted his glass, holding it in front of him for several seconds, I noticed what he was wearing. Dressed in all black, he exuded darkness, as if issuing a silent but bold threat to anyone coming near him.

He tossed every drop into his mouth, closing his eyes as he swallowed. Even the way he handled his alcohol reeked of superiority, utter domination. After placing the glass on the bar and sliding it in my direction, he reached in his pocket, pulling out a wallet and tossing a hundred-dollar bill in my direction.

"Keep the change."

For some reason, that pissed me off. I pushed the bill back in his direction. "Don't worry about it. The drink is on me."

I'd surprised him, his eyes opening wider than normal. When a slight smile curled on his upper lip, I stood as tall as possible, daring him to try to give it back to me.

No, he had to make certain that everyone in the room knew we had a connection. He slid the tip of his index finger under my chin, lifting it gently.

Lovingly.

As if we'd been lovers the night before.

I wanted to slap his face but knew better than to cause a scene inside this bar. Stiffening, I managed to keep my eyes locked on his, but every muscle was tense, and I was shaking like a leaf. As he leaned further across the bar, I could swear the man was going to kiss me.

"Ty ochen' plokhaya devochka, moy ognennyy shar." His whisper was hoarse, yet the tone was another round of soft velvet floating across my skin.

I closed my eyes briefly, taking several tiny breaths for fear of crying out. "I don't understand."

He chuckled, the vibrations sweeping through me. "You are a very bad girl, my fireball. We will deal with that soon enough."

With that, he turned around, his moves almost robotic, and walked toward the exit.

And no one dared to challenge him.

I exhaled, leaning against the bar after he'd left. His words continued to shift through my mind, leaving me breathless, my skin tingling. I envisioned another unbridled round of passion, wallowing in the afterglow of raw ecstasy.

"Candy."

Sean's voice dragged me out of the fog. I turned around, surprised at how much concern was on his face. "I was just helping a customer."

He inched closer, shaking his head. "Do you understand who that was?"

"I… I have no idea." It wasn't time to start telling the truth now. I could only imagine how well that would go.

"He's mafia. Bratva. He's one of their enforcers. Kirill Sabatin."

Kirill Sabatin. Why hadn't I made the connection the night before? The Kozlov Bratva. I hadn't needed to live in New York very long to hear about their brutal methods of handling anyone who crossed them. Every soldier, enforcer and assassin, as well as the male heirs to their illustrious throne had a black dragon tattoo carved on their backs. Kirill's was dynamic in design, the sweeping arch of the dragon's wings a true work of art.

But the dragon's single eye was as bold and dangerous as the man who'd just been sitting in front of me.

All my thoughts and fears had proven to be true. I did what I could not to react in any way, which was next to impossible. I was ready to jump out of my skin, my blood pressure rising. The mistake I'd made wasn't just a tiny one I could fix any time soon. It was huge. Gigantic. I decided to act stupid, or least like that naïve little girl so many of my family believed me to be. "What does that mean?"

My stomach continued to lurch, another round of terror settling in. The Bratva's reputation wasn't just about their savage methods of handling business, but also their primal needs when taking their women. Taking was the operative word. They always took what they wanted, bragging about their conquests as if each member was trying to top the other.

And I'd become another notch on the man's thick leather belt.

"It means he's extremely dangerous. I could tell you stories of their heinous deeds, but I don't want to give you nightmares. I'll just say he and the other thugs leave a trail of blood a mile wide. He's made many a widow in this city. From what I know, Kirill handles the family's… issues," Sean continued, studying me carefully.

Issues. Which meant I'd been right from the first moment I'd seen him. He was a killer. Butterflies continued to swarm in my stomach, but I found myself glancing toward the door more than once. I was lightheaded, forced to grip the edge of the bar. I had to think of something to say. Anything. Sean would immediately go to my cousin, telling him every detail of what he'd seen and heard. Then all hell would break loose. That couldn't happen. I had to figure this out on my own.

If that was possible.

It was obvious Kirill had his sights set on me, but why had he risked walking inside this bar?

"What was he doing in here? He didn't seem like he belonged." The man hadn't acted like he'd cared or was worried by the words of hatred spewed at him. This was no time to panic. Kirill had left, likely gone on some mission to bite the head off a snake before gunning down a man or three.

Sean rubbed his eyes, taking another look at the door as if he expected Kirill to come back with backup and guns. "I don't know why he was here, but that concerns me, and it should you as well. As far as why he and his kind aren't accepted, it's a long story, but the Irish and the Russians don't mix. We're oil and water, the hatred going back for centuries. You should ask Michael about the years as a boy when he was still in Ireland. They're... pretty nasty. Anyway, they usually keep to themselves. There's something going on." He narrowed his eyes as he stared at the door then swept his gaze toward the small safe located under the cash register.

The lockbox didn't just keep the night's cash and credit card proceeds. It also contained a gun. I'd seen it twice before. My God. Would he use it on a member of the Bratva?

"What do you mean? Why do you think something is going on?" As soon as I asked the question, it was obvious Sean knew more than he was willing to tell.

"As I said, it's a long story. Just do me a favor. Stay away from him. You don't want to mess with that kind. He'll tear you apart."

I held up my hands, backing away. "I don't have any intention of talking to him again."

"Good."

"Oh, but put his drink on my tab." When he glared at me harshly, I shrugged. "He tried to give me a huge tip. I said no."

"Be careful playing with fire, Candy. Around here, you will get burned."

CHAPTER 6

Kirill

Vladimir Kozlov wasn't the kind of man to be fucked with, but over the years he'd softened to some degree, allowing his sons to handle a good portion of business operations. On this night, he sat in his giant leather chair, drumming his fingers on the armrest.

"The bastard is lucky I didn't slit his throat," Alexei stated, referring to the meeting with Walsh and the assholes who'd kept their smirks when we'd turned to leave.

"Your tolerance was necessary, Alexei, and you know it," Vladimir huffed. "Until we know what we're dealing with, we're not starting a war. However, it is important to find out who attacked us. I believe Kirill had that under control." He shifted his gaze in my direction, studying me intently.

PIPER STONE

His accent was as thick as mine, a direct contrast to all but one of his children who'd been born in the States after Vladimir had escaped the tyranny of daily blood-lettings that Russia had succumbed to. He'd had one child in tow, another on the way, but he'd swept me off the streets after my family had been slaughtered in a crossfire.

To this day, I had no understanding of why he'd taken a kid he'd barely known as another dead weight, forced to walk several miles before catching a train. My loyalty to him was without question. I'd become another son to him, which I knew had eventually irritated the oldest brother, Viktor. He'd returned to Russia to handle certain business operations without hesitation. That put his life in extreme danger, but he was determined to regain some of our lost power in the country after Vladimir's departure.

"Understood, but the new development is disconcerting. The casino will provide additional legal revenue." Alexei lifted a single eyebrow as he tipped his head toward me.

I'd told him about stopping by Killian's, finding one of the bastards from our meeting with Walsh inside. While I'd been unable to tell whether there was a direct connection to Candy, there were too many circumstances regarding the last twenty-four hours, which remained troublesome.

Vladimir knew when I was irritated, the look of amusement on his face highlighting the indication he sensed I was fuming. "Tell me about the woman."

"There's nothing to tell. She lives downstairs. She works at Killian's." My words seemed hollow, stark. I was pissed

Alexei had relayed the news before I'd had the chance, but blood was thicker than loyalty of service.

"Does she have a last name?" he asked, swirling his index finger around in circle after circle. Vladimir was a brutal man, including to his sons. While he'd never been violent with me directly, he refused to take incompetence on any level. I'd realized only after I was in my twenties that he'd become a role model. I'd learned to be ruthless, unforgiving to anyone.

"If you're asking if she's a Walsh, you already know the answer, but she's an external relative," I answered carefully.

Now Alexei seemed amused at my choice of words and my terse tone, laughing softly as if I'd told a joke for the first time in my life.

"Then who is she?" Alexei asked. I'd grown up with Alexei and his older brother, educated at the same schools, provided with everything I needed to become a man. However, I'd never be blood, no matter how Vladimir treated me and there were times Alexei never let me forget it. "It's no coincidence the son of a bitch standing with Walsh was in that bar, Kirill."

I knew better than most there was no such thing as coincidences. "If I had to guess, I'd say he was in Killian's looking for Rian Walsh."

"Rian Walsh. I heard Daddy Walsh has been pushing his youngest son into following in his footsteps. We need to watch the kid," Vladimir said, grousing under his breath.

"The girl is nobody," I said in a gruff voice. "Just a girl living and working in New York. However, I'll find out if she knows anything."

"Good," Vladimir said almost in passing, which continued to piss off his son. "I agree with you, Alexei. This construction project must be completed on time and without continuous issues. Maybe your... connection will be of use, Kirill."

Connection. The correct term was possession. Seeing her pawed over by other men had shoved that fact into my face. I'd wanted nothing more than to break the necks of every asshole who'd dared take a second look. Especially the assholes she'd been serving. They'd watched me the entire time I was there, one in particular never taking his eyes off me. A part of me regretted I hadn't stayed, waiting until the asshole had left for the night.

"Are you seeing her tonight?" Alexei's question made me snort.

"We aren't dating, my friend; however, I'm heading for her apartment." While I had no intention of providing my agenda to him, I definitely had plans for her, the kind that would take me all night long to handle. I kept the smirk on my face as I glanced toward Vladimir. He seemed to approve of my methods.

"Just make certain whatever you discover is the truth. You know how the Irish lie." His statement was met with laughter between the two men.

There wasn't a soul on Earth who didn't lie if it suited them. I had a knack for knowing when that happened. Men. Women. It didn't matter. I always knew. And it handled the situation appropriately. Candy would be no different.

I would peel away her layers, exposing every piece of what made her tick. She'd soon learn that bedding a monster had both consequences as well provided her with everything she desired.

As I turned to leave, Vladimir cleared his throat. "Stay for a minute, Kirill."

Alexei grinned as he walked by, patting me on the shoulder. Very few people got a one on one with Vladimir and when they did, it usually wasn't a pleasant experience.

The powerful patriarch waited until his son had walked out, closing the door behind him before standing. I towered over the man, but that didn't make his stature any less formidable.

"You know you're like a son to me."

"I know, *Pakhan*." While I rarely used the term, I thought it in my best interest.

"There's no need to be formal. This isn't as much about business as it is about you."

Now he had me curious, although I had a feeling he wasn't finished with giving advice regarding Candy. "Okay."

"I know how losing your men affected you. You take your job seriously, but you can't let the anger I sense in you destroy all the good work you've put into improving your life."

He knew about my nightmares and continued need for revenge given the death of my parents and little sister. He'd counseled me over the years, his tutelage reducing some of the anger, but no one could ever take it away. "It's crossed my mind more than once. I assure you that I will hunt down the men responsible for the attack."

"I'm certain you will. I've always respected your work ethic, Kirill. I also value your loyalty, which is why I'm certain you'll do the right thing in your search efforts."

I wasn't entirely certain what he was getting at, but the man's penchant for revenge was almost as extreme as mine.

"I'll do what's necessary," I said through clenched teeth.

"I sense you like this girl."

The man also had a way of cutting through my carefully secured layers. "Men like me don't have the luxury of enjoying anything but a piece of ass. No one will interfere with business. No one."

"Dear God, boy. I'm not concerned about that in the least. You've never failed me and don't give me that look. What happened at that warehouse no one expected. I don't doubt your efforts will go as planned. They always do. As I said, this is personal. You deserve a life."

I laughed. "I have a life, a good one." I wasn't certain what he was getting at. The man wasn't known for riddles, but I had the feeling there was a dual meaning behind his words.

"You work all hours of the day and night. You need more. If this girl entices you then by all means explore the relationship. Make her your own. Just allow yourself to feel for once. That will do you some good. Take it from an old man. I know what I'm talking about."

"I'll take that under advisement."

"I'm glad to hear you say that." When he leaned forward, I took a deep breath. "It's vital that we stop the unions. The project must succeed. However, if it's necessary to eliminate collateral damage, then you have my blessing. Women are fine treasures, Kirill, but with a single mistake, they can be the sharp blade gutting you in the middle of the night."

There was nothing else that needed to be said. As I walked out of the room, I continued to remind myself that I wasn't interested in a relationship with anyone.

Ownership was an entirely different matter.

And as far as collateral damage, I'd never made a wrong decision in my life, and I wasn't going to allow that to happen now.

* * *

Candy

. . .

Sean's words continued spiraling through me the rest of the evening. I'd gotten myself in jams before. I'd skipped school more than once. I'd ventured out to parties with friends, climbing through my bedroom window. I'd even gotten pretty close to third base with a boy when I was in high school, but this was in a league of its own. What I wondered the entire time I was on the subway was whether it was possible to put the genie back in the bottle.

By the time I reached the sidewalk in front of my apartment building, I knew the answer.

Not a chance in hell.

I glared up at the windows to the fourth floor, cringing to the bone. There were lights on, which indicated he was home. Great. At least I didn't need to walk by his door, but who could say whether he was staring at me from his perch, waiting to pounce like a tiger. The analogy wasn't doing me any good. I hurried inside, taking the back stairs toward my floor, easing open the door to the stairwell then counting to five before I found the nerve to peek out quickly.

It was late enough there was no one on the floor. I breathed a sigh of relief, remaining as quiet as possible, tiptoeing my way to my door, easing the key into the first lock then the second. When I opened the door, the scent of the vanilla air freshener greeted me. When I closed and locked it behind me, another fragrance assaulted my senses.

Him.

He was here.

That's the moment I realized the light I'd left on had been shut off, but as my eyes grew accustomed to the darkness, I was finally able to make out his hulking silhouette. He'd dragged one of my chairs closer to the window. He had been watching my arrival, waiting for me. And the bastard had broken into my apartment. Mine. I'd stood watching my detective cousin installing the lock he called impenetrable, yet here the brutal Russian was.

I was temporarily frozen to the spot, trying to think of something witty to say.

"Hello, *printsessa*."

Kirill had the ability to make me swoon by saying only a few words. Tonight was no exception. Maybe a small part of me had wanted to see him, or was hoping he'd come knocking on my door, but breaking in was an example of how possessive he was.

I remained exactly where I was, my legs unwilling to take orders from my brain. Seconds later, I heard his intense exhale. The man was already annoyed with me. When he flipped on the decorative light I'd been so happy to find at secondhand store the day after I'd arrived in town, a slight wave of anger rushed into me. I was finally able to walk closer, noticing he'd made himself at home with my booze. How dare he?

"What gives you the right to break into my place and drink my liquor?"

My demand was met with the man lifting his glass, allowing me to hear the clinking of ice against the thin crystal before he consumed the entire contents. Then he leaned forward, placing the glass on the cheap table I'd brought with me. Even though he hadn't used force, I flinched nonetheless, which he caught, lifting a single one of his dark eyebrows in response.

"Are you still frightened of me, *moy malen'kiy ognennyy shar*?" he asked.

"I don't like people who aren't who they say they are," I retorted, instantly regretting it. I couldn't expose the fact I knew who he was under any circumstances. I could only imagine what he'd do if he knew. "And don't call me your fireball." At least I remembered the phrase in Russian. Oh, God. What did it matter?

He leaned over, spreading his legs then easing his elbows against his knees. When he folded his hands, placing them under his chin, he took enough time doing so that I became lost in his eyes once again. "We've found something in common. What would you prefer I call you?"

"Anything but that."

"Let's start with your last name. That might enable me to determine what name would suit you."

"Yours first."

Kirill didn't budge an inch, nor did he blink. He just kept his cold, hard stare directed on me. "Candy Lancaster," I finally said. While I couldn't be certain, it would appear he accepted my answer.

After a few seconds, he took a deep breath. "I will warn you, Candy Lancaster, that what we talk about tonight is considered private. You cannot repeat what you hear to anyone. Understand?"

It wasn't a real question. I knew it. He knew it. "Of course."

"Good. Also, as I mentioned last night, I will know if you lie to me."

"As I told you, I don't make a habit of lying."

I still had my bag clenched so tightly in my hand that the strap was cutting into my skin. I could swear the man was reading my mind.

"Put your bag down, Candy, and come to me."

God, I hated his authoritative attitude, but I did as he demanded, placing the bag on the floor and remembering I had a can of mace inside. What I hated the most was the effect his voice had on me. My panties were already soaked, the wetness sticky, a reminder of the way I'd felt after he'd filled me with his seed. When I was only a few feet away, he lifts his heated gaze, his glorious eyes piercing mine. Sadly, they seemed tortured tonight, as if his day had been rough.

I wondered what that meant for the rest of the world.

Even though I was wearing the same uniform he'd seen me in earlier as well as the night before, I felt naked around him tonight. The thought was far too arousing, my nipples aching more than they had since last night.

"Who do you belong to, Candy?"

Was this some kind of trick question? Was he expecting me to fawn over him like a chicklet, gushing that he owned me? Not a chance. "I don't belong to anyone."

He took another deep breath, and I could sense he was losing his patience. "Who are your parents?"

The question would ordinarily seem out of the blue except for the oddity of a portion of our limited conversation the night before. Fine. I'd play his game. Then I'd ask him to leave. As a wave of scalding heat flushed my face, I knew I'd just told myself a lie. "My parents are Mallory and Robert Lancaster."

"And where are you from?"

"Pennsylvania. Born and raised in a little town. Why?"

"Because I need to ascertain if you're a threat."

At least he'd finally told me something concrete. I thought about Sean's words all over again. The Irish and the Russians didn't get along. What horror stories did Michael Walsh have to tell me? Maybe it was best that I left that side of my family out of the conversation. "I don't know how I could be a threat to anyone."

"Why are you in New York?"

"Why are *you* in New York? You're obviously from another country." *Nice, Candy. Insult the man.*

He lifted his head for a few seconds, his eyes flashing. "I'm here because I have no family left in Russia. They were killed and I was orphaned."

His frank words stunned me more than I would have thought. Maybe I'd assumed a killer like him didn't have family or couldn't have real feelings. "I'm very sorry to hear that."

"That's what happens in life, *printsessa*. After that experience I will never let anything I consider precious to be taken away from me. Ever."

His statement was another promise.

"I'm here because I plan on being an actress, or so I'd like to hope. I keep auditioning for parts on Broadway, but I've never gotten a call back. I keep trying though." There was no reason for me to spout off about my goals in life, but it seemed to please him. Maybe that meant he wouldn't kill me tonight. "Lofty, stupid goals. Right? That's what my parents told me anyway."

"Nothing that you desire should ever be considered stupid, *moya krasota*. Tell me about the three men you were serving."

I'd been right about the assholes. "Tonight was the first night I'd ever seen them in the bar." He didn't blink and I wasn't certain he was even breathing. Five seconds ticked by.

Ten. Hell, maybe twenty.

"I believe you. However, I still need you to undress."

"What?"

"It's quite possible that the men at the bar could be considered our enemies."

My God. The man thought I was working with those assholes? "I don't know who you mean as far as your enemy, but I'm not in the habit of consorting with bastards. Well…" I was digging myself a grave. Lordy. "You think I'm carrying a weapon, don't you?"

"I've been attacked by women before. I do not intend to allow that to happen again."

"Does mace in my purse count?" I could tell he wasn't in the mood for my corny jokes, but that's what I did when I was nervous, and this man made me anxious in the worst way. He wasn't budging on his demand. All I could see was the upper half of his face at this point, but I was coming dangerously close to irritating him.

I turned around, although that seemed ridiculous. He'd already seen me naked. Still, the thought of him watching me was more terrifying than his questions. My fingers were stiff as I crouched down, untying my tennis shoes. Nothing could feel more awkward than what I was doing. A single bead of perspiration trickled down from my forehead as I stood, fighting to kick the heavy canvas from my feet, finally jerking and tossing it.

Everything seemed like a massive blur as I tugged on my shirt, the stench of beer lingering on my skin adding to the nauseous feeling. I closed my eyes, reaching around my back and unfastening my bra. He was breathing heavy, which meant he was enjoying humiliating me. I bit my inner cheek, praying I didn't make a single sound. When I unfastened my skirt, I took several deep breaths before being able to lower it to the floor.

Now I'd wished I'd worn sexy panties instead of the cotton ones that made me feel inferior. My stomach lurched when I slipped my fingers under the elastic. I just couldn't do it. I just couldn't. When I turned around, I knew he could see my lower lip quivering. I hated myself for being so terrified but fighting to breathe was difficult enough. I covered my breasts with one arm as I turned around. "I know who you are."

"I imagine you do. There wasn't a man in that bar who didn't know who I was or the people I work for."

"Are you a dangerous man, Kirill? Are you a killer like they said you are?"

Very slowly he rose to his feet, walking toward me with the gait of a predator. "I *am* a very dangerous man, Candy, but not on this night. At least as long as you are who you say you are."

He didn't answer the killing part, but he didn't need to. When he came closer, I understood just how small I was in comparison to his large frame. He stood in all his masculine glory, dressed in black slacks and the same ebony shirt he'd worn into the bar, only he'd removed his jacket and rolled up his sleeves. He was far more intimidating in appearance than when he was wearing only gym shorts the night before.

I tilted my head, studying his expression as he closed the distance, sliding one hand behind my neck, rubbing it back and forth across my skin before tugging on the ponytail, then weaving his fingers through my hair. While he was searching for a hidden pin or some small weapon, the touch was so gentle and soothing that I closed my eyes.

He continued his exploration, rubbing his long digits down my chest and under my breasts. I took a quick glance down, mortified that my nipples were fully aroused, swollen and so pink they almost appeared dyed. I could tell he'd taken notice by the smirk on his face. When he started to slide his hand between my legs, I threw back my head.

"Relax, Candy. I'm not going to hurt you."

At that moment, pain wasn't what I was worried about. He dared to cup my cotton-covered mound, depressing the material with several fingers. He knew he was driving me crazy, his eyes darting up to mine every few seconds.

I wasn't expecting him to lower his head, pressing his lips against the side of my neck. His touch scalded my skin immediately, hot flashes rolling through every cell in my body. He continued teasing me, sliding his fingers up and down my pussy as he nipped then bit down on my skin.

The flash of pain was strangely alluring, my legs trembling as he growled, his deep baritone warming the rest of my body. He continued kissing me, pressing his lips against my collarbone and shoulder, lowering his head until he was able to take my hardened nipple into his mouth.

I was forced to grip his shoulders to keep from falling, my body swaying to the point I was fearful I would fall. He continued taunting me, kissing and licking, driving away the strangled fear. I wasn't certain what he was trying to prove, but I never wanted him to stop.

Kirill shifted to my other breast, swirling his tongue around my nipple before pulling the tender tissue between his teeth. The second rush of anguish was just as exhilarating as the first, driving me into a beautiful wave of pleasure that I hadn't expected. I was suddenly aware he'd dropped to his knees, trailing his fingers down my stomach until he gently rolled the waistband of my panties over my hips.

I sucked in and held my breath as he tugged on the fabric, gingerly rolling it down further until he was able to lift first one foot then the other, freeing me of the unwanted confines. I was bleary-eyed, incapable of processing why his touch felt so right when everything about the man was so entirely wrong.

He held my panties to his mouth and nose, taking a deep breath. I'd passed the point of being thoroughly embarrassed, his filthy actions arousing me even more.

"You're very wet, *printsessa*. I would have to say you enjoy your body being commanded."

I might be somewhat blinded, but I was able to catch the smirk on his face. The bastard was making fun of me.

The second I pushed against his shoulders in some lame attempt to break free from his hold, he gathered my buttocks into his hands, pulling me closer. Without hesitation, he buried his head in my wetness, immediately thrusting his tongue past my swollen and aching folds.

"Oh. Oh…" Within sweet seconds, he'd already provided more pleasure than I knew existed. I gripped his shoulder with one hand, holding the back of his head with the other. While he wore his hair short, the luxurious feel of his curly locks tickled the tips of my fingers. As he licked up and down the length of my pussy, finally concentrating on sucking on my clit, I pulled on his head, pressing his face firmly against me.

His guttural sounds were a sweet indication I'd pleased or surprised him. I lolled my head at first, fighting the growing number of stars sweeping past my eyes. Then I threw it back, staring up at the ceiling as he continued licking and sucking. I realized my hips were grinding against him involuntarily, my hold tightening as much as his. He dug his fingers into my bottom, quenching his thirst as if I was the only liquid he'd received in days. Weeks.

I shouldn't be shocked any longer by the way he brought me to an orgasm within seconds. He had a way about him, his abilities unlike any other enraptured pleasure I'd felt in my entire life. When he dared to break the hold, looking up at me with some crazed baited anticipation, I almost begged him to continue. I didn't need to bother. He resumed his carnal duties, driving me to the very edge then pulling back just enough to heighten the desire. By the time he was ready to allow me to indulge in a sweet release, I could no longer feel my legs.

The pressure built until I couldn't take it any longer, issuing a strangled whimper that floated toward the ceiling.

He refused to stop, pushing me harder to accept that he was in full control of my body. As soon as one climax stopped, a second took over, slamming into me like a tidal wave. I had no voice left, only the breathless whisper of a sated woman. When he was finally finished, he rubbed his lips against one inner thigh then the other.

When he finally stood, I clutched the front of his shirt, trying to control my breathing as well as keep from falling. "What are you doing to me?" I managed, lifting my head so I could look him squarely in the eyes. "I'll know if you're lying to me."

This time, his smile was broad, almost as much as his shoulders. "*Printsessa*, I'll be the man to ruin you if you're not careful."

I wasn't certain I minded the thought.

"You're so… magnetic. I don't understand," I whispered in return.

"Does that mean you enjoyed the moment of bliss?"

"Uh-huh." My answer was met with a single hard snap of his hand against my bottom. "Ouch."

"I think you need to answer me with more respect."

I stared at him, still delirious from the incredible moment of ecstasy. "Yes. Yes, very much."

He smacked me twice more, the force he used pressing me against the thick bulge between his legs. "Once more with meaning."

"Yes, sir. I loved it."

"Mmm... Much better. You can be taught."

While the single word should annoy me, it did just the opposite. I was so turned on, the scent of my desire wafted between us. The man was completely intoxicating, driving me to the point of madness. "What else are you going to teach me?"

This time he smiled wryly then lowered his head, pressing his lips against my ear, licking the shell then whispering, adding to my excitement, "I'm going to teach you that fucking is so much better than having sex."

"Is there a difference?"

He chuckled, the warm whisper and the heat of his body creating a giant flame. Suddenly, I was like the moth, drawn to the light and heat, prepared to give up its life in exchange for one special moment of pure sin.

"The difference is that when I'm finished, you'll be screaming out my name, begging me for more."

He was finished teasing me, providing an appetizer when he preferred the main course. He gathered me into his arms, cradling me as if I was a bride being taken over the threshold, finally able to provide the single gift he would cherish the most. The man knew exactly where my bedroom was, which of course he would since our apartments were similar. I was reminded the villain lived so close, able to keep an eye on his prize.

His long strides echoed in the hallway as he hurried into the room, gingerly laying me on the bed. He flicked on the nightstand light, hovering over me and leaning down. The way he brushed his lips across mine was surprisingly tender. Then again, I wasn't certain anything about him would truly surprise me any longer. He was an anomaly, a killer, yet held a soft side underneath his layers of protection and anger. I darted my tongue across his lips, the ache inside increasing.

When he pulled back, I could tell he had no fear I'd try to get away like the night before. Damn him, but he was right. I wanted to feel the same bliss as before, the utter free feeling of floating as I soared into new heights of pleasure.

I craved the feel of his thick shaft as he drove his cock deep inside. However, I wanted to see him up close, to be able to bask in the beauty of his inked skin and carved muscles. I moved onto my knees, my action resulting in a slight look of disappointment flashing in his eyes until he realized I was staying put.

He never shifted his pointed gaze, staring at me as he unbuttoned his shirt, peeling back the edges and exposing his beautiful physique. Every tattoo had a purpose, a story that could only be told over hard liquor and long nights. But he wore them proudly, badges of honor for whatever accolades and accomplishments he'd earned over the years.

There was something unique about the way he folded his clothes one piece at a time, placing them on my dresser with care. When he was completely naked, I found myself dragging my tongue across my lips, crawling closer to the end of the bed.

Kirill rolled his open fingers down his chest, lightly stroking his fully engorged cock. I was still amazed that his massive shaft had fit inside me, but I would never forget the sheer ecstasy. The little voice inside my head was still nagging me, issuing jabs that I was crazy for not only allowing him to touch me but wanting more. I'd already thrown all caution to the wind. Another incredible night of passion wasn't going to damn me any further into hell at this point.

"Where did the scars come from?" My voice was dripping with husky need.

"My life isn't pretty, Candy."

"How can you stand it?"

"Because it's all I know."

"You can do something else."

He thought about my statement then lowered his head, the look on his face so carnal I knew he was planning on devouring me for hours. "No. I can't."

My dirty little secret was becoming even more intoxicating. Sadly, what I knew about hiding things from people who cared is that one day they would be exposed. I shuddered from the thought even as I reached for him. As with almost every other action I'd taken, he seemed amused, swaggering toward me, the heat of his need written all over his face.

I felt that thrill between my legs, my pussy muscles clenching and releasing several times. I almost slipped my hand between my legs to find another moment of relief, but I had a feeling the man holding me as his possession wouldn't allow my naughty action. The thought was wicked and powerful at the same time.

As I wrapped my hand around the base of his cock, my mouth watered, my throat tightening. He was pure male, every single inch of him a clear reminder. No longer were my touches tentative like the night before. My cravings were just as intense as his, the jolts of electricity we shared when around each other earth-shattering. I squeezed my hand as I pulled my fingers all the way up to his cockhead, sliding a single finger back and forth across his sensitive slit.

He wasn't moving, but his eyes were ablaze as I pumped him up and down, twisting my hand, creating friction. I felt it in the palm of my hand, the dazzling sensations crawling through me. When I slipped my other hand between his legs, cupping his balls, he finally let off a series of groans that turned into husky growls. I took my time fondling his balls, rolling them between my fingers then squeezing as I lowered my head.

When I blew across his cockhead, he placed both hands on the sides of my head. I knew he wouldn't allow me any amount of control for long. I took his tip inside my mouth, using my strong jaw muscles to suck as I swirled my tongue.

"God, *moya krasota*, your mouth is so hot. Keep sucking me. Take all of me."

I tried to relax my throat, squeezing his balls to take some attention away as I struggled to get more of his shaft into my way too tiny mouth. I hadn't realized how small it was until just now. I continued stroking the base as I sucked, laving my tongue in a lazy manner. His guttural sounds increased, becoming more animalistic. When he guided my head down by another two inches, I could swear there was no way I could fit all of him inside.

But I suddenly had no choice. He pushed my head all the way down until my bottom lip rested on his balls, the tip slammed against the back of my throat. While the shock stripped away my breath, forcing me to gag, within seconds, I was able to breathe easier.

"That's it. Relax. Just relax." His command was softer than normal but a command nonetheless. The wonderful blur of what I was doing, the image of my filthy act floating into my mind, only added to the crazy sense of losing all my inhibitions. He was now in full control, face-fucking me, but taking his time, ensuring I could handle his huge size.

His shaft throbbed inside my mouth, the trickle of pre-cum sweet and tangy, the combination the most powerful aphrodisiac. I had no idea how long the moment of pure sin lasted, but I could tell by the way his body was tensing that he could soon flood my mouth, filling my throat with his seed. As much as I wanted to taste him, licking his cock clean, I needed him to fill me.

Fuck me.

Allow me to learn what it felt like to scream out his name.

And as he'd done before, he read my mind, pulling out completely then within seconds, crawling me up further onto the bed.

"Now, I fuck you. Are you ready, *printsessa*? Are you prepared for utter ecstasy?"

"Yes."

"Then beg me. Tell me what you want."

I rolled my fingers down his chest, circling his belly button. There was no point in denying the way I felt even for a few seconds. "Fuck me. Please, sir. Just fuck me."

CHAPTER 7

*K*irill

Raw, primal sex.

I hadn't broken into her apartment with full intentions of fucking her like some crazed animal. Or maybe I'd been lying to myself. All it took was one look at her shimmering face, the slight fear shown in her eyes, and I was hooked on the uproar of desire building deep within my loins. She had an unassuming way of digging a dull spoon straight through my sternum, carving out small portions of my heart.

Again, maybe that was just some insane need, a desire that would never be allowed or accepted. This wasn't about pleasing the Kozlov family or living by their rules. This was my rule. The only rule I'd mandated of myself over two dozen years before. No one would ever get close.

There were legitimate reasons, fear of the weakness being used against me, but that wasn't the most disturbing of them. It was the fact that in allowing someone to enter my world, I could destroy them with ease. I would ruin my lovely fireball. It was only a matter of time, but it was too late to turn back the clock.

The feel of having her in my arms, the lightness of her aura was enough to slay the dragon in me. That had never been done before. Maybe it was all about her goodness, an innocence that couldn't be faked, but if that was the case, I'd just shattered her world along with mine.

She'd tasted of sweet cherries, succulent and ripe, and her scent lingered, swirling through my system. I was incapable of pulling away from her, even though I knew it was best for both of us. While I believed her story, I had a feeling she didn't understand how close she was to being in the middle of a war where few would survive. I could be forced to drag her somewhere safe if I wanted to keep her.

My pet.

My prize.

My possession.

The thought was riveting as I crawled up the length of the bed, pushing the pillows away. She was entirely different than the night before, no longer hesitant to touch me or to take what she wanted. Everything about her was entirely too delicious but feasting on her was all I could think about. I eased her legs apart with my knees, remaining on my palms, keeping the full weight of my large body from hers. I felt like I could crush her, but I needed to feel the explosive heat we shared. When she wrapped her leg around me, using her muscles to guide me down, I was ready to pound into her like a wild man. I'd never wanted a woman to this degree.

She always seemed to wear a perpetual smile, even when she was tossing barbs in my direction. I had to admire a girl with such spunk, refusing to allow her fear to get in the way of what she craved or accepting crap from anyone. I still had the jealous streak running through me just like I did the night before, but from now until the end of time, no man would ever touch her again.

The way she raked her nails down my chest created a firestorm burning brightly inside of me. I was trying to maintain some level of control, but it was impossible at this point. When she tugged on my shoulder, arching her back, that was all I could take.

"Be careful what you ask for."

"You've already warned me of that," she murmured. "I'm not asking. I'm begging."

The playfulness was appealing, sending the beast dwelling deep inside of me to the surface. I allowed her to guide the tip of my cock to her entrance, hesitating long enough to drive the anticipation to a frenzied state. I couldn't take it any longer. As I pushed inside, she pressed both hands against my chest, her fingers kneading my muscles. My body was tense, every muscle aching from trying to maintain a tight hold on the brutal man I'd become. With her, everything was next to impossible.

I eased in two inches, then another. My patience was sucked dry, leaving me nothing more than a true savage. I thrust the entire rest of my cock inside, throwing my head back and roaring from the way her muscles constricted around it.

"Fuck. Yes… So tight. So fucking hot. I could fuck you for hours. I think I will."

"Okay. Yes," she murmured, tossing her head back and forth. Her entire face was shimmering, the sheen iridescent. She was truly a beautiful woman.

I remained buried deep inside, her muscles pulsing from the roughness I'd used.

Mewing, she wrapped her other leg around me, her thigh muscles surprisingly strong. "Don't stop."

"Baby. I have no intention of stopping. I'm just getting started." Grinning, I pulled all the way out, slamming into her again. When I repeated the move, she clung to my shoulder, lifting her body off the bed. Her eyes were like oversized jewels, her pupils dilated. As I began to fuck her long and hard, she did everything she could to buck against me, creating a round of friction, current sparking in all the right places.

We were tangled with one another, body and soul, two strangers who had no business being together. That made the moment dangerous and more exciting. I almost laughed at the thought. I hadn't been able to afford risking something like this and doing so in this location could sign my death warrant, but I'd die a happy man.

I lifted onto my arms, wanting to watch her as she shifted from one round of ecstasy to another. I was rewarded for my efforts within minutes, her entire body shaking and her eyes rolling into the back of her head.

"Oh, yes. You're going to make... me... come." Candy laughed as she bit her lower lip, dragging her nails down my chest several times. I'd wear her marks like she would wear mine. The moment continued to increase in intensity and seconds later, sweet cries erupted from her mouth. That wasn't good enough for me.

I rolled her over, forcing her to straddle me, gripping her hips and yanking her up and down. "That's it, my beauty. Take all of me. Let go. Just fucking let go."

She continued to shake, lolling her head as her pussy muscles spasmed. I lifted my hips, driving into her brutally. When she threw her head back, reaching her arms toward the ceiling, I finally heard what I'd longed to hear.

"Kirill! Yes, don't stop."

A satisfied smile crossed my face as she shifted from a single orgasm into a second. She was even more lovely when she climaxed, her mouth twisting and her brow pinched. When she gasped for air, smashing her hands down against me, the look she gave me was completely feral. I continued pumping her up and down until she stopped shaking. Then I tossed her off, wrapping my hand around the back of her neck and dragging her toward the headboard, pulling her onto her knees.

After planting her hands over the edge of the wooden platform, I leaned in, nuzzling against her neck. "Don't move."

Panting, she tossed her head over her shoulder, licking her luscious lips in some effort to tempt me into doing even more vile things than what I had planned. She didn't understand that if she unleashed the beast, the creature would never be satisfied. She would learn soon enough.

I tangled my fingers in her hair, taking my time to drag my tongue across the base of her ear then down her neck. Then I nipped her skin, moving from her collarbone to her shoulder. My cock was aching to the point I couldn't think straight, my balls so swollen they battered the inside of my thigh when fucking her. My needs were too significant to wait for much longer.

Wrapping my hand around her long locks, I kept my firm hold as I licked down several inches of her spine. As if testing me, she pulled away from the headboard, reaching back in order to touch me.

"Mmm... You will need to be trained." I smacked her bottom several times, enjoying the tingle in my hand and the way her bottom jostled from the force I was using. I gave her several additional cracks of my hand, enjoying her soft whimpers and the way she'd returned her hands to the headboard, her fingers now white knuckled from the rugged hold.

That was it. I couldn't handle the wait any longer. I shoved my cock inside, gripping her hip with my other hand as my shaft expanded, swelling even more. My heart raced, thudding to the point of echoes. I was tight as a drum, every muscle burning from the need coursing through me. I slammed into her again, my balls slapping against her legs.

"Oh. Oh..." she whimpered. I could tell her eyes were closed, the look of extreme pleasure on her face as heightened as it had been before.

When my cock was thoroughly coated with her juice, I pulled out, sliding the tip between her ass cheeks.

She bucked hard against me, doing her best to obey my command yet the fear crossing her face extreme. "I've never... I mean..."

"Relax, *moya krasota*. I'll be gentle." At least for the first time. The fact that I was the first one to take her in her forbidden place only heightened the pleasure even more. I'd never wanted anything so badly as this, to fill her with my seed. The thought yanked on the brutal side of me, but I kept my promise, guiding the tip in slowly.

Candy was trembling all over, kicking her feet up and down on the bed. I released my hold on her hair, running my fingers down the length of her back. As I lowered my head, I whispered words of passion in my native language. It didn't matter that she wouldn't understand. The sound should provide some level of comfort, a soothing moment as she realized that even a monster like me could keep his promises.

She was so fucking tight that if I was rough with her, the pain I'd cause would be damaging not only for her body but also for her spirit. That wasn't going to happen. Never in my life had I held back my intensity on anything. That wasn't my nature, but she'd pulled it out of me. Her beguiling smile and rebellious attitude made me want to provide nothing but sheer joy, ecstasy that would last with her for hours. I pushed in another inch, hitting the tight wall of muscle.

"You're so damn big. So big," she whispered, taking several shallow breaths.

"Just breathe. Do that for me."

Her breathing was nothing more than ragged pants, but after I pushed past the ring, her muscles started to relax, pulsing around the circumference of my cock. The heat continued to build, the fire burning between us threatening to consume us in an intense blaze.

But nothing would stop me from taking what I wanted.

She murmured several words that I couldn't hear, twisting her head in order to try to see what I was doing. When I was finally seated inside, I realized I'd been holding my breath. Very slowly, I developed a rhythm, taking it nice and slow until she finally seemed to relax.

"You feel so good, Candy."

"Mmm… It's amazing." She laughed, shocked at both my actions and her words. When she started meeting every thrust with one of her own, I let go of the tight hold I had on my control, jutting my hips forward. The incredible moment could last all night as far as I was concerned, but my body wouldn't take it.

I powered into her for several additional strokes, savoring every damn sensation she was providing. Then I finally gave myself permission to release. As I erupted deep inside of her, the moment was far sweeter than I'd imagined. Beads of sweat ran down both sides of my face as my balls finally got the relief they needed. As I pushed my body against hers, I ripped her away from the bed, cupping her breasts.

"You're not going anywhere," I growled into her ear.

She panted several times then laughed. "You forget. This is my place."

Her slight laugh was another wave of sweet music. What she didn't understand is that soon enough, she wouldn't reside in this clunky apartment any longer. She would learn about the finer things in life, wanting for nothing. As long as she learned to obey my every command, my *printsessa* would have the world at her fingertips.

Even if I had to slay the dragon in the process.

* * *

Candy

. . .

Bam. Bam. Bam!

I woke with a jerk, hissing as I sat straight up, gasping for air. I'd been dreaming of something incredible, although I couldn't remember a single detail. Maybe the noise I'd heard was in my dream and nothing else. I took a deep breath, the sun streaming in through the window indicating I'd slept later than normal.

Then I remembered in vivid detail why I was lounging in bed with everyone else was busy with their day.

Kirill.

He'd kept me awake for hours, taking me several times. The man was completely insatiable with his needs. I turned my head toward the other pillow, moaning when he wasn't beneath the covers. I couldn't remember him leaving. Maybe my brain was a little foggy from the wine I'd consumed after the second round of sex, or the third. No, the hard fucking. I knew he'd correct me.

I dropped back onto the bed until I heard the sound again.

Bam. Bam. Bam.

Whoever it was on the other side of the door was desperate to get inside. They also had a death wish. I rolled out of bed, woozy from the lack of sleep and the savagery my body had experienced. Wow. I could barely walk. I managed to grab my robe from the chair where I'd tossed it the morning before, trying to walk a straight line as I headed into the living room.

My eye caught the glass he'd used. I hadn't noticed a bottle of bourbon remained on the floor. I tied the sash hurriedly, trying to smooth down my hair enough to look presentable. When I looked through the peephole, I cringed, trying desperately to keep from making any noise.

But I knew he wouldn't go away.

"I know you're in there, Candy. You need to open this door right now. Do you hear me?"

Shit. Rian. He was pissed. No, he'd probably been pissed when Sean had told him what had happened the night before. Now he was Irish angry, which wasn't a good thing for anyone. I took a deep breath and unlocked the door, opening it casually as if nothing was any different than another day.

"Rian. What are you doing here?"

He glared at me with fire and brimstone in his eyes. "You know perfectly well what I'm doing here. Why didn't you call me? Why? You can't mess with people like that."

"Shhh... I don't want the entire building hearing your tantrum." I jerked him inside, closing the door hurriedly. The truth was I didn't want my vicious neighbor from upstairs to overhear him. And Rian's voice was loud, booming.

"Tantrum? This isn't a tantrum, cousin. This is an outright demand that you tell me everything that happened."

"Nothing happened. I served a customer at the bar. So the fuck what?" Oops. There went my bad girl language again, but he had a way of getting under my skin.

"And you bought him a drink. Do you have any idea who that was? Do you?"

"Trust me. Sean made certain I knew who *that* was. So what? He deserves to be served like any other person."

I knew that would make him angry, but I was furious too. How dare he act like he had a say in the matter?

"Well, maybe he didn't do a good enough job explaining it to you so allow me to do it. That man is like all the other Russians in the Bratva. They are animals, pure and simple. Hell, I think they eat their young for breakfast, for God's sake."

"Oh, give me a break. I know for certain there are plenty of corrupt Irishmen in our clan." Uh-oh. I'd gone and done it. I could tell by the fury in his eyes that I'd pushed him too far.

He started walking toward me, forcing me to back away. His glare was as brutal as I'd seen on Kirill's but he was family, at least sort of.

"You will not see that man again."

"That man," I repeated for no other reason than to buy me time to figure out what to say to him.

"Kirill Sabatin." He narrowed his eyes, his cold stare studying every movement I made. I could feel the damn twitch on the corner of my mouth, an absolute dead giveaway when I was nervous. "He's the Kozlovs' enforcer. Do you know what that means?"

"How the hell should I know what that means? As you continue to remind me, I'm from a hick town in Pennsylvania so I couldn't possibly protect myself or be able to sniff out a bad guy." I could tell that my defiant statement had irritated him, but for the first time since I'd come into town, a hint of embarrassment flushed his cheeks. He'd treated me like some wayward innocent fawn when I was anything but.

"That means," he said, softening his voice to some degree, "that means he controls a deadly group of soldiers, men who have no qualms about killing anyone who the head of the Kozlov Empire even thinks is an enemy. They are trained assassins, their operations as close to military as I've ever seen. They don't care about who gets in the way. They kill innocent people, Candy. Including women." He stared at me, waiting for the information to sink in.

Women?

Was he serious? A single quiver shifted down my spine as I thought about the two nights I'd spent with the man. With the killer.

Swallowing, I took my time addressing him, but when he lifted his head, I could swear he was able to tell I was lying. "Until Sean told me who he was, I'd never heard of him." I wouldn't put it past my cousin to already know the man lived directly above me.

A few seconds later, he exhaled. "Just stay away from him. You will not see him ever, and I do mean never again." He was giving me an order. I didn't like to be commanded to do anything.

Then why did you enjoy Kirill's dominance?

Damn it. The nervous tic remained but his demand really pissed me off. "I'm not seeing him, Rian, and you're not my father. Just back off. I'm not a stupid girl." Had he really killed women? I don't know why that bothered me anymore than the fact he'd killed a man or ten thousand, but it cut right through me like a sharp blade.

"No, you're one of the most intelligent women I've met, but yes, you are vulnerable. Plus, you're my cousin and I was tasked to take care of you so that's what I'm going to do whether you like it or not." He sucked in his breath, cursing after issuing the statement.

His words finally sank in and I sucked in my breath, trying to keep my temper from flaring out of control. When I finally released the deep breath, I narrowed my eyes. "First of all, you're my second cousin and…" Hold on a minute. I was floored by what he'd just said. "What did you say?"

"Fuck," he hissed. "You heard me. Your parents made certain that I be put in charge of you."

This was ridiculous. "Put in charge of me? That's ridiculous. I'm twenty-four years old. I don't need a babysitter."

He looked over my shoulder and I'll be damned if he didn't home in on the glass. He stormed toward it, yanking the bottle into his hand. "I know you don't drink bourbon, but I know who does. That fucking Russian. You did not spend the night with me. Tell me you did not."

I resisted the urge to tighten the sash, instead planting my hands on my hips and lying my ass off. The funny thing was that the bourbon was mine, but only for cooking purposes. As if that mattered right now. "I did not spend the night with him. Period." Technically, I wasn't lying. I hadn't spent the entire night with him. A fleeting thought stifled my breathing. What if Kirill remained in the bathroom? Oh, dear God. I knew exactly what would happen. Or maybe I didn't. Would Kirill pull out a gun?

He rushed toward me so fast, I was taken aback. "Then what is this doing here?"

"You have no right to ask me who I keep company with. Now, I need you to leave." I pointed toward the door, feeling more awkward than I'd ever felt around him. Rian was protective, caring. He'd only met me once before I'd decided to move, yet he'd offered me a job even before I'd left Pennsylvania. Still, I refused to tolerate being told what to do.

I thought for certain he was going to toss the bottle against the wall given his Irish temper, but he slowly lowered it to the table, taking several deep breaths. When he walked toward me, I resisted budging from where I was standing. It was past time for me to take control of my life.

Maybe I was far too vulnerable. Damn it. I had to end things with Kirill before... Jesus. There were no good scenarios. None.

"Candy, I know you're eager to make your way in this ugly world. I was exactly like you when I was your age. However, there are dangerous men out there who will take advantage of your generosity and kindness. I have no intention of telling you how to live your life, but I can be concerned. That's what families do. We care. We watch out over each other. And if necessary, we intervene in order to prevent damage or disaster. I don't want to see you go down a bad path."

His words almost gutted me except I sensed he continued to believe he could be my overlord. "What path is that?"

"Getting involved with the Russian Bratva will only lead to pain. Whether physically or emotionally, it doesn't matter. That man will crush you after he's finished enjoying whatever twisted experience he believes is owed to him. I suggest you keep that in the back of your mind as you're making adult decisions."

Goddamn, the man could infuriate me more than most, yet I couldn't ignore what he'd told me. Kirill was demanding and forceful. What would he do if I dared to try to stop seeing him? I watched as Rian headed toward the door, cursing under his breath. Still, my gut told me that the Bratva had a beef with Rian's father. He was certainly a formidable man.

"I'm curious, Rian. What business relationship has the Walsh family entered into with the Bratva?" I knew within seconds I'd hit home, his body tensing.

He didn't bother turning around, only tilting his head so I could see a portion of his face. "I'll give you one last *recommendation*. Stay in your lane."

My lane? What the hell was that supposed to mean? When he slammed the door, I jumped, closing my eyes briefly. Things had just gone from really bad to insufferable.

CHAPTER 8

Kirill

Construction.

I'd worked enough of it to know my way around a commercial site. Vladimir had made certain all the boys in his family worked in an extremely physical field. He'd told us it would make men out of us. I'd felt more like an indentured servant at the time, but after reflecting years later, I'd learned to appreciate the value of hard work.

Not that protecting the Kozlov Empire wasn't strenuous. It had proven to be difficult no matter the situation. Long before Kozlov had fled Russia, bringing his family to the US, other mafia organizations had already established a firm hold on New York. That included the Italians, their third-generation family holding court above all the others including the Bratva. While they were dangerous, considered our number one enemy, the way Michael Walsh had graduated from his life as the New York police commissioner to the head of the largest union had taken a significant toll on our organization.

Another early morning call had interrupted my schedule. My mood was already surly, wanting nothing more than to provide the union with a message they wouldn't soon forget. As I pulled my GTO into the parking lot of the massive casino under construction, I had a feeling that lesson would come sooner than anticipated.

Alexei was engaged in what appeared to be a heated conversation with two men. That didn't concern me. The man could handle himself without issue. What did were the four men standing in the shadows while a solid two dozen of our workers gawked at the argument. While many of the workers hired by the Kozlov family and what I considered to be a worthless superintendent were highly skilled in their various trades, they weren't fighters. They were only on the job to earn a paycheck, some if not all risking being threatened by the high and mighty unions. The reason they risked admonishment and worse was because Vladimir had insisted that the workers be given a salary even the unions couldn't match.

Besides, many of them were in serious debt with the Kozlov Empire.

I'd known the meeting with Walsh had been a mistake. There was no reasoning with the man. Not that I gave a shit. Before exiting my vehicle, I grabbed my weapon from the seat beside me, popping in a fresh clip. While the

Russians were known as savages, the Irish were unpredictable, their fury often getting in the way of rational thinking.

The brute inside of me was ready to start a war, but that wouldn't stop the bullshit the union was tossing our way. Between the various trade unions, they outnumbered us. While only a small percentage was as corrupt, they provided enough influence over powerful politicians that the casino and our other two projects could be shut down permanently, buried in red tape. That wouldn't bode well for the bottom line and even as hotheaded as Alexei was, he'd accepted that fact.

Still, they continued to encroach on our territory in an entirely different way than members of other mafia organizations. That made them equally if not more dangerous given certain unknowns.

However careful we were required to be, that didn't mean we couldn't handle egregious issues one at a time and in complete privacy. Which is why I suspected the head of the Bratva cleanup crew had also been called. Vassily Morkoff was known as the Savage for his methods of operation. He remained in the background, leaning against an earlier delivery of metal studs. Perhaps he was sizing up pine boxes for body parts. I snickered at the thought as I headed toward the increasing group of men.

I snarled as soon as I got closer, glaring at the worthless superintendent. He was useless in matters of negotiation, his balls the size of peanuts. I still couldn't understand why Alexei kept him around.

"Get your men out of here," I ordered, giving him zero opportunity to talk back to me. He knew better. It had taken one incident in the parking lot for him to learn to be terrified of my methods.

While I noticed he glowered out of the corner of my eye, he obeyed almost instantly, directing his men to go back to work. I moved closer, hissing under my breath when I noticed the asshole from Killian's, the same shithead who'd been at the bar. I'd overheard the crap he'd given Candy. It had been difficult not to bash his head in. Given he was standing next to four other men I didn't know, I'd say Walsh had sent him as the representative from the construction trade council.

The last man moved out of the shadows seconds after my arrival.

Rian Walsh.

The owner of Killian's Bar and Grill.

The meeting with Vladimir and Alexei returned to my mind. His appearance wasn't coincidental. My instant rage was blinding, creating the need to spill blood. While I'd learned to control the darkness I called my beast dwelling inside of me, Rian's purposeful appearance was only fanning the flames. With one word out of his mouth, I couldn't be certain I'd be able to maintain control. I took a deep breath, the stench of the man repulsive.

Even worse was the fucker dared to smile at me. He thought he'd found something to hold over my head. Perhaps he was closer to Candy than I wanted to learn. I'd checked through her things in her apartment before leaving. There was no indication she'd been lying to me, although the fact she was an actress had been disconcerting. She could be anybody she wanted to be. While there were also no pictures that had raised a red flag or any union material, I still had questions.

And I could tell by the smug look on his face that he was gunning for me.

If Rian even attempted to do anything, the fucker would learn what challenging a man like me would do for his lifespan. I took a deep breath, holding it as I walked closer.

While I'd expected my appearance would be discussed as well as cursed, I didn't think the younger Walsh member had the balls to confront our organization without his daddy protecting him. From what I'd experienced, he'd left the politics up to his father, law enforcement to his brother. I cocked my head, giving him a hard onceover. Maybe things were changing.

He locked eyes with mine, studying me just as intently. The one thing I could say about the Irish, they usually wore their emotions on their sleeves. I could tell what he was thinking and what he was planning.

The kid wouldn't make it within a block of me before I'd be able to detect his stench.

I moved closer, listening in on the conversation, my eyes never leaving Rian.

Alexei tipped his head in my direction, his expression ice cold. "The order for steel girders we placed two months ago was suddenly canceled."

"Was it now?" I asked, giving all six men a hard stare. We'd been successful building our brand by issuing harsh punishment quickly and efficiently. The game of playing politics was disparaging our reputation as much as the attack could. I walked closer to the men, unbuttoning my jacket and allowing them to catch a glimpse of my weapon.

While most were appropriately afraid of the threat, both Rian and the man from the bar maintained their smiles.

"You know the requirements of this city," Rian mused, his eyes remaining locked on mine.

"There are no legal requirements for anyone to join a union, Rian. In addition, blocking as well as canceling our order is considered extortion. I don't think I need to tell you how our organization feels about that."

"I'll make a suggestion," Alexei stated. "That you take Michael Walsh a message, unless of course you'd like for me to do it personally. Let him know that if that shipment doesn't arrive within forty-eight hours, then we'll be forced to use countermeasures."

I cocked my head, noticing a flickering in Rian's eyes. He was here for a personal reason, not because he was a part of his father's hold on the unions.

"I'll relay the message, but rules are rules," he said, barely acknowledging Alexei.

"Yes, they are," I said, closing in on his personal space. When I noticed one of the assholes reaching for a concealed weapon, I reacted without hesitation, snapping my hand around his neck then slamming him against the stack of wood. Then I grabbed his weapon and jammed it under his chin. "I don't think you want to do that."

The man wheezed, keeping his hateful glare.

Suddenly, everything went deathly quiet in a two-hundred-foot radius. No one dared utter a word. Not one of the assholes who'd come to threaten us. Not one of the construction workers. They knew better than to cross me when I was pissed. They'd heard of my lack of patience and my creative methods for handling anyone who broke the rules.

I squeezed my fingers against the man's pulse, twisting my hand a few degrees. With just another fifteen added, I would snap the man's neck with ease. While he was large in stature, I was huge in comparison. "If a single one of you ever consider pulling a weapon again, the pain you experience will last for a very long time. Do we understand each other?"

The asshole continued to wheeze, his face turning red. I snapped my head in the other direction, locking eyes with each man before returning my attention to the idiot.

He huffed and puffed. "Yes," he finally managed.

Alexei chuckled from behind me. "Perhaps now we understand each other."

A part of me didn't want to release the asshole, but I did, hissing before taking a step away, shoving his weapon into my pocket.

"Now, get the fuck out of here," I snapped. I didn't need to make a single additional sound before five of them, including the bastard from my hold stumbled away. At least the asshole was still coughing. Only Rian remained. I had to give the man credit for having more balls than I'd remembered. Maybe he was following in his daddy's footsteps after all.

I turned sharply, moving to within a few inches of him.

"Is there something you need to say to me?"

For a full minute, the silence remained, other than the ongoing construction in another part of the site and the light breeze fluttering through shipment labels on already opened supplies.

Rian was no match for me, and he was well aware of it. However, he stood his ground, refusing to back down.

"I have one piece of advice for you, Russian. Stay away from my cousin. She's off limits."

He wasted no time backing away, but the smirk on his face was something I'd remember for a long time.

Cousin.

While not extremely close, she'd been confirmed as an important member of the Walsh family. How I handled her from here on out would need to change. I took a deep breath, holding it for several seconds until I felt Alexei's presence behind me.

"It's obvious we have two issues to deal with. I suggest you handle the extraction of information as well as the hunt. I'll handle the construction."

I nodded, turning my head to look at the assholes slinking away. "Then I handle it my way. Period."

"I don't think Pops would want it any other way. That girl you like is collateral now whether she knows it or not."

He didn't need to tell me. Collateral damage. Candy had no idea that she'd placed herself in harm's way and into the arms of a monster.

As he walked away, I shoved my hands into my pockets. Whether or not the meeting had been coincidental no longer mattered. It had been a perfect storm, an awakening so unexpected that even thinking about her proved to make everything else that much more difficult. I was a man of action and significant violence. I'd long ago forsaken any concept of humanity or even decency.

That's also when I'd made the promise to myself to never get close. That promise would need to be broken for the sake of the family.

Candy hadn't realized the nature of the savage she'd confronted, but she would soon learn what nightmares entailed.

I'd felt it before with no conviction. Now it was all I could think about.

And the beautiful fireball with shimmering eyes and a body like a goddess would have no choice in the matter.

She'd entered the beast's lair.

Now it was time to capture his prey.

Tonight, she would begin her new life.

After all, I always took what I wanted.

* * *

Candy

Anger.

My Irish temper remained close to the surface the entire day. I'd purposely left the apartment as soon as I was showered and dressed, refusing to have another member of the Walsh family try to tell me what to do. I was my own person. I made my own decisions. And I couldn't believe my parents had 'hired' Rian to watch out over me. I should have guessed that was the case when *they'd* suddenly changed their minds about allowing me to go and one of *them* had stopped by on a regular basis. I'd thought it was wonderful that Finnegan regularly drove past the street as a member of law enforcement, although red flags should have been raised given he was a first grade detective.

He didn't do a beat. He didn't patrol streets on a regular basis. No one believed I could take care of myself. Gggrrr... I was still hot, and I had to work tonight. Maybe it was time to find another job. I'd held my cell phone in my hand several times, almost calling my mother to berate her, but I knew how concerned my parents had been in accepting my move.

I'd gone shopping for hours instead of staying at home. And I'd spent way too much money that I didn't have when I should have been learning my lines for an upcoming audition in a couple of days. My entire schedule had been disrupted and all because I'd dared to knock on the door of a stranger in the middle of the night.

You did this to yourself.

The little nagging voice inside my head wasn't helping reduce my fury. However, she was right. If I'd minded my own business, maybe I wouldn't feel so suffocated. I pulled into the parking lot of the bar, glaring into the rearview mirror. What would happen if Kirill showed up again? I had to shove that aside. I didn't see the man as someone looking for a fight. Then again, I didn't know him at all.

Except carnally.

Shuddering, I cut the engine, remaining where I was as I allowed my thoughts to shift back to the one person I should definitely push out of my life for good. Somehow, I knew that wasn't going to be possible because *he* wasn't going to allow that to happen.

He. Him. Killer.

As I closed my eyes, visions rushed to the surface of my mind, every one of them sensual. No, they were downright sexual in nature.

His hard, muscular body.

His dark, demanding gaze.

His voluptuous lips.

His big, fat cock.

This was hopeless. I'd enjoyed the brutal sex more than I should have, relishing the way he made my body feel. He was a master of using his tongue. A heated shiver twisted through my body with such force, my mouth was suddenly dry. I wanted to say I didn't like the daydreams but that would be a lie. My mind was constantly filled with the same image of the emerald-eyed Adonis with a body carved out of the finest stone.

Unfortunately, my fantasy was always interrupted by the realization he had no soul and a heart of ice. The man was a killer. Proven. Maybe. Could I believe anything Rian had told me or was he just trying to scare me? At this point, it didn't really matter. I'd need to put on my big girl panties and figure out how best to get myself out of the twisted, terrifying situation.

Strangely, I wasn't as fearful of Kirill as I should be after hearing what Rian had to say. I winced at the various thoughts before launching myself from the car. I'd stay as far away from Rian as possible and would refuse to take any additional bullshit.

I was a big girl and could handle my own problems.

At least that's what I continued to tell myself.

As I walked inside, Rian didn't approach me, and then started to say something. I waved my hand, charging toward the small locker room to dump my gear. When he appeared in the doorway, I didn't bother looking in his direction.

"Where the hell were you?" he demanded.

"Were you checking up on me again?" I didn't bother looking at him, concentrating on yanking my hair into a ponytail. Then I decided against it, tossing the hairband into my purse and slamming the door. Fuck the rules. I was finished with playing games.

"I wanted to confirm you accepted your duties."

That was the line drawn in the sand. I snapped my head in his direction, moving to within two inches of him. He usually had a jovial look on his face, always smiling. Tonight, he had a serious, almost malevolent look.

"You and I need to get something straight, Rian. While I appreciate the fact you gave me an instant job and watch out over me, I think it's time I did things on my own."

"What the hell does that mean?"

"That means as of tonight, I'm giving you my two weeks' notice." I made certain my statement was solid as a rock.

Just like Kirill's body.

Jesus. Everything seemed to revolve around the mysterious Russian.

"You… You…" he sputtered, which was a rarity. "You can't do that. I won't let you do that."

"So what? You're going to chain me up in a backroom, maybe making the storeroom my new apartment. Is that what you really mean?" I stood as tall as possible, although he had several inches on me.

His glare was as harsh as some I'd seen from Kirill. He said nothing for a few seconds then jerked back by two feet. "I don't want to see you get hurt. That's all. I do care about you."

While he'd softened his tone, his expression was still harsh and unrelenting. "Thank you, Rian, but that's not necessary. I have a plan and I'm sticking to it. Now, if you'll excuse me, I don't want to be late for my shift. My boss can be a real jerk." I shoved past him, cringing from using such hateful words.

"You need to rethink this."

My anger was about to get out of control. "What is this really about, Rian? You know I'm not stupid with regard to your family."

"It's your family too."

I almost laughed. I'd always heard blood was thicker than water but at this point, I wasn't so certain. "Yes, you're right. However, your warning smells of something else. Why can't you tell me?"

The expression on his face gave me far too much information. His visit wasn't just about warning me with regard to Kirill. The family was involved in some shady operation. I'd bet on it. The thought sickened me.

"Stay out of family business. You aren't involved. Just heed my warning."

My natural defiance remained in place. "As I said to you before. Stay out of my life. I'm perfectly capable of making my own decisions."

There was a wave of tension that seemed an impenetrable wall. When he shifted from one foot to the other, his reddened face an indication of his anger, I turned away disgusted.

"Kirill Sabatin takes what he wants. He wants you. He's marked you. And he's going to kill you when he's finished with you, Candy. That's what he's done to every woman he's ever been with. Just ask Finnegan. He'll tell you the gory details, although I don't think you want to hear them."

My throat immediately closed, my heart skipping several beats. Could that really be true? I fisted my hands, making certain they weren't visible to him. I just couldn't believe it. "Warning duly noted."

As I walked into the bar, I scanned the small crowd, trying to keep the slice of fear in check.

What if it was true?

* * *

My good luck. The night was nothing special. No rowdy crowds. No assholes like the night before. I was surprised no one groped me, which was a nice change. However, I still couldn't wait to get home and lock the doors.

I wasn't certain what I was more afraid of at this point, being tormented by my extended family who'd I'd never been close to in the first place or the evil man living over my head. I needed time to think.

And to plan.

I was the last waitress, only the assistant manager and the night's bartender remaining. I didn't say a word as I grabbed my things, using the back door to escape the environment. I was still knotted inside, the anger mixing with terrible anxiety. I couldn't shake the anger or the shadows that had crowded around my vision, dragging me into a dense fog.

As I hurried toward my car, the light breeze tingling the naked skin of my arms, several gripping sensations rushed through me.

Someone was watching.

Lurking.

Stalking me.

I felt like some stupid chick from a horrible B-rated movie, turning around in a full circle and gawking into the night. While the parking lot was well lit, that didn't mean assholes weren't hiding in the scruffy foliage surrounding the property. Years before, someone had obviously tried to make the setting like some garden oasis, but no one had kept up with the plantings. Now everything was a freaking mess, what few flowers bloomed overtaken by thorny bushes. That didn't provide any comfort.

My breath skipping, I continued to scan the area as I hurried to my car. I dared not breathe a sigh of relief when I managed to open the door, tossing my purse inside. The skin on the back of my neck prickled, my mind swirling with the warning Rian had issued.

He was here. I could feel it.

Trying to pretend I wasn't bothered, I slid my hand inside my purse, grabbing the can of mace, which I'd never used. "Leave me alone, Kirill. I just can't with you."

Oh, yeah. What a stupid thing to say.

The play by play of the horror movie continued to roll as the only sound I heard was the light breeze rustling the bushes. Swallowing, I threw a look over my shoulder, unable to see anything in the glare of the overhead light.

But I knew he was there.

My hand remained gripped around the can, flipping the top and pressing my finger on the small stem. I could only imagine what punishment I'd receive if I managed to spray the powerful villain in the eyes.

When nothing happened, I tossed my bag onto the passenger seat, still clinging to the can. Then I heard a voice, deep and ominous.

"So you were expecting him to come to your rescue, the fucking Russian. I heard you were sleeping with him."

Sleeping with him. Oh, my God. Did this have something to do with Rian? Did my cousin put him up to this? A wave of nausea smashed into my system.

Inhaling, I held my breath, trying to remember why I recognized the terse tone. The night before. The asshole from the table of men, the ones Kirill thought I was somehow involved with as an enemy. Oh, dear God. Still violently angry from everything that had occurred earlier, I swung around, never hesitating before I began spraying in a wide arc. Tiny beads of the substance formed a slight fog in the light, but I didn't need clear vision to realize there were three men standing only a few feet away.

They seemed much larger than when they'd been sitting at the table. My throat continued to tighten, and I glanced toward the back door.

Rory seemed to notice. "No one is coming to save you, Candy. That's something you should accept."

Fuck. The man knew my name. This was about Rian.

And Kirill.

What did you do, girl? What the hell did you do?

"What are you talking about?" I asked, trying to keep the quiver out of my voice.

One of the others laughed as he gazed up and down. I didn't need to see his expression to know what he was thinking.

Rory laughed as well, taking a step closer. "You shouldn't have done that."

I'd never felt much fear while living in my parents' house, other than the occasional nightmares about mythical creatures that even haunted me in the daylight. Even coming to New York hadn't given me anxiety over criminals lurking in the darkness. But over the last two days, the time more like years than mere hours, I'd learned that often monsters didn't crawl out from under beds or slide beneath cracks underneath a closet door.

They were big and bold, brawny and ripped with sensuality, although a mere look in their eyes allowed you to understand just how dangerous they were.

But right now, the strange feeling that the three men standing in front of me like hulking masses of violence was almost paralyzing. I realized the can was knocked out of my hand, even though two of the bastards wiped their eyes furiously.

"What the hell is this?" I struggled to say, my chest already aching from the difficulty catching my breath, remnants of the spray assaulting my eyes. At least the burn was real. This was nothing but a yank of my sanity.

Rory was obviously leading the pack, the other two his lackeys. He took another step closer, far too close. In the harsh light, the grin on his face reminded me of the Riddler, stupidly lopsided and full of a sickening kind of knowing. This had been planned out, the bastards waiting for me to leave.

Alone.

He smelled of alcohol and rage, the stench repulsive. Yet he wasn't drunk enough to be able to pass this off as a horrible mistake.

"This," he said, his tone even more dark and menacing, "you might call an intervention."

"What the fuck does that mean?" The damn music inside the bar was loud, far too much so for David to hear me. While there were other businesses close by, none of them were open this time of night. I was all alone in a den of vipers. One of them was blocking direct access to the back door, but that didn't mean I couldn't sprint toward the front of the building, racing inside. David was a large dude, plus he had access to the gun Rian kept.

The fucker took another step toward me. "That means, sweetheart, that you're coming with us."

"Over my dead body."

"That can be arranged if you aren't a good girl."

Good girl? Was the fucker kidding me? The last thing I refused to do was remain an easy target, a victim of disgusting abuse at the hands of some crazed boys pretending to be men.

So I took a swing.

It was obvious Rory hadn't anticipated my spunk or the brutal punch since it knocked him back by a few feet. My action was enough of a surprise to cause the other two jerks to snap their heads in Rory's direction as he stumbled backward. That was my cue, likely the only one I'd get, to run the hell away.

Little did the bastards know I'd been a long-distance runner in high school and college, able to outsprint a good number of the boys on the team. As I took off running, I was grateful I'd forced Rian to allow me to wear my favorite sneakers. They were a definite advantage as I bolted around good ole Rory, allowing my legs to fly as I headed for the front of the building.

Nothing could have surprised me any more than when one of them managed to wrap their hand around my hair, jerking me with such force that stars floated in front of my eyes, the pain blinding. I screamed, but within seconds, a hand was placed over my mouth and I was dragged by my hair several feet.

I did everything I could to fight the attackers, flailing my arms as the asshole jerked me over one of the thick timbers surrounding the property and onto a bed of gravel. I felt the sharp pebbles digging into my legs as I was pulled at least a dozen feet more.

My vision blurry, I kicked out, but nothing I did mattered.

Then I heard Rory's laugh echoing in my ears. When he leaned over me, I blinked even as tears of agony formed in my eyes.

"You're going to make a fabulous prize," he huffed. "Dump her in the trunk."

"No," I said meekly, still fighting although almost all my energy was sapped.

I heard another snicker and a metal click. When I was hoisted into the air, I yelped one last time, praying to God anyone heard me. The hard thud as my body was tossed sent another blast of anguish slamming into every muscle.

Rory peered over me for a second time, the single blinking light attached to the building next door allowing me to focus on the demonic look on his face. "Don't bother screaming. No one is going to give a damn."

When the trunk lid was slammed shut, I immediately smashed my fists against it, screaming at the top of my lungs, which I continued doing when I heard the rumble of the engine. As the car was jerked backward, tires squealing, a part of my hope began to drift away.

While I wasn't certain why the horrible men had abducted me, I realized that something I'd done had been the reason.

I'd just traded one monster for three others.

And there was no doubt in my mind that I wouldn't survive.

CHAPTER 9

Kirill

Danger.

I'd sensed Candy was in danger almost immediately after I'd left the meeting at the construction site. Call it a sixth sense, but Rian's exclamation had bothered me all day. I'd expected to find her at home, although likely behind a locked door. She'd left in an obvious hurry, dropping her damp towel on the floor in the bathroom, the cup of coffee she'd started to drink remaining half full on the counter.

When she didn't return, the rage had started to build. I'd planned on taking her away from the apartment and to somewhere safer, but she hadn't given me the chance. And I hadn't been given the opportunity to intercept her at Killian's before she'd taken another shift. Other pressing business had kept me from scouring the streets in order to find her. An informant had information he thought I'd want to hear.

While I was angry she'd obviously kept portions of the truth from me, my protective side was struggling with the need to do my job.

I'd weighed the option of whether or not I believed she'd be safe inside the fucking sleazy bar in order to handle the situation. There'd been silence on the streets of New York, even though I'd scoured the city several times, making certain the few assholes we'd trusted enough to become informants understood that they owed their loyalty to the bratva.

So I'd gone.

Finding the asshole with a bullet between his eyes had pushed buttons no one wanted to push. It had also been nothing more than a goddamn decoy.

I roared into the parking lot just as a car screeched out of the parking lot next door.

Candy's car door was open. I slammed my hand on the steering wheel, jerking the car into reverse, spinning the wheels with enough force the rubber burned on the pavement. As I floored the accelerator, screeching out of the parking lot, I pulled my weapon into my hand.

The fuckers thought they could outrun me. My hand remained wrapped around the steering wheel as I shoved the gear into fifth. I was already doing eighty in a thirty-five zone. While the last thing I needed was to be hassled by the police, if I'd been two minutes later, there wouldn't have been a chance in hell to find her. Not in this damn city.

The last thing I was going to do was allow Candy to be taken. I skidded around a corner following them, now only a few hundred yards away. When they made another turn, I realized they were heading out of the Irish-controlled community and into Russian territory. The driver was also headed to the freeway. I couldn't allow that to happen.

Speeding up, all I could think about was getting to her. They were headed into a commercial area, the only businesses open the twenty-four-hour pharmacies. When I was only fifty yards back, the shooting started.

Even more concerning was that they were using assault rifles, which meant whoever had taken her were professionals. I weaved back and forth, hissing when a bullet smashed through the windshield. I was finished with playing games. Within seconds, I careened beside them, slamming the car into the driver's door.

The quick movement allowed me to take a quick glance into the car, a splash of illumination coming from streetlights. While the gaze was quick, at least I knew who I was dealing with. The three assholes from the bar. What I didn't see was Candy. There was no way they'd had the opportunity to drop her anywhere, which meant she was being kept on the floor or in the trunk.

The anger slammed against my insides, gnawing at my gut as I smashed my car into the driver's side again. This time, the force I used was enough to shove the bastard off the road, his front right tire jumping the curb. The fucker tried to stop, the screech of brakes easy to hear through the hole in the windshield, but he couldn't control it, careening into the brick-sided wall of the building.

I was already out of the car, racing in their direction.

Within seconds, the three men jumped out, two of them raising their weapons at the same time I did. Unfortunately for them, I was a crack shot and hell of a lot faster. The two men went down hard, one shot between the eyes, tossed backward from the impact. The other I caught in the throat, his body crumpling to the pavement, gagging on his own blood. Dropping and rolling, I shifted my attention to the third asshole, powering off three shots in a row.

I never missed.

The first shot shattered the asshole's shoulder, pummeling him against the wall. The second tore through his chest. And the third was a direct hit to the center of his face.

I took a deep breath, jetting toward the vehicle and peering inside. Fuck. Then I heard an intense moan.

I hit the unlock button on the key fob and rushed to the trunk. When I opened the lid, her angelic face peered up at me.

"Candy."

Her lower lip quivered, her eyes enlarged. I gathered her into my arms, gently easing her to the ground. While she continued to whimper, my first glance indicated the bastards hadn't hurt her, just minor cuts and bruises. "It's okay. Everything is going to be alright."

She said nothing as she clung to me, taking shallow breaths. I scanned the area, hissing as I yanked out my phone. The area needed a quick clean, hopefully before the police arrived. "Vassily."

"Kirill. I'm surprised to hear from you."

"No time for bullshit. I need you at the parking lot on the corner of Second and Alcove."

"How many?"

"Three, plus a vehicle. I also need a sweep at Killian's Bar and Grill. There's an older Chevy Cruze that needs to be removed and stored."

"You've been a busy boy," Vassily said, laughing.

"Just do it. As a side note, I need ID on the three fucks. One of them works for Michael Walsh directly. Rory something."

"I'll see what I can do. I'll check around with some of the boys."

'The boys' was the term he used for spies. They'd been cultured over time to infiltrate other crime syndicates, corporations and even to a small degree law enforcement.

If something was brewing on the street that we hadn't been made aware of, they would know.

"Just make sure you find something. These fucks didn't act alone." I shoved my phone into my pocket, walking her toward my car. I kept her close, constantly scanning the street.

Candy pulled away from me, folding her arms and staring in horror at the three bodies. I could tell she was fighting a scream, pressing the back of one hand over her mouth. While I should shield her from the carnage, she needed to understand what I was dealing with and what she'd gotten herself in the middle of. "Who are you?"

"Nobody special. Don't fight with me, Candy. We can talk later."

"That's a lie, Kirill. You told me you'd never lie to me. You're Bratva. Aren't you?" When I didn't answer right away, she struggled in my hold. "Aren't you?"

"Let's just say I'm an important man who has dozens of enemies. That means I need to get you out of here."

Her mouth twisted in uncertainty and frustration, but she remained where she was as I walked closer, flinching only when I lifted her chin.

"I don't know you," she whispered. "Just like I didn't know them. Leave me alone."

"You know more about me than almost anyone, Candy. There will likely be more of those men, which mean you're in danger. Now, can you trust me?" I could tell she'd been dragged across the parking lot, gravel imbedded in a few scrapes. Damn it. The assholes didn't deserve to die so quickly.

"How can I? You just murdered three men in cold blood. Just like you murder women."

Women? Who the hell had told her that? Rian.

I cocked my head and waited but could only allow her a few seconds more. This was the last place I wanted to remain without cover or backup. "Candy, those men abducted you, tossed you into the trunk of a car, and I assure you that where they were taking you, I wouldn't have located had I not followed my gut that you were in danger. What do you think they were going to do?"

"I don't know," she snapped then took another look at all three men before turning away. "What I do know is that you're a monster."

Up to this point, she'd come at me with all the fury she could muster. Now she showed her vulnerable side, her lovely face pinched with uncertainty. There was no longer any doubt about who I was, although she'd already been told. She'd been forced to accept that I wasn't just the mysterious, dangerous man who'd awakened her passion, but also a brutal killer, her head filled with even more atrocities than I'd committed.

"We need to go, Candy."

"Where?" she asked, tipping her head and finally locking eyes with mine.

"Somewhere safe." When I took her arm, she jerked away a second time, shaking her head.

"I'm not going anywhere with you. Just leave me alone." Even in the dim but harsh light, I could see her eyes widen in fear, her distrust understandable. But at this point, her rebellious behavior had become intolerable.

"We don't have time for this. You are coming with me whether you understand or appreciate why."

She backed up a few additional feet, almost tripping over asshole number three. Yelping, she turned as if she was going to run down the sidewalk. I couldn't allow that to happen. I lunged toward her, snagging her wrist and yanking her with enough force she slammed into my chest. Then I snapped my hand around her mouth. Her scream would draw more attention than the car crash. I shook her gently before lowering my head, my tone harsher than it likely needed to be.

"I'm going to get us both out of here, but you will need to trust me. Those assholes won't be the only ones coming. And next time, they won't fail. I'm your only lifeline at this point. I suggest you accept that or your stay with me will become very uncomfortable."

Her entire body remained trembling, but she nodded. I could tell she was shutting down, trying to rationalize what she'd seen and experienced. She was forced to crawl in through the driver's door. While the GTO was battered, it would get us to our destination. One thing was certain; I couldn't take her back to her apartment or my fake one.

Candy had just been given a jumpstart into my life, one that would ultimately ruin her in the end. Sadly, I had no other choice.

* * *

She'd remained quiet the entire ride, peering out the passenger window, occasionally glancing at the bullet hole in the windshield. The only reaction I noticed was when I headed out of Brooklyn over the bridge, driving into Manhattan. That's when she'd turned her head, shifting her eyes back and forth as she'd studied me.

When I finally slowed down, heading into an underground parking lot, she tensed.

"It's safe here," I assured her.

"Where is here?"

"A secure building."

"I'm not stupid and I'm not a child, Kirill. I'd appreciate if you wouldn't treat me like one."

"Fair enough," I said, sighing as I pressed the button, waiting for the gate to slide out of the way. I'd purchased two condos in the high-rise years before, the building chosen because of its many layers of security, including that no one knew who owned the units in the building, our identities protected.

I couldn't allow anyone to know who I was or where I resided. The cost was too high, my anonymity an asset to the Kozlov Empire. Bringing her here was risky, but I refused to drop her in one of the safehouses. She deserved better and I refused to allow her out of my sight.

Not only was I pissed off that she'd been taken, but I was also deeply troubled by the way she'd been handled. I would have understood had members of the Walsh family intervened, taking her against her will. This was something else entirely.

I knew enough about Rian to know he wasn't typically into violence. Then again, things might have changed. As I pulled into one of my spaces, she leaned forward on the seat, glancing at two of the other vehicles.

"Are they yours?" she asked, her voice still trembling.

"Yes, they are."

She gave me another look, the same curl appearing on her upper lip that I'd seen before. When she narrowed her eyes, her expression was unreadable, but I could swear she was laughing at me.

"And you live here. I mean really live here."

"Yes, Candy. I do, at least a portion of the time."

"You lied to me. You're rich."

"I make a decent living, nothing more, nothing less."

"You make it sounded glorified." She fisted her hand, moving as close to the door as possible.

"Nothing about what I do is glorified." A part of me wanted to reach out and touch her. What good would that do at this point? She knew more than she was telling me. There were far too many red flags. "Why do you think I kill women?"

She shot me a look, her glare harsh. "Something I heard."

From Rian, no doubt. "The acts I've been required to perform are brutal, but they are also selective. Whether or not this gives you any comfort, I've never harmed a woman before in my life. That is a line I refuse to cross." Her eyes held no glimmer of belief, but she slowly lowered her gaze, issuing a single nod.

With that, she tried to get out the passenger door, yanking it several times.

Sighing, I eased onto the concrete, taking a glance around the private garage as I would any other location. Nowhere was completely safe, no matter how many men were on my detail, or the security measures installed. If I had a price on my head, the bastards would find a way to get to me.

The easiest way was through the people I cared about. I'd broken my rule, but for the first time in my life, something else mattered more to me than just business.

"Come on, Candy. Let's get you settled."

At least she didn't fight me when I helped her out of the car, but her solid, hateful stare remained, her eyes now full of questions as well as venom. I led her to the private elevator, pulling the key card from my wallet. I'd ordered two of my men to stand guard in the parking garage until we arrived. They would remain close to the building, acting as my security detail.

I knew they likely appeared ominous to her, both wearing dark suits, their weapons in clear display. While she stared at them, she didn't react other than shaking her head.

"Does it ever bother you being a killer?"

I'd expected the question, only not so soon. "It's complicated, Candy. You don't necessarily choose to become an enforcer with the Russian Bratva."

"No freedom of choice. Why bother being in this country?" Her tone was accusatory, but oddly enough, she had a good point.

"Because everything here is more beautiful, including the women."

"I don't need bullshit any more than I need lies." When the doors opened, she stepped inside, no longer shaking.

When I entered the cold steel box beside her, she stayed as far away from me as possible, never looking me in the eyes.

It was difficult for me not to study her as I'd done the first night. Her lips remained pursed and all I could think about was having them wrapped around my cock. She'd just been kidnapped, her life shattered and all I could think about was Candy sucking my cock. What did that make me?

Certainly a bastard, a term that had never bothered me before.

The elevator came to a halt, requiring me to slide my secure card into the slot for a second time, another measure of added security. When the doors opened, Candy remained where she was, her breathing shallower than it had been before.

"Come. As I told you, you will be safe."

"I don't think there's such a thing any longer. Is there?" She tipped her head, her lips pursed and an entirely different fire in her eyes.

"Maybe not." I walked out, giving her time to follow, which she did seconds later. I could sense her every movement, the feel of just having her around me slamming my system more than any electric jolt could do. I'd asked my housekeeper to prepare the space, providing provisions I thought Candy would like.

I had no concept of her preferences, nor had I ever allowed anyone else to visit my condo except for Alexei and a few members of my team. I headed into the kitchen, yanking out a bottle of water then grabbing wine from my wine cabinet.

Observing her was fascinating. She was a touchy-feely kind of woman, touching several surfaces as she walked past, heading for the window. I had one of the most beautiful views of the city, the venue providing a one-hundred-and-eighty-degree picture, including the Hudson River. She remained pensive, wringing her hands as she peered out the glass surface. I noticed she remained two feet away, as if the soaring height bothered her.

I found being forty stories above the rest of the city comforting, but the amount of time I'd spent inside the condo had been limited. As I walked in her direction, she tugged on her long ponytail, pulling it over her shoulder and running her fingers through the long strands. She'd never appeared more vulnerable than she did at this moment. When I tried to hand her the glass of wine, she shrank back.

"I don't need anything from you," she huffed.

"Take the glass, Candy. I'm not in the mood to play games."

"And you think I am?" She shot me a hateful look, her features softening when I kept the glass in front of her. When she finally wrapped her hand around the dense crystal, our fingers touched. I was amazed how much a simple brush of her skin could ignite the fire within me. I could tell she felt it as well, her breath skipping.

She hid behind the glass for a few seconds, taking several sips. "Why do you have a beef with my family? Why did they kidnap me? And don't tell me you're a bad man because I already know that. They want something from me, don't they?"

A part of me had been prepared to launch into her, grilling her about questions regarding Rory and his cohorts as well as what else Rian was into, but there was complete truth in her questions, continued concern in her eyes.

I chuckled, glaring at the bottle of water. The tasteless liquid wasn't going to cut it tonight. Fuck my rules. When I moved toward the bar in the corner of the room, I sensed her eyes following me.

"To answer your question honestly would place your life in even more danger."

"Yet you want me to trust you. That can't happen unless I actually know you."

Her retort was just as I would have expected. I poured my drink then leaned against the bar, studying her. "You already know a good deal about me, Candy, and who I work for."

"But what exactly do you do for the Kozlov Bratva? An enforcer. You clean up messes created by the aspects of the Kozlov business."

I took a sip before answering. Her fire had returned, refusing to allow the events of the evening to dampen her spirit. My cock ached even more than it had before, the hard pinch against my trousers forcing me to shift my legs. "You're very astute. I handle business situations that have gone wrong, doing what I can to fix them."

"Then everything I heard about you was true. You kill people for a living."

"I do what's necessary in order to keep the peace."

She huffed, shaking her head. "I'm not certain what that even means."

"That means that you and your friends can continue living their everyday lives without fear that monsters will crash through your windows. It means that blood won't rain in the streets on a daily basis."

"Please."

"Please what, Candy? Please pretend that what I'm telling you isn't the truth? I can't do that. You want the truth, then be prepared for the answers."

Her quick glance in my direction was riddled with anxiety. I didn't need to be any closer than I was to gather a whiff of her fear. She should be afraid of me, which is why I should never have placed a finger on her.

"Your enemies are out to get you, using any method they can," she whispered. "So you're on a high alert, taking down whoever gets in your way."

"Yes, at least mostly."

"Mostly. Which means you kill innocent people as well."

"I've done everything in my power not to allow that to happen."

"Why? I would think eliminating any collateral damage would help you sleep easier at night."

I swirled the liquid in my glass, studying her intently, her words striking a different chord with me. Was there anyone truly innocent? "Nothing allows me to sleep at night, Candy. Nothing." I hated that my thoughts continued to drift to the past but with her presence, it was difficult to think about anything else. "Sit down. I need to make certain you don't have gravel imbedded in your skin." When she hesitated, I pointed to the chair, keeping my eyes locked on her until she obeyed.

I pushed the drink onto the counter. "Stay right here. Do not move."

She laughed. I was able to hear the sound as I headed to the half bath, gathering everything I needed. When I returned, she remained in the same place, staring out the window, unblinking. I moved closer, placing the hydrogen peroxide and several towels on the table. When I bent down, she bristled, fisting one hand, the fingers she had wrapped around her wineglass shaking.

Very tenderly I cleaned the scrapes, picking out several pieces of gravel, more furious than ever how she'd been treated. When I was finished, I shoved the items aside, brushing the back of my hand across her knee.

Candy immediately pulled it away, chewing on her bottom lip.

I returned to my drink, uncertain how to handle her. As before, my mind refused to let go the possibility she was playing me, but with every second that passed, I became more certain her near abduction had nothing to do with Rian attempting to be protective. Why take her? What good would that do?

Unless the target was actually the Walsh family.

The possibilities were endless.

"What are you fighting and why am I involved? Because I know you?"

"That's possible, Candy, and it's something I need to find out. That's why I need you to be truthful with me."

"Truthful. Just like you were with me." She stood, walking away from me and toward the window. I sensed exhaustion was settling in, her body swaying.

At this point it wouldn't matter what I said to her. She still needed time in order to process what she'd experienced.

Including with me. She was a fascinating woman in several regards. One minute she was fire and brimstone, prepared to take on the world. The next she was fearful, trembling even though she tried to hide her terror. As she stood in front of my window, she was experiencing both, hating me one minute then longing to indulge in the passion the next.

She took several sips of wine, her brow furrowed. Every subtle nuance intrigued me, enticing the continuing hunger I already had for her. If she had any idea what effect she had on me, it was impossible to tell.

"Why were you staying in that apartment when this is your home?"

Her question was a fair one, even though answering was more difficult than I'd imagined when I'd played out this scenario. "This is my private space, a location few people know exists. I need it to remain that way. My anonymity is what allows me to stay alive. The apartment was necessary in order to conduct business."

"You were keeping tabs on someone or some entity. Right?"

"Smart girl. You are correct."

"That includes my family." Very slowly she turned her head in my direction, apprehension in her voice.

I took a deep breath before answering. "Your comment is one of the reasons we're here. If I'd known you were associated with the Walsh family, I would have turned you away."

"I'm not just associated with them. They are my family, although right now I'm not certain I care to admit it. And would you have turned me away?"

Now she'd caught me in a lie. I wouldn't have given a shit what family line ran in her blood. That's how strong my feelings had been. And they were only increasing. "I do what is required."

"That's not an answer and you know it."

"Don't ask questions you don't want to learn the real answer to."

"Don't, Kirill. That's just some mantra you learned. How many times have I asked you, begged you to tell me the truth? You came into my life like a bulldozer, pretending to be something you weren't."

"First of all," I said as I walked closer. "You came into my life. Second, I've never pretended to be anything but a brutal man. If I'd laid out my lineage, would you have turned away?"

She opened her mouth, her lips forming a perfect O. Then she closed her eyes. "I don't honestly know."

"Fair enough. Why didn't you tell me the truth about your family?"

"Because I didn't think it mattered for one thing. The other is that I'm not close to them. At all."

"I'm not certain I believe you."

"Fine. Don't. I learned that Rian, my second cousin who owns Killian's, was required to keep tabs on me. Second, he confronted me about you, as if the man had any right to tell me who I could spend time with, and third…"

She bit her lip instead of finishing, a pained look crossing her face. I moved even closer until I was positioned in front of her. Her words rang true, which was rare in my world. I lifted her chin, lowering my head to ensure I could study her eyes.

They never lied.

"And third?"

The fact she appeared even more uncomfortable sent up red flags. "And third, I think Rian is the reason those horrible men grabbed me out of the parking lot tonight. That asshole Rory and his buddies were in the bar when you came in. You should have heard them. They went on and on about you. Nothing of importance, but they acted like you were enemy number one."

She was right again. The three had been sent to gather information. There were more of them. Who the hell had they been working for?

Immediately, my hackles were raised. Whether or not she knew more remained to be seen, but she would tell me everything. In truth, whoever Rory was and the entity responsible for giving him orders to abduct Candy, I suspected the order hadn't come from anyone in the Walsh family. Call it instinct, but given Rian's genuine anger and concern, even confronting a man he'd been taught could snap his neck with one hand, I seriously doubted he'd condone what had been done to his own cousin.

"Why do you believe your cousin had anything to do with it? And I want to know the full truth, Candy."

"I don't know who they were, other than overhearing the asshole's name and the trash talk they were throwing out like every other bully I've encountered in my life. That's the damn truth, Kirill. They came into the bar that night then tried to kidnap me the next." She looked away, her brow furrowing.

"What is it?"

"The girl who works with me said they're trouble. They really are your enemies, aren't they? The ones you mentioned to me last night."

I shouldn't have said a damn thing to her. "As I already told you, I have many enemies, so does every member of the Bratva."

"Who wanted me taken, Michael Walsh?"

"Why would you think that?"

Her mouth twisted as she tried to think of an answer. "Just because he's powerful. At least that's what Rian told me."

I doubted she was lying at this moment, but in not telling me her full identity, she'd placed herself in harm's way. "Michael Walsh believes himself to be the god of unions. He's causing significant issues with a construction project. Do I think it's possible he ordered your abduction? I would ordinarily say anything is possible, but the Walsh family prides themselves in being close-knit." Was I just telling her what she wanted to hear? "I can't imagine he'd go that far."

"Why would that matter to you? It's not like there's a union for assassins or crime lords." She slapped her hand over her mouth, fearful of my reaction.

At that moment, she seemed even more innocent than before, almost gullible but I knew better. I laughed softly, unprepared for handling her like I thought I would be. She needed to understand that this was no game and that her life remained in danger, but the last thing I wanted to do was to break her spirit. Unfortunately, I also needed her controlled. That would mean being more forceful with her. If she believed me to be a monster, perhaps it was time to reinforce it. That might be the only way to keep her alive.

"The Kozlov family is in the business of construction, as well as other profitable organizations that are entirely above board. I think that's all you need to know."

She stared at me with wide eyes, a hint of amusement in them. "Interesting. So you're the enforcer who kills anyone who fucks with your legitimate businesses. Does that mean my family has stood in your way? Are you planning on killing all of them?" Her smirk was pushing my level of irritation. While her quirks were adorable and her smile able to light a part of the darkness dwelling within me, I was exactly as she believed me to be. To think otherwise would be a weakness others would be able to smell a mile away.

"It's not your place to question how and what I do, Candy. The fact you lied to me doesn't sit well with me. In fact, it earned you a stern punishment." If Rian was behind her mistreatment, it would be impossible to keep from hunting him down like the dog he truly was. I bristled, trying to keep my anger in check, but I was losing the ability quickly. It had just become even more important to keep her safe until I found out exactly what I was dealing with.

But she needed to believe that I was the villain, then so be it. I couldn't waste time in pretending or sugarcoating my existence.

Her eyes opened wide, but there was no fear in them, only her continued defiance. "You don't own me or get to tell me what I can do or am required to tell you. I'm not in some cage."

"Look around you, Candy. While this condo is secure and comfortable, and you'll be provided with everything you need to survive, this is a cage. Your cage. You will be required to follow my rules at all times. Any infraction will result in harsh punishment. There is no alternative. None."

"That's not fair. I have a life."

"As of now, this is your life. I am your life."

She glared at me for a few seconds then looked away, the quiver in her lower lip returning. "What rules?"

"You will stay in this condo at all times. To ensure that happens, there will be two guards waiting at the bottom of that elevator if you try and escape. If you do, I assure you that the punishment you receive will remain with you for a long time. There are no phones here, no other method of communication. I keep my computers locked away. Even if you were able to access them, the system installed is highly sensitive and secure. There are two people under my employ who keep this place cleaned, food and necessities purchased. One or the other will be here. Do not try and take their private cellphones or attack them in any way. I assure you that both are highly trained and will do whatever is necessary to help you follow my rules. As you might imagine, I have business outside of this house. There are books to keep you entertained, music available to you, but there are no televisions." I waited until she blinked in recognition. I could sense her growing hatred, which a part of me loathed but this was necessary. The fear of me would keep her alive.

"What else?"

"You will not deny me in any way. Never. Did I make myself clear enough this time?" I heard the harshness in my tone, knew the look on my face was villainous. To see the look of horror followed by shock in her eyes was troubling, more than it should be.

I should have anticipated her reaction given her rebellious nature. When she tossed the wine in my face followed by issuing a hard slap, I closed my eyes, taking several deep breaths. Then I tossed my glass against the wall as well as hers, not giving a shit whether they shattered or not. When I grabbed both her wrists, yanking her onto her toes, her gasp was a clear indication that I'd gotten her attention.

She quivered in my hold and at that moment, all I wanted to do was to wrap my arm around her. As I lowered my head, she winced. I'd never paid much attention to the monster I'd become or the face glaring me back in the mirror, but at that moment, I longed to be anyone else but the assassin I was. However, I couldn't change what I was or the circumstances.

I pulled her even closer until her body was crushed up against mine. "I don't know how to make this any clearer than what I'm about to say. Listen to me, Candy. Someone is out to use you as a pawn. And in my experience, if they don't get what they want, you will be killed. I assure you that if bastards like those three men get ahold of you again, I doubt I can save you. I'm your only lifeline at this point and you will need to trust me. Now, I'll ask you one last time. Do. You. Understand?"

Goddamn it, I cared about the woman but not a single person, including the Kozlov family members could know how I felt. There was still a snitch inside our operation. People attempting to provide information were killed, another indication of a leak. News like this would be a reason to take another chance for a hit, only it would be direct. She was innocent, I was convinced of that, but given our connection had been broadcast to God knows who, she could be used by several entities.

I was finished with playing nice all the way around.

Her face fell, as if she finally understood the truth. Hatred set in, shutting down several of her emotions. She closed her eyes briefly, her lower lip quivering. Then she gave me nothing more than a simple nod.

CHAPTER 10

Candy

Prisoner. The cage might be pretty, but that's exactly what it was, a cage.

I tried to comprehend his change in demeanor as well as his level of cruelty, but I couldn't fathom how a switch had been flipped. Had everything we'd shared been a total lie? I was aching inside, hurt from his brutal words. Tears threatened to form but there was no way in hell I was going to allow that to happen.

He didn't deserve anything from me. Not one thing. Not that it was going to matter. It was obvious he was going to take what he wanted.

Never deny him.

It was as if all the passion we'd shared had been a lie. Had he been using me to gather information? No, that was insane. He was right. I'd gone to him. Was it possible he'd purposely annoyed me? Hell, I didn't know. I couldn't stand not putting the pieces together. Everything was unraveling. Could the Walsh family be as corrupt as the Bratva? I wouldn't know.

His words were terrifying, even more so because of the inflection in his voice. My heart was ready to explode, the fear unlike anything I'd known before. I studied him carefully, fisting my hands and longing to pummel them against his chest but his hold was too strong. I forced myself to try to relax just to be able to get out of his clutches. My cage. Had I traded one for another?

The same questions rolled through my mind in a never-ending loop.

Random thoughts splintered my mind. Why would Rian do this? Was he involved in something as sinister as Kirill's occupation? Could I even call what the brutal Russian did for a living a job? I closed my eyes, still able to see the ugliness of the three men shot dead, their vacant eyes staring up at the darkened sky.

He was so violent and uncaring, but I'd seen another side. Or maybe I'd convinced myself that he was capable of anything other than violence.

Killing those men had seemed so easy for Kirill to do. Just another day at the office. A nervous laugh threatened to bubble to the surface, but I managed to squelch it. When I started to squirm, he shook me once, issuing a guttural sound.

"Breathe for me, Candy. While I am going to punish you, I don't intend on hurting you unless you give me no other choice."

"Maybe you already have."

He sighed, looking away briefly. "A necessary part of my job."

"What am I supposed to say, that I forgive you for uprooting my life or saving me from a different species of bad guys?"

"As I said before," he said quietly, loosening his grip, "I need you to tell me everything you know about the man you called Rory. Everything, Candy. Do not leave anything out."

"I wasn't paying that much attention as they were dragging me by the hair toward their damn vehicle."

My forceful words yanked at the beast inside of him. He hissed, every part of his body tensing. He was intimidating yet sexy, the heat he exuded wrapping around me. I had the feeling of lust again, the connection unbreakable even by his change in demeanor.

He took a deep breath before speaking. "Try and think about it, Candy. It's important. I need to find out who they are. Did they say anything to you before they dumped you in the trunk?"

I thought about the question, hating the fact I had to remember the horrible event. But I did, the entire few moments flashing in my mind in vivid color. "That they were providing an intervention and that I'd make a fabulous prize. What the hell does that mean?"

His snarl was a terrifying sound, his upper lip curling. Then he placed his hand on the back of my head, forcing my face against his chest. As he held me, sweeping his long fingers down in even strokes, I was finally able to breathe easier. A moment of softness returned to his actions, but he'd already done enough damage. He didn't care about me. I was nothing more than a method of obtaining information.

Or worse.

"You're safe now."

With him? That was never going to be possible. I don't care how much passion we'd shared or how lurid my thoughts had become. He wasn't my savior.

He was my captor.

I was now his prize, instead of being the prize of the horrible man who'd dumped me in the trunk. What was the real difference? I'd become more daunted by him than I was before, his size overwhelming where it had been sexy before. But a part of my frazzled brain was locked in the two nights we'd shared, which was utterly ridiculous.

I pushed hard against him, managing to encourage him to release his hold on my head. I wanted to see his eyes. You could tell everything by a man's eyes. They weren't just a window to his soul; they were a clear indication of truth.

As well as good versus evil.

He was strange combination of both, a tortured conscience that he'd never been able to appease. In those seconds, he decided to kiss me, catching me completely off guard. When he crushed his mouth over mine, I was frozen stiff for a few seconds, longing to have the strength to shove him away, but around him, taking control was impossible.

He tasted like bourbon, the liquor bitter yet inviting at the same time. I was drawn to him as I'd been before, a moth to a flame. My heart flickered as he thrust his tongue past my lips, engulfing my mouth completely. He wasn't just a powerhouse in providing damage to anyone who dared cross him. He was also an extreme source of power in everything he did.

Including kissing.

I was quivering to my core, everything inside of me pulsing erratically. The fire we'd shared before had remained active, now doused with gasoline. The deep need I'd felt before hadn't subsided, now even more desperate. I curled my arm around his neck, my body swaying as he held me close. The heat was almost oppressive, pulling out the same darkness I'd seen in him.

What the hell was I doing with this man? I couldn't want him, especially now, but there was no avoiding the extreme sensations or the intense longing. As he dominated my tongue, sweeping his back and forth, I'd never felt so lost in my life.

I wanted to feel dirty, as if every time he touched my skin, I'd given away a part of me, but the reality was that he completed me in some crazy way. As the moment of passion continued, a few seconds of rationality finally set in. I managed to break the kiss, the flash of anger on his face a reminder that I was nothing more to him than a way to find answers.

I had every reason to hate him. I was also horrified at what I'd fallen into. When I tried to slap him again, he grabbed my wrist, twisting my arm enough I cried out.

"I thought we had an understanding. I guess I'll need to make it much clearer to you." His tone was darker, deeper and I sensed his irritation given he was about issue a proclamation.

Or a warning.

"Please do," I countered, trying to find my voice. I wanted nothing more than demonize him because I knew if I managed to do that, I'd find it easier to hate him. But every time I looked into his eyes, butterflies swarmed my stomach, lust replacing the loathing I'd felt only seconds earlier. He was staring at me in amusement, a slight smile curling across his lips. "Go ahead."

He let go of my arm but remained only a few inches away. "I can tell you're going to remain defiant, *malen'kiy ognennyy shar*. Very well. Have it your way. Undress."

As I'd seen before, his expression changed, none of the amusement I'd seen earlier remaining.

"What gives you the right to order me around?"

He huffed. "The *right*? Is that what you asked me?"

I expected him to come at me, to release the obvious anger he'd been holding since releasing me from the trunk, but he grew sad instead. Or maybe haunted. Swallowing hard, I had no decent answer. I couldn't make any demands, but he pulled out entirely different emotions in me than anyone else ever had. I backed away, no longer finding my voice.

As I'd seen before, there was something primal about him, but the darkness had encased him. I'd pushed one button too many.

"What are you going to do to me?"

I could tell he was debating, studying me as if uncertain of how I'd react to being punished. He'd spanked me before, but the moments of pain had added to the extreme pleasure we'd shared. I doubted what he would do this time would lead to anything resembling what we'd shared before.

The intensity of the look in his eyes was as unnerving as the man. I wished he would get on with determining what he was going to do to me. Spanking me. Fucking me. Whatever it was, I couldn't take the heavy anxiety. Getting it over with would make things much easier. The lump remained in my throat as I slowly started backing away.

Even his breathing was entirely different, the raspy sound unlike any normal sound. I could swear he was turning into an animal before my eyes.

"I'm going to fuck you."

His statement shouldn't have surprised me, but it did. "I don't want to have sex with you, Kirill. There is no way after what happened and after finding out who you really are that I can even stand the thought of being intimate with you."

He walked closer, matching every backward step I took. When I was finally incapable of going anywhere else, the wall preventing me from escaping his clutches, I slammed out my hands as soon as he approached. He allowed my palms to stop him, but I knew not for very long. He could easily take what he wanted.

"As happened from the first minute you walked in through my door, your body betrays you. Don't you think I can tell by the way you look at me or when your mouth quivers how much you crave my touch? Your nipples are already hard, sweet Candy, your pulse rapid."

I bit my cheek as I'd done so many times around him, darting a look at the stupid, torn tee shirt, the outline of my nipples easy to see through the thin fabric. The very core of my being was pulsing, the longing even more intense. I was swept up in his scent just like before.

"And your pussy is wet. Isn't it?"

He didn't bother waiting for my answer, sliding his hand between my legs. As he rocked it forward and backward, I bucked against his indecent touch almost instantly, moans slipping past my lips. He knew exactly how to drive me crazy with desire, incapable of making any rational decisions.

"Answer me, my little rebel."

Of course he knew the answer. I imagined his fingers were slickened from my juice. The seductive nature of the man as well as his voice made me want to answer him, to concede that he drove me crazy.

"Yes."

His smile was at least a small reward for being a good girl.

"Then it's settled. First, I fuck you. Then I spank you."

The brutal man tossed me over his shoulder with ease, acting as if I weighed nothing in his arms.

There was no sense in fighting him. It wasn't just about how strong, powerful, or dangerous he was. Another wave of excitement had surged through me. I couldn't seem to get enough of him, and he knew it. He was using my attraction to him to keep me in line. What could I say or do? Nothing.

He moved from one massive space to another, walking into what had to be his private quarters, the other used for business maybe? I tried to lift my head, paying attention to my surroundings. While his condo was gorgeous, windows on several sides, it was as austere as the apartment above mine. There were at least two flashy cars in his private parking garage, and I gathered the furniture was terribly expensive, but there was nothing personal about it.

It was as if the life had been sucked out of him, everything merely functional.

After carrying me into a bedroom, he immediately tossed me onto the center of the bed. I moved onto all fours, staring at him as he ripped off his jacket, tossing it aside, wasting no time in unbuttoning his shirt, merely peeling it over his shoulders. Everything about him was entirely different, including his roughness. I reacted as I'd done the first time, scrambling to get off the bed.

Kirill snagged my wrist, yanking me back with ease. Then he cupped both sides of my face, his breathing ragged as he rubbed his thumbs across my skin with enough pressure that he twisted my mouth.

"You shouldn't fight me any longer, *moya krasota*. That will only make your punishment that much worse." He lowered his head until our lips were only centimeters apart.

I snapped my fingers around his wrists as I rose onto my knees, thinking I could pull away his hands. I should have known better. He kept the pressure as he pressed his lips against mine. I was surprised when he kept his kiss gentle, brushing his lips back and forth. Still, I sensed his hunger was heightened, becoming even more insatiable.

There wasn't a part of me that wasn't tingling. He continued the soft touch, darting his tongue across the seam of my mouth, and everything seemed far too intimate. My mind was ready to explode, my body incapable of shutting down like I'd fully intended on doing. Everything seemed desperate, his needs greater than before, yet so perfectly controlled that I knew at some point he would crack.

He slowly forced my lips to open, to accept his tongue's domination of mine. Then the kiss became more insatiable and unyielding, his mouth capturing mine. There was something about this connection, this moment we were sharing that seemed as different as his kiss.

Not just personal, but as if he was ensuring I accepted that I belonged to him. His two-day beard scratched my skin, but the subtle discomfort added to the extreme arousal. I found myself clinging to him as if he was my only lifeline, raking my nails down his sides. If he was experiencing any pain, there was no way I'd know it even if every sound he made was like a wild animal, guttural and predatory.

I melted into him, the heat of his skin skimming against mine, creating another wave of searing electricity. He took his time exploring my mouth, losing himself in the pleasure without fear of interruption or time constraints.

Whatever this was exploding between us, I sensed a complete change in our roles. He'd allowed me to play before. Now he was asserting his full authority, nothing off limits. I closed my eyes, enjoying the various vibrations. When he pulled me even closer, I arched my back, savoring the feel of his throbbing cock pressing against my chest. He pulled me back onto my feet, crushing his body against mine. I was small and helpless in his arms, forced to accept his power over me.

I continued to shiver, my nipples aching from the way my bra shifted back and forth. I rolled my hands over his shoulders, marveling in the feel of him, so rugged. So muscular.

When he finally broke the kiss, the look in his eyes was raw and uncensored, so easy to read, the vile and filthy things he had planned for me disgusting.

Exciting.

My God, I was fatigued from the continued shots of electricity coursing through me.

He released his hold, but only for a few seconds, grabbing my shirt and ripping it over my head. Another growl left his mouth as he cupped my breasts, dropping his head and engulfing my nipple.

"Oh, God." I was powerful in his hold, my mind racing as he filled me with an entirely new, heightened sense of need. I craved his cock filling me, taking me completely. Even though I wanted him, I'd been unable to get the ugly visions out of my head. Three dead men. The look in Kirill's eyes when he'd pulled me from the wretched darkness had been almost as terrifying as the ordeal I'd just gone through.

The man had no soul, no remorse for killing those men. And I hadn't cared about what he'd done, at least not at first. I'd wanted those bastards cut down for what they'd done to me. I'd relished seeing their lifeless bodies, blood oozing on the pavement. But that wasn't reality. At least it wasn't supposed to be mine.

All the years I'd believed myself to be a good girl had faded away in a single instant, replaced with vile anger and hatred. And now? I felt confusion and uncertainty, but I didn't fear Kirill, no matter how hard he was attempting to try to terrorize me. Maybe there was a growing sickness inside, my body now controlling my mind. Whatever was happening, I couldn't shut down my feelings.

Or the crazy desire that continued to surface every time I was close to him.

I threw my head back, blinking several times although it was impossible to focus. A silly little laugh rushed up from my throat as I gripped his shoulders, digging my fingers into him for fear of falling.

As if he didn't have a firm hold on me.

The thought made me dizzy, the stars floating across the ceiling making me lightheaded. The second he bit down on my nipple, I whimpered, but the pain instantly shifted into incredible bliss, the carnality of what he was doing so enticing.

Growling, he shifted his mouth to my other nipple, using his teeth to yank down the lace on my bra, exposing my hardened bud. He squeezed both breasts, holding me in place as he sucked and nipped. I heard the slight ripping of material and gasped.

He chuckled and breathed across my skin before flicking his tongue back and forth. When he pulled away, I could tell how tense his body was.

"I suggest you finish undressing, my little fireball. If you do not, I'll take care of that for you. And I won't be the gentle man you're used to experiencing."

There was even more darkness rushing to the surface, a different look in his eyes.

I stumbled backwards, darting my eyes across his. He was being serious. The man would rip my clothes into shreds. Everything about him continued to throw me, keeping my heart racing. It was as if a switch had gone off in him. I couldn't read his expression as I'd done before, at least not entirely. While there was lust in his eyes, there was something else that finally troubled me.

Remorse. Or guilt?

While I wasn't certain, when he yanked off the rest of his clothes, I remained frozen. His physique continued to draw me in, creating extraordinary heat, but his change in demeanor continued to startle me. I was forced to remind myself that this wasn't some fantasy or a chapter in a romance book. This was dangerous. He was dangerous. Nothing good was going to come out of this.

And maybe there'd be additional deaths.

The air vanished in the room, the only sound my heart. He was far too beautiful, in my mind blissful perfection, but I reminded myself that there was nothing perfect in this life. I turned my head on purpose, refusing to be drawn by his good looks or captivating gaze. Every time I reminded myself that I was nothing more than his prisoner was enough to drag me out of the moment of reverie. He didn't deserve that.

I closed my eyes, almost laughing that the only thing he'd seen me in had been the same ugly green tee shirt, khaki skirt, and tennis shoes that had been with me for almost two years. My parents weren't wealthy. There was no trust fund, no huge sum of money in my bank account. They'd spent every last dime paying for my apartment for a year. Their generosity had been unexpected, but it also meant my father couldn't retire early as he'd wanted. Perhaps the guilt was killing me, which had allowed me to make bad decisions.

I heard Kirill's impatient deep breaths as I fumbled to untie my shoes, falling back on the edge of the bed in order to rip them off my feet, peeling away the socks. When it came to everything else, I had just as much difficulty performing the simple task. There was no reason to feel embarrassed around him, but it hit me hard tonight, prickles covering almost every inch of skin.

Maybe because this change meant something else altogether. It meant the loss of freedom, being tied to his world. An ugly world.

I bit my lip to keep from spewing off my usual rebellious quips. It was time to stop pretending he was anything but what he was.

A killer.

He could easily end my life if I presented a problem. However, if I earned his trust, maybe I'd find a way to escape his prison eventually. I hadn't asked him what he was going to do with me. Maybe I didn't want to know. As I folded the clothes, placing everything neatly on the huge dresser, it suddenly dawned on me why a man like Kirill couldn't have anyone special in his life. He couldn't handle having anything or anyone as a weakness.

How lonely that must be. No wonder there was nothing that resembled a man with a real life outside of killing people. This beautiful condo that likely costs millions of dollars was nothing but a glorified hotel.

"Am I your whore?" I don't know why the question came to my mind or why in God's name I allowed myself to ask it.

I expected his anger, maybe for this round of punishment to begin earlier, not the booming laughter coming from deep within his chest.

"Why would you ask that, *malen'kaya ptitsa?*"

"I can't understand you, Kirill. I hate not knowing the horrible things you say to me. It's not fair."

He cocked his head, real confusion crossing his face. "I called you my little bird, Candy."

"No longer a rebel? I see. Because I'm a bird in a cage."

Now it was easy to see I'd angered him, the hard clench of his jaw adding to his dangerous persona. Gone was the moment of frivolity, replaced by his usual scowl. "You are not my whore, Candy. A whore leaves after I've paid for her for whatever satisfaction she can provide."

"That means you've had a lot of them." I looked away from him, angry with myself for such a ridiculous question but hurt, even jealous. He hadn't used a condom.

Fuck. I felt his looming presence as he walked closer. What limited air was in the room was stagnant, forcing me to struggle for enough air.

"No, little rebel. I don't make it a habit of paying for sex, nor do I pick up women in bars. No one has drawn my attention for many, many years."

Was I supposed to believe him? He forced me to look into his eyes, his thumb and forefinger pulling my chin toward him. I'd be damned if there wasn't sincerity in his sinfully gorgeous eyes. Every time I thought I'd found a way to hate him in order to shut down my desire, he surprised me. I expected given his dark mood that he'd toss me onto the bed, but he guided me instead, yanking back the covers all the way to the bottom of the bed. When he eased me down, his expression was full of shadows and darkness, but just as primal as before.

He remained standing over me for a few seconds, sliding two fingers down the length of my arm, issuing a deep sigh. "Do not move."

Where would I go if I did? The place was an utter fortress. I watched as he walked away, unable to stop thinking about his gorgeous butt and muscular thighs. And the dragon. It was silly of me, but the beast's eyes made me think they were watching me, relaying every inch I moved to his master. The sensations were uncanny, almost frightening. As much as I wanted to look away, I couldn't. The savage man with the raw, unforgiving look and the cold demeanor was an incredible specimen.

Every move he made was methodical. He took long strides toward the dresser, glaring down at my clothes. "You'll never wear this garbage again. No woman of mine should be forced to wear something so unflattering."

There it was. His woman. He'd meant what he'd said. I wasn't his whore, but I was his possession. Did he plan on parading me around when appropriate, showing me off like a prized china doll? I couldn't stand the repulsive thought.

I sensed a moment of anger rushing inside of him. Then he shoved my clothes aside so hard they tumbled to the floor, smashing his fist on the dresser's surface twice before reaching his hand inside a drawer.

He was magnificent in everything he did, and tonight was no exception. His actions reminded me of a man preparing for his last meal before execution, determined to enjoy every moment before the end came. I couldn't tell what he was retrieving until he turned around slowly, returning then crawling onto the bed.

A long piece of fabric. The asshole was going to tie me to the bed. I bit back a whimper, refusing to let him know I was horrified, angry and uncertain I could remain some good little girl like he wanted. Yet as the explosive heat we shared smashed into me again, I drank in his musky essence before turning my head away.

"Don't turn away," he commanded. "Never look away from me."

More rules.

But I found myself obeying him. The man was irresistible, and I was incapable of ignoring him.

As he loomed over me, I licked my lips, which caused another sly smile to cross his face. He pushed me onto my back, pinning me down with the weight of his body. The feel of his cock positioned between my legs kept my body shivering. I didn't fight him as he pulled one arm over my head then the other, giving me his usual dominating stare. He didn't need to provide any reminders. I knew what was expected of me. Full submission.

I wasn't certain I had the capability. I'd never been that kind of girl. Then I reminded myself that I'd already done that on several occasions.

He tied my arms as expected without tethering me to the bed. Obviously satisfied, he kissed me as if he'd never done so before, hungrily and without remorse. I found it difficult not to lower my arms in order to touch him. I was powerless underneath him, his massive body easily able to crush mine if that's what he wanted.

When he pulled away, he continued to tease my mouth, nipping my lower lip then pulling it partially between his teeth. He raked the back of his fingers down my arms, creating wave after wave of shivers, finally releasing his hold on my mouth then biting down on my chin. I was flooded with vibrations that sent a series of electric shocks through me. He continued taunting me, crawling between my legs and leaning over.

His smile was almost evil as he tweaked my nipple, twisting first one then the other. I was ashamed that the glorious moment of pain further excited me, and he knew it, his eyes reflecting he heard the sound of my scattered moans.

He was never going to allow me to go anywhere. Right now, with the glorious moments of bliss tearing through me, it didn't seem so bad.

"Are you wet for me?" he asked.

"Never." Just like when he'd asked the question before, he always knew the answer. He was toying with me as he'd done before, proving that my body couldn't ignore the intensity of our connection or the electricity soaring through me like bottle rockets.

Ignoring him was tough but denying him would never be possible.

"Hmmm... Then I can see I have my work cut out for me." His words were barely more than a breathless whisper, the velvety tone like gentle caresses of a light breeze. I was already on fire when he crawled his hand down between my legs, cupping my bare mound. "You're not a very good liar, my little rebel. Soon, I'll teach you that the consequences of lying to me aren't in your best interest."

While there was no malice in his words, I knew he meant them. He'd punish me for any infraction, ensuring I follow his damn rules. I had no further chance to ponder his statement. Still keeping his palm in the same position, he used a single finger, swirling it around my clit. Seconds turned into two full minutes. He remained quiet as my body started to writhe, the sensitivity so intense that I jumped several times.

Maybe I'd been a good enough girl because he rolled his thumb up and down, grazing the tip between my swollen and aching folds, yet refusing to thrust it inside.

"You're torturing me," I threw out, my breath so ragged I couldn't think clearly. I was shocked the simple touch had provided so much pleasure, bringing me to the edge of a climax. But he was a damn expert, shifting his actions just as I was almost ready to succumb to the bliss.

"This is torture?" he growled. "Then I need to continue fucking you long and hard so you can understand the difference."

Minutes went by. I was desperate to climax and he knew it. Stars were floating in front of my eyes, wiggles and other shapes tumbling back and forth. I couldn't believe this simple gesture had made me so lightheaded. He was in total control of every aspect of my pleasure, and I was exactly where he wanted me to be.

"Are you ready to come for me, my beautiful rebel?"

Was he kidding me? Panting, I realized I could no longer focus when I glanced down. "Yes. Please."

"Please. I like that, but you're going to need to convince me. And I'm not convinced easily."

When I lowered my arms out of desperation, he pulled his hand away.

"Remain in position, Candy. You need to learn restraint."

I obeyed him, shoving my hands over my head, wrapping my fingers around two of the metal bed posts.

"Now, convince me." He resumed what he was doing, this time flicking his finger from one swollen pussy lip to the other.

"Please. Finger fuck me. Allow me to come." Nothing changed. I glared down at him, shifting my hips. He pinched my clit as a response, driving me up from the bed. "Oh, God. Fuck me. Just fuck me."

"Then come for me, Candy. Come."

Even in my haze, I could tell he was finally pleased with my answer. He continued to roll his thumb around my clit as he thrust two fingers inside. Two fingers. That was all he needed to instantly drive me into an intense orgasm.

"Yes. Yes!" My scream floated away toward the high ceilings, the sensations one incredible rush of vibrations after the other. I was tossed high in the sky, pushed all the way into a moment of ecstasy. He continued pumping several times, waiting until I floated down like a soft petal from the air above us.

As he crawled over me, he shoved his slickened fingers into his mouth, his guttural sounds becoming a perfect orchestration.

Yet the moment was unnerving.

I was his captive, his prisoner.

I should hate him and all he stood for, but that wasn't the case.

Not only had the man captured my body, but he'd taken something else as well.

And the terror of admitting it had already gutted me.

CHAPTER 11

Kirill

The woman was tearing apart my layers one at a time. Being with her was more dangerous than I'd originally thought, but not for the reasons I'd brought her here. She had a way of getting under my skin so completely that any concept of rational thinking had been tossed aside.

I'd wanted her to hate me. That would make it easier on both of us, but I'd seen the look in her eyes. I could tell the sexual game we'd both enjoyed playing had already shifted into something else altogether.

I should walk away right now, return to business and stop thinking about her. I could ensure her safety and provide her with food and clothing. That should be good enough.

Except it wasn't.

Every time I looked at her, I wanted more. Every. Single. Freaking. Time. It made no sense. Then again, what had in my life?

Just like now. I should walk away and close the door behind me, but my need was far too great.

I parted her legs even more as I eased down, putting the full weight of my body over hers. Candy whimpered, but not from the fact I was crushing her with my hefty size. She was already longing to reach down and touch me.

That would only make things worse. I had to think of her as a possession and nothing more or I wouldn't be able to carry out my missions with the same advantage as usual. My cold, stark methods of hunting then killing my prey were well known. People feared a man they'd never seen. All they knew was if the man with the green eyes appeared, you could kiss your ass goodbye.

A dull rumble crawled into my chest, as if I truly had a beast living inside of me. As I peered down at her, I was surprised her eyes had yet to focus, as if she'd fallen into a permanent dream state.

Only this was no dream for an innocent like her. This was a nightmare.

I remained on my elbows, the lust only increasing with every passing second. The tip of my cock seemed to have a mind of its own, shifting against her wetness, throbbing in eagerness. Who was I to deny my needs? I thrust into her in one long, brutal drive, my actions much more aggressive than I'd been with her before.

She bucked against me, gasping for air. "God, so big."

I pulled out, waiting for her to catch her breath before slamming into her again, the force shoving her small body into the mattress. I enjoyed being able to see every inch of her. The third time was just as savage, pushing the air out of her lungs. Then I slowed down, developing a rhythm, yanking one of her legs around me.

Candy kept her eyes open, her mouth pulled into a rounded O, the look sexy as hell. I remained on one elbow, yanking her folded leg up even further, taking my time to press kisses along her heated skin. She was so damn hot to the touch, which pushed my needs into overdrive. After licking across her knee, I eased her leg away and pushed myself up onto my palms. As I pumped into her long and hard, she seemed to regain her control, her breath skipping as she stared into my eyes.

The connection was entirely different, the closeness something I'd never felt with any other woman. I'd been shocked she'd asked such a terrible question. How could I think of her as a whore? She was far too delicate and refined, her innocence like a babe in the woods. She was precious, something to be kept perfect. Growling, I both hated and understood why I still considered her a possession and nothing more.

I couldn't change who I was, and she would never be able to tolerate a monster sleeping next to her in bed. As soon as the novelty wore off, she'd run as fast and far away from me as possible.

That is, if I allowed her to get away.

A strangling sense of anger rushed into me, the various emotions something I needed to shove aside. She'd lied to me. That had to be handled. It was funny I had to keep reminding myself of that fact.

I pulled all the way out, sliding my arm under her, jerking her up and onto all fours.

"What are you doing?" she dared to ask me, as if anything was going to change.

"I'm fucking you." I pressed my hand on her back, driving my cock back inside. Her muscles were tighter tonight, and she was so wet I craved feasting on her all over again. That would come later.

After I returned.

After I handled business.

I pounded into her, taking everything I wanted. I planted my hands on her hips, holding her in place as the slick sheets constantly forced her body forward.

She was panting, her moans still filtering into my ears. There was nothing more that I enjoyed than hearing her cries of pleasure. Within seconds, there was no chance I could hold back any longer. I would take her again.

And again.

It was my right.

I closed my eyes, yanking her back to meet every brutal thrust, the sound of my balls slapping against her skin the only thing I could concentrate on. The animal was living up to his reputation. I threw my head back, glaring at the ceiling, wishing the damn pain would go away, the ache in my heart increasing.

Now she was adding to the anguish because at some point I'd be forced to let her go.

As my balls swelled, I issued a guttural roar, a direct expression of the sweeping agony. And even as I filled her with my seed, I was forced to face that the devil incarnate could never be allowed a mate.

Or a lover.

Only gilded possessions were allowed for soulless creatures.

My heart pounded in my chest as my body shook and I continued to snarl at the ceiling, as if I'd find some sort of answers, a release of the anguish. What a fool I was.

I draped my body over hers, both of us trying to catch our breath. The sensation of her crowded against me was one of the best feelings I'd had in a long time, one I'd remember until the day someone put a bullet between my eyes.

Even though I wanted to remain exactly where I was, that wasn't possible. This wasn't about love.

Or was it?

Half laughing, I finally moved away, easing off the bed and raking my hands through my hair. Goddamn it. What the hell was wrong with me? When I glared at her, taking gasping breaths, all I could think about was fucking her again. She continued to clutch her fingers around the bottom sheet, tugging at it as she dropped her head.

When she looked over her shoulder, I could see trepidation in her eyes. She knew what was next. Rules were meant to be obeyed. I dragged her closer to the edge, shoving one of the pillows under her stomach and gently pushing her down.

"I won't lie to you again," Candy said in a much demurer voice than she'd used before.

"No, you won't. I think the use of my belt will help you remember."

She threw her head over her shoulder again, glaring at me. Good. She was finally accepting that I wasn't some lover she'd picked up on the street but a man who required rules to be followed at all times.

I grabbed my trousers, yanking the belt from the loops. She never took her eyes off me, nor did she whimper even once. Everything about the woman surprised me, including her refusal to give into her fear. She had to be out of her mind with terror, yet since arriving here, she'd acted as if the incident had been no big deal.

She had no way of understanding that men like Rory and his buddies would likely never have let her go. They weren't playing a game any more than the Bratva were. Still, something nagged at me, pulling on my sixth sense.

I'd find answers by the time noon crawled into the sky.

Or else.

I slapped the strap once before folding the leather in my hand. Her breathing was heavy, her face pinched as she stared at it.

"We'll start with twenty tonight."

She turned her head away, muttering under her breath. She was the kind of girl who refused to back down to anyone. Another trait I admired. I rubbed my hand from one cheek to the other, marveling in the feel of her soft skin against my rough fingers.

Then I took a step back, snapping the belt across the width of her bottom.

"Oh, fuck," she moaned, kicking her legs several times. "You're a bastard."

I couldn't help but smile. Her nasty words turned me on, my cock already rising to the occasion. I cracked the belt across her bottom twice more, regaling from the slight blush already creeping up on her dazzling unblemished skin. The bastard in me wanted her to wear my marks. Hell, I'd love to tattoo her with my name, so every man knew she belonged to me. The thought was sinful and arousing, but not possible.

"I hate you." While she issued the words, she closed her eyes, a moan escaping.

"Good. Keep hating me, Candy. That's what will keep you alive."

She bristled, my words obviously startling her. I brought the belt down again.

And again.

Her cries of pain shifted into ones of pleasure, her pussy glistening from building desire. When I eased my hand from one side of her bottom to the other, she shivered.

"You enjoy pain," I half whispered.

"I..."

"You're wet. Tell me the truth. You crave my firm hand, the feel of my belt against your beautiful bottom."

She threw her head in my direction, panting. "Yes. Okay? Yes..."

For several reasons my muscles tensed, especially from the thought of someone trying to hurt her. That would never happen again. I moved closer, rubbing both cheeks even though she growled at me.

She'd actually growled.

I was delighted, which was ridiculous, but she was formidable, not the kind of woman who was comfortable in stilettos and fur, diamonds and expensive clothes. She was a real woman, one with verve and a lust for life, capable of making a goddamn pair of tennis shoes, red no less, look sexy as hell.

My cock continued throbbing, driving me fucking crazy. She did this to me. No other woman had ever before. I couldn't get enough of her, hungering to take her for hours on end. I wanted to push us both to the outer limits of what we could tolerate, the passion unequaled. I craved having her skin stained with my cum, her body filled with my seed.

Maybe I'd pick up an ass plug on my return. I fisted my other hand, the sinful thought far too delicious. I'd wanted to be as rough with her as humanly possible, but I'd fallen for her spell all over again.

Damn it. That couldn't happen.

"*Ty uznayesh', chto ya nastoyashchiy monstr,*" I whispered.

You will learn I'm a true monster.

I only hoped that when she did and accepted who I was she wouldn't already be broken.

Maybe I did have a conscience after all.

I snapped my wrist, savoring the whooshing sound as the belt jetted through the air. I could be a cruel man. Everyone knew that. Hell, I could be a damn serial killer given the way I handled needed assassinations. I had no guilt over them whatsoever, but the single thought of hurting her had ripped away the thick armor, targeting the man inside. Even teaching her a lesson was entirely different than any other experience. She was mine to keep.

Mine to protect.

And I would not hurt her.

Goddamn it, woman. What are you doing to me?

The words slammed into my mind as I peppered her with four in a row.

She kicked out once again, gasping for air, her moans becoming ragged. "I'll be good."

"I know you will. Only a few more."

I brought the belt down three more times, struggling not to drive my cock back into her sweet pussy.

As I stumbled backward, I threw my head back, glaring at the ceiling as the ugliness of who and what I was continued crushing in on me.

Her back heaved as she took several deep breaths, the sound unlike anything I'd heard before. I'd broken men of all sizes, forcing them to blubber and beg, even promising me everything they owned if I didn't kill them. Hell, I'd had more than a few piss their pants. Nothing had bothered me. There hadn't been a single time that I'd even second guessed my decision, pulling the trigger or dragging a blade across a man's neck without looking back.

But this.

This...

"Please. Just fuck me," she said, her voice dripping with lust as her need continued to build. She turned over, her voluptuous mouth pursed, her eyes glassy from the crazed need that had already consumed both of us.

I closed my eyes, trying to yank in the beast. I moved toward her again, easing onto the covers. Another part of me was ripped away by the realization that she'd like it. The domination. The pain. She craved what only I could give her.

And I couldn't imagine spending a day without her by my side.

"You deserved the punishment, and you know it." My growl was laced with the same level of desire her voice held and as our eyes connected, there was no real need to speak. No one would ever be able to tear us apart.

God help them if they tried.

"Why? Because I didn't know you were a ruthless killer? Because it didn't dawn on me that my cousins made such a difference in your life? Really?" She glared at me with all the defiance I'd seen since day one, but there was an entirely different spark inside of her that continued to manifest itself in a spiraling jolt of electricity. Together we were fire.

And I needed more. So much more.

"Stop fighting," I said as I moved to untie her. She flailed against me and once freed, she smacked her small fists against my chest several times.

"You bastard. You're such a fucking bastard. How could… How could this happen? You? You fucking happened in my life. You ruined my life because…"

While she didn't finish, there was no need. I'd never lied. I'd told her that one day I'd ruin her.

I allowed her to smack me several additional times then pulled her toward me, cradling her in my lap.

When she jerked her head up, the fire in her eyes matched the flames singing my insides.

Then she dug her nails into my chest as I wrapped my hand around the back of her neck.

This time, her request would be rewarded.

"Fuck me."

* * *

Candy

Love. Hate.

The fine line had just gotten thinner.

He was dangerous and powerful, yet I'd seen a few moments of tenderness.

As if I'd changed him somehow. But I knew the brutal man remained just under the surface, his darkness a threat that continued to terrify me. He wasn't the one who'd changed.

I'd been the one, no longer accepting the common sense of my inner voice.

It was as if he was my breath of life, the tether that held me together. And I couldn't seem to get enough of him.

If I had any rational mind left, I knew I should hate him, doing anything in my power to keep him from touching me. But the attraction was too strong, my needs increasing every time he brushed his hand across my cheek, or I gazed into the lust-filled looks in his eyes that inflamed my senses. Today was no exception.

Even the brutal spanking hadn't deterred my hunger. My body had betrayed me as it had done from the first night, my pussy and my nipples aching. The pain had sparked a burning need that I could no longer deny.

As he crushed his mouth over mine, dragging me against his heated body, I tangled my fingers in his hair, holding him as if being separated for even a second was too long. I wrapped my legs around his hips as he pulled me onto his lap, every cell exploding, the sparks becoming a firestorm.

He swept his tongue across mine, our breathing ragged. The moment of passion was just as intense as a few minutes before, unfurling the last vestiges of a sacred hold on what I thought I should be as a person.

As a woman.

Without hesitation, he yanked me down, his cock spreading my muscles, the ache to have him as deep as possible clawing at my system. He rocked me, his fingers digging into my skin, his hold possessive.

There was nothing like the feel of him filling me, the anticipation of his seed spilling into me. As the kiss became a frantic state of need, every sound he made that of a savage, my core continued to ache for more. There was no sense of why I was so aroused, why the spanking had driven me to desperate yearning. The man was merciless, unyielding with everything he did.

Yet with me his actions were entirely different.

His cock continued to swell, throbbing against my pussy walls as my muscles clenched and released. When he finally broke the kiss, he kept our lips only centimeters apart, his hot breath cascading across my skin.

I was lightheaded, the vibrations pulsing in my system driving me to madness. I licked across his mouth, savoring the taste of him, his musky scent adding to the sinful moment. Everything about him was intoxicating and once would never be enough.

"Ride me, baby. Take all you want."

Even his gruff voice kept me fully aroused, his command exactly what I needed. I pulled my head back a few inches, able to stare into his eyes, the gorgeous green burning into my soul. There was nothing that I wanted more than this. He was intimidating in his power, a threat to everyone but the one woman who'd managed to capture a small portion of his soul.

"I can't want you," I whispered.

"But you do."

"No. Never."

"You're lying, *printsessa*."

He'd seen through me the very minute he'd locked eyes with mine nights before. He'd instinctively known what I craved, had stripped away every layer of anger and uncertainty, allowing me the sweet feel of freedom.

Yet the fine line of love and hate remained. With only a few words, he could make me loathe him all over again. I'd sensed him watching me all the time, gauging my reactions, daring me to defy him.

And I had.

My world was infused with his and I was required to play by his rules, no matter the circumstances.

The punishment had been required.

As he raked his fingers down the side of my face, I leaned in, the touch enigmatic. I couldn't stop shivering as he slowly eased his hand to my hip. As he took full control, shifting the angle, within seconds I was thrown into another incredible wave, the bliss pushing me to another climax.

I threw my head back, gasping for air, still struggling to make sense of the insanity. But there was no holding back, the orgasm sweeping through me with the force of a tidal wave.

"Oh. Oh!"

"That's it, my angel. That's it. Scream out my name." His deep baritone was soothing, enticing, the pulsing sensations increasing until I was breathless. As he pushed me into a deep arc, I dug my fingers into his shoulder, so lightheaded I couldn't focus. This was what raw ecstasy was made of.

"Kirill. Yes. Kirill!" How could anything so sinful be the exact thing I couldn't live without? I hadn't been alive until he'd taken me into his world and the thought was damning.

Panting, I blinked several times as he slowly grabbed my long strands, fisting my hair at the scalp. He remained rock hard even after spilling his seed only a few minutes before. There was an even more crazed look in his eyes, his savage needs unleashed. I'd awakened a monster and there would be no way to restrain him.

He fucked me long and hard, his hooded eyes never blinking, the veins on the side of his neck pulsing from the intensity of his actions. Sweat beaded along his hairline, drops sliding ever so slowly down both sides of his face, yet he refused to stop. He was mad with need, incapable of being rational.

At least for a few minutes, we were as one.

I palmed his chest, watching him as he continued the throes of passion, his body finally shaking as he lost control.

Just as he was ready to erupt deep inside, he cupped both sides of my face, every word spewing from his mouth spoken in his native language. While I couldn't understand what he was saying, it no longer mattered. I knew he was allowing me to understand a small part of him and that was priceless.

As I squeezed my muscles, I was rewarded with a husky bellow, his body spasming. When he stopped shaking, I pressed my face against his neck, traying to catch my breath.

He was my kryptonite.

A villain.

The devil.

And I knew that whatever happened, I would never be the same. He hadn't just ruined me.

He'd nearly broken me.

* * *

Kirill

"I need to leave, but you will obey my rules." The words slipping from my mouth were commanding, refusing to allow the few moments of extreme pleasure to taint what needed to happen in my world.

A world of violence and bloodshed.

Candy stiffened, jerking her head away, her eyes searching mine. "Rules. That's all you are about is rules."

"As I've told you before, they are necessary in order to ensure your safety."

Her pinched face highlighted her frustration, an anger that she couldn't deny. "You're an asshole."

"So you've told me many times." When she tried to jerk out of my hold, I gripped her arms.

"Get away from me. I don't want to have anything to do with you. I thought you gave a shit for some crazy reason," she blurted out, a single tear sliding down her face before shaking her head. She wiped it away furiously, her eyes no longer holding the moment of passion. "No more. I'm not going to cry over you or anything you do to me. I was fooling myself about you. Stupid me. Stupid. Fucking. Me."

As she wiggled in my lap, all I could think about was fucking her, sliding my cock so deep inside that it would give her a decent reason not to be able to breathe. Fuck. Fuck! What the hell was going on with me? I'd lost all sight of who I was and what my life was supposed to entail. This woman had done that to me. This woman.

There was no logical reason why, but that meant shit no longer.

She reared back, managing to claw my face, her eyes full of venom. The sting was sharp. If I had to guess, I'd say she'd drawn blood. I snapped my hand around her wrist, preventing her from repeating the rebellious act.

Candy darted her eyes back and forth, hissing as she continued to glare at me, fighting with everything she had to get out of my hold.

I refused to let her go, digging my fingers into her slender arms. She needed firm discipline but all I could think about was kissing her, holding her.

"Stop, Candy. Just stop. You're exhausted. You need your rest. And I have work to do."

"Rest?" she spit at me. "Here? Are you insane? I have nothing of my own. Nothing. I can't. I just..." She looked away, sucking in her breath. Several seconds ticked by, her body going limp in my hold. "You're going to kill him, aren't you?"

"Who?"

"My cousin. Rian. Because of what I said?" She was shaking from adrenaline as well as anger, unable to continue processing anything rational at this point.

"Aspects of my work aren't something you need to learn about."

"Damn you. Promise me you won't kill him. Do it! Please. Please do this one thing and I'll do anything you want. Anything."

Promises. I wasn't in a position to make her any other promises than keeping her safe but as I looked into her eyes, I allowed myself to be pulled into them. She was an angel born of light. I was the devil dwelling in the darkness. Somehow just being with her had complicated things in my own mind. "I won't kill him." Unless he forced me to.

She studied my eyes, digging at my irises in order to find the truth. "You better not lie to me. If you do, I promise you I will find a way to slit your throat."

"As I mentioned, *printsessa*, lying isn't in my best interest either. But in providing this gift to you, I expect something in return."

"What can I give you that you haven't already taken from me?"

I shook her again, barely able to control my lust. "You've called me a monster several times. When I return, you're going to learn just how right you are."

Her fire had almost as much effect on me as her innocence. My balls were instantly swollen. I would take her again when I returned whether she was prepared or not.

That's what she was for, to please me in every way.

"Fine. You can take whatever you want from my body, but you will never have anything else. Never."

I pulled her into my arms, holding her against my chest. She refused to look at me, keeping one hand pressed against me as if it was able to protect her from the devil.

After tossing the pillow back in position, I eased her onto the bed, gently pulling the covers up and over her.

She immediately rolled over, closing her eyes even though I knew she was just trying to get away from me. I reached down, ready to slide strands of hair from her face but pulling back. She was right that she had nothing that would possibly make her feel comfortable. That would need to change.

I noticed her clothes on the floor and sucked in a growl before leaning over, pulling them into my hands and carefully folding them like she'd done before. Then I grabbed her tee shirt, adding it to the pile before collecting my clothes. After moving toward the door, I turned and studied her.

I didn't need to worry about whether I could break her. I'd always started the process.

As soon as I flipped off the light, I heard the rustle of sheets.

"I hate you," she whispered.

This time, I knew she meant it.

I closed and locked the door, providing her with a slight understanding of what being inside a cage felt like. Then I pulled my phone from my pocket. I didn't give a shit what time it was. I needed answers. Fucking now.

Vassily answered on the third ring, which pissed me off. What the fuck was he doing? I'd given him a direct order.

"You better not be sleeping," I barked as I padded through the condo, moving into the laundry room, removing my wallet and weapon before dropping my things.

"There's no sleep on this job, Kirill. You should know that better than anyone."

"What did you find?"

"Well, first of all, it was a wee bit dicey cleaning up your mess, especially since someone called the fucking cops. That damn parking lot was right across from a twenty-four-hour drug store. Did you know that? Could you have picked a different place to take care of business?"

"I wasn't exactly thinking about finding the sweetest spot in the city, fucker."

"Yeah, well, I had to sweet talk two cops by calling for their supervisor. I don't think the two junior cops were too thrilled the case was ripped out of their hands. Both of them were salivating."

"Is the supervisor on our payroll?" I asked as I moved into my private bathroom.

"Fucking thank God he is. Everything is cool. About your boys. They weren't carrying proper identification with them."

Hissing, I flicked on the light in the bathroom, staring at my reflection. "You better shake the trees because I will hunt those bastards down. Concentrate on the people Michael Walsh associates with or has employed under him on the trade's council."

"Fine, I'll do it, but maybe you need to put the hunt on hold for a little while. In my job tonight, I think I found someone with information regarding the attack."

Every hackle was raised, bile forming in my throat. "Who. Is. It?"

"Just a guy who walked up to me and asked if I wanted to pay for some information." Vassily laughed. "Needless to say, I put him on ice. I figured you'd want to handle it yourself."

"Yeah, I do. Keep him on ice. I have a few things to do beforehand." What the hell was going on? First one informant who'd been killed, now this. It felt like a goddamn trap.

"Like playing a little house with a beautiful girl?"

"Don't you fucking ever dare say shit like that to me. Never. Do you hear me?"

Vassily whistled. "What the hell is wrong with you, Russian?"

Russian. Vassily was tossing that in my face as an insult considering he was born in Belarus, his family forced into Russia when he was a kid. He'd accused me of being too Americanized more than once, which had caused us to come to blows.

"I don't need that shit thrown around, patriot."

He hesitated, but I could tell his blood was boiling. "Yeah, I hear you. Not a word from me. I have your new friend in the safehouse. I'll keep a couple of my men on him until you get there. Call me before and I'll enjoy being of service."

"Good enough. Keep searching for the Irishmen."

"You're sure they're Irish?" he asked.

To be honest, I wasn't certain at all. "No, but I might have a way of finding out."

"I'll keep searching. Even the VIN didn't give me shit other than tell me it was a stolen vehicle."

I took a deep breath before starting the water in the shower. A stolen vehicle for an abduction. That smelled of a much larger plan. "Find out where it was taken from."

"That I can do. I'll call you when I find something."

The call ended, I tossed the phone on the counter, hunkering over and glaring at myself in the mirror. Looking at my reflection was like looking into the eyes of a man without a soul. However, tonight there was something different laced in eyes just like my mother's.

Something human, a man who could feel again after all the years of being dead inside. Sighing, I rubbed my jaw, then studied the scratches Candy had left, able to smile from how deep she'd managed to go. My little hellion. My cock stirred all over again, the want and need mixing together, the insatiable combination even more dangerous.

That could lead to mistakes.

I headed into the shower, planting my hands against the marble surface and dropping my head. I'd made the water as hot as possible. I wanted to burn on the outside the way I was seared on the inside. Still, a part of me wanted to carry her scent with me for an eternity. Laughing, I smashed my fist against the wall several times. Even the horrible pain couldn't calm the rage or the need.

The beautiful woman had broken through my last barrier. She'd fucking found a way to lasso my soul, dragging it from the quicksand.

I continued to smash my fist harder until my knuckles were bloodied and raw. Nothing took away the agony of how I felt.

Everyone who'd touched her would die by my hands. Then I'd set her free, sending her to another place where I could keep her protected at all times.

In another pretty little cage just like she'd accused me of before.

But if that meant keeping her alive, then that's what I'd be forced to do. She could hate me all she wanted but at least she'd have her life. My budding little actress.

As I lifted my head, staring at the ceiling, another flash of memories shifted into my mind, horrible visions.

And the screams.

They never left. They never allowed me to sleep.

My cross to bear.

CHAPTER 12

Kirill

Long Island.

The epitome of luxurious living. The number of mansions was astounding, the security encompassing the dozens of homes outstanding.

At least usually.

I'd often found it interesting that between the Bratva and their families, the Italian mafia and various cartels, most of the billions of dollars spent on real estate had come from corrupt organizations.

Not that everyone residing in the posh palaces would admit to the reasons behind their good fortune.

While Michael Walsh still resided in a modest, albeit expansive home on the outskirts of Long Island, the very location where all his children had been raised. His place of residence wasn't opulent by any standards. If I had to guess, I'd say he was attempting to stay grounded, appearing as nothing but a working man for his union supporters. Meanwhile, he owned a yacht that was currently parked in a pristine club in Fort Lauderdale.

However, his sons were all down to earth, Rian no exception. He owned a quaint home in the heart of Brooklyn, a fixer upper that he'd handled himself. I had to give the man credit. He had talent in woodworking. I snickered at the thought as I made myself at home inside his bright kitchen.

I'd even made myself a cup of coffee, although the lack of fresh cream did annoy me. Still, beggars couldn't be choosers.

Not that I would beg the prick for anything except the acceptance of his death.

I continued to be enraged by whatever level of involvement he'd had in Candy's abduction, whether by direct orders or because of his father. However, I'd remain cautious in making the determination as to whether he should live or die.

Keep your promise.

Jesus.

As I sat in one of his kitchen chairs, I had a perfect view of his garden. I certainly didn't take the man for the gardening type, which could mean he had a girlfriend. I wasn't in the mood to handle additional collateral damage but would if necessary. I flexed my hand, staring down at the bruises that were already forming. The dull ache was a dim reminder of my lack of humanity.

I planted my feet on the edge of the table, leaning back and finding that I was actually enjoying the flavored coffee. You could learn a lot about a household by the coffee they kept. Hazelnut. A further indication that Rian had someone else in his life. Fortunately, there wasn't a second car in the driveway. I'd made a full pot. I had a feeling that Rian and I had a lot to talk about.

I was surprised the Irishman slept in so late. Then again, he did keep odd hours. I pulled the mug to my lips, swirling my finger over the weapon I'd positioned on the table. I thought about Candy, allowing the moment of peace to help me think clearly.

I'd returned to her room, standing in the shadows until the first rays of ginger and fuchsia hues had drifted across the horizon, erasing the darkness. She'd tossed and turned for a good portion of those two hours, finally falling into a fitful sleep. And still, I'd been unable to take my eyes off her, the hunger churning inside when I knew the last thing either of us needed was another round of passion.

While I'd wanted her to hate me, now I wasn't so certain I could handle her venom or fear of being in the same room with me. Yet I was no fool. While I'd saved her life, I'd given her every indication that my intentions were malicious. There was no way she'd ever learn to trust me.

Especially not after my proclamation. She deserved better. She deserved everything, but I wasn't the man to give it to her. The same argument continued in my head. I fisted the bruised hand, images of the hurt in her eyes flashing into the back of my mind. So what? Better she learned now than later when…

When what? When she cared and wanted to stay? When I couldn't live without her, keeping her in the perfect cage for the rest of her life?

I'd checked on her identification, finding her parents still residing in New Hope, Pennsylvania. Even the name was far too quaint, matching the population. While I'd had limited time to utilize our network system, enabling me to find more detailed data, I felt confident that she wasn't a spy, unless she was doing so for her own family. By all accounts, she'd started working at the bar three days after her arrival in town. Her parents' names were on the lease of her apartment, so at this point everything she'd told me was true.

Sighing, I couldn't seem to get the images of her face out of my mind.

When I finally heard a noise, I didn't bother glancing toward the doorway.

I wasn't necessarily surprised that he'd remained quiet, probably trying to keep from shitting in his pants. I had that effect on a lot of people.

After twenty full seconds had passed, I took a deep breath, deciding to address him. "Come join me, Rian. We have a lot to discuss. I took the opportunity of making coffee. I hope you don't mind. There is almost a half pot left."

"What in the fuck are you doing here?" he demanded, his anger making his voice tremble. I noticed a flash out of the corner of my eye and sighed.

It would appear my stealth skills needed attention.

"If I were you, I'd put the gun on the counter before joining me." When he said nothing for a few seconds, I tipped my head in his direction. While he had the good sense to lower his Beretta, I had a feeling his trigger finger was itchy. "You really don't want to cross me today, Rian. Let's just say I woke up on the wrong side of the bed."

Sleeping. It would be a sheer joy if that was possible.

I could sense he was weighing the odds that he could shoot me for breaking into his house before I had a chance to grab my weapon. Fortunately, he had the common sense to follow my orders, placing his gun on the counter then walking closer.

"Grab a cup of coffee. I think you're going to need it." I wasn't making a request and he knew it. After taking another sip, I returned my attention to the window, surprised at the number of butterflies in his garden.

After a few additional seconds of hesitation, he moved away, yanking a mug from his cabinet. I stared down at mine, chuckling under my breath as I read the saying on the exterior.

My level of sarcasm depends on your level of stupidity.

I had to admit the words gave me a smile.

I could smell his anger as well as the appropriate amount of fear as he jerked out the chair, sitting down with a hard thud.

"I'm going to ask you one more time," he started again. "What the fuck are you doing in my goddamn house?"

After taking one more sip, I realized the taste had turned bitter in my mouth. I jerked my feet off the table, swinging around to face him then shoving the mug across the table with enough force it almost toppled off in his lap.

He glared at it, shaking his head. I studied him, noticing how hard he was trying to hide the nervous tic on the side of his mouth.

"To answer your question, Rian. I thought talking in private would be a much better choice than me threatening you then you acting like you'll come after me on a fucking construction site. Here's my answer. You fucked with the wrong man." I pulled my weapon into my hand, yanking the ammunition clip out by several inches then slamming it back in. I was delighted to see there was a single bead of sweat rolling down the side of his face.

"I don't like you any more than you like me, Russian, but that tells me shit."

"Well, we could start by the fact you've become your father's lackey. Didn't he tell you that making threats to anyone of Russian descent wasn't in your best interest?" I kept my eyes on him, able to keep a smirk on my face.

He snorted as if insulted. "I did my father a favor and nothing more. However, I agree with his assessment of what the Kozlov family is doing should be stopped. You're using your own labor. That goes against everything the union stands for and all we've tried to help facilitate over the years. You know that unions were created to keep workers from being abused by unscrupulous employers. I can only imagine what you or your family experienced in Russia. I've heard the work environment there is reprehensible."

I wanted to rip the man's throat out for just assuming he had any clue what kind of life people were forced to endure, but I held off, rubbing my fingers across the barrel of my Sig Sauer instead. I did lean forward before answering. "I appreciate your commitment to ensuring workers have a decent wage, benefits and are treated well, but that only matters if the organization they're working for had any scruples left after being forced to pay hefty union dues. As far as life in Russia, anyone involved in a business similar to an organized union would be captured and killed after they were tortured for information including the names of every member."

It was obvious he had no idea what to say to me. I hated the fact the fucker had managed to get under my skin. I wasn't in the mood to play word games about how much better our employees' lives could be by conforming to their bullshit.

"Then your site will continue to have problems."

The man had balls. That was something. "I don't think you're really in the position to threaten me, Rian. It's not in your best interest unless you're ready to leave this world."

He half laughed, looking away then shoving his mug against mine. "My family will crush the Bratva."

Sighing, I rubbed my jaw. I had other business to attend to. "I'm going to make the purpose of my visit very clear for you. Candy Lancaster is no longer your concern."

Rian snapped his head in my direction, jerking up from his chair so quickly that the force almost toppled the table. His face was the shade of sun dwellers who'd forgotten to wear sunscreen on a bright, cloudless day. As he sputtered, his body shaking yet so tense his actions were almost comical, it was easy to confirm that he had no idea that Candy had been attacked. I'd use that to my advantage, pushing him even further.

"If you dare touch her... I'll..." Saliva oozed from his mouth, which wasn't a good look on him. However, it was further evidence that he'd been warning her against the sins of the Bratva more in its entirety than knowing I'd touched her in a carnal manner. There was no reason to lie to the man. It would serve no purpose.

"Not only have I touched her, Rian, but as of now, your cousin belongs to me. However, I'm not here to discuss her living or employment status, although she will not work another day in your seedy bar. What I am here to discuss is the fact she was kidnapped last night by three frequent flyers in your establishment."

There was real shock in his eyes, the second round of anger just as genuine. He'd had no knowledge of what had occurred.

"I suggest you sit. The. Fuck. Down." Hissing, I picked up my weapon, aiming it directly at the center of his chest.

Swallowing hard, he did as I demanded, his body shaking from rage. "What do you mean?"

"It's simple. Three customers tossed her in the trunk of their car. Fortunately, I was in close proximity, able to take her to safety. However, they won't be the only ones that attempt to harm her. The question is why?"

Rian seemed befuddled at first then closed his eyes, taking a full twenty seconds to calm down. "I had nothing to do with that, Kirill."

Interesting. Now I was more than just a disgusting Russian. "Then who did?"

"I don't know. I have no idea. Why would anyone want to hurt Candy?" His question hung in the air. Then he smirked. "Unless this has to do with you."

I ignored his jab. It would serve no purpose to become irritated over something holding no merit. "What my instinct tells me is that you are behind the attack, whether for personal controlling reasons or to use her as your father's pawn in his greed and desire to obtain more power. However, if you believe those assholes had any intention of letting her go after your little game was finished, you're dead wrong." This time, I pointed the barrel of my Sig in between his eyes as I rose to my feet.

He threw his hands up, also standing. "You're a motherfucker if you think I'd do something like that to my own flesh and blood. You're the only animal I know who'd eat their young."

I laughed. "Your attempts at insulting me mean nothing. It's entirely possible that her near abduction had a direct connection to your father's unscrupulous activity surrounding the trade council. If you ask me, I think he pissed off the wrong people. Not accounting for the Kozlov family of course."

"That's bullshit. My father…" He exhaled, doing his best to keep his gaze pinned on me. I could tell by the doubt in his eyes that he didn't necessarily approve of his father's activities. Good. That would also work to my benefit.

"Does the name Rory ring any bells?"

At first, he acted like he had no clue. Then a light went off in his gaze. "I don't know him, but he does some work for my father."

"Interesting. Here's how we're going to play this, Rian. In exchange for your life as well as that of your cousin's, you're going to find out the identity of the three men who were involved. While I'm certain you'll want to ask your father who they are, that's not going to happen. As soon as you discover the information, you'll contact me directly."

"Why can't you track them down and ask them yourself?"

Grinning, I leaned further over the table. "They don't seem to be in a position to answer any questions at this point." I allowed the information to sink in. "However, there is no doubt they didn't act alone. In addition, you're going to advise your father that it's in his best interest to stop leading the attack on the Kozlov construction projects. Nothing good can come of his continued interference. Do I make myself clear?"

"How in the fuck am I supposed to identify these assholes? What does it matter anyway?"

"Today is your lucky day, Rian. I'm in a generous mood. Ask your good buddy and manager friend about him. Candy served him the night before last. With any luck, they paid with a credit card. As far as why it matters, well, I do think that's obvious. They're either working for your father directly or are a rogue group of individuals." Another light popped on in his brain as he realized that his family might be the direct targets. Maybe he'd do the work for me.

I moved around the table, lowering my weapon. When I was only a few feet away from him, he squared his shoulders, trying to assert whatever authority he believed he had in his tee shirt and boxer shorts.

"I'll do what I can to find out what you need, but you better keep your slimy hands off her. She's a good girl. She doesn't deserve to be touched or even forced to stay in the same room with scum like you."

The asshole had a way of riling me. I took a deep breath instead of smashing the pistol against the side of his head. I would try to keep this civilized.

For now.

I offered a smirk and closed the distance. We were of the same height, our weight approximately the same, but the man was no match for my training and he knew it, backing down almost instantly. "Don't hurt her."

"I have no intention of hurting the lovely Candy as long as you keep your end of the bargain." As I moved toward the door, I gave him a hard glare over my shoulder. He was already preparing to grab his weapon. "Tsk. Tsk, Rian. You will learn that fucking with me will only end with your family forced into selecting your coffin. And Candy's." I walked out, confident he'd follow my orders.

If not, there'd be no place on this earth where I couldn't find him in order to fulfill my end of the deal.

* * *

I stood outside the apartment building, scanning the buildings and street around me. If Rian had been part of her attack, he'd already called the people he was working with, which could mean an ambush even though it was almost noon. But if I had to guess, I'd say he was demanding he talk with his father right about now, determined to find out what he'd been forced into the middle of.

While nothing seemed out of the ordinary, I had a sense that the building was being watched. It felt like a twisted game of cat and mouse.

After a few seconds, I moved inside, taking the stairs and heading toward my apartment first. Dimitre's message had been of interest. Just as I slipped my key into the lock, my phone rang again. Dimitre. I opened the door and immediately he swung around, the weapon in his hand.

Snarling, he lowered his phone, shoving it into his pocket. "Goddamn it, Kirill." He continued to walk closer, cursing in Russian.

What the hell has gotten into him?

"Who were you expecting?" I growled, slamming the door and remaining where I was. Dimitre wasn't the kind of soldier to allow anything to get under his skin. When it did, that turned him into a formidable assassin. He continued to hold his weapon in his hand, glancing over his shoulder toward the door.

"Let's just say someone managed to get inside. Where the hell were you? You were supposed to be here last night gathering information."

"I had something more pressing to handle, Dimitre. Don't push me."

"Don't push you? That's bullshit."

Something had crawled up his ass.

"How the fuck do you know someone got in? And why are you so rattled?" Nothing seemed out of order. In circumstances of this nature, the place was usually tossed if for no other reason than to show off their entrance abilities.

He lifted a single eyebrow before nodding toward the boxing bag. As I headed closer, I was forced to walk around to the other side to see what he was talking about. Then I chuckled. "At least there's no need to decipher their bullshit."

One word had been cut into the thick leather with a serrated knife.

DIE

"Yeah? Do you know the last time a single location where I lived had a breach in security like this?" His anger was only increasing. I shot him a look before returning my attention to the bag.

"I have no clue but I'm certain you're eager to tell me."

Huffing, he started pacing the floor, waving the weapon around more carelessly than I was used to. "Never."

"Maybe that's because you spent most of your time at the Kozlov estate."

"Fuck you! That's my job. Fucking a mark shouldn't be one of yours."

I bristled, my tension soaring. "What the hell do you mean a mark?" He looked away, visibly cringing.

"You heard me. Old man Kozlov has no intentions of allowing that girl to live if the shit with the casino goes south."

His words seemed like a challenge. Dimitre knew better than to ever issue me a challenge. "I'm going to give you approximately three seconds to tell me what the fuck you're talking about before you and I are going to have words." When I walked toward him, he flicked on the safety, shoving his weapon behind his back into his waistband. Maybe he was afraid I was crazy enough or pissed off enough to end our tense words in gunfire.

"Alexei. He told me point blank last night there would be a hit placed on that girl if you didn't do something about it."

It. The woman wasn't an 'it.' Either Vladimir had lied to me, or Alexei was stepping in the middle. The man enjoyed tossing around his authority, another thing that pissed me off about him. My relationship with the second in line to the throne was rocky at best, but this could tip it over the edge. He usually let me do my job and I stayed out of his shit, but his project was in the crosshairs, and he wasn't in control. The construction project was the single overlap where our duties were concerned for a reason.

One day we would kill each other.

The realization that Alexei was out to strip her away from my life only made me gravitate toward wanting to keep her. As I'd told most of men under my command, they had to think with their head, not their dicks. What the hell was I doing?

"Did Alexei say anything else?" I was more demanding than before.

"He didn't have to. You know how he is."

Yeah, I knew better than some. I'd thought of him as deranged, but my opinion didn't matter worth shit. "I'll deal with Alexei on my own terms. Any idea who got in?"

"Well, they didn't leave a second love note, if that's what you mean. No. I got here a little over an hour ago. That's when I called you the first time. I guess you were too *busy*."

I was beginning to dislike his attitude. "How I spend my time is my business, Dimitre. I suggest you remember that." I was driven back to the thought that she'd provided someone with a layout of the apartment, but given they'd entered for a single purpose, in my mind it was all about keeping us going in different directions, never able to focus on who was playing us.

Everyone in the fucking family as well as those closest were all on edge. What I knew about the slice in the bag was that it was a personal message directed at me.

"Yeah, I hear you loud and clear. What the fuck did you do, beat the crap out of someone?" he asked, pointing toward my knuckles, grinning as if my battered hand was a badge of honor.

"It's not important."

"Nothing ever is with you. By the way, staying in this apartment is bullshit."

"But in a good location."

"As if you're going to spend another night here."

"That's not up for discussion. We might have a possible leak regarding the attack."

His face brightened. "Oh, yeah? How so?"

"Vassily secured someone with information. That's where I'm headed next."

"Maybe I'll join you. I need to get rid of some rage."

"Suit yourself," I hissed then took another good look around the living room. "First we find out information. I don't need another bloodbath. If this asshole had anything credible, then I want it. Do you understand me?"

He tilted his head, laughing under his breath. "Even the woman hasn't been able to soften you."

I checked the other rooms before heading back into the main area.

"I heard about the attempted kidnapping. Any idea?" he asked.

"If I had to guess, I'd say it's the same people who wanted to make certain I knew there were more of them waiting in the shadows."

"What in the hell do they want, the girl?"

"I honestly don't know." That was the sole reason for my continued rage. Now I knew someone was interested in trying to keep me on that precipice. If there was anything people outside of the family knew was that my anger was often uncontrollable. Up until now, it hadn't been a weakness, but everything involving Candy was shifting that way.

"Maybe she's more valuable than you know," he continued.

"Maybe."

"I'm serious, Kirill. Maybe the attack and the crap being pulled on Alexei's jobsites are connected."

"Already thought of that."

Dimitre walked closer, the damn smug look on his face something I was ready to wipe off with my fist. "I hate to say this, but did you also think about the possibility that Candy isn't who you think she is?"

It was all I could do to keep my anger in check. "I've checked on her information. She's exactly who she said she is. Do not mention this to me again. Ever. I'll hunt down the people responsible and handle the situation. That's what needs to be done. The girl stays with me and anyone who fucks with her will face my wrath."

He glared at me but nodded. "You can't handle this with three men and no backup."

I wanted to laugh. He made the operation sound as if I couldn't handle a few Irishmen who thought they could infiltrate the Bratva. "Then what are you suggesting, Dimitre?"

He looked away. "I know you don't think the men who work for me have the same elite capabilities as the men who were killed, but they know their shit and could prove to be useful."

It was the first time I'd realized that Dimitre took pride in being tasked with keeping the family secure. He'd been a street kid himself, working the streets of Russia then finding a way to America all by himself. He'd done damn well. Vladimir trusted him without question.

"If additional men are required, I'll keep that in mind." I gave him a respectful nod, although I could see doubt in his eyes. While the Kozlov Bratva wasn't as structured as most still holding power in Russia and other Eastern European countries, clout and position both had value.

"I'll stay here tonight, but Vladimir has a party tomorrow night."

A party. It was more like a reminder to those the patriarch had in his pockets that the Kozlov family was owed their loyalty. There wouldn't be a single invitation that wasn't accepted. "Any invitations sent to the Walsh family?"

Dimitre narrowed his eyes then grinned. "I can find out."

"Do. I might attend myself."

"Alexei won't like it."

"Ask me if I give a shit if Alexei approves or not. I'm getting a few of Candy's personal items. Then I'm heading to the safehouse."

"Vassily does have a sense of humor."

"Let's hope for our unlucky informant that this isn't a wild goose chase."

"Be careful, Kirill," he said in his more jovial tone.

"As I said, I can handle any situation."

"I'm not talking about business or the goddamn bloodlust you have. I'm talking about the girl. You might need to make a decision that you won't like. I know you. That will drive the final stake into your heart."

I took a deep breath before answering. "Then so be it. I'm already dead."

As I headed toward the door, the same demons I'd been fighting my entire life breached the surface again.

Through my eyes I could see only one color. Red.

Blood red.

CHAPTER 13

Kirill

Bloodlust.

I'd had more than one person accuse me of being too savage in nature, preventing me from providing any aspect of mercy. The phrase wasn't tossed around in admiration but out of fear of the lengths I could go to.

The scent of blood had remained in my nostrils the entire time I'd been talking with Rian. A part of me had wanted nothing more than to slice him ear to ear, watching as the blood stained his perfectly white tile floor. The restraint I'd used in deference to Candy weighed heavily on my mind. She did owe me.

Hissing, I stepped out of my car, studying the safehouse. We used that term loosely, the location centered in a section that bridged the Italians as well as the Armenians and Polish forces. The house was used by spies who'd infiltrated the Polish mob but had recently been vacated. Our spies were moving up in the world.

Dimitre pulled up right behind me, immediately getting out of his car. "The place looks like shit."

Snorting, I had to agree with him. "It's supposed to look like shit."

We moved to the back door, and I knew it would be unlocked. I heard nothing as I walked through the downstairs, finally opening the door to the basement. The area was perfect for handling certain aspects of business, including interrogation. We found Vassily and two of his men waiting, but I could tell all three were itching to provide punishment for not supplying information.

Granted, I'd run out of patience, my eagerness to get back to her increasing every passing minute. If the fucker wanted payment, then whatever he had would need to hold merit.

I nodded toward Vassily, who grinned and moved away.

"Looks like we're going to have a party," he said, nodding toward Dimitre.

"I'd prefer a piece of rare beef and full bottle of cabernet," Dimitre huffed.

At this point, so would I.

After a few seconds, I walked in front of the man, glaring down at him. They'd worked him over, likely for his arrogance in thinking he was owed anything. While that usually pissed me off since I preferred handling this business myself, at least conditioning him would likely loosen his tongue. If not, then he'd be tossed into the trash like anyone else refusing to cooperate.

"What's your name?" I asked, as if I cared.

"Roger. Roger Guthrey."

"Well, Roger, it would seem you have information you believe is worth money. Why don't we get straight to business? How much money do you believe this prized information is worth?"

He thought about my question, as if I was being serious. "Twenty k."

One of the other soldiers started to laugh. While they were in standby in case a cleanup was needed, that didn't mean they didn't appreciate the value of a man being taught a lesson.

"That's a hefty sum, Roger. I suggest that you start talking."

He glanced from Vassily back to me, already quivering. That was a dead giveaway he knew better than to ask for that kind of money. Allowing him to live was payment enough.

When he continued to hesitate, Dimitre smacked him in the jaw. I threw up my hand, shaking my head. "Roger, I do think it's in your best interest to start talking. You have five seconds to do so." I didn't bother telling him the consequences if he ignored me.

Four.

Three.

Two.

"There are some shit Italian assholes out to get you," he sputtered.

The few words were enough to drag out my curiosity. "Go on."

"They want to bring you down piece by piece."

I gave Vassily a quick look. The man rolled his eyes. Who didn't want to bring us down piece by piece? Unfortunately, the fucker was lying. I hated when anyone lied to me. When I'd looked carefully into his eyes, I'd notice that he was doing his best acting performance, hired by someone to try to instigate a war with the Italian mafia. What wasn't widely known, including by lower-level soldiers within the Bratva was that we had an unspoken pact with the leader of the Italian Mafioso.

While I hadn't been told the details, it didn't matter. The knowledge allowed me to realize when a stupid fuck like this was lying. What the hell? I'd play along. I wanted to know just how far down the rabbit hole he'd been told to go.

"I suggest you give me more. That means nothing to me, Roger." I took a deep breath, leaning over even further until the stench of his sweat-stained clothes and piss was almost too repulsive to tolerate.

"The attack. They attacked you, right? The bastards took out some of your men."

Okay, so Roger was getting warmer to the real prize. I cocked my head, tired of asking the questions already. Plus, the clock was ticking. I had more pleasant tasks ahead of me.

I pulled the knife from my back pocket, flicking it open. Time to up the game, so to speak. "Roger. I am a businessman and as such, my time is valuable. I suggest you provide me with names, or our discussion won't be going any further." I flicked open the blade, turning and twisting it in the single overhead bulb used for a light.

Dimitre sighed, hovering over the man as if longing for the chance to cut him.

"Michael Walsh! He's responsible." Roger gasped for air, his puffy face twisting.

Maybe two days ago I would have salivated on the juicy information, but I was no fool. Too much had happened over the last forty-eight hours. I could tell Vassily was chomping at the bit, hungering for bloodshed.

"Is that so?" I asked before jamming the point under the man's chin.

Roger whimpered, trying to keep from fighting with the rope digging into his wrists but failing, allowing the sharp tip to dig into his skin. I watched as a single trickle of blood slid down the length of his sweaty neck.

"Yes, sir," he whispered.

I liked that. Respect.

At least he understood what he was facing.

"Unfortunately, Roger, you're still lying to me, which as you might imagine is not in your best interest. Now, you may ask how I know you're lying. For one, the nervous tic on the corner of your mouth gives you away. Another might be the fact you've pissed your pants at least twice. But the real *coup de gras* is all about the knowledge stored in the back of my mind. You see, we have a long-standing truce with the Italians. You might say we're buddies."

His eyes opened wide, the terror in them appropriate.

When he twisted his mouth, I dug the blade in tight against his throat. "As far as Michael Walsh, I don't think that's the truth either. Michael uses the power of the pen instead of guns."

"I can... Let me explain. They made me do it."

"They," I repeated, every muscle tense. Even the thought of ripping this man's throat out wasn't providing a sense of satisfaction.

Only one thing could do that.

One person.

He tried to swallow, his body shaking to the point I could hear the man's teeth chattering. "Irish. Fucking Irish. I don't know who they are, but they're big and ugly." His choice of words was comical.

"And why would you do a goddamn thing the Irish said?"

"I have my reasons."

While I wasn't known for allowing mercy of any kind, most men in this predicament wouldn't hesitate to spout off exactly why they'd been stupid enough to put themselves in this position. This man was... far too stoic for my liking. Whether he'd been threatened or given a million dollars was inconsequential at this point.

"I'll ask you one last question, Roger. If you get this one right, I will consider allowing you to return to your paltry life." I didn't need to provide the other option. "Who is really behind the attack?"

"I don't... know."

He looked down for a split second, but it was his last act of betrayal. Without hesitation, I dragged the serrated edge across his throat, exhaling as I stood back.

"Do you buy the shit about Walsh?" Dimitre asked.

"No. He was given a lifeline in case his original story wasn't bought." Was it possible the Italians had stepped over the line, breaking the treaty made years before? Maybe, but my instinct told me otherwise. Still, it wouldn't hurt to remind Cesare Vincheti about the deal he'd made with Vladimir. I knew just how to make that happen without starting a war.

"I don't know, Kirill. Walsh has been making some outlandish claims at various rallies he's attended over the last few days. He certainly has the connections to form a posse in order to gun down your men," Vassily added.

Posse. Like we were in the Wild West. Maybe we were, but our weapons were far superior. I thought about sending a message to those who were responsible.

Then it came to me.

I wrapped my hand around the front of Roger's blood-soaked shirt, ripping it away with ease and exposing his chest. Then I went to work, creating artistry.

When I was finished, I stood back, basking in the piece I'd created.

"Dump his body in the heart of the connection between the Italians and Irish fucks. Perhaps they'll get the message."

"And if not?" Vassily asked, his grin widening. He knew when I'd reached the edge, incapable of holding back my need for revenge.

"Then I'll resort to more extreme methods of punishment."

"You heard the man. Get moving," Vassily instructed, still keeping the grin on his face.

"And make certain you clean this shit up," I stated as I moved toward the stairs, taking them two at a time. There was no doubt things were about to get messy. Whether or not Vladimir wanted a war on his hands might be forced into the background. It would seem some unknown faction of the Irish community had made it their mission to strip away our control.

Hell would freeze over first.

* * *

Candy

The bastard had locked me in the room. I'd infuriated him, pushing him past the limits of the smidgen of humanity I'd seen. I'd never felt so lonely or helpless in my life.

I could only tell several hours had passed by the waning sun and the gnawing in my stomach that continued to increase, my nerves so far over the edge that drinking water had become difficult. I stood by the window in the bedroom, which is where I'd been for almost two hours. I'd awakened to find a tray of pastries and fruits waiting for me. While my mouth had watered, I hadn't been able to eat a bite. I'd noticed there wasn't any silverware. Maybe whoever was watching over me had been instructed that I might use one as a weapon.

Being in the room was like being in a vacuum or a tomb, not a single sound permeating the thick walls. I'd tested them, pounding my fist on one side then the other. It was obvious they'd been reinforced, likely for the sole purpose of keeping anyone from hearing bloodcurdling screams.

I chewed on my lower lip, another thing I'd been doing almost the entire time I'd been awake. The taste of blood spilling into my mouth allowed me to remember where I was and why I was here.

As well as the fact a brutal killer had promised to protect as well as keep me.

The sound of the door engaging forced me suck in my breath. At some point he had to return. I had difficulty thinking his name, let alone speaking it. The differences in his temperament the night before had been unnerving. He'd acted like a man on the very edge of a cliff, shutting down all emotion for fear it would drive him over.

Even worse was my mind and body's continued craving for him. No matter how hard I tried to hate him, the fact he'd saved my life as well as the incredible passion we shared always seemed to get in the way. I slowly turned my head as a woman entered the room, a tray exactly like the one that had been placed on the dresser in her hand. When she noticed the uneaten food, she scowled, muttering something under her breath in Spanish.

I turned toward her, suddenly needing information more than air. As I walked toward her quickly, she seemed surprised, jerking her head up even before she had a chance to replace one tray for another.

"Where is Kirill?"

She acted as if she didn't understand at first.

"I know you can understand me. Where is he?" I didn't care how demanding I sounded. When I moved to within a foot of her, she narrowed her eyes, glaring at me hatefully.

"Mr. Sabatin is otherwise engaged." While her accent was thick, she spoke English flawlessly.

"When will he return?"

"I do not know."

"And you wouldn't tell me even if you did. Would you?"

She remained smug, ignoring me then resuming her purpose for being in the room.

"Have you worked for him long?"

"*Si, señorita.*" She'd been trained not to say anything to me.

Hassling her would prove to be futile, even if I wanted to lash out at anyone in my path. I didn't bother barraging her with questions, but I did contemplate bolting out of the room, staring at the door as she finished her task, which of course she noticed.

"Mr. Sabatin has instructed me to allow you free roam of the house."

"Did he now?" I asked, more excited than I wanted to let on. At least I'd get an up close and personal tour of my spiffy cage.

"Yes, but you may not leave the premises," she stated as she walked quickly toward the door.

"Of course not." And what would happen if I tried? She certainly didn't seem like a trained killer.

She stopped just inside the door, acting as if she wanted to say something to me. Then she disappeared, once again muttering under her breath. I sagged against the wall, staring down at the plate of food. A sandwich, a bottle of water, a glass of milk with an apple on the side. Milk? I grabbed the water, cracking it open and taking a huge gulp. At least the cold liquid soothed my throat.

Unfortunately, nothing could do that for my heart.

The lure of the open door continued to draw my attention even though my stomach continued to rumble. I replaced the water with the apple, taking tentative steps toward the hallway. As I walked down the expansive space, the walls complete devoid of photographs or art of any kind, I'd never felt so claustrophobic, but the intensity of the silence was overwhelming.

As I walked by at least six rooms, I tried the doors, finding two of them locked. The other four were more like storage areas than anything else, but at least one had floor-to-ceiling bookcases, hundreds of books positioned on the gorgeous dark shelves. Perhaps this was going to become his library. I glanced at his selection, drinking in the various titles. As with everything else, his taste in books was infinite.

Classicals.

History books.

Travel books.

The only single modern book I could find was one from Tom Clancy. I don't know why that would surprise me. Perhaps I'd expected to find everything printed in Russian. I trailed my fingers across several of the spines, finally pulling out one. Even more surprising was that it was a first edition. The man was a true anomaly. As I replaced it in the shelf, I realized just seeing some of his things allowed me to feel closer to him. While it shouldn't matter, it did. Everything about the man intrigued me.

After turning around in a full circle, I backed out, continuing my search. What I didn't find was anything that looked like his bedroom. I knew for a fact the room where I was staying was either meant as a prison or a guest room. There were no clothes in the closet, the few toiletry items in the bathroom unopened.

He'd mentioned there were two condos that he'd had turned into one. Maybe he had an entire wing to himself.

I hurried along the various corridors, noticing the huge living room and small kitchen, which appeared as if it had never been used. When I stepped foot into the foyer where he'd brought me in, I stared at the elevator for several seconds. Kirill had saved me from God knows what, but I couldn't spend my entire life as his prisoner, no matter what he called it or what kind of danger I was in.

Exhaling, I glanced from right to left then moved toward it, pressing the button. I half expected one of his goons would be standing with an automatic rifle behind the steel doors, but it was empty. I took a series of deep breaths, realizing that if I somehow made it outside the building, I'd have to run far away. Could the Walsh family keep me safe, or would that start a crazy war? I didn't know.

The nagging voice inside my head told me to back away, but I moved inside, staring at the two buttons I could press. My hand was shaking as I made my selection, slapping my fingers across it then moving against the back wall. As soon as the doors started to close, I lurched forward, throwing my arm between them and pushing. Still shaking, I returned to the foyer, waiting until the doors closed once again. A part of me didn't want to leave. A huge part.

What did that say about me?

I backed away, folding my arms and chastising how foolish I'd been. Thank God I hadn't gone through with it. After taking a few seconds to collect my shit, I continued my tour, unable to stop thinking about him. We'd been so intimate, but this was personal. He was allowing me the opportunity to learn more about him, something he'd never done. I shivered from the thought.

There was more character, including dark gothic pictures adorning the walls. I saw no one as I continued my venture, but I felt eyes watching me. Maybe there were hidden cameras I hadn't noticed.

As I crossed into another long hallway, I looked over my shoulder before continuing. I knew everything I did would be reported to the master of the house. Maybe the woman would get a gold star for tattling on me. Several of the rooms on this side were also locked, but a single door stood ajar. There was no reason to be afraid of going inside, but I suddenly felt like I was trespassing.

Half laughing, I bolted inside, ill prepared for the beautiful, majestic view that almost assaulted my senses. Everything within the room was rich in detail, the dark furniture appearing heavy yet the exquisite detailing of the woodworking taking my breath away. I was drawn inside, no longer caring who found me here. His bed was massive, larger than I suspected the majority of king-size beds were. The comforter reminded me of crushed velvet, the deep burgundy meant for royalty.

The stupid nervous girl in me wanted to jump on the bed, raking my hands across the surface, testing the softness. I didn't dare to do something so childlike for fear of being punished. The thought brought a chill down my spine. I wasn't certain of the right adjective to use regarding the look of the room, but 'old world' came to mind, but instead of feeling stuffy, I envisioned sweltering nights of passion.

My actions still tentative, I moved toward the closet, hesitating for almost thirty seconds before opening the two doors. The man had dozens of suits, all in dark colors, dozens of crisp long-sleeved shirts hung in perfect formation, and ties in every color. They were all lined up, the entire closet completely organized. It was another moment where I wasn't certain what I'd expected. Leather? The thought gave me a small laugh. I threw another look over my shoulder before opening one of the drawers from a massive built-in dresser.

Tee shirts folded as if they'd been pressed. I pulled one into my hands, running my fingers across the front. There was no screen print gruff saying. From what I could see, none of them had any statement or admiration of a sports team printed anywhere. I pulled the soft material to my nose, his scent lingering even though I knew everything inside this room had been dry cleaned or washed, everything kept exactly the way he wanted.

The way he demanded.

I closed my eyes, trying to keep from crying. I'd never been that kind of girl, refusing to whimper even when I'd broken my arm. My mother had called me far too tough for my own good, yet here I was blubbering like a fool.

Breathe. In and out. In and out.

Every time I did, I inhaled more of his musky scent. All that did was leave me aching inside. I returned the shirt, trying to place it exactly the way I'd found it, taking one last look before walking out.

His bathroom was another creation of beauty, Venetian marble in stark black accentuated by the cold, hard color of steel, the shower larger than my kitchen in the apartment. There were four showerheads, other small indentations in the wall indicating even more capability for water flow. The single picture was as austere as the room, the nearly naked woman standing with her back toward the artist, one hand over her shoulder, her head slightly turned. I'd believe the piece was a photograph of someone he cared about except it was a painting, rich in detail and beautiful. Perhaps he'd hired someone to create it for him.

What intrigued me about the picture was the look in the model's eye. She appeared terrified. Is that what I looked like? Vulnerable?

The room was dark, as foreboding as the man.

Even the large borderless mirror did little to reflect the small pendant-style lights. The space was appropriate and very much like the man. I glanced at the picture again, then studied my reflection, exhaling as I noticed the glow on my skin. He'd done that to me.

After a few seconds, I wandered out, moving toward the huge window that had another gorgeous view of the city. Then I noticed another door. This time, there was no hesitation before I headed toward it, surprised to find it unlocked. Maybe I'd expected to find his private office. The gym, complete with a punching bag, was a welcome surprise.

This was his private space, somewhere that allowed him to be the man he'd been turned into, the area far removed from his duties or other requirements. If I had to guess, I'd say no one was allowed inside the hallowed space.

I felt more comfortable in here, closer to him, even though I doubted anyone had ever gotten but so close to Kirill. This section of the condo wasn't a mirror representation of the other side, which made it seem even more special, a hidden gem. There were still sweeping views of the city along one wall, another holding a bank of oversized mirrors. Inside this room there was almost too much light, the glow accentuating the cold vibe in the room, but I liked it. A lot.

I'd seen my cousin, Jack, boxing only once, practicing another time, but I'd enjoyed every minute of the brutal event. Nothing about the circuit Jack was on was fake, the blows bloody and body altering. I moved closer to the bag, realizing it was an exact duplicate of the one Kirill had hung in his 'fake' apartment. Fisting my hands, I issued one punch then another, exhaling from the blunt force driven into my fingers.

"Whew," I breathed, shaking my arms and pacing the floor for a few seconds. Then I repeated the action, bending over and taking several deep breaths. How in the hell could anyone do this?

Whap. Whap.

The sound of my fists hitting the thick bag wasn't nearly as loud as the ones Kirill had issued and I was standing right next to the swinging hunk of leather. I doubted I'd be able to quit my night job. The thought brought a strangled laugh, the entire situation ridiculous.

"You can do this," I said, taking another deep breath then smashing my fists against it again.

Even though pain rolled up both arms, my muscles already feeling the effects of facing the concrete-like object, I repeated the two punches. There was a freeing feeling about it, the violent action allowing me to get rid of some of the anxiety. I shook my arms then smacked it again. And again. "Ow." Half laughing, I flexed my fingers several times, staring down at them as if I'd expected instant bruises. Those only happened deep inside your heart. But I had a feeling I'd feel the effects of my foray into the world of amateur boxing within hours.

I wasn't certain why I'd bothered in the first place, but a portion of the dense sensations I'd felt all morning long had disappeared. Maybe I needed to feel closer to the man, to feel the kind of anguish I sensed he carried with him. Even if I did, that wouldn't provide any answers or make things easier.

I sucked in a breath, sensing a presence, just like had happened at the bar.

When I lifted my head, I was startled by Kirill's appearance in the mirror, his reflection entirely different than before. He exuded danger as always, his presence even more formidable, a force to be reckoned with. He also seemed detached, as if he'd performed a heinous act and would soon find it necessary to explain the reasons why.

And he was angry, furious with me. He'd been told or had found out that I'd almost attempted to escape.

I couldn't take my eyes off him. There was the same sense of arousal, but there was also an entirely different level of urgency in both of us.

How long had he been watching me? Wanting me? He remained the same as before, determined to have me follow his orders or face consequences. However, he seemed impassive as to the fact I was standing in his private space. Or perhaps he was furious with me, so much so he was preparing how to handle the egregious infraction, his anger so intense that he was ascertaining whether he could control himself around me. The brutal man wore no expression but the stark, icy look in his eyes was mirrored by his change in clothes.

Seeing him dressed in dark jeans and a shirt so black it appeared to have an iridescent blue glow, the draw to him was as strong as it had been before, perhaps more so. Only it seemed as if he wanted me to continue fearing him.

Hating him.

I was forced to remind myself that his world revolved around brutality, using his position with the ruthless family to inflict pain as an everyday practice. Unfortunately, even that didn't change the way I felt about him. I'd fallen hard and even though it didn't make any sense, it was useless to deny it. He allowed his gaze to travel to the floor then back up again, obviously trying to control his emotions.

My throat was tight, trying to figure what to say. The last thing I wanted to do was find out that he'd ignored my plea. At least a full minute passed. I was now so anxious, I could no longer control that damn nervous tic on the corner of my mouth. He could steal my breath while standing still.

Kirill was so stiff, unmoving and that continued to add to my anxiety. Not only had I broken one of few rules he'd laid down like the law, but I'd also broken the limited trust he'd placed in me by allowing me to roam freely in his house.

My stomach churned, more than a trickle of fear remaining. I knew what he was capable of. Had I pushed him too far?

As soon as he took a step inside, I noticed his bruised knuckles and backed away. All I could think about was that he'd beaten a man to death, the images violent and bloody. As he took another step into the room, I flinched, expecting him to drag me into another part of the house, whipping me for whatever sin I'd committed. I wanted to scream at him to get it over with but held my tongue in another moment of defiance.

He remained silent as he closed the distance, shifting to a small cabinet nestled against the wall. With no mirror on that wall, his large frame blocked my ability to see what he was doing. When he finally turned around, there was a roll of athletic tape in his hand.

"Hold out your arms," he instructed.

I was confused, uncertain what he had planned. Then I noticed what had to be dried blood on his neck, a few speckles on his jaw. My gaze was immediately pulled down to his shirt, able to gather a slight coppery smell. What had he done?

"I said hold out your arms, Candy."

"I…" No, I couldn't challenge his authority, not now. He was too wired.

While I obeyed him, my stomach churned even more. When he touched my hand, gently rolling his finger across my knuckles, I finally allowed a single moan. He flicked his eyes into mine then continued caressing first one hand then the other. As he started to wrap the tape around my hands, I couldn't have been more shocked.

"You must be careful when using the apparatus, Candy. It's not a toy. I have every bag built to my specifications. They are not meant to be used for regular exercise. However, since you seem interested, I'll give you a single lesson."

Why were his words still so cold? Had he shut down so completely that there was no future possibility of breaching his armor? I had to get him talking. Maybe he'd open up.

And maybe you're dreaming.

"You're a boxer. A hobby?"

He chuckled, the sound still cold, impassive. I didn't expect an answer. "I've boxed since my early twenties."

"For money?"

"Not for money, Candy. To settle scores."

I shuddered from the thought of what kind of scores could be settled over beating a man until he was bloody. "Are you any good?"

"I'm still standing here, aren't I?"

A sudden wash of visions allowed me to invent a terrible scene where the loser would be stoned to death by the audience members after the event. My crazy mind was trying to figure out what the winner received.

"What happened to your hand? Is that where you went, to settle a score? Were you the winner?"

"There are some aspects of my life that you don't want to know about. As I'm certain you've already thought of, there are no winners in my line of work, only losers. And I never intend on being on the losing end."

"That means you killed somebody." I wasn't posing a question. I already knew the answer.

His sigh was one of annoyance. "Is that what you really want to know?"

"Yes. Don't lie to me. Please?"

"If you're asking whether I kept my promise to you, the answer is yes." He lifted his gaze to remind me of the payment he required. I'd once been able to get lost in his glorious eyes. That wasn't something that would ever happen again.

When he was finished, he reached over, pulling open another drawer and dragging out a pair of boxing gloves. I was surprised that his actions were tender, just as he'd been before. He took his time securing them, then pressed my hands together, peering down at me.

"Face the bag." He didn't wait for me to respond, shifting me around to face the stationary object. "Use careful jabs. Don't allow it to come back and hit you. I assure you the force will knock you down."

When he backed away, the experience didn't feel the same as before. I was stiff, uncertain how to make the first hit. It hadn't been like before when I'd used my frustration as the driving force. I felt inferior.

But I took a swing, the sensations rocketing through my hand entirely different. Then I took another. Within seconds, I believed I had the swing of it, pummeling my fists against it with the ferocity I'd used before. It felt good, damn good.

His eyes never left as I swung and he didn't take more than a few steps away. Maybe he was prepared for the possibility that I would turn on him, taking out my aggressions. Just seeing his reflection in the mirror did more for my resolve than the adrenaline flowing through my veins. I smacked the bag several additional times until my arms were exhausted, stopping too close to the swinging mass. As soon as the heavy object boomeranged back, he was there to catch me before I fell, dragging me out of harm's way then turning me around to face him.

His hold was firm, controlling, but he'd allowed true concern to replace his icy stare. "I think you've had enough. Besides, you've lost your freedoms for now."

He did know I'd tried to escape. Shit. *Shit.* Gritting my teeth, I turned around to face him. There was also a hint of amusement in his eyes, as if he'd won a bet.

He didn't need to tell me to hold out my arms. I did so automatically, still breathless from the experience as well as his heated mass of a man standing in front of me. I couldn't stop shaking, my nerves as much on edge as they'd been before. I was just as aroused as before as well, the sole reason I could tolerate him being so close.

Somewhere deep in my mind I was fully aware I had to fight my feelings, the needs that had become so unbridled I could barely breathe around him. But as with everything else about the man, I couldn't seem to shake the hunger.

"Did you enjoy searching through my things, *moy milyy* angel?" He took his sweet time untying the strings.

I should have known he'd have someone always watching me. "Do you have cameras installed in every room?"

He seemed amused, lifting a single eyebrow. "To answer your question, there are cameras in every room except for my suite. However, I make it my business to know when someone has invaded my space."

"Another trait needed by a trained killer?"

I hated the way he was staring at me, half out of amusement and half out of disappointment. I wasn't certain which was stronger. He pinched my chin between his thumb and forefinger, lifting my head. "Are you enjoying taunting me, *printsessa*? Do you want to push what little patience I have with you? If that is the case, then you should prepare yourself for the harsh consequences. I am finished with your disobedience. You were in my room going through my things. I think it's fair that I ask you that question."

I wasn't going to win this argument by being rebellious. What was I saying? I wouldn't win this argument at all. He had full control.

"I'm sorry. I shouldn't have invaded your space."

He stopped what he was doing, pulling out his phone, pressing several buttons. When he turned it toward me, I was frozen as I watched myself on the screen heading into the elevator.

"You must think me a fool, Candy. Allowing you to roam my house, a location where no other woman and only two men other than my employees have entered was my gift to you. A gift of protection for you that gives me time to find out the reason for your attempted kidnapping. It was also about trust. It was not meant as a gesture to be ignored or made fun of as you have. You are under my roof, which means you will follow my rules whether you like them or not. This is the last warning that I will provide. Make no mistake. I am an impatient and savage man. Everything I said to you before applies. I believe I've made my requirements perfectly clear."

The lump in my throat was the size of a golf ball. A part of me had tried to push aside the fact he was coldblooded, capable of doing monstrous things without thinking about them. "Yes, you have."

The darkness remained in his eyes, his stare adding pinpricks of pain. When he lifted my arm, his expression softened but only by a few degrees. "We're going out tonight."

"What do you mean out? Where?"

"We're going to dinner."

"What about protection?"

He laughed, his eyes flashing. "I assure you that several of my men will provide a level of security that will seem comparable to that of a standing president."

Just hearing his words allowed a further indication of his power. Sadly, I didn't want to go to dinner with him or anything else. I wasn't his girlfriend or anyone he considered important. I was what my mother used to call a happenstance.

I pushed against him, breaking the connection, fighting to remove the gloves myself. I was instantly frustrated that there was no chance I could yank them off. I needed his help. Damn it. He had the same look of delight on his handsome face. "Don't just stand there. Help me get these off."

He laughed, his tone more jovial. "Then don't pull away from me." With one jerk of his hand, he snapped me against his chest. He had a way of making me feel so tiny. As I peered up into his eyes, the haze of lust created shivers. With only a shift of my hips, I knew the power would be placed in my hands, his sexual needs overpowering his anger and disappointment.

As with everything else about him, I wanted to hate his stare. Not possible. Yet, I closed my eyes, trying to break the spell. "I don't have anything to wear."

"Yes, you do."

I waited for an explanation, but it wasn't going to come. Was this some other secret he was planning on keeping from me? After tossing the gloves aside, he brushed his finger down my cheek and narrowed his eyes.

"Go to your room, Candy. I expect to see you in one hour waiting for me in the foyer. Select one of the two dresses I purchased for you."

With that, he walked out, leaving me feeling cold and shaky.

CHAPTER 14

Candy

A princess.

I'd never felt like a princess in my life, other than dressing up as one when I was kid. As I stood in front of the mirror, I was shocked how entirely different I felt in a gorgeous designer dress and heels instead of my usual sneakers and cheap skirt. It had been a long time since I'd walked in heels. On this cloudless night, I'd never felt so shaky in my life.

Kirill had surprised me once again, not only with the exquisite purchases he'd made, including lingerie, but also by stopping by my apartment and innately knowing what I'd need or want. Everything in the small suitcase had been packed with care, neatly folded, and placed just so.

Why had he bothered? Why not dump things into a trash bag, pouring the items on the bed?

Nothing about the man made any sense.

Swallowing, I placed my hand against my throat, swishing one way then the next in order to catch a better glimpse of myself in the mirror. I'd selected the insanely beautiful red velvet dress, the soft material hugging every curve, the red heels the exact same hue. I'd checked under the bathroom light.

I had no idea where we were going, but wherever it was obviously had a dress code. I stood back, taking one final look before reaching for the matching clutch. The man had thought of everything, including a crimson lace thong, which was the only item possible to wear under the dress. Giving one final nod, I left the room, hesitating only a few seconds before switching off the light.

There was no reason to be nervous, but the anxiety rolled through me like a tidal wave. Whatever this was, I couldn't imagine it was an actual date. As I moved through the corridor, careful where I was walking, I held my breath. Going out in style meant he was attempting to flush out whoever was behind the trouble involving the Kozlov family and my abduction. Could it be my extended family? I wish I felt confident in the answer.

I rounded the corner, catching a glimpse of him already waiting in the foyer, his back turned to me. A dark suit. How could I have guessed? I resisted smiling as I walked onto the marble floor, the slight tapping of my heels drawing his attention. When he swung around, I half expected him to have the same stone-faced expression, but what I observed was indescribable. His look went way beyond lust into something darker, more possessive than before. With a simple flick of his gaze, he'd already undressed me, feasting on every inch, the heat between us building to an explosive level. I was hot and wet, my nipples aching and my panties already damp. I felt the pulse in my neck skipping and I pressed my hand against it, holding my head high. He'd done this to me. Him. My beautiful villain.

With. One. Single. Look.

Kirill remained where he was, his eyes narrowing as he slowly lowered his gaze. He looked at me with hunger in his eyes before, but his reaction was all about primal need. When he finally locked eyes with mine, I was only inches away, finding it difficult to breathe.

He said nothing as he closed the distance, lifting my hand into his then slowly curling my fingers, pulling my knuckles against his lips. As he rolled them back and forth, a series of explosive tingles shifted into every muscle, every cell. I was on fire, rapidly losing all sense of reality, the passion we'd shared before almost all I could concentrate on.

His silence was different than before, a quiet reverence instead of anger, but it was just as unnerving. He had that effect on me and I suspected he always would. When he let go of my hand, I shuddered audibly, the rush of warmth building across my neck and chin giving away my pang of anxiety.

"You look incredible," he stated, his tone dominating, proud, infused with raging desire.

"The dress is gorgeous."

"Not the dress, although it suits your personality. I was talking about the woman. Absolute perfection. Are you ready to go?"

"Yes."

As he guided me inside the elevator, dozens of if not more questions entered my mind, but for the first time while around him, I couldn't find my voice. When the elevator doors opened, Kirill led me outside and the sight of the stretch limousine was another surprise. I wanted to act like I'd ridden in one several times, but the truth was I hadn't. Even the jerk who'd taken me to the prom had arrived in his beat-up Dodge Ram thinking I wouldn't mind.

"I thought this would be appropriate." His husky voice soothed my nerves but the heated breath skipping along the back of my neck kept the fire ignited. He helped me inside, leaning over. "I'll be right there."

After he closed the door, I watched as four men approached, one the obvious driver. All were carrying weapons. Kirill was giving instructions, the men used as protection. I slunk back in the seat, pressing my hands down my dress, another wave of anxiety rushing in. Was this what it was like every time he went out like a normal person? Normal. I wasn't certain I even knew what that meant any longer.

He turned his head toward the limo, his eyes somehow glowing in the ugly fluorescent light of the underground facility. Just being around him was surreal.

When he finally climbed inside, he waited until the driver and another man moved into the seats up front, the engine starting and the window between us closing before he said anything.

"I assure you that we are safe."

His words weren't as comforting as he believed them to be. "Are you trying to convince yourself, Kirill, or me?"

He laughed, the throaty sound another reminder of how much he aroused me.

"Maybe a little bit of both. I don't normally go anywhere without driving myself."

"Then why are we?"

"Because tonight is… special."

We were barely out of the garage when he opened a bottle of expensive champagne. While I couldn't see the label, it wasn't necessary. The taste was incredible, the bubbles tickling my nose.

He moved in the seat in order to study me intently, remaining quiet. I had to admit he looked positively dashing in the suit, his crisp white shirt and stark red tie perfect complements.

I found myself licking the rim of the delicate glass, which of course he noticed, his eyes flashing.

"I will devour you tonight." His words were simple, possessive. While not demanding, they were just... what would happen.

The blush returned and I looked away, staring out at the city lights. "Why, Kirill? Why wine and dine me?"

"Because I do what I want, and what I need is for you to be happy."

Happy. I wasn't certain he understood the meaning of the word. "I assure you that I want that as well. Where are we going?"

"We are going to La Travitorria."

I turned my head, now studying him. "An Italian restaurant. Let me guess, owned by the Italian mob." I'd heard of the establishment from Finnegan Walsh, the five-star restaurant supposedly notorious as the location where the Vincheti crime syndicate to hold certain 'business' meetings.

There were those times that reading his thoughts was easy. This wasn't one of them. His look was cold, harsh like before, so when he lifted his champagne glass in a toast, I almost burst into laughter.

"Yes, Kirill. I actually listen to the news and occasionally pick up a copy of the *New York Times*. This, all this is about showing off your prize in the hopes that whoever has decided to become your new big enemy will play their hand so you can cut it off. Am I right?"

Now it was obvious he didn't like that I'd caught him in a subterfuge, which made me feel a little sick inside. Why not enjoy the evening? What the heck. Who knows when I'd have another opportunity to enjoy myself, or perhaps attempt to escape?

I knew better. Getting away from him was no longer an option.

I purposely turned away, hearing his heavier breathing. I'd confounded him once again. I leaned against the side, staring out the window and sipping on the champagne. When the driver turned down a street, I tensed. He would drive right past the George Gershwin Theater. "I almost had an audition for a brand-new Broadway show in this theater." I made the statement in passing, knowing he wouldn't respond, and I was right. "That was supposed to be today." My last words were nothing more than a whisper. He truly didn't care.

It was a pipe dream being on Broadway, and as a cast member of the most highly anticipated show of the last two years no less. Ridiculous. However, it had been my dream since I was tiny, singing and dancing my little heart out from the time I could walk. At least that's what my mother had told me. Sadly, the dream would be put on hold indefinitely, if not forever.

Today had been the last day to audition, the premiere of the show in less than two months. Oh, well.

No, it truly pissed me off. I'd worked far too hard over the years to just let my dream fade away.

There was so much yin and yang about him. The clothes were so gorgeous that for a few minutes I allowed myself to think we could find some kind of a fairytale ending, although I wasn't stupid enough to think it could last forever. Moments like the few seconds before leaving and this one were stark reminders that our worlds were completely different, our lives incompatible.

"How dare you," I said without looking at him.

"How dare I what?"

"Take away my life. I know it's inconsequential to you given you were programmed as a child to become a killer, but this is something different. Something special."

"Then why don't you tell me about it?"

I snapped my head in his direction, expecting him to be on the phone or staring at me drolly. But he was watching, forever watching. "Okay. I've studied drama, dance and piano and voice since I was six. Six years old. This was my big chance. I worked very hard to get an audition and now it's done. Poof. And don't tell me that there are other auditions because I'm sure there won't be. You'll find a way to keep me from going to those. I'm angry. I'm hurt. I'm stupid as hell." I started laughing, unable to stop. I laughed so hard I developed the hiccups, which just added to the ridiculousness of the situation.

When he handed me a cup of water, I almost threw it at him, but it was just a kneejerk reaction. I wouldn't want to ruin his spiffy clothes. I took several sips, trying to control my diaphragm just like I did for hitting the high notes. Finally, it worked.

Then we sat in silence just like before, but at least I'd gotten it off my chest.

"Nothing about you is stupid, Candy. You are by far the most intelligent, talented, and beautiful woman I'd ever known or would ever want to know. Sometimes things happen for a reason."

Yeah, and sometimes the devil takes control, another of my mother's phrases. Actually, it had been her warning to be a good girl. I'd failed miserably.

Enjoy the night. Just breathe and enjoy.

As the limo pulled in front of the restaurant, blocking in several vehicles, both the driver and the passenger climbed out. It was easy to tell they were looking for any issues prior to opening Kirill's door.

He leaned over, raking a single nail down my arm. "Just remember to be on your best behavior tonight. While I'm very aware of every player in every syndicate, my identity is unknown to most and it's going to stay that way. We are not here to interrupt their business in any way." He pinched my chin, forcing me to look into his eyes.

"Then why are we here?"

The smile crossing his face highlighted his dimple, which I'd only seen a few times. He exuded sexuality, his scent rocketing through me. As usual, just when I wanted to hate him even more, he refused to allow that to happen.

"We're here because this happens to be my favorite restaurant and I wanted to bring the most beautiful woman who's ever been in my life to my second favorite delicacy."

His words oozed of sexuality and truth, and I was suddenly breathless. "What's your first?"

He leaned closer so he could whisper in my ear. "You, my *printsessa*. You."

* * *

Kirill

Dangerous.

Some would say I enjoyed living dangerously. Perhaps I did. While what I'd told the stunning woman who graced my arm was the truth about my identity, there was always a chance that one or more of the customers inside would suspect my allegiance, especially after hearing my accent. While certainly not as pronounced as other members of the Bratva, any one of certain foreign accents was always a cause for curiosity if not alarm.

Given my keen observation skills, I'd know the status of our agreement with the Italians just by who was inside the restaurant. Friday nights were always busy, but I'd made certain the hostess knew that a table was going to be ready at precisely six-thirty. I slipped her several bills before she led us to our table, the view of the room perfect for my needs while also showing off my prize.

Candy's perceptive nature was a strong part of her, so it was no surprise that she'd questioned my choice of this particular establishment. However, I also hadn't lied to her. Seeing her in the dress, the light in her eyes and the way soft curls fell against her face had almost driven me into a frenzy. I wanted time with her outside of the normal confines of the bedroom.

For the first time, I craved getting to know someone.

What my little rebel didn't know was that I knew more about what her driving force was than she realized. I'd found the paperwork on the audition, the music and lyrics she'd been asked to learn, the few lines she'd been required to memorize. It was a small part and the pay was atrocious, but hearing her tonight, I realized just how important it had been in her life. I'd never aspired to be anything else. Then again, I hadn't been given the chance.

After we were taken to our table, I scanned every other one, able to identify at least four different individuals. I found it fascinating that the location was neutral. Not once had any blood been shed inside. From what I could tell, no business was being handled tonight. Then again, there wasn't an Irishman in the room.

The waiter arrived within seconds and I ordered a second bottle of champagne without thinking. Then I noticed her look of fury.

"Don't do that," she said quietly, a smile remaining on her face. "I am perfectly capable of ordering myself."

Everything about the woman drove me to a state of madness. "Fair enough, *printsessa*. Perhaps I was only trying to impress you."

"You can impress me by telling me something personal about you. And I don't mean about what weapon you carry. I also don't care about your favorite color or what aftershave you like. I want something personal that will help me believe you're anything but a killing machine."

The light of fire in her eyes sparked the lust that had been building since the moment I walked into my private room, finding her punching on the bag. Nothing was going to break her, including me.

And I wanted her even more than before.

"How about food?" I asked, the only personal thing that came to mind far too toxic to discuss.

Candy wrinkled her nose. "Fine. What would that be? Let me guess. Italian food."

Even the way she leaned over the table was sexy as hell, the slight shift allowing me to catch a delicious glimpse of her rounded breasts peeking over the bodice of her dress.

I rapped my fingers on the table. "Ice cream."

It didn't seem that my selection registered at all. Then she burst into laughter, her booming voice immediately drawing attention. I noticed and the insanely gorgeous bright pink spotting her porcelain skin forced my cock to twitch. She pushed the back of her hand across her mouth to muffle the sound, the same fire in her eyes burning into mine. "Ice cream?" she whispered. "A big he-man like yourself enjoys ice cream? What flavor?"

"Chocolate, of course. Decadent. Rich. Seductive."

"Mmm… Maybe that's what we need to have for dinner. Fine. I'll play the game. How about movies?"

I waited as the waiter brought the champagne, unable to take my eyes off her. There wasn't a single man in the room who wasn't hungering for what I had.

For what I possessed.

I lifted my glass, ignoring the waiter's comments. *"Die Hard."*

"Now, that makes much more sense. Violence. Brutality." She clinked her glass against mine, licking the rim before taking a sip. Even the way her long lashes brushed across her cheeks was alluring. Perhaps I'd drag her into the bathroom for a quickie.

My God. She had a way of turning me into a stupid kid in lust.

"Actually, it was the way the heroine punched the reporter that I liked the best."

She almost choked on her sip, forced to grab her napkin. "You do surprise me, Kirill Sabatin. As much as I want to hate you, I can't seem to hold firm to my commitment."

"Hate me, Candy. That's what you need to do." I said the words regretfully, although they were truthful.

Her expression changed as she turned thoughtful, but the powerful gleam never left her eyes.

I'd told her I was going to ruin her. The truth was she would be the one to ruin me.

There was no reason for me to believe the Italians were involved in the attack or any other devious behavior. We were able to enjoy our dinner without incident, finally free of unwanted attention. Was I able to breathe a sigh of relief? Absolutely not. Exactly the opposite. I felt like time was running out. Whether or not that was the truth was inconsequential. It was time to place the fear of God into every informant and those under our control to aid us in finding the truth.

And being careful in order to avoid a war wasn't my *modus operandi*.

"Do you trust me enough to allow me to go to the bathroom?" she asked after the last bite of food had been consumed.

"I assure you that even if you were daring enough to try and escape through the service or exit doors, you'd find one of my men waiting to retrieve you. This isn't about trust, Candy. This is about keeping you safe."

I'd known my statement would rile her, but it was necessary to remind her that her choices were limited. Her sense of danger wasn't where it should be.

Her nose wrinkling for a second time with an entirely different meaning, she jerked to a halt, tossing her napkin, glaring at me before walking away. As expected, she cursed under her breath as she left.

The waiter had been standing in the wings, waiting for an opportunity to approach. "Would you enjoy an after-dinner drink, sir?"

"Bourbon. Neat. Amaretto for the lady." I shot him a look and nothing more. He knew to move away from me quickly.

When I sensed a return only seconds later, I bristled.

When Valentin Vincheti slipped into Candy's seat, I lifted my head, staring into his eyes. As the firstborn son of the Italian Mafioso, he was set to take over as the head of the family upon his father's retirement. While his life was uncharacteristic of what anyone would expect coming from such a brutal upbringing, he was dangerous nonetheless.

"And to what do I owe the pleasure?" I asked as he placed two brandy snifters on the table.

"On the house," he said quietly, studying me intently. "I wanted to thank you for the gift you left on my doorstep."

Gift. He was nothing if not amusing. I remained quiet, waiting to hear what he had to say. At least the body had gotten his attention.

"I assume it was your handiwork," he added.

"And what if it was?"

"The warning didn't go unnoticed, Sabatin. However, I'm curious as to the reason."

"Let's just say I'm hunting certain people."

"I heard about your issues with the Irish clan. Can I offer assistance?"

Assistance? What was he getting at? Whatever the deal was between the two families was starting to irritate me given I wasn't privy to the reason behind it. "I'll play along, Valentin. What do you know about a rogue group attempting to slide into our territory?"

He took a few seconds before answering. "The gift you sent me provided that answer. He's a turncoat, his loyalty shifting to the Irishmen."

So the man had been one of the Vincheti operatives. I did find that interesting. "Go on."

"He owed a debt to the Irishmen that couldn't be repaid. As such, he indentured himself to someone else, hoping that would provide some… relief."

As usual, words were chosen carefully. There was always a chance some FBI agent or other operative was enjoying dinner at the same time. 'Irishmen' was nothing more than a code for the smaller Irish mob. They'd never made a push before, but they remained lurking in the background like the cockroaches they were. "Their intentions?"

"You and I both know there is no opportunity for new blood at this time. Therefore, and this is my opinion, they are making a play in an entirely different manner, attempting to bring down an even greater Irish power."

The Walsh family. The Saints.

If the Irish mob got control over the unions, they had a decent chance of overrunning the entire city. My instincts had been correct. "Are you aware of any plans?"

"Nothing concrete. However, be leery of gifts being presented in the middle of the night. Often a moment of carelessness is what allows changes in control. Also, I've found that the lesion in one's army is always caused by those who have nothing to lose."

His riddled answer was easy to decipher. Candy. Whether or not she fully understood, she'd been made the catalyst in the Irish mob's attempt at making a hostile takeover. I had decisions to make, ones that would test my loyalty. As far as lesions, I understood far too well that it was most often those placed under the radar who had the ability for betrayal.

"Why are you providing this fascinating information, Valentin?"

"I assure you it's not a gift, Sabatin. However, it is an opportunity to maintain the peace, which I believe is important to both families. I hope you enjoyed your dinner." As he rose to his feet, he pushed the snifter further in my direction, giving me a respectful nod then walking away.

And I remained seething inside.

CHAPTER 15

*C*andy

Something drastic had happened. The man sitting next to me had resumed his solitary role as protector, wearing his rage in a brazen fashion in order to warn all those around him to back away.

Only I'd become a player in his world. However accidental the happening, I'd become fully entrenched in the madness of his life. He hadn't spoken a single word since leaving the restaurant. While his actions had remained decent, even gentle, I sensed the discord from whatever had happened while I was in the restroom. His constant reminders that I should hate him were grating, but in his world, I believed they were necessary. He couldn't get close. That wasn't allowed.

It could mean his death.

I stared out the window as I'd done before, more pensive than ever. As the driver rounded the corner, the bright lights of the theater coming into view, another wave of sadness swept through me. How life could change on a dime.

"The theater is important to you," he stated, the tone of his voice darker, more foreboding than before.

It was also embroiled in a haunted tone, his deep pitch rumbling through me.

"It was. Now, I'm not so certain." I was shocked when the driver pulled to a stop directly in front of the entrance. "What are we doing here? Are you rubbing the fact I can't have this in my face?"

Kirill resumed his silence, exiting the vehicle in a dramatic fashion, buttoning his jacket before closing the door. Why would he do this to me?

The feeling of being a princess faded as he walked me into the theater, passing by the ticket office and moving directly inside. Two of his men trailed behind, remaining close yet providing enough room I didn't feel smothered. Yet their presence was undeniable. The danger was real. When Kirill led me to the orchestra section, I couldn't deny I was impressed. The tickets had been sold out for weeks. The fact he'd been able to obtain two of them meant he'd spent a premium price, which of course didn't bother him. He could obviously afford anything he wanted.

As soon as we sat down, the heat of his body became overwhelming. I had the feeling we were being watched, creepy crawlies tickling both my arms and legs. If that was the case, he didn't allow it to bother him in the least. While his arm touched mine, he didn't attempt to make contact in any other way, but his stoic body language was further acknowledgment that someone or something had pissed him off.

"I'm not certain why you did this, but thank you," I finally said, my upbringing requiring me to provide some sense of gratitude.

"I did this to make you happy."

"You did." If only for two incredible hours. "This is a magical place."

"Why?"

I turned my head, thinking about my answer. "I think because my mother loved George Gershwin. She always had big band or Broadway music on, her voice melodic. She encouraged me to become a singer, even when my father called my aspirations hogwash. I'd promised her that one day she'd see me on Broadway."

He didn't respond in any way, but I sensed he'd heard me.

As if that would matter.

The lights began to dim and the rush of excitement I'd always imagined came to life. I sat on the edge of my seat, allowing myself to slide into a perfect moment of fantasy. As the curtain rose, I could feel his eyes concentrated on my reaction. At that moment, I didn't care. Nothing would spoil the special occasion.

Yet it ended all too quickly, the lights in the theater lifting even before the curtains began to fall. I remained emotional, the dazzling musical fluid and dramatic, yet poignant. I wiped away tears as everyone else stood, preparing to leave. I found myself holding my arms, still trying to absorb the beautiful rendition.

"Did you enjoy it at all?" I asked in a breathless whisper, uncertain he'd even hear me.

"What I enjoy isn't important, *moya krasavitsa*."

"Yes, it is." I couldn't look at him, which was silly of me. He'd displayed no emotions that I'd been able to detect, but his constant stare had left me fully aroused, my heart skipping beats. If only I could truly hate him. That would make the experience of being with him much easier. "You deserve happiness. Everyone does."

"Not a man like me." He guided me to my feet, his grip on my arm firm. He remained protective, a force to be reckoned with as he led me out of the theater and onto the street.

I hated his silence, his brooding behavior. I loathed that he couldn't talk to me. And I wanted him. The entire situation wasn't just uncomfortable. It was also tearing at my heart. I'd never believed in 'instalove,' a saying I'd heard regarding all those gorgeous females who found the love of their life on the first few pages of a romance novel, but here I was, falling hard and fast. I knew it was wrong. I understood that it had no decent outcome. I was no fool. He wasn't capable of feeling the same way, but the tingling warmth that constantly spread from my tummy to my pussy and nipples was in total disagreement.

Maybe I still did feel like a princess after all, but the clock was ticking down to midnight. The gorgeous clothes would be gone, the reality of my cage returning. I'd never be his Cinderella.

Even after the driver started the engine, I continued to stare out the window at the bright lights, longing to fool myself for a little while longer. And still he was watching me.

"Would you like some champagne?" he asked, as if that was going to appease me.

"What I'd really like are answers, Kirill. Did you find out the Walsh family is behind whatever terrible things happened to the people you protect? Are you planning on killing them, or me? Why can't you tell me anything personal? Is that some unknown requirement that no one can get close to you? You want me to hate you, but that's impossible. And I can't love you because I don't know you."

I had no idea why the barrage of sentiments rushed out of my mouth.

Goddamn it. Why did he have to exhale and say nothing? The man was infuriating as hell.

I shifted closer, refusing to allow him off the hook. Whatever our strange, passionate connection had become at least allowed me the truth. Right? Or was I fooling myself again?

"Talk to me, Kirill. Tell me something, anything to help me understand you."

Another deep sigh.

Damn the man.

Just when I was ready to turn away, he slipped his index finger under my chin, brushing it back and forth. The touch was enigmatic, sensual, his eyes even more so.

"I'm not attempting to hurt you, little rebel. I have reasons to be a very private man."

"I know. Your job."

"Not just that. I can't risk losing anyone else."

I leaned over, drinking in the exotic scent of his aftershave, my head spinning. "What did you lose?"

An instant faraway look flashed in his eyes. While he continued to stroke my face, moving the tip from one side of my jaw to the other, he was miles away.

"My parents. My little sister. I remember very little except for their deaths."

I found myself shifting closer, a little hammer going off inside my head. "What happened?"

"There was a war on the streets in Russia. My parents had taken my little sister to the doctor. That much I remember. I was with them. They were caught in the wrong place at the wrong time." While he didn't look away, he lowered his gaze, his mouth pinched.

"I'm so sorry." I wrapped my hand around his, pulling it against the spot over my heart.

"I was a little boy, a mere child, but I understood terror. There were so many people running, trying to get away from the gunfire and carnage. We were suddenly separated and I was pushed forward with the crowd. I tried to get back to them, but I was too small. A man picked me up in his arms, whispering that I'd be safe. I screamed for my parents, trying to explain to my savior that I had family, but it was already too late."

His voice was softer than I'd ever heard, yet there was a hardness in his eyes, the memory dredging up the wretched moment that had changed his life forever.

He dug his fingers into my hand, his chest heaving. "I watched them being killed then trampled and all I could do was scream. I couldn't save them. I couldn't…"

His voice trailed off, his chiseled face holding an even harder edge.

"The man who saved you." I wasn't certain how to ask the question.

"Vladimir Kozlov."

BEAUTIFUL VILLAIN

Now I understood his extreme loyalty, his willingness to give up a good portion of his life in order to protect his savior. I wanted more, but he'd programmed himself to lock away all his emotions, refusing to accept or acknowledge that he had justified needs. I eased my hand to his face, cupping his jaw. He blinked several times, unable to look me in the eyes.

"Several of my men were executed recently by an unknown source. I couldn't save them, but I survived. They counted on me to protect them, and I failed." His admittance was gut-wrenching to hear, another reason he refused to allow me in.

When I inched even closer, I was surprised he didn't push me away. I pushed on the side of his face, forcing him to look at me. The swell of emotions I saw in his eyes was a tidal wave of images and feelings, desires and fear. His breathing was heavier, his facial features distorted.

Then he grabbed my arm, yanking me onto his lap, cupping my face with both hands.

"That's why I can't get close to you. My world will destroy you." Even though he said the words, he crushed his mouth over mine, his hunger knowing no bounds.

I gripped his wrists as he thrust his tongue inside, sweeping his back and forth, every action more dominating than before. He growled into the powerful moment, his actions become brutal and unforgiving. The swirl of emotions was intense, heartbreaking yet pulling us together. We were locked together in our own fortress, two people who had no business together yet couldn't get enough of each other.

I'd never felt so strongly about anyone in my life. I'd never been so exasperated or so overwhelmed, the fervor of our connection more breathtaking than any jolt of electricity. He drank from me hungrily, sucking on my tongue as he yanked in my essence, his savage moves forcing me back and forth across his lap. His cock was rock hard, the heavy beat as it throbbed against me sending several chills dancing down my body.

Within seconds, we were tearing at each other's clothes, neither one of us caring where we were or about the threats to our lives. Our combined sounds were guttural, like two beasts devouring each other. I was breathless as I tugged off my shoes, the haze around my eyes glittered in gold.

He broke the kiss, gasping for air as he fought to remove his jacket. I ripped his shirt, laughing softly as buttons went flying. He yanked me onto my knees, fighting to yank the dress over my head.

"God. I want you," he muttered then cupped my breasts, immediately pinching my nipples as he crushed them together, dropping his head and sucking on first one then the other.

I rolled my fingers across his cock then fought to unfasten his belt, the pleasure rolling through me more explosive than ever. Always impatient, he snagged my panties with a single finger, ripping them away just as I managed to unzip his trousers.

We were both in a crazy rush, the need unlike anything we'd experienced before. As soon as I freed his cock, he forced me to straddle his legs, giving me barely any time to position the tip of his cock against my dripping pussy. With one hard yank, he jerked me all the way down.

I threw my head back, gasping for air. "Yes. Yes…"

Kirill pressed kisses against my heated skin, snaking his arms around my neck and holding me in place. It was as if he'd never let me go.

And I didn't want him to.

I clung to his shoulders, every nerve ending on fire, my heart thudding. I felt deliciously filthy and oh-so alive as I rode him, rolling my hips forward, my pussy muscles clamping tightly around his massive, amazing, beautiful erection.

As he sucked and licked my nipples, finally biting down until I whimpered in pain, I could tell it wouldn't be long until he shoved me into a mind-blowing orgasm. The heat shared between us was explosive, every glass surface fogged. He gripped my hips, yanking me up and down, pulling me closer and closer to sweet ecstasy.

Panting, I lowered my head, wrapping my arms around his neck, holding the back of his head.

He whispered words in Russian that I couldn't understand, but every word dripped of passion and eroticism. I wanted to become lost in this man forever.

"Come for me. Slicken my cock with your sweet juice." He issued another harsh growl then captured my mouth, holding our lips together. He became a wild man, his cock swelling even more. Within seconds, I couldn't hold back any longer, ripping my head away and doing everything I could to stifle a scream.

The rush was sublime, tossing me straight into raw and beautiful bliss.

"That's it, baby."

I clung to his shoulders, my body convulsing from the power of the orgasm, one immediately shifting into another, this one earth-shattering.

"Oh. Oh. Oh!"

I was barely able to catch my breath before he tossed me onto the seat, forcing one leg around his hip, taking full control. His eyes bore into mine, glistening as the driver rolled down the brightly lit streets, reflecting light flashing in through the windows. I pushed my palms against him, holding him aloft so I could watch every expression as he powered into me.

He slowed his actions, filling me so completely I found it difficult to breathe. I was no romantic, but at that moment we weren't just lovers. It went much deeper than that, a need that burned so brightly I feared we'd be consumed in the flames.

"So beautiful," he whispered, several expressions crossing his face.

As I studied him, transfixed by the moment, a single bead of sweat trickled down his forehead, rolling along the bridge of his nose then splashing against my cheek. There was no reason for the small moment to feel so surreal, but it was as if he'd marked me as his for all eternity.

Unable to control his actions or his needs, he resumed fucking me savagely, the force he used driving me into the thick leather seats. Within seconds, I could tell he was struggling to hold back. Closing my eyes, I squeezed my muscles, delighting in the husky roar he issued just seconds before he erupted deep inside.

His body shook in time with mine, his face pinched. When he slowly crushed his full weight against me, I wrapped my other leg around him, holding him close, his whisper tickling my ears, the emotion in them more intense than the passion we'd just shared.

"Ty budesh' moyey navsegda."

* * *

Kirill

You will be mine forever.

I'd whispered the words. I felt them. No. I'd burned with them but in doing so, it was as if I'd sealed some ridiculous fate for both of us.

I rubbed my eyes, staring out at the Manhattan skyline, swirling the same glass of bourbon I'd had in my hand for almost an hour. In the space of a few days, I'd broken nearly all my rules, ones I'd abided by since I could remember. An angry hiss slipped from my mouth as I stared down at the watered-down drink. Even the slightly bitter taste didn't have the same effect on me I was used to.

I'd left Candy in my bed. My bed. The bed I'd told myself I'd never share with anyone. I'd lost my freaking mind. I purposely left the window. Staring out into space wasn't going to get me any closer to securing the identity of the bastards responsible for her abduction or the murder of my men. Valentin's words continued to play over in my mind. I'd gathered the Italian Empire was equally concerned about the possibility of the Irish mob getting any control within the union. Granted, there were already several members who'd been placed inside the organization, but to date, only grunt people, soldiers told to provide information.

I moved to my desk, placing my unwanted drink on the edge then moving toward one of my safes, punching in the code. After retrieving my laptop, I sat down and prepared to continue searching for information.

Alexei was damn good with business opportunities, his usual charisma and good looks opening doors for him and adding to the family's reputation. He also had a mind for sensing traitors, but I continued to have my doubts regarding the superintendent of the project. Being placed in a level of control, he'd been given access to almost every aspect of the business surrounding the project. I'd seen him on several others over the years. Alexei trusted him, the man's loyalty challenged on several occasions.

However, I'd learned a long time ago that often betrayal occurred because of a personal vendetta or an inability to curb a dark proclivity. I glared at the glass, realizing breaking my own rules was the first step down that path. It was usually about liquor, women, or gambling.

I'd made enough connections over the years to develop a network of my own, able to obtain almost any information I desired on everyone from enemies to corporate moguls. If they had a footprint, I could find them, tracing their actions over a course of time.

I sat back, beginning the search. There had to be something.

When I looked at my watch, I shook my head. Two hours had gone by. During that time, what had I found of value? Nothing. Jeff Parker was clean as a whistle. That didn't sit well with me.

I shifted to the employee files for the casino site, flipping through the names. Finding the name of the second person who'd been in the trailer would take time, including searching through the pictures of the employee files. It was time Alexei and I had a private conversation. At this point, a phone call wasn't enough.

Before I had a chance to head into my room to change, Dimitre called.

"What?" I barked as I walked out of the room.

"You're not going to like this," he answered.

* * *

Light was shifting over the horizon by the time I arrived at Alexei's residence. He'd remained in the city, his preference for the party life likely the reason. The condo was equally as secure as any other facility, no one gaining entrance without being approved.

"Can I help you, sir?" the guard asked as he moved to his feet.

"Alexei Kozlov. Now."

"Sir. Do you know what time it is?"

I pulled out my weapon, reaching across the desk and grabbing him by the throat. "Does it look like I give a shit?"

"Na… No, sir. I'll call him. Okay?"

Hissing, I kept my hold, squeezing until his face turned the same shade of rose that Candy's had earlier. I wanted to hurt somebody. When I let him go, he stumbled backward, his body shaking.

But he immediately reached for his phone.

I shoved my weapon back into my jacket, trying to take several deep breaths. Getting control was important, but I wanted blood. I could hear the fucker mumbling behind me, likely tipping off Alexei that a deranged man was in the lobby. Well, it was past time Alexei knew I was done with taking his shit.

Waiting while the well-trained guard made the call increased my agitation.

When the guard finally ended the call, he merely nodded toward the bank of elevators. He knew better than to open his mouth. As I stepped inside, I shoved my hands into my pockets, thinking about Dimitre's call.

He'd confirmed that Michael Walsh had been invited to Vladimir's party. The Russian patriarch had always found the best way to deal with his enemies was to provide a sense of what they'd be missing if they continued in their treacherous activities.

The party was no exception.

Over the years, I'd been to two of them before growing bored. I'd witnessed several deals made and others cut to shreds, relationships ending both eloquently and brutally.

However, it was widely known that declining the invitation would mean additional difficulties. Loved ones vanishing. Business arrangements failing. Promotions stalled. It wasn't beneath Vladimir to use whatever necessary in order to get what he wanted.

Alexei was a carbon copy of his father, his chaotic but brilliant methods of providing pain to his enemies creating a reputation that was as savage as mine.

Only we were entirely different.

The other reason for his late-night call had caused me to nearly jump off the deep end. I took several deep breaths, just as impatient for the elevator door to open.

I trusted few people in this world. That had been an early lesson taught by Vladimir. It had stayed with me, including aspects about my private life. There were four people who knew that Candy had been moved under my protection. All of them I trusted without question.

That included Dimitre. No matter his loyalty for the family or his love of the only Kozlov daughter, he would never betray my trust.

When the elevator finally pinged, I pushed the doors open myself, taking long strides as I moved down the hallway. As expected, I didn't need to pound on the door. As soon as Alexei yanked it open, I threw a hard punch to his jaw, the force pitching him backward and to the floor. After slamming the door, I yanked my weapon into my hand, pointing it toward his head.

"It's time for you and me to have a discussion."

CHAPTER 16

Kirill

"*Chto, chert voz'mi, s toboy ne tak?*" Alexei demanded.

"What the fuck is wrong with me? I was going to ask you the same goddamn question." I made certain he knew I was ready to pull the trigger. The rage rolling through me was unacceptable, but I had one damn good reason. "First, I find out you're bragging about issuing a kill order on Candy Lancaster. Then you have the fucking nerve to toss her apartment in your effort to take her off the street."

He didn't say anything at first, just sat up slowly, rubbing his jaw. There hadn't been a single week that had gone by when we were kids where we hadn't been pulled off of each other, our fists flying. We were more like brothers than the relationship he had with Viktor or Sevastian. That didn't mean we'd ever been close.

"Are you going to allow me to stand?" he asked, his attitude just as surly as mine.

I took a step away, waving the barrel, watching as he climbed to his feet. He tied the sash on his robe, cursing in Russian under his breath. "Do you want a drink? I sure as shit do."

I didn't answer him, watching as he headed into his living room. Seconds later I followed behind him, leaning against the doorjamb. The fact he hadn't denied either accusation was a clear indication Dimitre's call had held merit. He'd heard the assholes trashing her place. By the time he'd moved down the stairs, prepared to confront them, they'd left, but not before he'd overheard a portion of their conversation in Russian.

He poured a drink, lifting the bottle in my direction until I shook my head. "It's Saturday. Lighten up."

"We're not friends, Alexei, and I'm not here to play games."

"And I'm not playing games, Kirill. That woman could be an issue."

"She's not."

"You're right. We're not friends. We also aren't blood; however, I respect you. My father worships the fucking ground you walk on. You have your reign and I have mine. It would not be in my best interest as it wouldn't be in yours to cross into each other's territory," he snarled as he walked toward me.

"That's not a denial. Did you not state that you would need to handle the woman if I didn't?"

When he looked away, I had my truth.

"I should put a bullet in your brain right now. That woman is off limits. She had nothing to do with the situation."

"You're right, Kirill. I shouldn't have spouted off at the mouth, but after Rian Walsh threatened you, I became concerned."

"You stepped out of line."

"Yeah, I did." He walked closer. "As far as trying to extract her, that had nothing to do with me."

There was a ring of sincerity in his tone. "Then we have a serious problem on our hands."

We glared at each other for a full thirty seconds.

"Then we work together to solve it. Walsh was invited to the party," he said, acting as if it would surprise me.

"I'm aware. I had an interesting conversation with Valentin Vincheti. What deal was made with the family?"

"Vincheti? What the hell?"

I cocked my head, finally returning the safety. "You don't know."

"I have no fucking idea what you're talking about. Sure, Pops mentioned he's had conversations with Cesare

Vincheti, but I doubt a formal deal was made. What makes you think that?"

"Because he offered advice. He thinks the Irish mob is behind the attacks as well as framing the Walshes."

He whistled but didn't seem very surprised. "Not a bad plan. We spend time and effort turning on each other. They take a portion of our turf given our marred reputation and also claim control over the unions. Meanwhile, we just sit back and allow that to happen. How did Vincheti come by this information?"

"He didn't say but if I had to guess, I'd say they're experiencing the same pressure."

"I wouldn't put it past the Italians to double-cross us," he insisted.

My phone rang. Immediately my hackles were raised. "Vassily. I take it you have some information."

"Yeah. Rory O'Leary was the dude you were looking for. Kevin O'Connor and Parker Shay were nobodies as far as I can tell," Vassily stated.

"And Rory?"

"Well, his dad used to be the head of the trade council. He was pushed out, but that was four years ago. Might mean nothing."

I laughed. "It could also be a reason for revenge. What did he have to do with the trade council?"

"He was popular, served on the nominations committee."

"That means shit."

"Wait a minute. There is an election coming up and guess whose term is up?"

"Michael Walsh." Fuck. It was all about revenge but not against us. "Why was Rory's father pushed out?"

"That I don't know, but I do have another tidbit of information you might be able to use," he continued. "That stolen car carrying Rory and his buddies that night? Guess who reported it missing?"

"Keep talking."

"Jeff Parker."

I moved closer to Alexei, my fury just increasing. "Parker, huh?"

"Yep. It's getting far too interesting," Vassily said, laughing.

"I'll say."

"I'll call you if I find anything else."

The call ended; I took a deep breath.

"The snitch is Parker."

Alexei opened his eyes wide, immediately shaking his head. "I won't buy it. I check my employees every four months. He's had no payments made."

"Gambling debt?"

"The man is a born-again Christian, for fuck's sake. He had a wife and two kids. What the hell does Vassily think he knows?"

"Candy was attacked and abducted, which is why she's now under my protection. The car involved was stolen. Guess who it belonged to?"

Alexei snorted. "Jeff reported his car stolen from his house over a week ago. Don't go there, Kirill. He wouldn't be that stupid. It was legit. He was very upset."

I gave him a hard look as I thought about what had transpired. "Who was the man in the construction office with him the other day?"

"You mean Mikhail? I hired him a few months ago. His background, his bank accounts all check out. I think they knew each other before on another jobsite. He's a good worker."

What I'd also learned in my life was that the most dangerous threats were the ones that you least suspected, including those designed by friends. Which is exactly what Valentin had been getting at.

"Was he connected to the union? Rory O'Leary was the man who abducted Candy. He was the son of the past president of the trade council."

"If you're insinuating Mikhail is involved somehow, I'm not certain what he could gain," Alexei responded.

"Maybe nothing unless he's working for the Irishmen. Maybe his payoff is coming later."

"Wait a minute. O'Leary. Patrick O'Leary. I had run-ins with him building the first casino five years ago. The man killed himself after he was forced off the council. Because he was accused of being tight with the Irish mob." He lifted his head, curling his upper lip. "We need to make a connection to—" When he stopped short, I could see the rage forming in his eyes. "I think know who our snitch is."

"Meaning?"

"Meaning the man who recommended I hire Mikhail. He was the same man who knew about the mission you were on when your men were killed before being able to eradicate the snitches. The fucking bastard sold us out to the Irishmen."

The Irish mob had been behind the attack on my men, not the Walsh family and his followers. The perfect setup indeed. I curtailed my rage. Now was the time to think clearly. "Mikhail was relaying information about when to attack the construction site."

"Goddamn it. That's the reason for the recent incident."

"Another incident?"

"A fire earlier this evening. What a fucking fool I've been." Alexei cursed in Russian.

I wasn't going to tell him I agreed with him.

"Let me get dressed. We have business to attend to." He walked closer, holding out his hand. "We might not be friends, Kirill, but we are brothers. We need to work together. I know why your men were attacked and how. Now, I need your to help us fix this problem."

I stared him in the eyes, finally accepting his gesture. Brothers. I'd accept that, especially coming from Alexei. "Who is this traitor?"

"The only man other than family I ever trusted. I won't make that mistake again." He gave me an entirely different look, as if he'd just realized that I belonged in the family. He started to walk out of the room then stopped. "Not trying to give you advice, Kirill."

"Good, because I'm not in the mood."

"If you like this girl, really like her, be prepared to let her go. If there's any chance you could fall in love with her, do it sooner versus later. If you don't, you'll ruin her life. You should know that being in a Bratva family doesn't allow for love. Find a woman, marry her, but never, ever fall in love. It'll ease the heartache."

As he walked away, I realized two important things. One was that I didn't know Alexei at all and two…

It was already too late.

Maybe we'd ruined each other.

* * *

While it was still early morning, there was already some activity on the casino construction site, several men still handling the cleanup from the earlier fire. The Irishmen were certainly enjoying their attempt at keeping us on our toes. I continued to seethe, my desire to shed blood and break bones fueling the rage churning inside. He'd told me about his soldier, Yuri Romanoff, involved in the Bratva for over a decade.

Alexei had dug deeper into the man's accounts, finding several direct payments from one of Shane's shell companies that very few people knew he owned. It was enough to confirm what we already knew.

As I got out of my car, I stared at the massive buildings beginning to take shape. The design was utter perfection, the accomplishment one that would be the crowning glory of the Kozlov family's empire. I thought about Alexei's words, his indication he'd accepted me as his brother and smirked. Time would tell if that came to pass.

We didn't bother talking. There was no reason to go over our intentions or the outcome. This was simply a matter of business, getting rid of unwanted baggage.

We found Mikhail on one of the floors under construction, the light breeze blowing through the completely open fifteenth floor facility. We moved in silence, our approach stealthy. The fool was on his phone, his back turned to us. He was the only man on the floor and gauging by his hurried tone, he was finishing with a conversation he wanted no one else to hear.

But we did.

"Everything is set. There's a party tonight so neither Alexei nor anyone else in the core group will be anywhere close to the facility." He hesitated, nodding to no one. "I know what to do. Yes, I'm ready. The money better be in my bank account tomorrow. Yeah, well, I did my part. Now, do yours." He ended the call, cursing in Russian. He and his buddies had been responsible for breaking into my fake apartment as well as tossing Candy's. Another attempt at leading us astray.

Alexei darted a glance in my direction, his need for blood just as strong as mine.

"Mikhail." My booming voice carried across the space, the wind unable to push it away.

He turned with a start, immediately shoving his phone into his pocket. "I wanted to get here early," he bothered to say, although even in the early morning light, it was easy to gather a sense he was terrified.

As he should be.

"You betrayed us," Alexei said almost casually as we both closed the distance.

"I don't know what you're talking about," he insisted. He was standing behind a pallet of steel girders, the last ones located on the property given the holdup caused by the trade council. As I approached, I noticed two cement trucks actively pouring a concrete floor below.

"You're working for the Irishmen. There is no sense in denying it." I itched to drag out my knife, taking my time inflicting pain, but we still had other business to contend with. I moved around the girders, blocking him in on one side.

Alexei remained where he was, easing his weapon into his hand. "What is the name of the man you're working for?"

"I'm not working for anyone," Mikhail insisted.

I took my time taking my weapon out of my pocket, not bothering with a silencer. There was no need given the noise on the site. "Do you know what happens to rats who betray us, Mikhail?"

"You're crazy. I would never betray you."

I shook my head, allowing him to hear a tsking sound. "A name. Now."

At least his body started to shake, but his jaw was clenched. He was a hardcore Russian, determined to take what he knew to his grave. It didn't really matter at this point. He was only a small cog in the wheel, taking his orders from Yuri, Alexei's second in command. I could tell how much it pained my brother that one of his own, a man he'd claimed as his friend, could betray him. And for what? Money? He was paid well, like the rest of us. A higher position in the Irish mob. Doubtful.

Just like this fuck. His stupidity would cost him his life.

"*Russkaya krysa khuzhe tarakana*," Alexei snarled.

A Russian rat is worse than a cockroach.

The statement was very true.

I took the last long stride toward him, pointing the barrel of my weapon directly in the center of his face.

Then I fired.

It always seemed to amaze me that it took a body several seconds to understand that the life had just been yanked out of it, sent straight to hell. As he started to fall, tumbling over the edge, I moved closer, only somewhat satisfied when his body was tossed into the wet cement. At least I'd have the satisfaction of knowing his dead body would be buried in the muck.

I wiped my face then turned toward Alexei. It was moments like this that could make a normal man question his profession.

But I wasn't normal.

Without talking, we left the floor. The next item on the list would prove to be more… enjoyable.

Yuri's position had allowed him to enjoy numerous luxuries in life, including a modest home near the water, a medium-sized watercraft tied to his massive dock.

Alexei kicked in the front door, moving with ease through the man's house. He'd undoubtedly been here a number of times, saluting the accomplishments and planning for future business endeavors. While I'd had limited dealings with the man, he'd seemed honest and loyal to a fault.

Maybe that was the issue. He was too loyal.

"Yuri," Alexei said, obviously surprising him.

"Alexei. What are you doing here?" He stood in shorts and a tee shirt. Perhaps this was his day off.

Alexei glanced around the room then outside, staring at the dock through the all-glass door. "Why don't you show us your new boat? I think Kirill would enjoy seeing the watercraft."

Yuri swallowed then glanced from one to the other, dropping his gaze then moving toward the set of doors. He said nothing as he led us to the dock, hesitating only when he was just outside the boat.

"What is this about, Alexei?"

"Betrayal. You're working with Shane Dunnigan," Alexei threw out. The Irishmen's leader was young and aggressive. He'd grown up in the States, pretending that he'd been born in Ireland. He had a ruthless reputation, but up to this point, he'd never made any inroads into a single major territory. Maybe he was finally spreading his wings.

Time to clip them off.

Yuri didn't need to answer. I could see terror creeping into his eyes. He turned, moving onto the boat. "Just don't hurt my family."

"They will be well taken care of. That I promise you," Alexei stated.

The ride was pleasant, slightly chilly, but blood was pumping through my veins.

"Stop here," Alexei directed.

He did as he was ordered, turning to face us, giving a nod of respect. "I'm sorry, Alexei."

"It doesn't matter why you did this, Yuri. Enjoy your time in hell." Alexei turned toward me, blinking only once.

He knew how much I enjoyed perfecting my knife skills, providing food for the fish.

**

Candy

Shifting, I finally opened my eyes, almost immediately jerking to a sitting position. There was too much light in the room. Still fuzzy, I struggled to pull myself into the moment. Then a swell of emotions as well as dancing vibrations drifted all the way down to my toes. The night with Kirill had been… amazing.

Not just the passion, although there'd been several mind-blowing orgasms. The entire night had been a beautiful foray into filth and truth. As I pulled the sheets against my naked body, I took a deep breath, still able to gather an incredible whiff of our sex. Even before turning my head, I knew he'd left me alone in his bed. His bed! I thumped down against the pillows, still dreamy.

Being in the theater had been a dream come true, even though I wasn't on the stage, singing or performing. His surprise had meant more to me than I'd told him. I pressed my hand across my mouth, giggling like some stupid kid. I'd seen yet another side of him. How many more existed?

After a few seconds, I tossed back the covers, enjoying the ache and wetness in my pussy. Good God, the man had ravaged me for hours. Just forcing myself to press my feet to the floor was a feat. I stared at his closet, unable to keep a smile from crossing my face. With purpose in mind, I headed toward the doors, swinging them open, justifying what I was about to do.

I had no robe, at least inside the room. I had to wear something to roam the house. Right? I rolled my eyes, taking my time in selecting one of his long-sleeved shirts. The crisp cotton felt delicious against my skin. I took a few seconds, rolling the sleeves to my elbows, finally taking a look in the mirror.

I looked like a chick who'd been fucked hard and put away... wet inside at least. The stupid giggle remained as I took long strides toward the door.

The quiet in the hallway was almost unnerving. He wasn't like me, who needed music. Kirill enjoyed the quiet. I had a feeling the silence was necessary to keep his anger from breaching the surface.

As I headed downstairs, I thought about what he'd told me about his family. How awful. How tragic. The horrible moment had defined him; however, he wasn't a man who didn't deserve love.

Love.

What was I thinking?

I couldn't possibly have fallen in love with such a brutal man. Maybe I was just lying to myself. He was rough and tough, yet capable of being gentle when necessary, gorgeous to a fault. Damn it. I wanted to be with him. Did it really matter what he did for a living?

As soon as I reached the bottom of the stairs, I could swear I felt him close by. A swell of emotions, including joy flooded me. I scurried into the various rooms, scowling when I couldn't find him.

Then a light caught my attention. I found myself skipping toward it, slowing only when I was close. I ran my fingers through my hair before moving to the doorway.

I was no fool. I'd understood that in his profession, he was responsible for killing people. He'd made certain I was completely aware that he was a bad man who did terrible things, but seeing his face and neck covered in blood was gut-wrenching. It also managed to stop time from moving forward.

He stood in front of the mirror, wiping his face. His shirt, his bloody shirt had been dumped in the sink, but it was the sight of his stoic reflection that chilled me to my core.

As he shifted his gaze in my direction, I couldn't move, paralyzed other than the hard thumping of my heart. He continued wiping his face as he stared at me, his chest rising and falling evenly, content with whatever horror he'd inflicted.

In those seconds that seemed like forever, I was forced to face exactly what he was, and the ugly realization wasn't one I could forget or forgive.

He wasn't just a monster.

He was a coldblooded killer who enjoyed exacting revenge. There was no reason for me to walk inside, no point in confronting him or saying anything. I couldn't change things. There was no chance he'd become a different man, no matter how much I wanted to believe he could.

This wasn't a beautiful love story. This was nothing more than a moment in time.

I caught a glimpse of my reflection, my skin pale and my eyes open wide. I couldn't hide my look of horror as trickles of blood slid into the drain.

Sinner.

Killer.

Monster.

The three words should be all I needed in order to find the courage to run as far away as possible, although he was never going to allow me to leave. I'd be locked in the nightmare forever.

"I never lied to you, Candy. The business I'm in requires making difficult decisions." He turned toward me, rubbing the towel across his neck.

I had no idea what to say.

There was still a chaotic beauty about him, his stare exuding tremendous passion, his presence commanding everything and everyone around him. Only his eyes reflected his intent to keep me captured, yet the thought of this lasting forever was heartbreaking. There would be no simple joys, only pleasures of the flesh. Our house wouldn't be a cozy representation of our love, it would be a fortress. And there'd be no happily ever after, only tragedy and death.

I would love him until the day I died, a deep penetrating love that time and space would never erode. In the darkness of the night, I'd hunger for him, longing for the brush with perfection, the sweetness of ecstasy.

But I'd allow him to become a bittersweet memory and nothing more. Anything else would destroy me.

I couldn't take that. Being with him would break me, shattering every aspect of my being.

"I care for you deeply. Being with you penetrates inside my soul. There is nothing more I'd like to do than give you everything you deserve, but that won't change who I am. You are so special, a gift that I don't deserve." His words were heartfelt, the deep rumble of his tone prickling every inch of skin.

When he reached for me, I threw out my hand, the hard pounding in my heart intensifying. The electricity soared between us, the breathless moment not that different from the intimacy, but suddenly, everything had changed. Everything.

I lifted my gaze, staring into his.

I knew without a shadow of a doubt, he was a man who had no soul.

And I did what was necessary to keep my heart intact, refusing to risk losing myself to the man I'd fallen deeply in love with.

I turned and fled, praying to God that he'd leave me alone.

CHAPTER 17

Kirill

For a man who'd reveled in the darkness, the shadows continuing to build inside the car were oppressive. Every time I darted a glance toward Candy, I was forced to accept that she'd shut down completely. She'd finally seen me for who and what I was, but the harsh reality had been too much for her.

And so, she remained silent.

She'd followed my instructions, donning the second dress I'd purchased for her. The moment she'd walked into the foyer, my possessive side had erupted to the surface, my hunger out of control. But I'd left her alone, allowing her to fall deeper into her despair. Tonight would mean the beginning of the end. If Michael Walsh didn't accept the deal we offered, the only choice he had, then we'd stand back as he was ruined, most of his power stripped away.

Then the Kozlov family would act, ensuring he didn't rise again.

I'd seen the incredible rush of joy in finding me then the despair of what she'd learned. The brilliant, beautiful light had drifted away from her eyes. I'd never felt so alone in my life, even though her closeness kept me aroused, my hunger insatiable.

Sighing, I tapped my fingers on the steering wheel, unable to find any words of comfort. I'd been right to attempt to shove her away, forcing her to hate me, but I'd been lying to myself that I could follow through with what was necessary. Soon, I would release her, ensuring that she was safe and happy. Then I would walk away.

But when I did, I'd be a broken man.

I took a deep breath, shoving aside the feelings as I pulled onto the long driveway leading into Vladimir's estate. I'd purposely waited, arriving almost an hour after the event had started, incapable of enduring the small talk and suffocation of being surrounded by dozens of people.

This was business, not a social event. After parking, I studied the area, noticing the number of soldiers. I loathed the tension that remained in my gut. It was only a matter of time before Shane and his goons realized that Yuri was no longer their bitch. The deal needed to be in place with Walsh.

When I opened the door, Candy didn't look at me, barely responding when I eased her from the passenger seat. I pulled her close despite the push of her hand against my chest. While a small part of me continued to long to ease her pain, tonight wasn't that night. She had to be on her best behavior at all times, especially around Walsh.

I lowered my head, using two fingers to force her head in my direction. "I don't think I need to tell you that you are here to provide comfort for Walsh. He needs to know that you're doing well, enjoying the time you've spent with me. Do not reach out for help or decide to become rebellious."

"I know. If I do then you'll punish me. I guess I'll get used to that." As hard as she tried to make her voice sound impassive, there was no mistaking the hurt and confusion she felt. She was such a strong woman, but she seemed even more vulnerable in my hold, the glisten in her eyes nearly tearing me apart. She was stunning, even more so than the night before, the longing running like wildfire through my veins.

I longed to capture her mouth, thrusting my tongue inside and driving us both into the throes of ecstasy, but I'd committed to myself that I'd never touch her again. She certainly deserved better than me.

She didn't fight me when I pressed my hand against the small of her back, leading her inside, but she remained tense.

As expected, there were several politicians, members of law enforcement and even a few celebrities. I continuously scanned the rooms as I walked her through, finally guiding us toward one of the bars.

"So this is what crime will help pay for."

I wrapped my hand around her arm, squeezing, tugging her close against me. There was nothing I could say at this point. "What would you like to drink?"

"Wine. Red wine." Her terse answer was in reference to the blood she'd seen.

As I caught Vladimir's eye, his attention immediately shifted to Candy. Then a smile broke out across his face. He pushed his way through the crowd, heading in our direction.

"Kirill. You're finally here," he said, glancing at the bartender. "Make certain they are well taken care of. They are family."

I sensed Candy tensing, uncertain what he meant.

"Has our guest arrived?" I asked, noticing both Alexei and Sevastian moving through the crowd, the brothers almost carbon copies of each other.

"Yes, he's annoying everyone in another room. We'll get to business momentarily, but first things first. So this is the woman who captured my boy's heart. I'm Vladimir Kozlov. I understand you're Candy Lancaster."

I'd never seen Vladimir this way, gregarious, his eyes lighting up as he took Candy's hands into his. He'd also never called me his boy.

For the first time, Candy seemed flabbergasted, although she recovered quickly. "Sadly, I'm not entirely certain Kirill has a heart."

I noticed Vladimir's daughter approaching, Dimitre not far behind. He grinned seeing Candy then lifted his eyebrows when I gave him a harsh look. At least Candy wouldn't be left alone to fend for herself.

Vladimir glanced into my eyes, thoroughly amused. "Just like I heard. She is full of life. She'll keep you on your toes, Kirill. While this is a party, if you'll excuse Kirill for just a few minutes, there is one small piece of business that needs to be handled. I'll leave you in the capable hands of my daughter, who decided to grace us with her presence, finally able to take a few days away from the New York City Ballet. Tatiana, this is Candy. Candy has aspirations of being on Broadway."

"That's amazing," Tatiana beamed. "Come with me. I know where it's not so damn stuffy."

"Daughter!" Vladimir huffed.

It seemed everyone knew my business. There were no secrets inside the family. None.

Tatiana giggled and grabbed Candy's hand. There was something almost normal about the moment, although I wasn't a good judge. When Candy turned her head, her eyes held the same sense of longing that I knew could be seen in mine.

Sighing, I ordered a bourbon, more out of appearance than anything.

"She's beautiful," Vladimir stated. While he flanked my side, he remained turned in the other direction, keeping a close eye on the room.

"She wants nothing to do with me." My God, the sound of my voice made it almost unrecognizable.

He darted a quick glance. "That's too bad. I can tell how important she's become to you. You'd be surprised what some time apart can do."

"I'm not holding my breath. I assume we're making the offer tonight?"

Vladimir waved to someone in the room. "Yes. News of Yuri's disappearance has already spread."

I gritted my teeth. "I should have known it wouldn't remain off the radar for long."

"These things never do. I suggest we get this over with so we can enjoy the evening."

I waited for my drink, searching until I caught glimpse of Candy before trailing behind him. Alexei managed to convince Walsh that it was in his best interest to follow us into Vladimir's private office, Sevastian closing the door after everyone was inside. He would ensure no one entered the room.

"If this is your attempt at coercing me into giving you carte blanche with regard to your project, you don't know me very well," Michael huffed then guzzled some of his drink. I was able to gather the stench of scotch from where I stood. "And if you think you're going to influence me with Candy's presence, then think again."

Jesus Christ. The man couldn't care less about his own flesh and blood. Bastard.

Alexei chuckled and moved to one of the chairs, making himself at home.

"Mr. Walsh, it would seem that you have no understanding of what is actually going on within your precious council." Vladimir continued to beam. The man was in his element.

Michael snorted, lowering his head and inhaling the fumes from his drink.

"Why don't we make it easier for the man," I said, keeping my tone flat. "I'm certain you're aware of the name Shane Dunnigan."

He laughed, as if I was telling a joke. "That pompous pinhead? He's worthless."

"No longer the case," Alexei added. "Your boy, Rory O'Leary. Do you realize who his father was?"

"Of course I do. So what?" Michael asked, still laughing. "His father was ousted long before I came into the picture."

"Ah, but that's not true. Is it?" I grinned and walked in front of him, staring him in the eyes. "You were the one who leaked the information that he was involved with the Irish mob, the pinhead you were talking about? Only that was nothing more than a fabrication. Correct?" I loved it when I was right. "It would appear that Rory found out. Now, since his father killed himself after losing almost everything, Rory took it upon himself to take revenge on the person who was responsible. You."

"That's bullshit." Michael tried to walk away, but Vladimir stopped him from moving.

"I suggest you listen to what the man has to say," Vladimir said quietly.

"Not only did Rory abduct Candy, but he planned on running for your seat in November, and from what I understand, he had enough support to win."

"However, that was only the beginning. You see, Rory was tightly connected with Shane. In fact, they were very good friends. They even grew up together," Alexei took over from me.

"I just saw Candy a few minutes ago. You're bluffing." Michael cursed under his breath.

"Think again, old man. Kirill is the only reason she's alive. She's currently under his protection, where she will stay unless you don't accept the deal we're prepared to offer you," Alexei stated, grinning.

"If you dare hurt her, I will kill you." Poor Michael's face turned beet red.

"You don't have enough followers, Walsh. Nobody cares about your commitment to the union, although I'm beginning to wonder if the sole reason for that is because of the kickbacks you receive." As soon as I saw the nervous tic appear in the corner of his mouth, I knew my hunch was right. I could tell Vladimir was grinning, rolling forward and backward on his feet.

"That's... a damn lie!" he sputtered.

I moved around him in a full circle. "Is it now?" I wanted him good and nervous. "I can only imagine what the scandal will do to your career and even those of your children. You don't seem to fully appreciate just how far Shane's tentacles reach, or the damage he's done already."

The man didn't deserve to know the details or the plans already in motion for Shane's ultimate demise.

It took almost four minutes before he sagged. "What deal are you talking about?"

Alexei jerked to a standing position, more excited than I'd seen him in a long time. "It's simple, really. The Irishmen have plans on attempting to take over the unions in their entirety. As you might imagine, that's making several different communities very nervous. We're in the position of making certain that doesn't happen."

"In exchange?" Michael sounded like a beaten man.

"In exchange," I continued, "for you supporting our construction projects. It's a simple as that. We'll also make certain that you aren't troubled any longer."

He was actually debating his answer. I glared at Alexei, wanting nothing more than to teach the man a lesson; however, this wasn't the time or the place.

"What about Candy? She is innocent in all of this."

"As of right now, Candy belongs to me. Period. She isn't a part of this equation and you will make certain your son leaves her alone."

I glared him in the eyes, remaining unblinking.

He took his time, polishing off his drink then moving to Vladimir's desk, slamming it down on purpose. "You have a deal, but my warning about Candy remains. She is a good girl, sweet and loving. She certainly doesn't deserve to be turned into your whore."

Vladimir knew the limits of what I could tolerate.

I wrapped my hand around Michael's shirt, able to lift him off his feet by several inches. The sound of material tearing was the least of my concern. I dragged him as close as I could stand, snarling for effect. "Mr. Walsh. I pay for my whores. Candy is utter perfection. She's my princess."

Just saying the words drove a stake through my heart. Goddamn it, I wanted her with me. I needed to feel her body curled up against mine, to have the joy of tasting her sweet mouth every morning.

Fuck.

I loved her.

Hell, I wasn't certain I could live without her.

He nodded, the fear of God finally driven into him. I let him go, jerking away from him and turning around. I couldn't stand the sight of him any longer.

"If you honor the deal you made, Michael, we will have no issues in the future," Vladimir said more in passing, but the unsaid meaning was clear.

"While I appreciate your generosity in inviting me here. I think I've developed a severe illness," Michael snarled before walking out. I studied his reflection in the window, barely able to control my anger.

Alexei chuckled. "I think we have him under control."

"For now," I said. "But don't be fooled by his 'aw shucks' attitude. He will strike again."

"Kirill is right. Perhaps you'd enjoy spending time with your lovely princess instead of being here. Maybe on the way you could determine where our guest will be spending the rest of his evening."

I took a gulp of my drink. "I think I'll do that." I wasn't in the mood to hear what he might have to say if he learned that by this time tomorrow, Candy would be on her own.

As I headed out of the office, finally catching a glimpse of her a few seconds later, I could hear her laugh. She seemed entirely different, enjoying spending time with Tatiana. For a fleeting moment, I allowed myself to wonder what it would like to consider her family.

Then I shoved it aside, remembering Alexei's warning. He was right. Falling in love would do nothing but bring me additional pain.

I moved through the crowd, touching her on the arm. The same chemical reaction occurred, electricity bolting through both of us. Yet when she lifted her head, she'd managed to hide her emotions.

"I'm afraid we need to go."

"No fair, Kirill. I think Candy and I can become good friends," Tatiana whined.

"There will be another time," I insisted, pulling on Candy's arm.

"Nice to meet you," Candy said after I'd already pulled her away. "Why the hurry?"

"Concluding business. Then I'll take you home."

"Not my home. It's your home."

I held back any further comments, taking long strides toward the front door. When we moved outside, I was able to catch a glimpse of Walsh's car before he sped off. I eased her inside my vehicle, jogging to the other side, jumping in and immediately starting the engine.

"What's wrong?" she asked, barely snapping her seatbelt before I took off.

"We initiated a deal with Michael Walsh that will be beneficial to everyone, you included."

"What exactly does that mean?" she asked, her tone softening.

I rounded the corner, pressing down on the gas, able to see Walsh's taillights in the distance. I'd never had to hide my emotions before. I'd never cared about anything enough to need to. "You'll be set free."

The words were more difficult to say than I'd ever imagined.

When I didn't hear anything, not a breath or a squeal of joy, I glanced in her direction. Darkness was all around us, but I managed to see a single tear trickling down her face.

I'd seen enough combat that when my hackles rose, I knew I had an issue to contend with. Hissing, I glared into the rearview mirror then all around me. Something was definitely wrong. I yanked my phone into my hand, dialing Dimitre.

"What's wrong?" she asked.

"Maybe nothing." Oh, there was something alright. Just as I pressed send, I noticed two pairs of headlights in the distance approaching rapidly, at least one more up ahead.

"What's wrong?" Dimitre asked, answering after only one ring.

"I think I have an issue."

The two cars from behind slammed on their accelerator, I did as well. "Ambush," I managed, snarling as one of the vehicles attempted to pass me. I couldn't allow that to happen.

"Oh, my God," Candy muttered.

"Jesus," Dimitre snarled. "On our way."

"Hold on, baby. Just hold on." Tossing the phone on the dashboard, I kept two hands on the wheel, glancing out the windshield. I was gaining on Walsh's car. Suddenly a flash of light caught my attention. I knew exactly what it was. "Fucking Molotov cocktail."

Flames instantly erupted inside Walsh's car. As he started driving erratically, weaving from side to side, I captured another flash in the rearview mirror.

"Get down!" I roared, doing everything I could to keep us from crashing. The bottle tumbled over my car, pitching into the woods.

But not the second. The boom as it was driven through the window was like an explosion.

Candy screamed. The two cars from behind suddenly slowed, the one from in front of Walsh's car ready to pass on the driver's side. Walsh couldn't keep control of his vehicle any longer, jerking to the left and careening into a patch of trees. Flames engulfed the back seat. I had to get us the fuck out of here.

As the assailant's car whizzed past, the asshole took the opportunity to fire an assault rifle. Candy's continued wails echoed in my ears, and I struggled to keep some control. "Hold on, baby. Just. Fucking. Hold—"

Whoosh!

Boom!

I managed to jerk the car to a halt, but not before slamming it against the hill on the passenger side. Smoke was rolling from the engine. I had to act fast. "Are you okay?"

"Uh-huh," Candy moaned, her head lolled forward. I yanked at my seatbelt, fighting with hers, the smoke turning black. I'd have one chance to get her out. I threw open the door, sliding both arms under her and yanking. Fuck. I heard tires squealing behind us. The motherfuckers were coming back.

"Come on, baby. Just hold onto me."

She managed to drape her arm around my neck, digging in her fingers. I jerked back, stumbling then turning away, racing away from the fire. The blast shoved me forward, but I managed to stay on my feet, fighting to get her to the side of the road.

"You need to get Walsh out," she said as I eased her down.

I threw a look over my shoulder, unable to see anything but blazing orange.

And I heard two powerful engines.

"I'll do what I can. Stay here. Do not move. Don't fight me. They're coming back." I had no time to waste. Yanking my weapon into my hand, I took off running, almost immediately blinded by the dual set of headlights. There was little I could do. I took a stance in the middle of the road, lifting my weapon, waiting. Still waiting. When I knew they were in close enough range, I started firing.

Pop! Pop! Pop! Pop! Pop! Pop! Pop!

And I kept firing.

Both drivers finally lost control. I managed to jump to the side, the first vehicle driving straight into the craggy rock portion of the hill, the other flying off into the ravine. The blasts were horrific, but far away from Candy. Gasping, I shoved my weapon into my pocket, racing toward Walsh's car. He'd managed to dump his body out the door, his leg caught by a portion of the vehicle.

While he was breathing, he was unconscious.

A part of me wanted to leave his sorry ass there, but I'd made a promise to the woman I loved. The smoke was so thick, it burned my eyes, but I felt my way until I realized why he was caught. I jammed the weight of my body against the seat, barely moving it. I had maybe four seconds left before both of us would be incinerated. I shoved again, pulling with everything I had. When his leg was freed, the force I'd used pitched us both down the side of the ravine.

Taking gasping breaths, I closed my eyes as the car exploded, finally rolling him over and pressing my fingers against his pulse. "You're alive, buddy. You better not cross us." I fought to get up the hill, just reaching the edge when I heard her scream. I reacted, my adrenaline pumping, refusing to allow anything else to happen to her.

I took off running, able to hear several vehicles approaching. At least the fucking cavalry had arrived. When I was within fifteen feet, I stopped short.

"That's far enough, Russian."

With the only light the fire from my vehicle, the darkness shrouded his identity, but I was clearly able to see he had his arm wrapped around her neck, using her as a shield, his weapon pointed at her temple.

I raised my gun, trying to figure out how best to handle this.

"Let me go," Candy hissed, struggling with him, almost pulling away.

"Shut up!" the man snarled.

Whatever he had planned, this wasn't going to end well.

The others were forced to stop their vehicles several hundred yards away given the horrific debris, but I sensed their approach on foot.

"In about five seconds, you're going to be surrounded. Let her go and I'll allow you to live," I said, the deep husk in my tone unrecognizable.

"We're not playing by your rules. We're playing by mine," he answered. "It's simple. You choose. You or the girl will die. Which do you prefer?"

I took a deep breath, praying that I hadn't used the last bullet in the clip. "Neither." I pressed the trigger, releasing a single bullet. When she screamed again, I lunged forward, realizing I was out of ammunition. Even though the asshole was tumbling to the ground, he was preparing to fire, killing Candy.

I jerked her arm, freeing her from his hand, kicking the weapon out of his hand as it discharged.

"Oh, God." She clung to me, gasping for air.

"What the hell?" Alexei snarled, taking aim and killing the assailant.

I pulled her away, hiding her face. "They came from both... sides." Winded, I nodded to Dimitri and Sevastian as several other soldiers approached. "Walsh is in the trees. He's alive but needs an ambulance."

"Jesus Christ," Sevastian huffed. "That's Shane Dunnigan."

Fuck. Whether Walsh had been the intended victim or not no longer mattered.

"Get them out of here," Alexei huffed, walking closer and nodding several times. "You are a one-man killing machine."

At this moment, I didn't take it as a compliment.

As I turned away, she lifted her head, smiling as she cupped my face. "You're my hero. Twice."

I was also no hero, but at least I'd saved her life, which I would try to continue doing, even if it was from afar. I gathered her into my arms, cradling her against my chest. "Let's get you home."

What she didn't know is that I meant her home, although that would come after she recovered. Only then would I back away, doing my best never to see her again.

CHAPTER 18

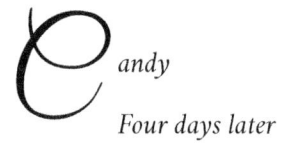

Candy
Four days later

Quiet.

The condo was far too quiet as far as I was concerned. While I'd had everything I'd needed to recover, including the best medical care, Kirill had purposely stayed away most of the time. But I'd felt him at night, watching over me, making certain I was okay. He'd kept his promise, able to save Michael seconds before his car exploded, but that was almost the only thing Kirill had told me.

Then it was as if he'd retreated from my life. I couldn't understand if I'd done something wrong or if becoming my savior on two occasions had forced him into an ugly realization that I was nothing more than an anchor around his neck.

Maybe I shouldn't care, but all I could do was think about him.

Him, the monster, savior, sinner, and saint.

And the man I loved.

I remained in the bedroom, the first one I'd stayed in, only because I didn't feel comfortable anywhere else. Seeing him was wonderful, but when he'd walk away, it broke my heart every time. I heard a light rap on the door and brightened, my stomach lurching.

"Ms. Lancaster. *Señor* Sabatin told me to bring you this. He said to change and meet him in the foyer in one hour."

I was immediately saddened, slumping against the wall. Another dress. Another occasion. I hated to admit it to myself, but I was fearful of seeing whatever he'd purchased for me. Maybe it was a wedding dress for all I knew. Then I'd be imprisoned for the rest of my life. Would that be so bad? No, except I wanted to be the one to make the choice. And it was something I wasn't prepared to do. I also knew all the passion we'd shared was gone by his choice.

"Thank you, Desiree. I appreciate it."

"*Si, señorita*," she said, smiling for the first time since I'd been here. I remained standing at the window, allowing my thoughts to shift to all the fond memories I had of Kirill. At least they were enough, but a part of me wanted more of the man. His passion. His dominance. Sighing, I finally found whatever courage I had left to take the bag off the dress.

For some reason, it wasn't what I'd expected. It was beautiful, but sequins seemed an odd choice. Maybe he was taking me to another show.

"Stop it."

He'd thought of shoes and lingerie. Laughing, I gathered the items, moving into the bathroom. Something was very strange, and I couldn't quite put my finger on it.

I took my time getting ready, styling my hair for the first time since the accident. Accident. What a ridiculous thing to call it. The people had tried to murder us and almost succeeded. Shivering, I stood back glancing at my reflection. I felt like a big band singer from a long time before, but I had to say, the dress was absolutely perfect for my figure, the deep emerald color highlighting my eyes.

The man had exquisite taste.

After gathering my purse, I stood in the room, trying to calm my nerves. Maybe I was making him wait just a little longer as well. Laughing, I finally headed down the stairs. The man was pacing, glaring at his watch.

When he heard me, he jerked up his head. "You're late."

"Just by a few minutes. I was… teasing you." I could tell he was angry, frustrated with me. Even stranger, while he was dressed nicely in his usual dark suit and shirt, he wasn't even wearing a tie. What the hell was going on?

"Come. We need to hurry."

"Why are you being this way?" I asked. No, I was demanding.

He shifted his gaze and while I didn't know him but so well, I could swear he had a smirk on his face, like he was hiding something from me. As usual, he remained quiet on the short elevator ride, pressing his hand against my back and guiding me into the garage. There was no limo, but there was a waiting SUV, the windows blacked out.

As soon as we approached, one of his men jumped out of the passenger seat, opening the door and allowing Kirill to usher me inside. This time, there was no conversation between the men, Kirill easing in beside me. There was no champagne, only bottled water and he remained rigid as the driver headed out of the garage.

"Where are we going?" I asked.

He handed me one of the bottles. "Drink this. And it's a surprise."

"O-kay." I did as I was told, remaining jumpy as hell. Was he selling me off to the highest bidder? At this point, I wouldn't put anything past him. I hated thinking that way, but with the lack of conversation, my imagination had gone wild. I could tell he wasn't going to say a damn thing to me. Not a single word.

I crushed myself against the seat, sipping water, longing for champagne or wine, anything to make this a celebration.

He'd risked his life to save mine. Twice. Twice!

Now he wouldn't talk to me.

I twisted my hand around the bottle, enjoying the crunching sound, wanting nothing more than to toss it into his face. Maybe that would get a reaction.

Good idea.

So I did.

Shocked I actually went through with it, I slapped my hand across my mouth, laughing until he turned his face in my direction.

But he remained silent, merely studying me with narrowed eyes and a heaving chest. There was the same amazing electricity crackling through us, but his eyes were cold.

While he wiped his face, brushing the remnants on his trousers, he didn't react. No yanking me over his lap. No pulling me into his arms. I didn't know what to think.

I took a deep breath, forced to realize whatever was going on, he had no intention of telling me. As I concentrated on looking out the window, I realized he was headed down the road leading to the Gershwin Theater. Was he trying to torture me with memories? My stomach was in knots, my mind one huge blur similar to the way it was the first night I met him.

Now I hated the memories.

But they continued, one coming after the other.

When the driver started to slow the engine, prickly sensations coursed through my body. Then the SUV was pulled to a stop directly in front. "What are you doing? It's dark."

"Dark?"

"The theater is dark. The show is closed, and another isn't opening for two months."

"Ah." He climbed out, closing the door.

What in God's name did he have up his sleeve?

Frowning, I folded my arms as he opened the door, sticking his arm inside. I refused to take it.

He leaned down, giving me a look that indicated I better obey him. I looked away.

Then he crouched down. "Candy. You have a dream that's amazing. I want that for you so much. I'm sorry for the partial charade but I know you well enough that if I'd told you about the surprise, you would have fought me the entire time."

"What are you talking about?"

He smiled, brushing the back of his hand across my cheek. The tingling sensations were just like before, desire swelling deep within.

"Trust me. For once, can you do that?" He lifted his hand again, giving me a nod.

"I do trust you, more than you know." *And I love you. I love you. I. Love. You.* Why was it so hard to say?

BEAUTIFUL VILLAIN

I took his hand, allowing him to lead me onto the sidewalk. Then he wrapped his arm around me, leading me toward one of the side doors, issuing two hard knocks.

"Please tell me what this is," I begged.

"This is your audition. Your private audition."

What? What had he just said?

"Are you fucking out of your mind? That's not possible. I don't know the music. I mean, I do, but not well enough. I haven't practiced in a lifetime. At least a week and a half. And what's with this dress? That's like the clothing the... lead would wear and I'm not auditioning for the lead so..." At first, I was blabbering away, nervous as could be. Then my words trailed off.

"You are auditioning for the lead. I happen to know the producer very well and told him about your magical voice. He made time in his schedule for a private audition."

"You mean you threatened him."

He laughed, the booming sound the one I remembered. "I did not threaten him, little brat. This is your time. You can do this."

I opened my mouth twice, squeaking like some damn mouse. "I'm terrified. I'm not good enough. I'm going to faint. I'm going to throw up. I'm going to-—"

He pressed two fingers against my lips, shaking his head. "You're going to be incredible." As he lowered his head, pressing his lips against mine, I said it just a second before the kiss.

"I love you."

The feel of his arms was amazing, but I wanted more. So much more.

The sound of the door opening interrupted us.

"Ms. Lancaster? Mr. Chevelle is expecting you. Right this way."

I smiled at the girl, reaching out and gripping Kirill's hand. "You are coming with me, aren't you?"

"I wouldn't miss this for the world."

Over the next several minutes, I *was* sent to a magical place, Kirill's gift holding a special place in my heart for all eternity.

Being on the stage had meant everything to me, but seeing his face sitting in the fourth row, listening to me sing and watching me dance gave me the courage I needed. I'd never enjoyed anything so much. While I knew this was for not, it didn't matter. What Kirill had done was unforgettable.

He had a heart.

And a soul.

And I loved him.

When the song ended, I lowered my head, able to hear the hard beating of my heart.

Time ticked away, anxiety returning.

"Ms. Lancaster. I'd like a word with you," Mr. Chevelle said seconds later.

"Of course." As I walked down the stairs, I couldn't seem to take my eyes off Kirill, his eyes just as piercing even from the distance. As Mr. Chevelle began to talk, I fell into a fog, terror and joy, love and happiness, sorrow and anger rushing into me.

Broadway. It had been my place of dreams, everything I'd ever wanted. Now I was going to be the lead in a play. On Broadway. And I knew it had more to do with Kirill's relationship with the producer, but I was determined to make them both proud.

"We'll see you in a few days," Mr. Chevelle stated as he shook my hand.

As I walked toward Kirill, for the first time I saw tears in his eyes.

This was his special and last gift, one that set me free.

He was saying goodbye.

* * *

Two months later

. . .

"Woo hoo! A star is born!" Rian shouted it out to the entire bar. I wanted to kill him. "My cousin, my beautiful cousin has her debut on Broadway tonight!"

There wasn't a person in the bar who wasn't clapping. I think they knew Rian would kill them if they didn't.

Still, a blush crept up my cheeks. I was scared to freaking death to go on stage. I'd been perfectly fine until earlier that morning. Now I wanted to run into the bathroom, shut the door, and never come out.

"Whoop! Whoop! Whoop!" one of the rowdy customers yelled, swinging his fist in the air.

Tanya laughed as she walked toward me. "You have fans already."

"Yeah, yeah." Not the right one. My thoughts drifted to Kirill, which I hadn't allowed to happen in almost a month. I'd been far too busy. Between catching as many shifts as possible at the bar and rehearsing on the play, I barely had time to sleep.

But now, the thoughts crowded in, slamming me hard with longing. He'd been so sweet after the audition, taking me to dinner as a celebration. Then he'd driven me to my apartment, explaining that it had been ransacked but that he'd bought some new things and he'd have the remainder of my clothes returned within a day, which he had.

He'd had the entire apartment refurbished, purchasing new furniture that I never would have been able to afford.

He'd even had a baby grand placed in the center of the living room. He'd thought of everything.

But he wasn't there. Ever.

The apartment upstairs had been vacated before he'd taken me home. The goodbye had been more like so long. No passionate embraces or words of adoration. Just… goodbye

And I'd spent the night under the covers crying my eyes out.

Then I'd realized that he'd given me several gifts, including my freedom. But tonight was different.

"What's wrong?" Tanya asked. "You're going to do great. You have your entire family there to cheer you on." Sadly, my mother and father couldn't afford the trip.

"Ugh. Don't remind me." I half laughed, grateful that they were so thrilled.

"But you want *him* there. Right?"

"Him?"

She rolled her eyes. "The godlike figure you mentioned, the one that was in here. The bad boy of the mafia world."

I shook my head. "That's been over for months."

"Two months, sugar. Two. That means nothing in the scheme of life. Just admit it. You miss him."

"Fine. Okay. I miss him. A lot. That means nothing right now. I have a career to worry about."

"Right. I hear you talking but you're lying." She backed away, grinning. "You never know what might happen. Just allow fate to take over. I think tonight you're going to become a star."

Fate. Uh-huh. See where that had gotten me.

I totaled my receipts and took a deep breath. Maybe I was ready after all. A star. I liked the sound of that. Only it would be more wonderful if I had someone to share it with. As I gathered my things, I was surprised to see Rian standing in the doorway.

"I'm proud of you, kiddo," he said.

"I'm proud of me too."

He shook his head. "I never apologized for what I said to you. It was wrong. You are more than capable of living your life. You've proven that more than once. You're very strong."

"If you mean because I was able to walk away from Kirill, please just drop it."

There was a thoughtful look in his eyes. Then he smiled. "Kirill isn't such a bad guy. He did save my father's life."

"Yeah, he did, and he was wonderful to me."

"Love has a funny way of finding you when you least expect it. Enjoy this ride, cuz. Second chances don't come around often."

"No, they don't."

Not for me anyway.

* * *

Exhilaration.

Applause.

Cheers.

As the audience erupted, getting to their feet, I did what everybody told me to do. I basked in the moment, recognizing my fellow actors before taking a bow. While there'd been a few glitches, the night had been incredible, the performance sold out.

And my parents had been in the first row. They'd surprised me after all. I'd seen tears in my mother's eyes, and she'd been the first one on her feet, her cheer heard over everyone else.

When the curtain came down, I fell to the floor, gasping for air.

"You did great, Candy!"

"What a fabulous job."

"We all did great."

The shouts were numerous, the entire cast excited. I was elated, happier than I'd ever been in my life. Then why was a single tear sliding down my cheek? I watched it fall before rising to my feet. This was just the beginning.

I scurried with the others, moving toward my dressing room. The flurry of activity was tremendous, the energy and loud voices like a marvelous party in full swing.

But sadness started to creep into my heart.

There were people everywhere, congratulations all around. It took me over ten minutes to wade through the number of people. When I finally reached my door, I sucked in my breath. My name was on the door. My name. Mine. I pressed my fingers across it, chuckling like a schoolgirl.

I opened the door, turning in a full circle then staring at my reflection in the vanity mirror.

"Candy. These are for you." The assistant had been a godsend the last few weeks, keeping us supplied with water and juice, making certain everything worked as it should.

When I turned around, I gasped. There had to be at least three dozen white roses if not more. "They're gorgeous. Who are they from?" A cold chill trickled down my spine. Was it possible?

"I don't know. There's a card. Where do you want them?"

"Right here is fine." The scent was incredible. I reached for the card then pulled away, biting my lower lip and snatching it into my hand. I held my breath as I opened it, expecting to see the Walsh family name.

As soon as I read the card, I was unable to stop the tears from falling.

. . .

Candy,

You were incredible tonight. You are the star I knew you'd be. I hope you enjoyed my surprise. Break a leg every night and know I'm thinking of you always.

Kirill

His surprise. Why did I have a feeling he'd brought my parents here?

"George. Were these dropped off?" I croaked.

"No. A guy gave me fifty bucks to hand deliver them to you."

"When? When did that happen?"

"Right after the show. I'm surprised you didn't see him."

He didn't want me to see him.

Fate.

Yes, fate had intervened. I took off racing out of the room, pushing and shoving my way through the crowd. "Please, let me through. Just let me through."

There was only one exit that he could go through connected to this area. I had to find him. Gasping, I took off my heels as the crowd thinned, running down the stairs and toward the exit. If he left this time, I doubted there would be a next.

Please let me find him. Please.

Then he was there, ready to leave my life for a second time. I leaned over the railing, struggling to breathe.

"Kirill!"

I was certain he hadn't heard me. When he stopped, I continued walking, struggling to keep from falling down the last few steps.

As he turned around, the tears continued to fall, staining my face.

For a few seconds, he acted as if he was going to walk out again. Then he lunged toward me, sweeping me off my feet.

"*Moy prekrasnyy ognennyy shar,*" he whispered.

My beautiful fireball. No words had ever sounded sweeter. He cupped my cheek, lowering his head.

"I've missed you," I whispered. "I couldn't stop thinking about you."

"I've missed you, my *printsessa*. You managed to crawl into my heart."

"My parents. You brought them here, didn't you?"

"I remembered what you told me. I wanted this to be special," he whispered, his scent intoxicating.

"I don't want this to end, Kirill. I can't... I can't live without you. I don't care about what you do or what could happen."

"There's no need for any more words. I have no intention of ever leaving you again. You are mine. Not just for now, but forever." Growling, he captured my mouth, dragging me against the heat of his body. All the passion that had been pent up inside, all the need and longing came bursting to the surface, tiny bottle rockets exploding all around us.

He pulled me onto my toes, the kiss becoming a passionate roar. The taste of him was even more incredible than I remembered, my body thoroughly aroused. When he finally broke the kiss, he nuzzled against my neck, nipping my ear. And his husky whisper was even more powerful than his tight hold.

"You will learn to obey me, my perfect rebel. If not…"

I shuddered. He didn't need to finish the sentence. I knew exactly what to expect and I couldn't wait.

After all, fantasies could come true…

The End

AFTERWORD

Stormy Night Publications would like to thank you for your interest in our books.

If you liked this book (or even if you didn't), we would really appreciate you leaving a review on the site where you purchased it. Reviews provide useful feedback for us and our authors, and this feedback (both positive comments and constructive criticism) allows us to work even harder to make sure we provide the content our customers want to read.

If you would like to check out more books from Stormy Night Publications, if you want to learn more about our company, or if you would like to join our mailing list, please visit our website at:

http://www.stormynightpublications.com

BOOKS OF THE BENEDETTI EMPIRE SERIES

Cruel Prince

Catherine's father conspired to have my father killed, and that debt to the Benedetti family must be settled. Just as he took something from me, I will take something from him.

His daughter.

She will be mine to punish and ravage, but when she suffers it will not be for his sins.

It will be for my pleasure.

She will beg, but it will be for me to claim her in the most shameful ways imaginable.

She will scream, but it will be because she doesn't think she can bear another climax.

But when she surrenders at last, it will not be to her captor.

It will be to her husband.

Ruthless Prince

Alexandra is a senator's daughter, used to mingling in the company of the rich and powerful, but tonight she will learn that there are men who play by different rules.

Men like me.

I could romance her. I could seduce her and then carry her gently to my bed.

But that can wait. Tonight I'm going to wring one ruthless climax after another from her quivering body with her bottom burning from my belt and her throat sore from screaming.

She will know she is mine before she even knows she is my bride.

Savage Prince

Gillian's father may be a powerful Irish mob boss, but he owes a blood debt to my family, and when I came to collect I didn't ask permission before taking his daughter as payment.

It was not up to him… or to her.

I will make her my bride, but I am not the kind of man who will wait until our wedding night to bare her and claim what belongs to me. She will walk down the aisle wet, well-used, and sore.

Her dress will hide the marks from my belt that taught her the consequences of disobeying her husband, but nothing will hide her blushes as her arousal drips down her thighs with each step.

By the time she says her vows she will already be mine.

BOOKS OF THE MERCILESS KINGS SERIES

King's Captive

Emily Porter saw me kill a man who betrayed my family and she helped put me behind bars. But someone with my connections doesn't stay in prison long, and she is about to learn the hard way that there is a price to pay for crossing the boss of the King dynasty. A very, very painful price...

She's going to cry for me as I blister that beautiful bottom, then she's going to scream for me as I ravage her over and over again, taking her in the most shameful ways she can imagine. But leaving her well-punished and well-used is just the beginning of what I have in store for Emily.

I'm going to make her my bride, and then I'm going to make her mine completely.

King's Hostage

When my life was threatened, Michael King didn't just take matters into his own hands.

He took me.

When he carried me off it was partly to protect me, but mostly it was because he wanted me.

I didn't choose to go with him, but it wasn't up to me. That's why I'm naked, wet, and sore in an opulent Swiss chalet with my bottom still burning from the belt of the infuriatingly sexy mafia boss who brought me here, punished me when I fought him, and then savagely made me his.

We'll return when things are safe in New Orleans, but I won't be going back to my old home.

I belong to him now, and he plans to keep me.

King's Possession

Her father had to be taught what happens when you cross a King, but that isn't why Genevieve Rossi is sore, well-used, and waiting for me to claim her in the only way I haven't already.

She's sore because she thought she could embarrass me in public without being punished.

She's well-used because after I spanked her I wanted more, and I take what I want.

She's waiting for me in my bed because she's my bride, and tonight is our wedding night.

I'm not going to be gentle with her, but when she wakes up tomorrow morning wet and blushing her cheeks won't be crimson because of the shameful things I did to her naked, quivering body.

It will be because she begged for all of them.

King's Toy

Vincenzo King thought I knew something about a man who betrayed him, but that isn't why I'm on my way to New Orleans well-used and sore with my backside still burning from his belt.

When he bared and punished me maybe it was just business, but what came after was not.

It was savage, it was shameful, and it was very, very personal.

I'm his toy now, and not the kind you keep in its box on the shelf.

He's going to play rough with me.

He's going to get me all wet and dirty.

Then he's going to do it all again tomorrow.

King's Demands

Julieta Morales hoped to escape an unwanted marriage, but the moment she got into my car her fate was sealed. She will have a husband, but it won't be the cartel boss her father chose for her.

It will be me.

But I'm not the kind of man who takes his bride gently amid rose petals on her wedding night. She'll learn to satisfy her King's demands with her bottom burning and her hair held in my fist.

She'll promise obedience when she speaks her vows, but she'll be mastered long before then.

King's Temptation

I didn't think I needed Dimitri Kristoff's protection, but it wasn't up to me. With a kingpin from a rival family coming after me, he took charge, took off his belt, and then took what he wanted.

He knows I'm not used to doing as I'm told. He just doesn't care.

The stripes seared across my bare bottom left me sore and sorry, but it was what came after that truly left me shaken. The princess of the King family shouldn't be on her knees for anyone, let alone this Bratva brute who has decided to claim for himself what he was meant to safeguard.

Nobody gave me to him, but I'm his anyway.

Now he's going to make sure I know it.

BOOKS OF THE MAFIA MASTERS SERIES

His as Payment

Caroline Hargrove thinks she is mine because her father owed me a debt, but that isn't why she is sitting in my car beside me with her bottom sore inside and out. She's wet, well-used, and coming with me whether she likes it or not because I decided I want her, and I take what I want.

As a senator's daughter, she probably thought no man would dare lay a hand on her, let alone spank her thoroughly and then claim her beautiful body in the most shameful ways possible.

She was wrong. Very, very wrong. She's going to be mastered, and I won't be gentle about it.

Taken as Collateral

Francesca Alessandro was just meant to be collateral, held captive as a warning to her father, but then she tried to fight me. She ended up sore and soaked as I taught her a lesson with my belt and then screaming with every savage climax as I taught her to obey in a much more shameful way.

She's mine now. Mine to keep. Mine to protect. Mine to use as hard and as often as I please.

Forced to Cooperate

Willow Church is not the first person who tried to put a bullet in me. She's just the first I let live. Now she will pay the price in the most shameful way imaginable. The stripes from my belt will teach her to obey, but what happens to her sore, red bottom after that will teach the real lesson.

She will be used mercilessly, over and over, and every brutal climax will remind her of the humiliating truth: she never even had a chance against me. Her body always knew its master.

Claimed as Revenge

Valencia Rivera became mine the moment her father broke the agreement he made with me. She thought she had a say in the matter, but my belt across her beautiful bottom taught her otherwise and a night spent screaming her surrender into the sheets left her in no doubt she belongs to me.

Using her hard and often will not be all it takes to tame her properly, but it will be a good start…

Made to Beg

Sierra Fox showed up at my door to ask for my protection, and I gave it to her… for a price. She belongs to me now, and I'm going to use her beautiful body as thoroughly as I please. The only thing for her to decide is how sore her cute little bottom will be when I'm through claiming her.

She came to me begging for help, but as her moans and screams grow louder with every brutal climax, we both know it won't be long before she begs me for something far more shameful.

BOOKS OF THE ALPHA DYNASTY SERIES

Unchained Beast

As the firstborn of the Dupree family, I have spent my life building the wealth and power of our mafia empire while keeping our dark secret hidden and my savage hunger at bay. But the beast within me cannot be chained forever, and I must claim a mate before I lose control completely…

That is why Coraline LeBlanc is mine.

When I mount and ravage her, it won't be because I want her. It will be because I need her.

But that doesn't mean I won't enjoy stripping her bare and spanking her until she surrenders, then making her beg and scream with every desperate climax as I take what belongs to me.

The beast will claim her, but I will keep her.

Savage Brute

It wasn't his mafia birthright that made Dax Dupree a monster. Years behind bars and a brutal war with a rival organization made him hard as steel, but the beast he can barely control was always there, and without a mate to mark and claim it would soon take hold of him completely.

I didn't know that when he showed up at my bar after closing and spanked me until I was wet and shamefully ready for him to mount and ravage me, or even when I woke the next morning with my throat sore from screaming and his seed still drying on my thighs. But I know it now.

Because I'm his mate.

Ruthless Monster

When Esme Rawlings looks at me, she sees many things. A ruthless mob boss. A key witness to the latest murder in an ongoing turf war. A guardian angel who saved her from a hitman's bullet.

But when I look at her, I see just one thing.

My mate.

She can investigate me as thoroughly as she feels necessary, prying into every aspect of my family's vast mafia empire, but the only truth she really needs to know about me she will learn tonight with her bare bottom burning and her protests drowned out by her screams of climax.

I take what belongs to me.

Ravenous Predator

Suzette Barker thought she could steal from the most powerful mafia boss in Philadelphia. My belt across her naked backside taught her otherwise, but as tears run down her cheeks and her arousal glistens on her bare thighs, there is something more important she will understand soon.

Kneeling at my feet and demonstrating her remorseful surrender in the most shameful way possible won't bring an end to this, nor will her screams of climax as I take her long and hard. She'll be coming with me and I'll be mounting and savagely rutting her as often as I please.

Not just because she owes me.

Because she's my mate.

Merciless Savage

Christoff Dupree doesn't strike me as the kind of man who woos a woman gently, so when I saw the flowers on my kitchen table I knew it wasn't just a gesture of appreciation for saving his life.

This ruthless mafia boss wasn't seducing me. Those roses mean that I belong to him now.

That I'm his to spank into shameful submission before he mounts me and claims me savagely.

That I'm his mate.

MORE MAFIA AND BILLIONAIRE ROMANCES BY PIPER STONE

Caught

If you're forced to come to an arrangement with someone as dangerous as Jagger Calduchi, it means he's about to take what he wants, and you'll give it to him… even if it's your body.

I got caught snooping where I didn't belong, and Jagger made me an offer I couldn't refuse. A week with him where his rules are the only rules, or his bought and paid for cops take me to jail.

He's going to punish me, train me, and master me completely. When he's used me so shamefully I blush just to think about it, maybe he'll let me go home… or maybe he'll decide to keep me.

Ruthless

Treating a mobster shot by a rival's goons isn't really my forte, but when a man is powerful enough to have a whole wing of a hospital cleared out for his protection, you do as you're told.

To make matters worse, this isn't first time I've met Giovanni Calduchi. It turns out my newest patient is the stern, sexy brute who all but dragged me back to his hotel room a couple of nights ago so he could use my body as he pleased, then showed up at my house the next day, stripped me bare, and spanked me until I was begging him to take me even more roughly and shamefully.

Now, with his enemies likely to be coming after me in order to get to him, all I can do is hope he's as good at keeping me safe as he is at keeping me blushing, sore, and thoroughly satisfied.

Dangerous

I knew Erik Chenault was dangerous the moment I saw him. Everything about him should have warned me away, from the scar on his face to the fact that mobsters call him Blade. But I was drawn like a moth to a flame, and I ended up burnt… and blushing, sore, and thoroughly used.

Now he's taken it upon himself to protect me from men like the ones we both tried to leave in our past. He's going to make me his whether I like it or not… but I think I'm going to like it.

Prey

Within moments of setting eyes on Sophia Waters, I was certain of two things. She was going to learn what happens to bad girls who cheat at cards, and I was going to be the one to teach her.

But there was one thing I didn't know as I reddened that cute little bottom and then took her long and hard and oh so shamefully: I wasn't the only one who didn't come here for a game of cards.

I came to kill a man. It turns out she came to protect him.

Nobody keeps me from my target, but I'm in no rush. Not when I'm enjoying this game of cat and mouse so much. I'll even let her catch me one day, and as she screams my name with each brutal climax she'll finally realize the truth. She was never the hunter. She was always the prey.

Given

Stephanie Michaelson was given to me, and she is mine. The sooner she learns that, the less often her cute little bottom will end up well-punished and sore as she is reminded of her place.

But even as she promises obedience with tears running down her cheeks, I know it isn't the sting of my belt that will truly tame her. It is what comes next that will leave her in no doubt she belongs to me. That part will be long, hard, and shameful… and I will make her beg for all of it.

Dangerous Stranger

I came to Spain hoping to start a new life away from dangerous men, but then I met Rafael Santiago. Now I'm not just caught up in the affairs of a mafia boss, I'm being forced into his car.

When I saw something I shouldn't have, Rafael took me captive, stripped me bare, and punished me until he felt certain I'd told him everything I knew about his organization… which was nothing at all. Then he offered me his protection in return for the right to use me as he pleases.

Now that I belong to him, his plans for me are more shameful than I could have ever imagined.

Indebted

After her father stole from me, I could have left Alessandra Toro in jail for a crime she didn't commit. But I have plans for her. A deal with the judge—the kind only a man like me can arrange—made her my captive, and she will pay her father's debt with her beautiful body.

She will try to run, of course, but it won't be the law that comes after her. It will be me.

The sting of my belt across her quivering bare bottom will teach Alessandra the price of defiance, but it is the far more shameful penance that follows which will truly tame her.

Taken

When Winter O'Brien was given to me, she thought she had a say in the matter. She was wrong.

She is my bride. Mine to claim, mine to punish, and mine to use as shamefully as I please. The sting of my belt on her bare bottom will teach her to obey, but obedience is just the beginning.

I will demand so much more.

Bratva's Captive

I told Chloe Kingstrom that getting close to me would be dangerous, and she should keep her distance. The moment she disobeyed and followed me into that bar, she became mine.

Now my enemies are after her, but it's not what they would do to her she should worry about.

It's what I'm going to do to her.

My belt across her bare backside will teach her obedience, but what comes after will be different.

She's going to blush, beg, and scream with every climax as she's ravaged more thoroughly than she can imagine. Then I'm going to flip her over and claim her in an even more shameful way.

If she's a good girl, I might even let her enjoy it.

Hunted

Hope Gracen was just another target to be tracked down... until I caught her.

When I discovered I'd been lied to, I carried her off.

She'll tell me the truth with her bottom still burning from my belt, but that isn't why she's here.

I took her to protect her. I'm keeping her because she's mine.

Theirs as Payment

Until mere moments ago, I was a doctor heading home after my shift at the hospital. But that was before I was forced into the back seat of an SUV, then bared and spanked for trying to escape.

Now I'm just leverage for the Cabello brothers to use against my father, but it isn't the thought of being held hostage by these brutes that has my heart racing and my whole body quivering.

It is the way they're looking at me...

Like they're about to tear my clothes off and take turns mounting me like wild beasts.

Like they're going to share me, using me in ways more shameful than I can even imagine.

Like they own me.

Ruthless Acquisition

I knew the shameful stakes when I bet against these bastards. I just didn't expect to lose.

Now they've come to collect their winnings.

But they aren't just planning to take a belt to my bare bottom for trying to run and then claim everything they're owed from my naked, helpless body as I blush, beg, and scream for them.

They've acquired me, and they plan to keep me.

Bound by Contract

I knew I was in trouble the moment Gregory Steele called me into his office, but I wasn't expecting to end up stripped bare and bent over his desk for a painful lesson from his belt.

Taking a little bit of money here and there might have gone unnoticed in another organization, but stealing from one of the most powerful mafia bosses on the West Coast has consequences.

It doesn't matter why I did it. The only thing that matters now is what he's going to do to me.

I have no doubt he will use me shamefully, but he didn't make me sign that contract just to show me off with my cheeks blushing and my bottom sore under the scandalous outfit he chose for me.

Now that I'm his, he plans to keep me.

Dangerous Addiction

I went looking for a man working with my enemies. When I found only her instead, I should have just left her alone… or maybe taken what I wanted from her and then left… but I didn't.

I couldn't.

So I carried her off to keep for myself.

She didn't make it easy for me, and that earned her a lesson in obedience. A shameful one.

But as her bare bottom reddens under my punishing hand I can see her arousal dripping down her quivering thighs, and no matter how much she squirms and sobs and begs we both know exactly what she needs, and we both know as soon as this spanking is over I'm going to give it to her.

Hard.

Auction House

When I went undercover to investigate a series of murders with links to Steele Franklin's auction house operation, I expected to be sold for the humiliating use of one of his fellow billionaires.

But he wanted me for himself.

No contract. No agreed upon terms. No say in the matter at all except whether to surrender to his shameful demands without a fight or make him strip me bare and spank me into submission first.

I chose the second option, but as one devastating climax after another is forced from my naked, quivering body, what scares me isn't the thought of him keeping me locked up in a cage forever.

It's knowing he won't need to.

Interrogated

As Liam McGinty's belt lashes my bare backside, it isn't the burning sting or the humiliating awareness that my body's surrender is on full display for this ruthless mobster that shocks me.

It's the fact that this isn't a scene from one of my books.

I almost can't process the fact that I'm really riding in the back of a luxury SUV belonging to the most powerful Irish mafia boss in New York—the man I've written so much about—with my cheeks blushing, my bottom sore inside and out, and my arousal soaking the seat beneath me.

But whether I can process it or not, I'm his captive now.

Maybe he'll let me go when he's gotten the answers he needs and he's used me as he pleases.

Or maybe he'll keep me…

BOOKS OF THE DARK OVERTURE SERIES

Indecent Invitation

I shouldn't be here.

My clothes shouldn't be scattered around the room, my bottom shouldn't be sore, and I certainly shouldn't be screaming into the sheets as a ruthless tycoon takes everything he wants from me.

I shouldn't even know Houston Powers at all, but I was in a bad spot and I was made an offer.

A shameful, indecent offer I couldn't refuse.

I was desperate, I needed the money, and I didn't have a choice. Not a real one, anyway.

I'm here because I signed a contract, but I'm his because he made me his.

Illicit Proposition

I should have known better.

His proposition was shameful. So shameful I threw my drink in his face when I heard it.

Then I saw the look in his eyes, and I knew I'd made a mistake.

I fought as he bared me and begged as he spanked me, but it didn't matter. All I could do was moan, scream, and climax helplessly for him as he took everything he wanted from me.

By the time I signed the contract, I was already his.

Unseemly Entanglement

I was warned about Frederick Duvall. I was told he was dangerous. But I never suspected that meeting the billionaire advertising mogul to discuss a business proposition would end with me bent over a table with my dress up and my panties down for a shameful lesson in obedience.

That should have been it. I should have told him what he could do with his offer and his money.

But I didn't.

I could say it was because two million dollars is a lot of cash, but as I stand before him naked, bound, and awaiting the sting of his cane for daring to displease him, I know that's not the truth.

I'm not here because he pays me. I'm here because he owns me.

BOOKS OF THE CLUB DARKNESS SERIES

Bent to His Will

Even the most powerful men in the world know better than to cross me, but Autumn Sutherland thought she could spy on me in my own club and get away with it. Now she must be punished.

She tried to expose me, so she will be exposed. Bare, bound, and helplessly on display, she'll beg for mercy as my strap lashes her quivering bottom and my crop leaves its burning welts on her most intimate spots. Then she'll scream my name as she takes every inch of me, long and hard.

When I am done with her, she won't just be sore and shamefully broken. She will be mine.

Broken by His Hand

Sophia Russo tried to keep away from me, but just thinking about what I would do to her left her panties drenched. She tried to hide it, but I didn't let her. I tore those soaked panties off, spanked her bare little bottom until she had no doubt who owns her, and then took her long and hard.

She begged and screamed as she came for me over and over, but she didn't learn her lesson…

She didn't just come back for more. She thought she could disobey me and get away with it.

This time I'm not just going to punish her. I'm going to break her.

Bound by His Command

Willow danced for the rich and powerful at the world's most exclusive club… until tonight.

Tonight I told her she belongs to me now, and no other man will touch her again.

Tonight I ripped her soaked panties from her beautiful body and taught her to obey with my belt.

Tonight I took her as mine, and I won't be giving her up.

BOOKS OF THE DANGEROUS BUSINESS SERIES

Persuasion

Her father stole something from the mob and they hired me to get it back, but that's not the real reason Giliana Worthington is locked naked in a cage with her bottom well-used and sore.

I brought her here so I could take my time punishing her, mastering her, and ravaging her helpless, quivering body over and over again as she screams and moans and begs for more.

I didn't take her as a hostage. I took her because she is mine.

Bad Men

I thought I could run away from the marriage the mafia arranged for me, but I ended up held prisoner in a foreign country by someone far more dangerous than the man I tried to escape.

Then Jack and Diego came for me.

They didn't ask if I wanted to be theirs. They just took me.

I ran, but they caught me, stripped me bare, and punished me in the most shameful way possible.

Now they're going to share me, and they're not going to be gentle about it.

BOOKS OF THE MONTANA BAD BOYS SERIES

Hawk

He's a big, angry Marine, and I'm going to be sore when he's done with me.

Hawk Travers is not a man to be trifled with. I learned that lesson in the hardest way possible, first with a painful, humiliating public spanking and then much more shamefully in private.

She came looking for trouble. She got a taste of my belt instead.

Bryce Myers pushed me too far and she ended up with her bottom welted. But as satisfying as it is to hear this feisty little reporter scream my name as I put her in her place, I get the feeling she isn't going to stop snooping around no matter how well-used and sore I leave her cute backside.

She's gotten herself in way over her head, but she's mine now, and I protect what's mine.

Scorpion

He didn't ask if I like it rough. It wasn't up to me.

I thought I could get away with pissing off a big, tough Marine. I ended up with my face planted in the sheets, my burning bottom raised high, and my hair held tightly in his fist as he took me long and hard and taught me the kind of shameful lesson only a man like Scorpion could teach.

She was begging for a taste of my belt. She got much more than that.

Getting so tipsy she thought she could be sassy with me in my own bar earned Caroline a spanking, but it was trying to make off with my truck that sealed the deal. She'll feel my belt across her bare backside, then she'll scream my name as she takes every single inch of me.

This naughty girl needs to be put in her place, and I'm going to enjoy every moment of it.

Mustang

I tried to tell him how to run his ranch. Then he took off his belt.

When I heard a rumor about his ranch, I confronted Mustang about it. I thought I could go toe to toe with the big, tough former Marine, but I ended up blushing, sore, and very thoroughly used.

I told her it was going to hurt. I meant it.

Danni Brexton is a hot little number with a sharp tongue and a chip on her shoulder. She's the kind of trouble that needs to be ridden hard and put away wet, but only after a taste of my belt.

It will take more than just a firm hand and a burning bottom to tame this sassy spitfire, but I plan to keep her safe, sound, and screaming my name in bed whether she likes it or not. By the time I'm through with her, there won't be a shadow of a doubt in her mind that she belongs to me.

Nash

When he caught me on his property, he didn't call the police. He just took off his belt.

Nash caught me breaking into his shed while on the run from the mob, and when he demanded answers and obedience I gave him neither. Then he took off his belt and taught me in the most shameful way possible what happens to naughty girls who play games with a big, rough Marine.

She's mine to protect. That doesn't mean I'm going to be gentle with her.

Michelle doesn't just need a place to hide out. She needs a man who will bare her bottom and spank her until she is sore and sobbing whenever she puts herself at risk with reckless defiance, then shove her face into the sheets and make her scream his name with every savage climax.

She'll get all of that from me, and much, much more.

Austin

I offered this brute a ride. I ended up the one being ridden.

The first time I saw Austin, he was hitchhiking. I stopped to give him a lift, but I didn't end up taking this big, rough former Marine wherever he was heading. He was far too busy taking me.

She thought she was in charge. Then I took off my belt.

When Francesca Montgomery pulled up beside me, I didn't know who she was, but I knew what she needed and I gave it to her. Long, hard, and thoroughly, until she was screaming my name as she climaxed over and over with her quivering bare bottom still sporting the marks from my belt.

But someone wants to hurt her, and when someone tries to hurt what's mine, I take it personally.

BOOKS OF THE ALPHA BEASTS SERIES

King's Mate

Her scent drew me to her, but something deeper and more powerful told me she was mine. Something that would not be denied. Something that demanded I claim her then and there.

I took her the way a beast takes his mate. Roughly. Savagely. Without mercy or remorse.

She will run, and when she does she will be punished, but it is not me that she fears. Every quivering, desperate climax reminds her that her body knows its master, and that terrifies her.

She knows I am not a gentle king, and she will scream for me as she learns her place.

Beast's Claim

Raven is not one of my kind, but the moment I caught her scent I knew she belonged to me.

She is my mate, and when I claim her it will not be gentle. She can fight me, but her pleas for mercy as she is punished will soon give way to screams of climax as she is mounted and rutted.

By the time I am finished with her, the evidence of her body's surrender will be mingled with my seed as it drips down her bare thighs. But she will be more than just sore and utterly spent.

She will be mine.

Alpha's Mate

I didn't ask Nicolina to be my mate. It was not up to her. An alpha takes what belongs to him.

She will plead for mercy as she is bared and punished for daring to run from me, but her screams as she is claimed and rutted will be those of helpless climax as her body surrenders to its master.

She is mine, and I'm going to make sure she knows it.

MORE STORMY NIGHT BOOKS BY PIPER STONE

Claimed by the Beasts

Though she has done her best to run from it, Scarlet Dumane cannot escape what is in store for her. She has known for years that she is destined to belong not just to one savage beast, but to three, and now the time has come for her to be claimed. Soon her mates will own every inch of her beautiful body, and she will be shared and used as roughly and as often as they please.

Scarlet hid from the disturbing truth about herself, her family, and her town for as long as she could, but now her grandmother's death has finally brought her back home to the bayous of Louisiana and at last she must face her fate, no matter how shameful and terrifying.

She will be a queen, but her mates will be her masters, and defiance will be thoroughly punished. Yet even when she is stripped bare and spanked until she is sobbing, her need for them only grows, and every blush, moan, and quivering climax binds her to them more tightly. But with enemies lurking in the shadows, can she trust her mates to protect her from both man and beast?

Millionaire Daddy

Dominick Asbury is not just a handsome millionaire whose deep voice makes Jenna's tummy flutter whenever they are together, nor is he merely the first man bold enough to strip her bare and spank her hard and thoroughly whenever she has been naughty. He is much more than that.

He is her daddy.

He is the one who punishes her when she's been a bad girl, and he is the one who takes her in his arms afterwards and brings her to one climax after another until she is utterly spent and satisfied.

But something shady is going on behind the scenes at Dominick's company, and when Jenna draws the wrong conclusion from a poorly written article about him and creates an embarrassing public scene, will she end up not only costing them both their jobs but losing her daddy as well?

Conquering Their Mate

For years the Cenzans have cast a menacing eye on Earth, but it still came as a shock to be captured, stripped bare, and claimed as a mate by their leader and his most trusted warriors.

It infuriates me to be punished for the slightest defiance and forced to submit to these alien brutes, but as I'm led naked through the corridors of their ship, my well-punished bare bottom and my helpless arousal both fully on display, I cannot help wondering how long it will be until I'm kneeling at the feet of my mates and begging them take me as shamefully as they please.

Captured and Kept

Since her career was knocked off track in retaliation for her efforts to expose a sinister plot by high-ranking government officials, reporter Danielle Carver has been stuck writing puff pieces in a small town in Oregon. Desperate for a serious story, she sets out to investigate the rumors she's been hearing about mysterious men living in the mountains nearby. But when she secretly follows them back to their remote cabin, the ruggedly handsome beasts don't take kindly to her snooping around, and Dani soon finds herself stripped bare for a painful, humiliating spanking.

Their rough dominance arouses her deeply, and before long she is blushing crimson as they take turns using her beautiful body as thoroughly and shamefully as they please. But when Dani uncovers the true reason for their presence in the area, will more than just her career be at risk?

Taming His Brat

It's been years since Cooper Dawson left her small Texas hometown, but after her stubborn defiance gets her fired from two jobs in a row, she knows something definitely needs to change. What she doesn't expect, however, is for her sharp tongue and arrogant attitude to land her over the knee of a stern, ruggedly sexy cowboy for a painful, embarrassing, and very public spanking.

Rex Sullivan cannot deny being smitten by Cooper, and the fact that she is in desperate need of his belt across her bare backside only makes the war-hardened ex-Marine more determined to tame the beautiful, fiery redhead. It isn't long before she's screaming his name as he shows her just how hard and roughly a cowboy can ride a headstrong filly. But Rex and Cooper both have secrets, and when the demons of their past rear their ugly heads, will their romance be torn apart?

Capturing Their Mate

I thought the Cenzan invaders could never find me here, but I was wrong. Three of the alien brutes came to take me, and before I ever set foot aboard their ship I had already been stripped bare, spanked thoroughly, and claimed more shamefully then I would have ever thought possible.

They have decided that a public example must be made of me, and I will be punished and used in the most humiliating ways imaginable as a warning to anyone who might dare to defy them. But I am no ordinary breeder, and the secrets hidden in my past could change their world… or end it.

Rogue

Tracking down cyborgs is my job, but this time I'm the one being hunted. This rogue machine has spent most of his life locked up, and now that he's on the loose he has plans for me...

He isn't just going to strip me, punish me, and use me. He will take me longer and harder than any human ever could, claiming me so thoroughly that I will be left in no doubt who owns me.

No matter how shamefully I beg and plead, my body will be ravaged again and again with pleasure so intense it terrifies me to even imagine, because that is what he was built to do.

Roughneck

When I took a job on an oil rig to escape my scheming stepfather's efforts to set me up with one of his business cronies, I knew I'd be working with rugged men. What I didn't expect is to find myself bent over a desk, my cheeks soaked with tears and my bare thighs wet for a very different reason, as my well-punished bottom is thoroughly used by a stern, infuriatingly sexy roughneck.

Even though I should have known better than to get sassy with a firm-handed cowboy, let alone a tough-as-nails former Marine, there's no denying that learning the hard way was every bit as hot as it was shameful. But a sore, welted backside is just the start of his plans for me, and no matter how much I blush to admit it, I know I'm going to take everything he gives me and beg for more.

Hunting Their Mate

As far as I'm concerned, the Cenzans will always be the enemy, and there can be no peace while they remain on our planet. I planned to make them pay for invading our world, but I was hunted down and captured by two of their warriors with the help of a battle-hardened former Marine. Now I'm the one who is going to pay, as the three of them punish me, shame me, and share me.

Though the thought of a fellow human taking the side of these alien brutes enrages me, that is far from the worst of it. With every searing stroke of the strap that lands across my bare bottom, with every savage thrust as I am claimed over and over, and with every screaming climax, it is made more clear that it is my own quivering, thoroughly used body which has truly betrayed me.

Primitive

I was sent to this world to help build a new Earth, but I was shocked by what I found here. The men of this planet are not just primitive savages. They are predators, and I am now their prey…

The government lied to all of us. Not all of the creatures who hunted and captured me are aliens. Some of them were human once, specimens transformed in labs into little more than feral beasts.

I fought, but I was thrown over a shoulder and carried off. I ran, but I was caught and punished. Now they are going to claim me, share me, and use me so roughly that when the last screaming climax has been wrung from my naked, helpless body, I wonder if I'll still know my own name.

Harvest

The Centurions conquered Earth long before I was born, but they did not come for our land or our resources. They came for mates, women deemed suitable for breeding. Women like me.

Three of the alien brutes decided to claim me, and when I defied them, they made a public example of me, punishing me so thoroughly and shamefully I might never stop blushing.

But now, as my virgin body is used in every way possible, I'm not sure I want them to stop…

Torched

I work alongside firefighters, so I know how to handle musclebound roughnecks, but Blaise Tompkins is in a league of his own. The night we met, I threw a glass of wine in his face, then ended up shoved against the wall with my panties on the floor and my arousal dripping down my thighs, screaming out climax after shameful climax with my well-punished bottom still burning.

I've got a series of arsons to get to the bottom of, and finding out that the infuriatingly sexy brute who spanked me like a naughty little girl will be helping me with the investigation seemed like the last thing I needed, until somebody hurled a rock through my window in an effort to scare me away from the case. Now having a big, strong man around doesn't seem like such a bad idea…

Fertile

The men who hunt me were always brutes, but now lust makes them barely more than beasts.

When they catch me, I know what comes next.

I will fight, but my need to be bred is just as strong as theirs is to breed. When they strip me, punish me, and use me the way I'm meant to be used, my screams will be the screams of climax.

Hostage

I knew going after one of the most powerful mafia bosses in the world would be dangerous, but I didn't anticipate being dragged from my apartment already sore, sorry, and shamefully used.

My captors don't just plan to teach me a lesson and then let me go. They plan to share me, punish me, and claim me so ruthlessly I'll be screaming my submission into the sheets long before they're through with me. They took me as a hostage, but they'll keep me as theirs.

Defiled

I was born to rule, but for her sake I am banished, forced to wander the Earth among mortals. Her virgin body will pay the price for my protection, and it will be a shameful price indeed.

Stripped, punished, and ravaged over and over, she will scream with every savage climax.

She will be defiled, but before I am done with her she will beg to be mine.

Kept

On the run from corrupt men determined to silence me, I sought refuge in his cabin. I ate his food, drank his whiskey, and slept in his bed. But then the big bad bear came home and I learned the hard way that sometimes Goldilocks ends up with her cute little bottom well-used and sore.

He stripped me, spanked me, and ravaged me in the most shameful way possible, but then this rugged brute did something no one else ever has before. He made it clear he plans to keep me…

Auctioned

Twenty years ago the Malzeons saved us when we were at the brink of self-annihilation, but there was a price for their intervention. They demanded humans as servants… and as pets.

Only criminals were supposed to be offered to the aliens for their use, but when I defied Earth's government, asking questions that no one else would dare to ask, I was sold to them at auction.

I was bought by two of their most powerful commanders, rivals who nonetheless plan to share me. I am their property now, and they intend to tame me, train me, and enjoy me thoroughly.

But I have information they need, a secret guarded so zealously that discovering it cost me my freedom, and if they do not act quickly enough both of our worlds will soon be in grave danger.

Hard Ride

When I snuck into Montana Cobalt's house, I was looking for help learning to ride like him, but what I got was his belt across my bare backside. Then with tears still running down my cheeks and arousal dripping onto my thighs, the big brute taught me a much more shameful lesson.

Montana has agreed to train me, but not just for the rodeo. He's going to break me in and put me through my paces, and then he's going to show me what it means to be ridden rough and dirty.

Carnal

For centuries my kind have hidden our feral nature, our brute strength, and our carnal instincts. But this human female is my mate, and nothing will keep me from claiming and ravaging her.

She is mine to tame and protect, and if my belt doesn't teach her to obey then she'll learn in a much more shameful fashion. Either way, her surrender will be as complete as it is inevitable.

Bounty

After I went undercover to take down a mob boss and ended up betrayed, framed, and on the run, Harper Rollins tried to bring me in. But instead of collecting a bounty, she earned herself a hard spanking and then an even rougher lesson that left her cute bottom sore in a very different way.

She's not one to give up without a fight, but that's fine by me. It just means I'll have plenty more chances to welt her beautiful backside and then make her scream her surrender into the sheets.

Beast

Primitive, irresistible need compelled him to claim me, but it was more than mere instinct that drove this alien beast to punish me for my defiance and then ravage me thoroughly and savagely. Every screaming climax was a brand marking me as his, ensuring I never forget who I belong to.

He's strong enough to take what he wants from me, but that's not why I surrendered so easily as he stripped me bare, pushed me up against the wall, and made me his so roughly and shamefully.

It wasn't fear that forced me to submit. It was need.

Gladiator

Xander didn't just win me in the arena. The alien brute claimed me there too, with my punished bottom still burning and my screams of climax almost drowned out by the roar of the crowd.

Almost…

Victory earned him freedom and the right to take me as his mate, but making me truly his will mean more than just spanking me into shameful surrender and then rutting me like a wild beast. Before he carries me off as his prize, the dark truth that brought me here must be exposed at last.

Big Rig

Alexis Harding is used to telling men exactly what she thinks, but she's never had a roughneck like me as a boss before. On my rig, I make the rules and sassy little girls get stripped bare, bent over my desk, and taught their place, first with my belt and then in a much more shameful way.

She'll be sore and sorry long before I'm done with her, but the arousal glistening on her thighs reveals the truth she would rather keep hidden. She needs it rough, and that's how she'll get it.

Warriors

I knew this was a primitive planet when I landed, but nothing could have prepared me for the rough beasts who inhabit it. The sting of their prince's firm hand on my bare bottom taught me my place in his world, but it was what came after that truly demonstrated his mastery over me.

This alien brute has granted me his protection and his help with my mission, but the price was my total submission to both his shameful demands and those of his second in command as well.

But it isn't the savage way they make use of my quivering body that terrifies me the most. What leaves me trembling is the thought that I may never leave this place… because I won't want to.

Owned

With a ruthless, corrupt billionaire after me, Crockett, Dylan, and Wade are just the men I need. Rough men who know how to keep a woman safe… and how to make her scream their names.

But the Hell's Fury MC doesn't do charity work, and their help will come at a price.

A shameful price…

They aren't just going to bare me, punish me, and then do whatever they want with me.

They're going to make me beg for it.

Seized

Delaney Archer got herself mixed up with someone who crossed us, and now she's going to find out just how roughly and shamefully three bad men like us can make use of her beautiful body.

She can plead for mercy, but it won't stop us from stripping her bare and spanking her until she's sore, sobbing, and soaking wet. Our feisty little captive is going to take everything we give her, and she'll be screaming our names with every savage climax long before we're done with her.

Cruel Masters

I thought I understood the risks of going undercover to report on billionaires flaunting their power, but these men didn't send lawyers after me. They're going to deal with me themselves.

Now I'm naked aboard their private plane, my backside already burning from one of their belts, and these three infuriatingly sexy bastards have only just gotten started teaching me my place.

I'm not just going to be punished, shamed, and shared. I'm going to be mastered.

Hard Men

My father's will left his company to me, but the three roughnecks who ran it for him have other ideas. They're owed a debt and they mean to collect on it, but it's not money these brutes want.

It's me.

In return for protection from my father's enemies, I will be theirs to share. But these are hard men, and they don't just intend to punish my defiance and use me as shamefully as they please.

They plan to master me completely.

Rough Ride

As I hear the leather slide through the loops of his pants, I know what comes next. Jake Travers is going to blister my backside. Then he's going to ride me the way only a rodeo champion can.

Plenty of men who thought they could put me in my place have learned the hard way that I was more than they could handle, and when Jake showed up I was sure he would be no different.

I was wrong.

When I pushed him, he bared and spanked me in front of a bar full of people.

I should have let it go at that, but I couldn't.

That's why he's taking off his belt...

Primal Instinct

Ruger Jameson can buy anything he wants, but that's not the reason I'm his to use as he pleases.

He's a former Army Ranger accustomed to having his orders followed, but that's not why I obey him.

He saved my life after our plane crashed, but I'm not on my knees just to thank him properly.

I'm his because my body knows its master.

I do as I'm told because he blisters my bare backside every time I dare to do otherwise.

I'm at his feet because I belong to him and I plan to show it in the most shameful way possible.

Captor

I was supposed to be safe from the lottery. Set apart for a man who would treat me with dignity.

But as I'm probed and examined in the most intimate, shameful ways imaginable while the hulking alien king who just spanked me looks on approvingly, I know one thing for certain.

This brute didn't end up with me by chance. He wanted me, so he found a way to take me.

He'll savor every blush as I stand bare and on display for him, every plea for mercy as he punishes my defiance, and every quivering climax as he slowly masters my virgin body.

I'll be his before he even claims me.

Printed in Great Britain
by Amazon